Children of the Mists

Alexandra
with love & best
wishes Lexa x

Lexa Dudley

Children
of the Mists

Matador
9 Priory Business Park,
Wistow Road, Kibworth Beauchamp,
Leicestershire. LE8 0RX
Tel: 0116 279 2299
Email: books@troubador.co.uk
Web: www.troubador.co.uk/matador
Twitter: @matadorbooks

ISBN 978 1785891 922

British Library Cataloguing in Publication Data.
A catalogue record for this book is available from the British Library.

Printed and bound by CPI Group (UK) Ltd, Croydon, CR0 4YY
Typeset in 11pt Aldine401 BT by Troubador Publishing Ltd, Leicester, UK

Matador is an imprint of Troubador Publishing Ltd

To Kit
For all your continued patience and help.
Thank you.

To the Spirit of Sardinia.
Just as I feel I have it in my hold at last
I know, like the breeze, it has already passed.

Naschet su Sardu suggetu a milli cumandamentos.
The Sardinian is born subject to a thousand commands.

To all the Sardinian people, who have retained their
independence, and pride through their strong sense of identity
and attachment to their beloved land.
Who, although they have been occupied since Nuraghic times,
have managed to retain their language, and are devoted to their
traditions and customs that, throughout their history, have
resonated in their hearts and souls.
May it always be that way.

ACKNOWLEDGEMENTS

My thanks to everyone who has helped with this book.
   To my doctor, who kindly gave me the medical information.
   To Signore Giacomo Mura living in Ozieri.
   To Cris Coe, who generously painted the cover for me.
   And to all my friends who have encouraged me to write.
   Thank you

Siamo Spagnoli, Africani, Fenici, Cartaginesi, Romani, Arabi, Pisani, Bizantini, Piemontesi.
Siamo le ginestre d'oro giallo che spiovono sui sentieri rocciosi come grandi lampade accese.
Siamo la solitudine selvaggia, il silenzio immenso e profondo, lo splendore del cielo, il bianco fiore del cisto.
Siamo il regno ininterrotto del lentisco, delle onde che ruscellano i graniti antichi, della rosa canina, del vento, dell'immensità del mare.
Siamo una terra antica di lunghi silenzi, di orizzonti ampi e puri, di piante fosche, di montagne bruciate dal sole e dalla vendetta.
Noi siamo sardi.

We are Spanish, Africans, Phoenicians, Carthaginians, Romans, Arabs, Pisans, Byzantine, Piedmontese.
We are the golden yellow gorse on the rocky trails that droops as large, lighted lamps.
We are the wild solitude, the vast and deep silence, the splendour of the sky, the white flower of Cistus.
We are the uninterrupted reign of the mastic tree, the waves that flow through the ancient granites, the reign of the rosehips, the wind, the immensity of the sea.
We are an ancient land of long silences, and also of wide horizons, of bleak plants, of mountains burned by the sun and revenge.
We are Sardinian.

Graize Deledda (Nuoro 27th Sept 1871 - Rome 15th Aug 1936)

INTRODUCTION

Sardinia is still the 'Unknown Island'. It is a land of immense beauty with majestic mountains, magical, ancient places and stunning beaches.

A land of people that has been occupied since the Nuraghic times. The coming of the Phoenicians changed their land forever, as the island came under someone else's rules and taxes.

The people who came took everything: their wealth, their lands, timber, minerals and people for slaves. Through all they have remained true to their culture, believing that *Furat chi benit dae su mare,* those who come from the sea steal. The true Sards are not fishermen, but the ancient farmers, keepers of their languages and traditions, which they have held on to with tenacity through difficult, and sometimes life-threatening times.

In April 1395 Eleanora d'Aborea laid out the laws for the Sardinian people, called the *Carta de Logu*; a document well advanced for its time, giving women rights to own land and to reject a forced marriage. No one could negotiate the sale of a horse in front of the animal, nor could a saddled horse be sold to a stranger; and this reveals an understanding of the Sards, their love of horses, and their long-held superstitions.

My love for Sardinia started in 1972 when I first visited the island with my family. I was amazed to find how proud these people are of their heritage. On being asked a question about some place or ancient site, they took pleasure in explaining everything they knew about it, then passing me on to someone else for further information. In my books, Sardinia is a character in her own right, and her strengths and weaknesses are all portrayed.

My friends in Sardinia say I am a Sard, and to me that is the greatest compliment I could have. I find them curious, friendly and loyal. If you make a friend of a Sard, then you have that friendship for life. Sardinia is the home of my soul. My love for the island and its people, is the reason I wrote *The Whispering Wind*, and this book, *Children of the Mists*, in the hope that others would find a little of what I have found and love about the island.

I have travelled all over Sardinia, taking whichever son happened to be interested at the time, or travelling on my own. I soon learnt that I had to pretend to be due to meet someone in another village as I was always offered food and drink. Although I spoke no Italian in those days, everyone made sure I had everything I needed. I have never felt threatened or afraid travelling on my own, or with my children. I knew there would be someone who would help me if I needed it; and I also learnt the Sards live more in the expectation of love, rather than death.

I have seen Sardinia change over the past forty-three years, as another invasion arrived in the form of the tourist. Many with just two weeks' holiday are content to sit on the beautiful beaches and take the sun, but those who can find time to travel the island will find themselves well rewarded.

Towns have grown; dirt roads have been concreted over, but the towns still hold on to their traditions and festivals. Their big Festas, like Sagra Sant' Efisio, Sartillia and Cavalcarta Sard, are still held for themselves, although everyone is welcome.

I hold Sardinia in my heart, afraid for her future as the young have to find work elsewhere, and they do not transplant well. They are born in paradise – why would they ever want to leave?

Independence is something I feel would benefit the island. Her taxes could be used for the local people and not sent to the Continent to be distributed as if a colony, an outpost of Italy. Where the Italians put everything they don't want on the mainland, and still regard the Sards as shepherds and small-islanders.

There are one and a half million Sardinians living on an island the size of Wales, but there are three million sheep and goats. It is still an agricultural land. Wine is produced, and has greatly improved since the 1970s. The cheese production is the greatest in all Italy. There *Pecorino Sardo*, also known as *Fiore Sardo*, was awarded Denominazione d'Origine in 1991 and granted protected designation of origin in 1996. They are still self-sufficient in the production of wheat, and their fruit and vegetables are second to none.

It is my fervent hope that there will be another Eleanora d'Aborea to take them forward into an independent island with a glowing future.

CANU FAMILY TREE

Carlo Canu – Teressa Matta
b:1791   b:1792

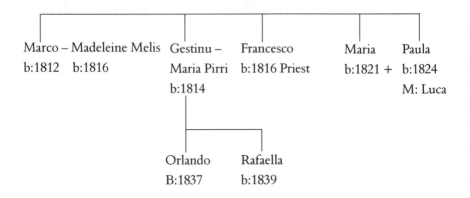

Marco – Madeleine Melis   Gestinu –   Francesco   Maria   Paula
b:1812   b:1816   Maria Pirri   b:1816 Priest   b:1821 +   b:1824
                           b:1814   M: Luca

                           Orlando   Rafaella
                           B:1837   b:1839

Giovanni Pinni – Maria

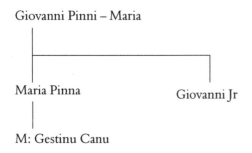

Maria Pinna   Giovanni Jr

M: Gestinu Canu

SANNA FAMILY TREE

Salvatore M: Gabriella Melloni
b:1816   b:1818

Antonio   Vitoria   Ignazio   Marina   Salvatore   Salvatore jr
B:March 1837   B: May 1838   b:1840 +   b:1841   b:1845 +   b:1855

PROLOGUE

At Sos Lampidos classes finished early, as the midday heat became oppressive. Raffaella had spent the morning looking out of the window, lost in a world of her own. She thought about Antoneddu, who had gone to help his father with the sheep. She had pleaded with Zia Paola to let her go too, but her aunt had been adamant that she stay with her brother and Antoneddu's sisters and not miss the lessons.

Now free at last, Raffaella ran from the farmhouse, down the wide track to the lower meadows below. She reached an old olive tree, and hitching up her skirt, she climbed up into its branches.

From her vantage point, she was in time to see Antoneddu riding up the meadow toward her. She called and waved to him, and smiled to herself. He looked so handsome with his strong, broad shoulders, and although only a couple of years older than her, looked more than his fourteen years.

Seeing her, Antoneddu reined in his horse and, dismounted and stood under the tree.

'What on earth are you doing up there? If your brother could see you now, you'd be in big trouble,' he said, looking up at her and smiling.

'I am Christopher Columbus in the foc'sle of his great ship. We learnt about him today. Come up here with me, and I will tell you about him. Classes aren't the same without you. Everyone is so serious, and they don't ask interesting questions like you do. Please come up and join me,' she begged.

At that moment, a swirling breeze raced up the valley, catching the olive tree, taking Raffaella's headdress and blowing it out of her reach, where it flapped against a branch in the gaining wind. The darkening sky, heavy with storm clouds, came chasing up behind the wind as the first large blobs of rain fell on the dry ground.

Raffaella made a grab for her headscarf, at the same time treading on another bough. A loud crack resounded as the branch gave way, and with a scream, she fell.

Antoneddu, who had watched her every move, caught her and held her in his strong arms. Her face was scratched and blood-smeared, as were her hands, making her look every inch the tomboy she was.

He smiled, and still holding the young slip of a girl, said with tenderness,

'I've got you, Raffaella. I've got you; you know I'll always keep you safe.'

PART ONE

CHAPTER ONE

Punta Néula, Sardinia Early April 1855

The Sanna family sat around the large, hand-hewn table. Their meal was ready, and the smell of the thick broth filled the room that served as both living room, and kitchen for the family.

Marina watched her father as he pulled her mother to one side and, leant forward over the fire to lift a heavy pot from its trivet, and carried it to the table, placing it in front of her.

Marina took the ladle to serve the broth, but the sound of barking from the dogs made her hesitate. Everyone strained their ears, trying to make out any unfamiliar noise above the increasing racket from the animals. In a moment, the barking stopped and faded to a muted whimper.

There came the sound of footsteps across the dust-baked yard; then scratching and clawing at the handle as someone tried to open the latch. Four pairs of eyes were riveted on the great wooden door. Salvatore leapt to his feet and, reaching up to the beam above where he sat, he took down his loaded shotgun from its hiding place. He signalled to his eldest daughter, Vitoria, to open the door and at the same time put his finger to his lips to make sure they all stayed quiet.

'Salvatore, be careful for pity's sake, it might be Antonio,' whispered Gabriella, fearing their son may have returned from the plains with the sheep.

'It's not Antonio; all the dogs know him,' growled Salvatore again, nodding to Vitoria, and at the same time waving his gun impatiently. Gabriella watched as her daughter pulled back the bar holding the latch. The door swung inward and a mud-splatted, blood-smeared young man fell to his knees on the old tiled floor. He clutched a wound in his right shoulder, and his face registered pain.

3

'Holy Mother preserve us, it's Cousin Gavinu!' cried Marina, dropping the ladle back into the broth and making the sign of the cross as she pushed past her mother, falling to her knees beside the young man. 'Oh, Gavinu, what has happened? It's Marina. You're all right now, and you are safe. Please, tell us what has happened!' wailed the young girl.

Salvatore stood watching his youngest daughter, his gun still pointing at the intruder. Gabriella stepped forward, took the gun from her husband and placed it in the corner out of harm's way.

'Help him, quickly,' she cried, trying to galvanise Salvatore into action. 'He's losing blood, hurry with some dressings.'

'I'll fetch them, Mamma,' called Marina as she took a lamp and fled to the large anteroom where Gabriella kept all her salves and herbs and Salvatore had his wine vats.

Vitoria, meanwhile, closed and barred the door and helped her father move Gavinu to the fireside. She then hurried to the shuttered window and flung it open.

'There's a light from the top window at Sos Lampidos,' she called to her father. 'The Carabineri must be there as someone has hung the warning lamp in the attic.'

'Bring a lamp over here, Vitoria, I need some light,' Gabriella called as she tried to look at the young man's shoulder.

Vitoria did as asked; fetched a lantern from near the fire and held it up for her mother. Gavinu groaned as Gabriella gently but firmly pulled his shirt away from the wound.

Marina returned with a collection of salves and bandages and helped her mother by holding Gavinu's wounded arm.

'How did you get this, Gavinu?' asked Gabriella in her soft manner.

'The Carabineri shot me, cousin. Ugo is dead.' The young man sobbed. 'They are after me. I gave them the slip at Sos Lampidos.' He winced, drawing in air between his teeth from the pain as Gabriella cleaned the wound with vinegar. Marina gave his hand a comforting squeeze and smiled at him.

'I saw Raffaella there,' he continued. 'She told me to cut down the ravine and double back at the ford. I set my horse free. The Carabineri won't find that crossing in the dark, so they will have to go upriver to the bridge, but they'll be here soon. Please, cousin, please help me. I beg you to give me the shelter of your hospitality.' He had a pitiful, pleading look in his eyes. Only a lad of sixteen, but the fearful look of a hunted animal added years to his young features.

Gabriella turned toward her daughter. 'Vitoria, take the lamp and help your father.'

Vitoria took the lamp and hurried to the storeroom to make good the hiding place for their cousin, while Gabriella and Marina bound the wound and bandaged the arm close to Gavinu's chest to stop any movement. Salvatore, returning from the storeroom, glanced towards Sos Lampidos and noticed the light had already been extinguished; meaning the Carabineri had indeed left.

It had been a long-standing arrangement between the two families, the Cannas at Sos Lampidos, and the Sannas here at Punta Néula. A white light meant the arrival of the despised Carabineri, while a red shade over the lamp meant they needed immediate help.

'We shall have to hurry,' said Salvatore as he listened for the sound of hoof-beats.

Gabriella finished the bandaging, and the two girls, with Salvatore, helped Gavinu into the storeroom and bundled him, without ceremony, into the family's secret hiding place.

Gabriella looked around the main room to make sure everything was in order and, collecting the soiled bandages and swabs, she burnt them. There could be no possible trace of their visitor.

Vitoria put her lamp back on its hook by the fireplace, next to the one Marina had taken to the storeroom; another final check and they returned to the table to resume their meal. They again sat down at the table, but the distinct sound of hoof-beats could now be heard above the increased baying of the dogs. The pounding hooves stopped, and a sharp command was given in Piedmontese. Loud oaths were followed by a repeated banging on the farm door as the visitors tried in vain to quieten the relentless barking from the dogs, and enter the relative safety of the house.

Gabriella watched as Salvatore rose from the table and walked to the door. He drew back the bar with the same slow deliberation, but the door was flung back against the wall with a deafening thud, throwing him off balance.

'Call off your dogs,' commanded the Captain holding his lantern high, the light catching his strong features.

Salvatore whistled to his hounds and called to them to go to their kennel.

'Now, where is he?' demanded the Captain. He stood large in the doorway. He came from the Continent, with his height and stature. The white cross-band of his distinctive uniform stood out in the dim light. The Captain took a step into the room. Marina noticed he carried not only his shotgun, but also a pair of pistols which were tucked into his broad leather belt.

'We know he is here,' continued the Captain, coming towards them and at last finding the courtesy to remove his red hackled hat, which he tucked under his left arm. His four subordinates followed their Captain into the room; they were older and also armed, and each one carried a lantern. They had a formidable appearance, with their dark bearded faces in striking contrast with their young Captain, who was clean-shaven except for his thin, waxed moustache; their features all picked out by their flickering lamps.

The Captain again stepped forward. 'You are his cousins, and it is obvious you will shelter him,' he snarled.

Salvatore turned to face the young intruder, and in his slow, deliberate way asked, 'First, under whose authority do you come into my house, frightening my family? And second, for whom are you searching?'

'We come, Pastore, under the authority of Savoy and the King of Sardinia,' replied the Captain, with an arrogant note of contempt creeping into his voice.

6

'But we have no dealings with the Piedmontese or the House of Savoy; I am a freeborn, land-owning Sard.'

'Come, peasant, don't waste my time,' cut in the Captain as he replaced his hat on his head and put his lantern at his feet. He then raised his shotgun to Salvatore's chest. 'We are looking for your cousin, Gavinu Piddu. He is wanted for sheep-rustling and attempted murder.'

Marina gasped and put her hand to her mouth. The Captain turned and gave her a long, enquiring look.

'I've not seen him for many months,' replied Salvatore. 'He came here in the autumn to help us round up our sheep, before my son drove them down to the plains of Chiliviana for their winter grazing. Let me see now – it would have been late October, early November. Gavinu was here for the feast of the dead, and talked with Antonio about going with him. It is a long walk to the plains and company is always welcome, and for all I know, he may well have gone with him for I have not seen him since…'

Salvatore's words were drowned by the Captain's orders to his men.

'Search the place; leave nothing unturned. Do you understand?'

Two men, carrying their lanterns, came forward and were dispatched upstairs, while the remaining two were sent to the sheepfold.

'Make sure nobody is hiding there. And don't forget to prod all the straw well. Turn over the dung heap if necessary, remember these vermin crawl in anywhere,' shouted the Captain, with a sharp note of sarcasm.

Marina watched the scene in silence, her heart beating fast, as she feared they would find Gavinu.

Salvatore walked across to the fireplace, reached up for his cigars from the box on the mantel and lit one, at the same time watching the Captain like a hawk. The Captain, for his part, stood clenching his fingers and grinding his teeth, making his moustache twitch from the pressure.

He placed his shotgun against the wall, picked up his lantern and ambled into the dimly lit storeroom. He collected a mug, then eyeing the two large casks in front of him, helped himself to the contents of the first barrel. He took a draught, and cursed aloud as he spat out the mouthful and tipped the remains of the mug onto the dirt floor.

'God in Heaven, will you damned Sards never learn to make a decent wine?' he exclaimed, drawing his hand across his contorted mouth in an attempt to rid himself of the vile flavour. He moved to the next cask and again helped himself. This one appeared to be more to his taste, for he drained the mug, then refilling it, he ambled back into the large room. He placed his lantern on the table and stood, his feet astride, in front of the glowing fire and let his eyes wander over the unfamiliar surroundings.

Dried herbs, gourds and figs festooned the ceiling, along with *bortarga*, dried mullet roe, which was considered a delicacy among the Sards. On the far wall, he could just make out a huge collection of lances, long rifles, and a great assortment of hunting knives, all making a formidable arsenal. Off the large room, next to where the wine casks stood, he could hear the unrelenting clip-clop of a blindfolded donkey, the *mollentu*, as it walked round and round in its monotonous chore of grinding the family's corn. The Captain sighed. Life had changed little on the island since Caesar's time. How in God's good name could they ever organise such a slow, barbaric people?

Marina watched the Captain, unmoved by his obvious disdain. She pulled the earthenware dish toward her, and was about to serve the broth, when the Captain put down his mug and strode over to the table, and taking the ladle from her, plunged it into the thick broth and drawing it to his lips, supped noisily.

Salvatore stood to rebuke him, but Gabriella waved her hand to stop his rebuff.

'Now, husband,' she said in a soft tone, 'men are always welcome to sup at our table. Remember, where there is a stranger, even if he is bad, there is God.' She smiled at the Captain, who made a faint effort to return the gesture. 'Even if they are Piedmontese pigs,' she added in *Sardu* with a smile.

The Captain slung the ladle back into the pot, about to give vent to his feelings, when his men returned from upstairs.

'We have searched everywhere, Captain; there is no sign of him, sir.'

At that moment, the others returned from the stables. They looked dishevelled and were covered with straw, and shook their heads.

The Captain scowled and turned to Salvatore. 'We will be back, and I promise you this, Pastore: if I find your cousin is here, or if he is seen in the area, I shall see that you suffer the full penalty of harbouring an outlaw. We will confiscate all your lands and stock, and your son will be sent to the mainland for war service. Is that understood?'

Without waiting for a reply, the Captain picked up his lamp, swung on his heels and marched out of the door, snapping his fingers to his men who followed behind him, the last of whom slammed the door. The sound of their horses' hooves faded into the night and peace once more settled over the little mountain community.

'Vitoria, you check they have all gone,' whispered her father, 'while I collect Gavinu.'

She did as her father bid her and went out into the star-flecked darkness. A solitary nightingale sang in the nearby olive grove, accompanied by a chorus of cicadas and frogs, but there hung a still, eerie silence in the valley without the sound of the sheep bells.

Vitoria looked towards Sos Lampidos and wondered about her beloved Orlando, and if he thought of her too. She smiled, and closed the door at the same time, drawing the bar across the latch to lock out any further intruders.

Inside, Salvatore busied himself in the storeroom. He slid out the front of the first large cask, revealing a cramped but adequate hideout complete with rough woollen bedding. Boards were laid across the bottom, giving a flat area on which to lie, while the space below was sealed. It was topped up regularly with the wine dregs so it wouldn't appear empty, but the wine was of dreadful quality, as the Captain had found to his cost.

Salvatore helped Gavinu back to the main room, and sat him at the table on the chair Marina had placed next to hers. Marina went forward and took the pot from the trivet where she had put it to reheat, this time placing it in front of her mother.

Gabriella waddled toward the table. Her baby was due in a few weeks and every movement had become an effort. With all the family grown up, this child was a gift from God. She gave her husband a tender look. Salvatore, a short, swarthy man in his late thirties with a soft voice and a twinkle in his button brown eyes, returned the smile with profound tenderness.

'I think we are ready to eat now, Mamma,' Marina said, collecting another bowl from the large plate rack hanging on the wall.

She removed the lid from the pot. The steam rose in a giant cloud, making the candles in the lamp above the table flicker and jump, giving the room a peculiar glow which highlighted the faces of those who waited for their food in the otherwise darkened room.

Gabriella handed each one of them a generous bowlful of vegetable and meat broth, together with a large slice of fine white bread, ricotta cheese and salami, with a glass of Salvatore's house wine. Silence fell over the table as Salvatore said grace, and they ate their way through the food; the peace broken only by the slurping of soup or licking of lips in appreciation.

First, Vitoria, the eldest at nearly seventeen. A tall, elegant girl with long, raven-black hair, which she tucked under her white linen headdress. She had large black eyes and delicate features; a natural beauty and an exact copy of Gabriella when Salvatore first met and married her. Next to Vitoria sat Marina, at fourteen, three years her junior; a slender, leggy creature like an overgrown colt with brown hair and eyes to match. Her curly hair escaped in tendrils from her cotton headdress in a rebellious mass. She sat beside Gavinu and helped him by breaking his bread into bite-size pieces and cutting his salami.

'Tell me, cousin, where did you get the idea for the cask? I've never seen anything like it before,' asked Gavinu, trying hard to delay the barrage of questions he knew they were all waiting to ask him.

'Before we discuss that, I must know why the Carabineri are after you,' replied Salvatore. 'And what's this you say about Ugo being dead? Did you kill him?'

Gavinu looked around the table at each one of them in turn until his gaze fell on Marina.

Her big brown eyes stared up into his face as she watched him intently. He looked so handsome to her, in his wild, unshaven way, for although only sixteen he sported a strong growth of beard. To her he had seemed such a romantic figure, for as long as she could remember. He came from the mountains, and had black hair and piercing blue eyes. Although they only saw each other at festivals and the sheep fairs, she found him far more attractive than his brothers. Now he was injured, she saw herself as his helper and would give him her undivided attention.

Gavinu looked at Marina and addressed his reply to Salvatore's question to her, flattered by her constant admiring looks.

'It's true, Ugo is dead, but I didn't kill him.'

The girls gasped at the news and crossed themselves.

'It was terrible,' said Gavinu, with a break in his voice.

'But how did it happen, and why?' asked Salvatore, bewildered by the news.

'It has been brewing for a long time. At Pinta Niedda, we have always grazed our sheep and goats across the common lands of the mountains and the valleys of Baddu Bunne, but then, two years ago, Don diVenti came to live nearby and has papers, he says, proving that he now owns all the Baddu Bunne.'

'He probably does,' said Salvatore, sounding tired. 'Is he wealthy?'

'Yes, he's wealthy, but no more than some of our old Sard families from this area. How can a man like Don diVenti own Baddu Bunne?' demanded Gavinu as anger started to well up inside him. 'It's common land, free for grazing and not bound by the feudal laws. They abolished feudalism twenty years ago. The enclosure laws surely don't cover common land.'

'Well, Babbu owns our land,' cut in Marina.

'I know that,' Gavinu replied, with an impatient edge to his voice, 'but he only owns the farmland. He doesn't own the valleys of Sos Lamparigos or Littischedos or the mountains of Perda Longa or Perda Viasu, because you share the common rights of those with all the neighbouring landowners. But Salvatore is a Sard; of course he owns his land. It is his by right, his family has owned and worked the land in this area for generations. However, Don diVenti is different – he is a Piedmontese, a baron landowner. How can he, a Continental, own our mountains and valleys, that belong to the Sard people? He doesn't even live here. He only comes for the shooting, and to organise the felling of the timber. Then the Pisans come to cut and pollard all that is left for charcoal.'

Salvatore sighed a deep sigh. He remembered his father saying the same words to him as he sat on his lap as a child, hungry from the famine that ravaged the island.

'Much of our land is owned by those from other countries,' said Salvatore. 'Many of them never live on the land they buy, but have others to farm it for them. They cut down our forests for the timber and lay waste the land. They strip the soil of all its growth; take the silver and the gold and raid the copper mines, returning to the island for their hunting and to collect their fat profits.' He paused to relight his cigar. 'People just take from Sardinia; they never give.' He sighed.

Marina watched her father as he became engulfed in the grey cloud of cigar smoke as he puffed on it to keep it alight, and the heavy smell of the rich tobacco filled the room.

Gabriella rose, collected her sewing and sat down again, listening to her family.

'One problem that will come, though,' Salvatore continued; 'the strangers do not know the ways of our land. When they strip the forests and take the wood, without a thought for the future, they will turn it into a dry, barren land. A wilderness where life will become hard and the sun-baked soil fruitless, is all that will be left for our future generation's heritage.'

A momentary silence fell across the table as they thought about the destructive violation of their beloved land.

'Tell us about Pinta Niedda,' begged Marina, moving her chair closer to Gavinu. She didn't like it when her father became serious, for his words often bore a prophetic ring. Gavinu composed himself enough to continue with his story, and looking at Marina, gave her an understanding smile.

'Don diVenti has many men to help him on the land,' he continued, 'and all of them come from either Piedmont or Savoy. They have cleared the land of stones, making wall enclosures where he keeps his pigs and cattle. He has walled and terraced vast areas, and planted vines that he brought from his native Piedmont. He has cultivated the olive trees and planted many new groves. He has built a large cantina to take the wine press, and another for the olives. People come from Sassari to buy his surplus, and he ships it from the island to Genoa and somewhere in France, where they say he knows the markets. He even has a separate outbuilding near the stables to house his mollentu for grinding the corn; he doesn't keep it in the storeroom as we do.'

Gavinu paused and took a sip of wine, and looked around again at the various pairs of eyes fixed on him in amazement at his story. 'Like you,' continued the young man, 'we let our sheep roam the common land.' He waved his good arm and shrugged his shoulder. 'Sometimes they go in among his olive groves and wander in his vineyards, I will own that,' he said, pouting, 'but Don diVenti says they cause damage. He has ridden over to us at Pinta Niedda several times to say he would either shoot the sheep, or keep them if they continued to roam over his land, and he or his men are always firing warning shots at us whenever we ride

13

too close. Do you know,' he said, wagging a finger at Salvatore, 'he doesn't even allow his hens in the vineyards? Babbu says he will have trouble with the beetle and it will destroy all the vines, not just his, but everyone else's in the area, just as it has in parts of the Continent, but he won't listen.'

Gavinu took another sip of his wine.

'Anyway, two days ago our sheep broke into his vineyard again. The following morning, I went out to find six of them with their throats cut and their carcasses thrown on our doorstep.

Babbu, Ugo and I left at once to go and collect what other sheep he may still have, but Don diVenti and his men were waiting for us. He accused us of sheep-stealing, then fired on us. The Don fired from the other side of the courtyard, and Ugo fell to the ground. I don't remember much after that. I know Babbu yelled at me to get out, but I wanted to see if I could help my brother. When I reached him, I knew there was nothing I could do for him. He was already dead. Killed by that Continental bastard.' His voice rose with his emotion.

Gavinu paused, trying hard to compose himself as the scene of that morning came rushing back with vivid and horrifying clarity. He took another swig of his wine in an attempt to stop his hand from trembling.

'I swung towards Don diVenti to avenge my brother's death. The Don had raised his gun to shoot me, but I fired first. I saw him fall, but then another shot rang out, and a terrible pain ripped through my shoulder. The Carabineri had arrived from nowhere. God knows, they must have been told we would be there. I saw Babbu make good his escape, and I took to the mountains as fast as I could. I know my way around here like the back of my hand, which is more than can be said for the Carabineri as most of them are Continentals. Although I hear they are recruiting young Sards as volunteers to join them now.' Gavinu looked pale, and tears stood out in his eyes as he recalled the tragic events.

'Are you sure Ugo is dead?' asked Gabriella, unable to take in all of Gavinu's story. She put down her sewing at her young cousin's harrowing tale. 'How could this happen to you?' she said, shaking her head, unable to believe it. 'You are such a law-abiding family, good people and honest folk.'

Gavinu nodded and wiped his hand across his face to wipe away any tell tale tears that might give away the emotion he felt pent up inside him, and was trying so hard to control.

'I don't know Cousin Gabriella, but he was only nineteen. He had his birthday last month,' said Gavinu, catching his breath, 'and now he is dead, killed by that Continental pig.'

'Well,' said Salvatore 'it seems that Don diVenti is not dead yet.' He touched Gavinu's arm to reassure his young cousin. 'You are only wanted for attempted murder according to the Captain, who came here tonight.'

'Be that as it may,' cried Gavinu, his words snapping with bitter sharpness, 'but I tell you this, Cousin Salvatore: Don diVenti killed my brother and I shall avenge his death, as soon as I am able. They can dig his grave now, for it is sure that he will be in it before the next full moon. He is a doomed man. I swear it by all the saints, and on my dead brother's soul, I swear it.'

A long silence fell over the table, then Gabriella said in her soft manner, 'You will have to rest until that arm has healed, and you will be safe here. Heaven be praised, that bullet passed straight through so it shouldn't take too long. Had it been a shotgun it would have been a different story.'

'Shouldn't we let them know at Pinta Niedda that he is here and safe?' asked Marina, concerned for Gavinu, who still looked upset.

'No, Marina,' replied her father. 'The fewer people who know he is here, the better for all of us. They will understand at Pinta Niedda, and know that if the Carabineri haven't found him and taken him into custody, then someone is sheltering him. I'll send word to them just as soon as I can, have no fear, and I will find out how Gavinu's father is too.'

Gavinu turned to Salvatore, bit hard on his lip and nodded. 'Thank you, cousin, for all your help.' Then after a short pause, he added, 'You were going to tell me why you had the store hideout. Will you tell me now?'

Salvatore sighed. 'My brother Angelo and I made it. He was a good carpenter and part of his job was to make casks and barrels for people to store their wine or oil. He lived in hiding with us for almost a year. The Carabineri never found him then. That was four summers ago now.'

'Why did he have to hide? What did he do?' enquired Gavinu, eager to know the details.

Salvatore shifted in his seat. It was not a story he relished telling. 'Angelo borrowed money from a Continental moneylender in Itteri,' he began. He took a piece of bread and wiped it around his bowl, savouring the last morsel of flavour. 'He needed the money for a month, to enable him to buy the land from his neighbour. He wanted it just until his sheep returned from the plains, and his lambs could be sold. He was too proud to come to me, the youngest brother, to ask for help, stupid fool; instead he asked a stranger, the man from whom he was buying the land. A Piedmontese, and eager to do the deal as he wanted to return to the Continent, he told him to see this moneylender, also a Piedmontese. They took the flock as security, saying that if the money wasn't paid in full by the end of the month, Angelo would forfeit not just the flock, but the land as well.'

Salvatore took a long draught of his wine; he felt all eyes on him, and clearing his throat, he continued. 'The end of the month came and Angelo had his sheep and therefore the money, so he went to the moneylender to repay his debt in full. It appeared the moneylender had left town, so he went to the landowner, but he had already left for Savoy. The man responsible for the land deals insisted the contract had been with the moneylender, and that Angelo would have to wait to see him on his return. The following day being Saturday, Angelo went to see the moneylender again, but his wife said he still wasn't home and to call on Monday. Angelo tried to leave the money with her, but she said she knew nothing of the contract or her husband's affairs.

'He returned on Monday, for being a good, church-abiding man, he obeyed the laws of God, and never carried out work on the Sabbath. Imagine his horror when he learned from the moneylender that his thirty days were up on the Sunday, and that he had lost both his sheep and his land.' Again, Salvatore paused, this time to relight his cigar.

To the family, the story was as familiar as the cautionary tales they had heard as children. They had lived through the events, and knew and loved their Zio Angelo, but the chance of a story; however well they knew it, and however sad, was a rarity to be savoured.

'Whatever did he do?' asked Gavinu, wide-eyed with disbelief.

'We went to see Gestinu Canu at Sos Lampidos,' continued Salvatore, 'but he could do nothing legally. His brother in Sassari tried to help. He is an important lawyer, with many Piedmontese clients, but all to no avail. Gestinu even went to the moneylender, but he wouldn't listen. He offered to double the money, but the man didn't want to know. Nothing, it seemed, would satisfy the land-greedy man. As you can imagine, my brother became desperate.'

Salvatore drew hard on his cigar, and his eyes misted over at the painful memory. 'A week later,' he said in a soft, deep voice with a slight break, 'they found the moneylender dead, shot with his own gun, and the contract and the money lay in shreds over his body. My brother had taken his revenge. It didn't take the Carabineri long to come looking for him. He came here and stayed with us in the mountains, and we made the hideout together. The Piedmontese took over the farm, then felled all the timber and made a vast profit, but left a barren land.'

'What happened then? Did your brother get away to the Limbara mountains to live with the other *fuori legge* or *banditti* that hide out up there?' enthused Gavinu, caught up with the romance of the outlaw bandit living in the wild, helped by his family or loved ones, for the sake of honour and his pride.

'No, Gavinu, he didn't go to the mountains. The Carabineri shot him when he visited his wife in Mores. She had taken the children and gone to live with her mother. They watched the place night and day. We begged him not to go, but he was headstrong and would have his own way. They gunned him down in front of the whole family. So, young man, you now know what happens to outlaws and *banditti*. It's not all romance,' concluded Salvatore, raising his mug and draining it to the last drop.

'When does Antonio come home?' asked Gavinu, eager to change the subject at the sight of his cousin's obvious sadness.

'We expect him any day now,' replied Marina. 'He promised he would be back with the herd before Mamma has her baby. Raffaella and Orlando came over from Sos Lampidos yesterday, asking the same question.'

Gabriella noticed Vitoria's face light up at the mention of Orlando's name, and recognised the same lovelorn look in Marina's eyes for Gavinu, and she smiled to herself. Vitoria and Orlando were promised to each other in marriage; in a contract made between Gestinu and Salvatore, as Salvatore had saved his friend's life when he first came to live in the mountains. Also, Orlando's mother, Maria, wished to join the two families as she had grown up with the Sannas. The *Cujugnu* or engagement would be soon, before Orlando left for Sassari to study law with his uncle, Zio Marco.

A sudden wave of tiredness washed over Gabriella, and she lifted herself from her chair and began to clear the table.

'No, Mamma, leave that, please,' said Marina, shaking her head and wagging her finger in a friendly manner. 'Please leave it and go to bed, you look tired. Vitoria and I will see to this, and we will make sure that Gavinu is settled for the night.'

Salvatore rose from his chair and walked over to a great chest in the corner of the room, where he took out a large sheepskin and handed it to Marina. 'Gavinu, you will be comfortable on this in front of the fire,' he said, then throwing his cigar stub into the dying embers, he kissed his daughters and followed Gabriella to bed.

Salvatore lay unable to sleep as his mind turned over the events of the evening. Perhaps, with good fortune and God willing, Antonio would be home soon. It would be good to see his son again. He worried about Gavinu and the likelihood of the Carabineri returning; if they found Gavinu at Punta Néula, Salvatore knew there would be trouble. The thought of Antonio having to go to the Continent for army service frightened him. Not until the early hours of the morning did he drop into a dream-filled sleep.

CHAPTER TWO

At Sos Lampidos, Raffaella Canu lay in her bed, suspended in that brief moment of time when sleep and waking merge into one, so she couldn't tell whether the sound of sheep bells was real, or if it came from her still dream-filled mind. All winter the valleys had been quiet, the sheep having gone to the plains, but now the familiar sound of tinkling bells filled the room.

Beams of light filtered through the holes in the wooden shutters. It caught the rough plasterwork and illuminated the pictures of her saints and the handwoven tapestries that covered the walls of her room. The vibrant colours of the hangings appeared blurred to Raffaella in her waking sleep.

A whistle, echoing up the valley and into her room, confirmed the reality she had been waiting for, and leaping from her bed, she threw open the creaky shutters. A flood of late spring light poured into her room, blinding her for a moment. The warmth from the sun felt comforting as Raffaella shielded her eyes against the glare, and searched the familiar landscape that spread before her.

Below this window was a yard filled with carts, and various implements for ploughing and reaping. Around the yard were the stalls which used to house the bullocks, and the vine-clad stables with their peeling plaster and neat terracotta tiles. The view of the mountains, was obscured from this window by a huge olive tree, double-dyed in pale green and silver, its shimmering magnificence shading the open area at the back of the house in the summer.

Although she couldn't see the river, Raffaella could hear it in the valley below as it grumbled and chattered its way over a bed of shiny, cold, grey stones; as it bubbled in the ravine with the fullness of extra water from the melted snows of the distant, haze-green mountains.

She went to the other window and flung the shutters against the vine-covered walls. The mountains, with their rich covering of *macchia* and cork forests, rose from all sides and towered over the small farmsteads that clung lovingly to the sides of the ravine. A mist still lingered in places around the valley, shrouding the vivid green of the flowering lentisk, bramble, Cistus rose, together with splashes of yellow euphorbia, and the pale asphodel. The granite rocks, jutting out from the green blanket of vegetation, rose like silent, ashen ghosts.

Raffaella reflected on last night's events and wondered if Gavinu had made it to Punta Néula. She had been the one who had slipped away and put the warning lamp in the attic window when the Carabineri arrived asking questions, while her brother Orlando and her aunt, Zia Paola, had kept them talking.

She looked across to the Sanna's farm at Punta Néula, which was perched on an outcrop of rock on the other side of the ravine, and bathed in yellow sunlight above vaporous, wispy clouds that still lingered in the shaded valley below.

Again, the shrill whistle echoed around the mountains. Raffaella strained her eyes as she peered out across the landscape. Now she saw what she searched for: hundreds of sheep moving down the pass. They were difficult to make out at first as they merged with the rock fall, but sure enough, on the small pasture where the Sanna's kept their sheep during shearing time, they were there.

The sound of their bells and bleating filled the valleys again after the silent winter. The clanging and tinkling bells from Gestinu and Salvatore's sheep became a background noise that melted into the spring and summer scenery, but when winter came the long, silent nights were still and unnerving.

Raffaella's heart leapt in pure delight. Antoneddu was back: he had been gone five months, and now she could see him again.

She washed and attended to her toilet, and then dressed in the new cotton shirt she had embroidered during the endless winter months, under the watchful eye of her Zia Paola. She pulled on her homespun *orbace* skirt and cursed under her breath as she fumbled with the laces of her bodice. She brushed her hair and put it up with combs, leaving her head uncovered. She often went without the traditional head covering, and was always being told off by Zia Paola and her father.

A quick glance in her mirror, she pinched her cheeks to give them a bit of colour. She tucked the hem of her skirt into the waistband, to keep it from dragging in the long grasses; slipped on her little shoes, and then fled along the corridor to see her brother.

'Orlando, wake up,' she cried, as she burst into his room. 'Orlando, for pity's sake wake up,' she cried again, desperate to shake him out of his deep sleep. 'Orlando! Antoneddu is back with Sergio and Ignazio – you can see your sheep and all the new lambs.'

Orlando stirred. He was never at his best in the morning.

'Oh hurry, do please hurry,' she begged, eager to be gone. She looked around the room, then noticing his wash bowl and jug, she grabbed his towel, soaking it in the cold water, and squeezed it over her brother.

Orlando, leaping from his bed, cursed the saints that he had such an ungodly young sister. Raffaella didn't wait to hear his rebuke, but raced downstairs and into the kitchen, calling to Zia Paola, who was busy helping Elena bake bread.

'Antoneddu is back,' she cried, as she took a piece of the newly baked loaf from the table.

'Not all day at Punta Néula, Raffaella – remember your father is coming home from Ozieri tonight,' called her aunt.

But Raffaella headed out of the kitchen door, past the veranda with its collection of pots, housing every variety of geraniums imaginable. Through the stable courtyard, with its fresh-sounding water running into the trough for the house and the animals, she went out of the gates, past an olive tree, and down the path that led to the lower meadows. The ground was still damp underfoot, with wet flowers and grasses that stung her feet and legs as she picked her way down the track to the pastures below. The whole area teemed with sheep and the air was full of their bleating as ewes called to their young, and they in turn searched for their mothers.

On she ran; up the stony path from which the sheep came on the last part of their journey from the plains. At the top of the ridge, she stopped to catch her breath. The early morning air caught the back of her throat, and the stitch in her side made her hold her ribs to stop the stabbing pain. Sure enough, coming through the pass were Antoneddu and her father's shepherd, Sergio, both riding and bringing up the stragglers of the vast herds.

Raffaella felt overjoyed, the pain gone in her excitement. Antonio, seeing her standing silhouetted against the haze-blue sky, dismounted and held his arms out to welcome her. She ran towards him in greeting. The next moment she was enfolded in his strong embrace, and she held onto him as if she wanted this moment to last forever. Antonio drew away, and held her at arm's length so he could have a good look at her. Raffaella drank in the sight of him with pleasure. He looked every inch a man with his broad shoulders and dark, deep-set eyes, although he was only two years older than her. His face was unshaven, and the heavy growth of beard added to his eighteen years. He was wearing his *berrita*, but it could not restrain his curling hair. His shirt was dust-stained and covered with horsehair, as were his white breeches and black kilt. Also, she recognised the all-too-familiar smell of sheep on his clothes. She smiled. He looked brown and well, and she sighed, happy to see him again.

'My dear little Raffaella, how you have grown, and how I've missed you this winter,' he said, taking her hand.

'Oh Antoneddu, I'm so pleased you're back. Orlando will be here any minute. Tell me, did you have a good winter? I thought about you a lot, and I've missed you too, really I have,' she enthused.

Antonio laughed. Raffaella always called him by his childhood name of Antoneddu, although everyone else called him Antonio, but he liked it, and was pleased with the intimate nature of the nickname.

'Tell me, *sa sposixedda mia*[i], has Mamma had her baby yet?' he asked, concerned.

'No. No, not yet, but she is very near. Zia Paola said last week that we'll be moving to Punta Néula soon to help Gabriella,' she replied, looking into his dark, searching eyes.

'Come here, Raffaella,' said Antonio, pulling her towards him; at the same time swinging his horse around so Sergio could not see them. 'My God, Raffaella, I've missed you,' he said, taking her in his arms and kissing her with a passion she had not, until that moment, experienced. When she drew away from him, she felt dizzy and a little shaky at the knees. Antonio noticed with pleasure that her dark eyes betrayed the deep, awakening feelings he aroused in her.

'I've run so fast before eating I feel faint,' she said in all innocence.

Antonio laughed again and ruffled her hair. 'You have a lot to learn, *bellaxeddu mia*[ii] and I will be happy to teach you.'

'I'm not so little,' she replied with an indignant air. 'After all, I will be sixteen in October and Zia Paola says I'm almost a woman now, Antoneddu.'

A cry went up from the ridge, and they looked up to see Orlando waving in greeting, with Vitoria and Marina. They too had heard Antonio's shrill whistle.

After all the embracing and greeting, and Orlando recalling the brutal way in which Raffaella had made him get out of bed, he and Antonio fell to talking about the business of the sheep with Sergio.

'All the sheep have the sign, Orlando, so Sergio and Ignazio can sort the herds when they need to, so they can roam the pastures with ours.'

'That's fine, Antonio, and thanks,' replied Orlando as he slapped his old friend on the shoulder. 'The weather must have been good on the plain, by the look of your sunburnt face and arms.'

'Not bad, not bad at all. Good, mild weather and plenty of pasture have made many strong lambs this season.'

'The snows have been gone from the mountains for three weeks now. We expected to see you earlier,' said Vitoria, looking at her brother.

'I would have been back sooner, but I had some business to attend to on the way home. Sergio and Ignazio also wanted to see their cousins at Badde Torzu, so we stayed there for a few days. Still, I'm home now and that's all that matters,' replied Antonio with a broad smile.

'Where is Ignazio?' asked Raffaella, looking around and searching for him among the sheep.

Ignazio, a child of the wild, was Sergio and Elena's son. He had inherited both his parents' fear and superstitions, and convictions that spirits lived in the dark where they hid in the caves. Much to the despair of Zia Paola, who found the habit he had of appearing out of nowhere unnerving.

'He will be along later. He is with the stragglers,' said Antonio, and he tweaked her nose with his forefingers, making her smile.

At Punta Néula, Salvatore embraced Antonio, and Gabriella cried out in her delight at seeing their son. She threw her arms around him in a warm welcome. Her obvious delight at having all her family under one roof again showed above all else as she clucked around her son like a plump mother hen. Antonio was her firstborn, and therefore special to her, and the winters always dragged when he was away. She turned to Raffaella.

'You look happy now, my dear,' she said with a tender smile.

Raffaella returned the look and then turned to Antonio, who gave her a broad wink.

The room hummed with gossip and idle chatter while the warm, comforting smell of cooking mingled among them. Marina told her brother about the arrival of their cousin Gavinu, and how the Carabineri had come looking for him. When there was a lull in the conversation she turned her attention once more to Gavinu. Salvatore again asked Antonio about their sheep and how the

25

winter had been, and whether they had lost any lambs.

They all sat around the fire, and while Gabriella cut Antonio's hair, he tried again to reassure his father that the losses were only a few lambs and a couple of old ewes.

Raffaella watched Gabriella. She felt a twinge of jealousy at the touch and attention his mother could give to Antonio as she trimmed his hair and beard.

'Antoneddu,' ventured Raffaella, 'please don't take off your beard. I do like it so much that way.'

'Do you now, *bellaxedda mia?*' he said with a large grin on his face. 'Hear that, Mamma? She likes it that way. Well, *sa sposixedda mia* if that's what you want; it can stay, but it must be trimmed, all right?'

Raffaella nodded, and felt a glow of triumph flow through her at his smile.

'You haven't grown your beard then, Orlando?' chided Antonio. 'Don't you like it, or aren't you man enough yet?' he teased.

Orlando laughed. Although he was the same age as Antonio, he knew he would never be able to produce such a luxuriant growth as his friend.

'I don't like beards,' cut in Vitoria, always ready to leap to Orlando's defence. 'I think they are untidy and give a man an ill-kept appearance.'

Antonio and Raffaella looked at each other and laughed.

Five months had passed since they were all together last autumn. With Antonio away on the plains and Orlando at school at Iterri, time had slipped by. True, there had been days when Marina and Vitoria had ridden over to Sos Lampidos for their lessons with Raffaella, for Zia Paola insisted on the upkeep of their studies. There had been times, too, when Raffaella had ridden over to Punta Néula, to see Marina and Vitoria and to spend a day in glorious peace and happiness with her beloved Gabriella, who always treated her like another daughter. But somehow it was never the same without Antonio. He made everything happen and encouraged everyone to join in; even Orlando and Vitoria came when Antonio organised them. The stronger character, Antonio held them all together. Orlando, on the other hand, was easily led. An acquiescent type, Orlando always followed the crowd, or the least line of resistance, with a love of the finer things in life and a loathing of hard manual work. Vitoria, too, had the same undemanding character, and for that alone they were well suited.

They were soon called to be seated at the table for the midday meal. Orlando sat next to Vitoria; Antonio sat in his usual place and pulled Raffaella down beside him. Gabriella noticed they were absorbed in each other's company since her son's return, and was happy for them. She knew that they shared the same strong, independent spirit, with a love of freedom and an acute passion for the wild.

Marina sat with Gavinu, for she had not left his side since his arrival; only to snatch a few hours' sleep, and to welcome her brother home. She had risen in the early hours of the morning to draw water for him and redress his wound.

Gabriella had taught Marina the art of healing with herbs so she would be able to carry on the work for the villagers after her death. She had learnt the art from her mother, Carmella, who had been widowed while still a young woman, and from her mother before her. Carmella, was the local *Accabadora*[iii], the woman who came in the night to send the sick and dying to a sweet death.

Marina had all the strong characteristics of her grandmother, with a great sense of loyalty and justice. Gabriella knew, deep down, that Marina would encourage Gavinu to seek revenge for his dead brother, and it worried her. She sighed. This 'calf-love' was more serious than the usual relationship between cousins.

That night, when Raffaella lay in her bed at Sos Lampidos, she turned the day's events over in her mind. In her hand rested a small wooden horse that Antoneddu had carved for her while he was away. Also on her side table were two new combs for her hair that he had carved from bone, and engraved with his name entwined with hers.

She had given him a knife. He had had his eighteenth birthday in March whilst away on the plains. She had worked hard over the past year, picking the wild asparagus in spring, and the asphodel in summer. She had helped the women to make their baskets, which Sergio and Ignazio sold in Ozieri, when they had taken their vegetables and carvings to the market. She had picked wool with other women from neighbouring homes, and helped to spin the yarn ready for weaving. She had worked hard in the garden for Zia Paola, and helped her to make the candles. She ran errands for her father, she had also helped Elena wash the linen in the river, and every *centesimi* went into her jar so she could buy Antoneddu the knife she knew he wanted.

Zia Paola had taken her to the knife-maker in Pattada, who knew Antonio, and told them which one he had often admired. Raffaella had counted out her hard-earned money with pride, and with a discount for friendship, she had been able to buy it herself.

The expression on Antoneddu's face when he opened the present was well worth all the hard work, and Raffaella had thrilled to the long kiss he had given her. He was home now, and they would be together every day. The thought filled her with unusual warmth, and a sense of well-being that she had never experienced before.

Raffaella had become aware that her childlike devotion to Antoneddu and her protective love had now turned into something different, stronger, and a warmth crept through her. The memory of Antoneddu's kiss came back to her again, giving her a deep, profound longing for the morrow.

CHAPTER THREE

Zia Paola arranged a large meal at Sos Lampidos for the Sannas and the Canus on Easter Sunday to welcome Antonio back and to celebrate the festival. Sergio and Ignazio roasted a suckling pig and the smell of the roasting meat hung in the air, whetting their appetites. Salvatore provided some of his excellent wine and Gabriella had made *Sebadas*[iv] the traditional sweet given to the shepherds when they returned from the plains, and *Sospiri*, sweets of almonds and honey, for dessert.

The windows and doors of the house were thrown open to let in the sun's warmth. It proved to be a beautiful day spent in the company of family and good friends.

The last days of April were full, and passed swiftly. They decided to accommodate everyone at Punta Néula. Zia Paola arrived with Raffaella and Orlando so they could help Salvatore, with the nearness of Gabriella's confinement, leaving Gestinu in the capable hands of Sergio's wife Elena, who ran Sos Lampidos with Zia Paola. Raffaella joined Vitoria and Marina in their room upstairs. Zia Paola had been given Antonio's room; he would be with Orlando and Gavinu in front of the fire on their sheepskin rugs. They all slept in beds normally, but when they were young at Sos Lampidos, they had often slept on the floor. Tomorrow, it would be Vitoria's seventeenth birthday, and she would attain her womanhood and celebrate the *Cujugnu*[v] when she became engaged to Orlando.

Today, however, they had decided to have a treat and to go to their secret pool with a picnic, leaving the adults to prepare for tomorrow.

Orlando gave Vitoria a large, silver filigree button for her costume, and was touched to see how much it pleased her. The others had worked hard and saved to buy her a silk shawl which Zia Paola bought for them on a recent trip to Ozieri. They decided to give her the presents today, as they all knew that tomorrow would belong to the adults with the festivities and engagement.

The excitement in the air became electric; even the dogs felt the sense of occasion and wouldn't leave Antonio's side in the hope he would take them hunting.

At last they were ready to leave, and Vitoria mounted behind Orlando on his horse. Marina rode in front of Gavinu so she could take the reins, as Gavinu's arm wasn't yet healed enough to handle Salvatore's spirited animal, but he made sure he put his good arm around young Marina's slender waist, and would whisper sweet words in her ear, making her smile and content to be in a world of their own.

The girls were wearing white linen scarves on their heads. Their fresh cotton shirts and beautiful coloured skirts made a striking contrast to the woodland green backdrop of the mountains.

Orlando and Vitoria were the first to set off, followed by Gavinu and Marina on Salvatore's horse. Antonio made some excuse about collecting something from the house, and when he returned, was pleased to see that the others were almost out of sight on the long path down to the river.

'Do hurry,' cried Raffaella, 'the others will leave us behind.' She patted *Bandidu*, Antonio's dog, who had returned from the retreating couples; he wagged his tail and jumped up, worried in case he should be left out.

'The day is too good to hurry,' replied Antonio as he mounted his horse from the usual mounting block. 'Come, give me your hand, *sa sposixedda mia*,' he said, leaning over and pulling her and her basket up behind him. *Bandidu*, seeing they were coming, raced off down the track to join the others.

Antonio's horse picked its way down the rugged sheep track to the river that divided their two lands. From this point Raffaella could see both houses. First, Sos Lampidos, where she had been born and lived all her life. The house, a large, imposing two-storey

30

building set back from the ravine, rose like a heavy outcrop of granite. The crumbling plaster work was covered by a vigorous vine, which ramped and twined its way over the old house, and added the only contrast, for even the roof was made of granite slabs.

Her father, a good farmer and lawyer, was well-known and respected in the area. He had come to Sos Lampidos on his marriage to Raffaella's mother, Maria, and the farm had been her dowry. The neighbouring farmstead, in the other valley and the lower valleys of Sos Lampidos, belonged to Papa Giovanni, Raffaella's maternal grandfather, and were joined so they could be farmed as one unit. Raffaella knew there would be no such dowry when she married, for Orlando would inherit the farm. She would have to be content with a few of her father's sheep and goats for her marriage contract.

Raffaella looked across the valley from where they had come. Second, Punta Néula now perched above them. A smaller farmstead, but with a startling freshness about it, with its neat, whitewashed walls and terracotta roof. All her earliest recollections were rooted in this collection of buildings and the people who lived and farmed here, for their lives were interwoven, like the intricate threads of her tapestries that hung on her bedroom wall.

Her mother, Maria, had died giving birth to her. Her father's sister, Zia Paola, had come to live at Sos Lampidos to look after her and Orlando. Zia Paola had been fifteen at the time and training to be a teacher. Now in her early thirties, she and Raffaella had become close, and the two adored each other.

Zio Carlo, Zia Paola's father, had sent her to the local convent as a child, where it was expected she would become a nun. Her brother Franco had also been sent to the seminary in Ozieri. However, when Maria died, Gestinu had gone with Maria's father, Papa Giovanni, and begged Zio Carlo to release Zia Paola from the convent so she could look after his young children.

No more than a child herself, she had insisted they all learnt to read and write from an early age. Zia Paola had taught them all the finer things of life, and how to sing and dance. From Zia Paola they also learned the names of the flowers and birds; while from Gabriella they learned the secrets of the plants' healing powers, and from Salvatore they learnt the ways of hunting, trapping and fishing.

Sergio saw to it that they knew about the bad spirits, and how to ward them off with the many other superstitions which ruled his life. The broom outside the back door to keep away evil spirits who would stop to count the bristles, but as they could only count to seven, it would occupy them all night until dawn, when they would run away. He also told them about the spirits who live in the wells, and would try to pull children into them.

He had been the one who insisted that Maria, Gestinu's wife, be buried with soap, a needle, thread and a thimble, afraid she would become *Sas Panas*, a woman who, after dying in childbirth, went to the river every night to wash her child's clothing for the next seven years. Anyone seeing her would condemn her to another seven years, so great care had to be taken not to disturb the spirits in the night. Father Franco had blessed the coffin, sprinkled holy water on it and read from the gospel, thus ensuring that no harm would come to Maria's soul.

Gestinu, who worked in Ozieri, tolerated all the comings and goings, for he owed his life to Salvatore. During his first year at Sos Lampidos, he had been set on by *banditti* and Salvatore had spoken up for him, and vouched for the 'stranger'. The family were always welcome at Sos Lampidos, although her father was at pains to point out to Raffaella that they, the Canus, were from Sassari while the Sannas were local landowners.

The two houses came into view again between the overhanging trees. The cliff-like sides that faced each other were steep and covered with a tangled mass of varied vegetation: lentisk, cistus, myrtle, bramble and hyssop, which gave a sweet and delicate scent that came intermittently on the air. From where they were, it looked impossible to climb such a sheer face, for the narrow little track was concealed from her searching eye.

She watched as the scene disappeared from view, obscured by the great bushes that flourished at the water's edge. Here, the willows and reeds mingled with the delicate flowers of the oleander, which looked like coloured stars in the milliard shades of green and silver-grey.

'What's the matter, *bellaxedda mia?*' asked Antonio, sensing her deep thoughts. 'You're very quiet behind me.'

She sighed and hugged him. 'Just thinking,' she replied dreamily.

They neared the river, and she could hear its loud burbling drowning the sweet, intermittent song of the warblers and the continuous rasping of the cicadas. They forded the stream and carried on up the meadow, over a small rise and down into another valley, where another stream rippled through the stones. A rock fall across the river made it easy for the horses to cross. The water rattled through the stones as it swirled and gurgled its way downstream, pulling the long sweeps of willow into the water in a graceful swaying motion.

Once across the river Antonio dismounted and led his horse along a narrow pathway up to the secret pool. They had found this by chance while out hunting one day when they were children, and since then, they came to bathe or spend carefree hours away from everyone and to enter their own private world.

The other horses were already grazing in a small clearing under the shade of a large, twisted willow. Antonio stopped and reached up for Raffaella, taking her in his arms to help her down. He looked at her with tenderness. His love for this young girl had grown as he had grown, and he hoped one day she would be his own. Raffaella was a tomboy at heart, a wild, free, loving spirit; which he loved, for she matched his untamed and unbridled love exactly. He was a creature of impulse, but his feelings for Raffaella ran deep and were sincere.

He held her against him, savouring the closeness of her, and then, placing her on the ground, reached up for his saddlebag. He grabbed her hand and pulled her up the rocky path to the ridge where the river divided. They sidled along the uneven path with its overhanging willow and oleanders. Below the pool came into view, sparkling in the sunlight like molten silver. The others were already in the water, splashing and laughing; their assortment of clothing scattered across the rocks and scented bushes.

Antonio turned to Raffaella, and kissed her cheek. 'Come on, let's join them,' he said, dropping to the ground below. He put his hand up to help her, but she brushed it aside, laughing, being as sure-footed as any mountain goat.

Antonio took their towels from his saddlebag and stripped to his cotton breeches, then dived into the water. 'It's lovely, Raffaella, come on, do hurry,' he called, treading water and watching her as she stripped off her shirt and skirt, leaving her in her cotton three-quarter-length embroidered petticoat. This she grabbed in one hand, then holding her nose with the other, she ran towards the pool and jumped in, surfacing a moment later amid a mass of bubbles and frothy white lace.

'Are you all right?' he called, laughing at her.

'Yes,' she gasped, trying to catch her breath from the coldness of the water. 'I'm fine, but by all the saints, it's cold, though.'

They all swam and splashed in the pool, and even the dogs found the courage to join their master and have a quick thrash in the now churning water. Gavinu waded at the water's edge, unable to swim because of his arm, but took delight in finding sticks and threw them to the dogs, watching as the animals steered themselves with their tails towards the floating objects.

It wasn't long before Vitoria decided she had had enough. Marina and Raffaella were happy to follow her, and collecting their towels, they rubbed themselves dry and then lay on the sun-warmed rocks to soak up some of their precious warmth.

Antonio and Orlando chose to have a diving contest, so it fell to Gavinu to judge. While Orlando practised his dive, Antonio sat at the water's edge and watched Raffaella's every move.

He couldn't help noticing how she was beginning to develop into a woman – not so much as Vitoria perhaps, but then his sister was a couple of years older than Raffaella. He had little doubt in his mind that Orlando noticed Vitoria's figure, for he often eyed her with obvious delight. He knew, too, that they had shared the joy of intimate love that he longed for with Raffaella.

He looked at her again; her wonderful smooth skin; her beautiful, trim breasts, which stood out under the thin, wet cotton petticoat that clung to every curve of her damp skin. The whiteness of the cloth contrasted with the brownness of her olive skin and long black hair that fell in waves to her waist.

Orlando swam to the edge where Antonio sat, and followed the gaze of his friend, watching Raffaella.

'Lovely young women, aren't they, Antonio?' said Orlando.

Antonio nodded. He became aware of the longing for Raffaella which now stirred in him, and dived back into the cold water to dampen his mounting desire. He longed to know the softness of Raffaella and the warmth of her love, but he knew she was too young and too innocent as yet.

'If you are going to do some diving, you'd better hurry,' called Vitoria. 'The food is all unpacked, and we're starving.'

The boys abandoned the idea, and swam to the edge of the pool and hauled themselves out of the water. They stood on the rocks and shook their heads so the water from their shoulder-length hair sprayed everywhere.

'You're like father's dogs, shaking like that,' cried Raffaella as the cold water fell on her sun-dried skin. Antonio made a grab for her, and whisking her off her feet, held her over the now-still pool. She screamed in fright and laughed at the same time, begging him to put her down.

'Ask me nicely, *sa sposixedda mia*,' he whispered to her.

'Please, Antoneddu, please put me down,' she wailed. 'Please, please let me go.'

He let her down, but still held her arm.

'Give him a kiss, sister, and then he'll let you go,' called Orlando.

35

Raffaella looked at Antonio, unsure of herself, and he smiled at her.

'No, I won't,' she said, the colour rising on her cheeks.

Antonio pulled her towards him and cradled her in his arms, not wanting to hurt her in any way. Raffaella, grateful for this protection, clung to him, for she could feel the heat rising still further on her cheeks.

'Why, my dear little sister, I would never have thought you would be so shy,' said her brother in a mocking tone.

Raffaella, still unsure of herself, threw him a stony look.

'Leave her be, Orlando. She is far more sensitive than you give her credit for, believe you me,' said Antonio, freeing her from his embrace. Raffaella, trying to compose herself, went to help Marina and Vitoria.

They had a good meal of cheese, meat, olives, bread and wine from Antonio's vineyard. Afterwards, they settled down to doze the afternoon away, or indulge in the small talk of which lovers are so fond.

Orlando and Vitoria lay apart from the others, their arms around each other, lost in their own private world. Marina lay spellbound next to Gavinu, who was telling her how they were related through their great-grandparents. Antonio flung himself on the ground in the full sun, while his head rested in the moving shade of the oleander. He put his arm out to hold Raffaella, and she lay against him, enjoying their closeness.

'Look,' he said, pointing with his free hand, 'up there, can you see the hawk hovering above the ridge?'

She nodded and snuggled even closer. They talked about the animals and the beautiful flowers, for they shared a great love and respect for the wild.

Raffaella watched as Antonio dropped into a sun-warmed sleep. She lay beside him, and could hear the dogs chasing through the undergrowth, their fevered searching punctuated by excited little yelps as they neared the scent of some poor unsuspecting prey. She sighed. All this would end soon. In a few days Orlando and Vitoria would be married and live in Sassari with Zio Marco so they could be together, and Orlando would start at law school. They would only come home for short visits at Easter, summer and Christmas.

It would be difficult for her to see Antoneddu without Zia Paola or Gabriella present. Worse still, Babbu had been talking about sending her to Itteri to his cousin's for schooling at a new academy for young women which had just opened, and was run by some well-respected spinster from Sassari. The thought frightened Raffaella. She had never been away from home or her beloved valley for any length of time; only to visit her Zio Marco in Sassari, or to Ozieri, to the convent with Zia Paola, and to see her maternal grandfather, Papa Giovanni. She would be cut off from everyone and everything familiar, and it made her heart sink from sheer terror.

Antonio stirred and turned toward her; she looked at his dark, handsome features, relaxed in sleep. His neat, trimmed beard hugged the side of his face, but hid the cleft she knew to be on his chin. His eyes were deep and large; his lashes were long and his unruly hair lay like a halo around his brown, weathered face. Dark hair lay close to his chest, giving him a much stronger and more virile appearance for his years. There was the large scar on his left arm from a sheep-shearing accident. His hands were large and work-worn, but he was a good-looking man, and she sighed again, but this time with contented satisfaction.

Raffaella turned her attention to Vitoria as she lay in her brother's arms. How different she was from Antoneddu. Her skin was a smooth olive colour and her hands, although showing signs of work, were small and fine. Her long raven hair fell in generous black waves over her shoulders and across her dainty frame. Vitoria looked delicate, almost frail compared with her brother; more refined. Yes, that was the word Babbu used. Little wonder that Orlando loved her.

Orlando too carried that look of quality about him, a natural polish which made him stand out from other men. He was tall and his hair, though long, was always pulled back into a neat ribbon. His eyes were topped by high, arching eyebrows, and his features were finely chiselled, with full lips. His skin was a dark golden brown, not sallow olive like Antoneddu's. He carried the Catalonia stance which gave him an air of dignity; inherited from Gestinu, for their paternal grandparents were all Sassarese; while their mother, a pure-bred Sard, was a native of these mountains.

There was little doubt in Raffaella's mind that Orlando and Vitoria made a perfect pair, and she was happy for them both. But she doubted whether Orlando, with his high ideas, could ever stir the same wild feelings deep in Vitoria as Antoneddu did within her, and she smiled. Still smiling, she rose to her feet, walked to the edge of the pool and collected her sun-dried clothes. The sun had started to dip in the late-afternoon sky, and she felt the change in temperature. Antonio noticed it too, and began to stir.

She became aware of him watching her as she dressed and combed her long hair. He watched the quickness of her fingers as she braided it and put it up with the combs he had made for her, and finally put on her scarf. Her every movement gave him intense pleasure, and he found her natural rhythm hypnotic.

The others busied themselves dressing and collecting their possessions. It didn't take long to round up the dogs and the horses and once more set off for home. As the steady procession wound up the path towards Punta Néula, Antonio turned to Raffaella.

'Orlando will be coming to look for a lost lamb tomorrow, *sa sposixedda mia*.'

'I know, isn't it exciting? I can't wait. I've finished my costume and shall wear it for you.'

'Our turn next, *bellaxedda mia*,' he called over his shoulder as he spurred on his horse to catch up with the others.

CHAPTER FOUR

Late spring in the mountains is a favoured time, with the vivid greens of the macchia and the fresh scent of the massed variety of wild flowers. The singing birds and bumbling bees make it near paradise. Flowers carpet the grazing areas with their patchwork of colours: windblown purples, yellows and white, that sway in the meadows and creep among the grey rocks, or fall and trail in the streams, which chuckle and gurgle in their waterways, hushed now after the rush from the distant snow-thawed mountains.

It held the promise of the approaching summer heat, when the passing breeze coming from the valley would be hot and dry, and the heat of the midday sun, combined with the lack of rain, would turn these lush, verdant valleys first to gold, and then brown. When people and animals sought the shade of leathery green olive or cork groves, away from the relentless, burning sun. However, today there was still the bright freshness that came with the late spring.

Raffaella rose early to help Antonio with the milking. She sang softly to herself, while Antonio whistled contentedly, as he collected the milk and carried it across the yard to the dairy.

In the farmhouse at Punta Néula, Marina blew life into the embers of the fire ready to heat the milk for making cheese and ricotta. She took a pan from the hook by the door and scooped some water from the barrel nearby, then placing it on the fire, she turned to Gavinu.

'Mamma wants to look at that wound and make sure it is all right,' she said with a smile.

Gabriella came forward to help. She undid the bandages while Gavinu watched, gritting his teeth against the anticipated pain.

Gabriella took the hot water from the fire and dampened the bandage to loosen the pieces stuck to the wound.

She was well-known in the outlying farmsteads for her herbal remedies and her healing powers. The local people often consulted her, for they had little or no faith in doctors, believing them to be nothing more than useless, and they charged too much money and never gave the patient an amulet or charm. Gabriella never charged for her services, but was always rewarded with a pot of honey or cheese.

Gavinu watched his cousin as she worked. Her full breasts rested on her round stomach, distended by the nearness of her confinement. Although in her late thirties, her long black hair was streaked with grey, all of which she pulled back into a neat bun at the nape of her neck.

He remembered with pleasure how he had watched his own mother, last year, when she carried his baby brother. How well women looked and how at peace with the world they seemed in their fulfilment. He remembered, too, the warmth he felt towards his mother when he watched her feed the baby at her breast, and how proud his father had been with the arrival of his new son. He recognised the same pride in Salvatore's eyes when he looked at Gabriella.

'When is the baby due, cousin?' asked Gavinu.

'Within the next week, that's for sure. He is near now; I can tell by the way he's lying.'

'Why do you say "he"?' laughed Gavinu. 'Surely you can't tell?'

'It will be a boy,' she said with disarming conviction. 'Another son for Salvatore, and he will be so pleased and proud.'

Gavinu winced and pulled back from her touch.

'I'm sorry. I didn't mean to hurt you. It is healing well you should have no more trouble with it.'

She leant over and put her hand into the large stoneware crock, and pulled out a generous helping of the pale green salve. It had a clean, pungent smell of lemon, thyme and honey, and the ointment, felt cool and soothing as she spread it on the wound.

'You still haven't answered my question, Gabriella. How do you know it's a boy?' he asked.

'Simple,' she replied as she again bandaged the wound. 'Girls are carried in neat little bundles in the front, hardly noticed, but boys; they are carried all round, like a barrel.'

Before Gavinu could reply, Antonio came in carrying a pail, brimming with the milk.

'Put half of that milk in the jug, Antonio, we need it in the house,' called Gabriella.

He did as he was asked. The rest he poured into the pan, which he returned to the fire to heat. When the milk was warm enough, he took one of the muslin bags his mother and Vitoria had filled with the dried leaves of lady's bedstraw, and stirred it in until the milk curdled, helped by the herb. He continued kneading the curd, then scooping it out of the pan, filled a nearby cork container which he sat on two pieces of wood across the bucket. The whey ran in small rivulets from the holes around the base of the cork container and splashed into the bucket below, as Antonio pushed on the curd, then flipped the cheese over and then pressed down on the curd again. Finally, he placed a piece of cork on top and weighted it down with a stone to press the cheese flat. He then continued to heat the whey until the curds of the ricotta formed and his work was finished.

Raffaella appeared in the doorway carrying a huge wooden pail of water and poured it into the barrel by the door. She disappeared outside again to refill the pail from the large container Antonio had loaded on the back of the house donkey earlier that morning, when they had both filled it from the spring.

'That bread smells good,' said Raffaella on her second entry into the kitchen. 'You must have been working hard with Zia Paola this morning, Vitoria.'

Unable to sleep with the excitement of the day, Vitoria had risen early. Everyone wished her a happy day, and one with good fortune. She had seen to her father and Orlando before they left for Sos Lampidos to see Gestinu, Orlando's father, to make the final arrangements for this evening. She now put the finishing touches to her baking with the help of Zia Paola, who was never one to languish in bed.

After breakfast, Orlando returned from Sos Lampidos with the gig; he and Vitoria were to go to Ozieri to see Papa Giovanni, for he and his wife would witness the civic marriage at the town hall. It had been arranged that they should have lunch together as Papa Giovanni couldn't get to Bantadda for the church wedding. Everyone waved them goodbye and then settled back into their work.

Marina busied herself in the morning by replacing the herbs and salves in the cupboard and returned in time to help with the meal. She collected the *prosciutto* from the cold room, plus one of the cheeses, *pane carasau*[vi] and olives. She prepared the table and carved the meat, and invited everyone to sit down to share the food, and enjoy the general conversation.

In the afternoon Marina and Gavinu spent their time together, Marina busy sewing her dress, which would, some day, be her bridal gown. Learning to sew was customary for the young girls, together with the skills of fine embroidery from their mothers; handed down from each generation, and keeping the ancient patterns and designs alive.

Marina and Vitoria always divided their time between mending the already patched everyday clothes and the finer work. Today, Marina chose to work on her dress, encouraged by Gavinu's flattering comments on the neatness of her intricate work. He, meanwhile, sat by her and tried to carve a wooden dish for them to eat off.

Zia Paola contented herself with preparing pasta for the evening meal. It was to be *Malloreddus*[vii], and a large basket was already full of the small, date stone-shaped pasta. She assured Raffaella and Antonio she didn't need their help, so they made their escape outside away from the rest of the family.

He chopped the wood and Raffaella helped him by stacking the logs into neat piles by the stable door. Later, they went to the pigpen and after much deliberation selected and prepared the two sucking pigs for the evening's feast. They lit the fire and put the halved carcasses of piglets on spikes which Antonio drove into the ground near the fire.

Salvatore returned in the late afternoon from Sos Lampidos. He unsaddled his horse and led it into the stable.

'Is that you, Babbu?' called Antonio from the dairy.

'Yes. Tell me, have you got those pigs ready yet?

'They're all prepared, Babbu, and cooking slowly,' returned Antonio.

'Good. I'll go and tell Mamma I'm back. Gestinu will be over later. He is bringing the notary from Bantadda. Is Vitoria back yet?

'Yes, she is upstairs. Orlando brought her back about half an hour ago.'

Salvatore was welcomed by his two hunting dogs, which he patted and then pushed gently to one side as he entered the house.

Zia Paola came forward to greet him.

'I understand everything is ready for tonight,' he said, giving her a quick, affectionate hug.

She smiled in return. 'Gabriella is upstairs resting. I sent her to lie down. She is looking tired now. Vitoria is upstairs getting herself ready. It seems they had a good day with Papa Giovanni.'

'You're a good friend, Paola, thank you,' said Salvatore.

He strode into the large inner room and helped himself to a glass of wine. He took a long draught from the glass, refilled it and greeted his youngest daughter, Marina, who jumped up to kiss her father.

'Oh Babbu, is Orlando going to ask for a lost lamb tonight?' she asked, her eyes wide with expectation.

'He is,' replied her father. 'I have just come back from Sos Lampidos where Gestinu and I have been making the final arrangements.'

Marina clasped her hands together and closed her eyes. 'Oh

43

lucky, lucky Vitoria. I wish I were the oldest.' She opened her eyes and looked straight at Gavinu. He smiled and gave her a broad wink, making the colour of the tincture Sarda flush on her cheeks.

'By the way, Gavinu,' said Salvatore, 'Sergio has ridden over to Baddu Bunne to see his sister and tell her to pass on the message that you are safe and well to your family. It seems the Carabineri is still in the area. Sergio will be here later this evening so he can give you the news.'

'Thank you, Salvatore. No doubt it will put Mamma's mind at rest – it's nearly two weeks since I left.'

Soon, they were all busy with their little jobs for the Festa. Salvatore donned his new *berrita* and finest traditional clothes for the occasion. He sat by the fire in the yard with Gavinu and helped with the suckling pigs, and the smell of the roasting meat filled the area. Branches of myrtle lay on the wooden dishes, waiting to infuse the cooked meat with their delicate flavour.

Marina put the finishing touches to the sauce for the pasta and set huge pots on the fire to heat the water for the *Malloreddus*.

'When you have finished that, Marina,' called Zia Paola, 'be a good girl and wake your mother. She will want to be down here when Gestinu arrives.'

Antonio and Raffaella had changed into their traditional dress and Antonio was now busy greeting the villagers as they arrived, while Raffaella went to help Zia Paola with the last-minute arrangements.

Gabriella entered the kitchen and tried to help Zia Paola, but was sent to find Salvatore, so she would be with him when the guests came.

First to arrive were Signore and Signora Piddis and their three young daughters and one son, followed by Sergio and his wife and then some of the many neighbours that would be dropping in all through the course of the evening.

About an hour later the sound of horses' hooves on the dry ground sent Marina to the window. They could not see a lamp at Sos Lampidos; nevertheless, Gavinu was dispatched to the storeroom for safety.

It proved a friendly knock at the door. Salvatore peered around it to greet his dear friend Gestinu Canu, and Orlando with him. A shadowy figure stood apart from the two friends, his face obscured by the darkness. The friends exchanged embraces and Salvatore asked what they wanted of him, adding, 'My house is small, but my heart is big. Welcome.'

'We come in search of a lamb for our flock. We think you have the one we are looking for here in this house,' said Orlando with a wide smile.

Salvatore threw open the door and beckoned them all to come in. Gestinu entered, followed by Orlando and the shadowy figure.

'Salvatore, this is Signore Gregorio, the notary,' said Gestinu. The shadowy figure stepped forward, and the two men shook hands. All the men were dressed in their traditional finery of embroidered white shirts, and sported either red or black waistcoats. A short, black, kilt-like garment fell over a pair of white cotton trousers, which in turn were tucked into heavy cloth gaiters or soft leather boots. On entering the house, they briefly doffed their *berritas*, but again replaced them in their own particular fashion.

The room buzzed with greetings. Marina went to collect Gavinu from the hideout, so he too could join in the festivities.

'Now tell me again what it is you seek, my friend?' asked Salvatore as he filled his guests' glasses with wine.

'We seek one of your lambs,' repeated Orlando.

'Well, I have this one here,' continued Salvatore. 'A little thin, I'll grant you,' he said as he pulled Marina forward and looked at her. 'Thin, yes, but fine-looking,' he added.

They shook their heads.

'What about this one?' said Salvatore, putting his arm around Gabriella and laughing, enjoying the age-old ritual that went with the *Cujugnu*. 'Perhaps not a lamb, but a fine ewe?'

They laughed, and Orlando shook his head, giving Gabriella a wink.

Salvatore intended to enjoy the ritual of the engagement. Out of the corner of his eye, he caught a glimpse of his daughter coming down the stairs. He offered each of his friends' daughters in turn and Orlando smiled, but kept shaking his head.

At last Salvatore waved his arms in a broad sweep around the room. 'Are you sure there is nothing here among the present company that you wish for?' he asked, as he distracted their attention.

Orlando followed Salvatore's line of gesture, searching the faces for the one he wanted. When he looked back at Salvatore, he saw Vitoria standing close to him. She looked shy, and even a little frightened.

'Oh, I forgot,' said Salvatore, laughing. 'Of course, there is this one, also a little skinny, but no doubt adequate,' he said, pride welling up in his chest as he looked at his eldest daughter. She looked breathtakingly beautiful in her finery that she had made, and he noticed, too, how all the men stared at her.

Salvatore tenderly took Gabriella's hand in his; their eldest daughter, seventeen years old and now a woman. The same age as Gabriella had been when he asked her father for the lost lamb twenty years earlier. How time had flown, and what goodness there had been in the family. Now, with one ready to leave, Gabriella had been blessed late in life, with a new addition to the family.

Orlando put out his hand and took Vitoria's; she looked pale and fragile and Salvatore noticed that she trembled as Orlando squeezed her small hand to comfort her.

'Yes, this is the lamb I'm seeking, Babbu,' he said, turning to his father.

But it was Salvatore who spoke. 'If you take this lamb,' he said, feeling a sudden pang of uneasiness tinged with jealousy, with the realisation that the affections of his daughter would be for another man now, 'you must promise, before us all, that you will always love and cherish her. For if any harm befalls her, by all the saints and the Holy Mother, you will pay for it. I swear it.'

Orlando stared at Vitoria, lost in the depths of her dark eyes. 'I promise, Salvatore. I shall love and cherish her all my life, and no harm shall come to her while she is in my care. If I should fail her, then may Heaven rain her wrath on me,' he said, never taking his eyes from her gaze.

'Then she is yours, Orlando, with my blessing,' replied Salvatore, his voice shaky as a twinge of fear caught him.

Orlando took a small gold ring, the *Fede Sarda*, from his pocket and placed it on Vitoria's engagement finger on her right hand. Later, at their marriage service, he would move it to the wedding finger on her left hand as a binding contract of his love. There was a long silence in which the two lovers read volumes in each other's deep, dark eyes.

'Come, Orlando,' said his father,' claim her, she is yours now. She has been yours since her birth, when your sainted mother asked for the union. God rest her soul. Welcome to the family, my dear Vitoria.' With that Gestinu raised his glass and drank the health of the young couple.

Orlando took his betrothed in his arms. He could feel her tremble under his touch, and he bent forward and kissed her on the lips.

A cheer went up from all present. Gabriella wiped a tear from her eye with the corner of her apron. Zia Paola sniffed into her handkerchief, while Antonio filled the glasses with wine for all the male company.

Orlando took Vitoria's hand and drew her to one side, at the same time pulling her towards him. He kissed her forehead and put a finger under her chin, lifting her face towards him. Her eyes were dark and inviting.

'I have a need for you. Tomorrow we marry – I hope you are happy?'

'Oh yes, Orlando, I'm happy, and I have a need for you too.

The Holy Mother has been kind to us, for we were chosen for one another and we love each other.'

'What's more,' he whispered, 'we know our love and have shared its joys and pleasures.'

Vitoria blushed and put her hand to his lips, preventing him from saying any more, frightened that someone might hear.

Antonio watched his sister with his lifelong friend and was happy for them, but needed to see Raffaella, and went to look for her. He found her in the storeroom filling a large flagon with wine.

'I hope to come to your house next year in search of a lamb,' he whispered in her ear. She felt a shiver of excitement tingle down her spine, and the thrill of expectation made her blood course through her veins. He felt her reaction, and it pleased him. She turned to face him, and saw his face, fraught with the conflict of his inner emotions.

'Oh, Raffaella,' he sighed, taking her in his arms and making her spill the wine from the flagon as he did so, 'I want you to know how I feel about you – *deu volu bene* – dear Raffaella, please let me ask your father if we can marry, I beg of you.'

Raffaella looked at him. She always looked up to Antoneddu as a brother; since early childhood they had shared all their secrets and innermost thoughts. She knew him better than she did her own brother. True, she missed him while he was away this winter, more than ever before, and when she saw him again this spring, she knew she felt differently about him compared with his return from past winters. She yearned for him so much, and ached in her longing for his touch. Yes, she needed him too.

He held her close to him, sensing what she was thinking, and he showered small kisses on her rosemary-scented hair. He roused feelings from the depths of her soul and stirred her inner mind so she no longer knew peace within.

'Could you love me, Raffaella?' he asked with such solemnity, she realised she could not toy with his affections.

'I'm still too young, Antoneddu. I have another three years

before Babbu will give his consent. Unlike Vitoria, I will have to be eighteen.' She paused and looked at him. 'Tell me, Antoneddu, do you want to marry me?' she asked in all sincerity.

'My dear, sweet girl, I have always wanted to marry you, but this winter, while away, I knew I wanted you above all else, for when I lay awake at night thinking about you, I would dream I was holding you. You haunted my mind until my brain became numb and my soul ached with its longing for you, as it does now.'

How strange, she thought, for in the velvety nights of winter she had often dreamt of being held by him, as if she were lying in his arms and feeling his warmth close to her.

He kissed her, tasting the sweet wine of innocent love.

'Come now, Antonio,' came a voice from behind them, and a large hand fell on his shoulder. 'You will have to be patient in your request for my daughter. She is still a child, and I have made no promises as to her marriage.'

Antonio let Raffaella go and swung around to be met with the stony faces of both his father and Gestinu. Without a word, he took the wine from Raffaella and taking her hand, he pulled her past the two men, leaving them alone.

'I tell you, Gestinu, my son has a love for Raffaella, the like of which I've never seen before in a man,' said Salvatore. 'He wakes at night, crying out her name, and there are times that he plunges into the depths of despair and loneliness over her. Tell me, Gestinu, do you know if Raffaella returns his feelings at all?'

Gestinu looked at his old friend with a faint smile. 'The notary has just sealed one deal. The wax isn't yet dry and the ink is still wet on the paper. Don't let us be in a hurry to repeat the exercise. Raffaella is like a young boy at the moment – womanhood has not yet caught up with her. She still spends her time in the meadows watching the animals and chasing butterflies, or helping Sergio and Ignazio with the sheep. I have plans for her to go to Itteri after Orlando leaves, so that she can learn to do the things all young *Bourgaise* women should know. As you know, her mother was an accomplished pianoforte player, and I want Raffaella to have the same chance. At Sos Lampidos, she is surrounded by men and dominated by a spinster aunt; although my sister, Paola, has some of the fine qualities that Maria possessed, but she does tend to spoil the child. They have learnt all they can from her, and I want Raffaella to have plenty of young feminine company and learn some of the ways of a lady. She is my only daughter, and it is the least I can do in the memory of her mother.'

Salvatore thought for a moment. 'Where in Itteri will you send her?' he asked.

'There is a school for young *Bourgaise* ladies opening in the summer. Now the road from Sassari is opening, great expansion is taking place. I believe, once the child has known the happy, elegant life of the sophisticated town, she will not wish to return to the mountains to live. My cousin lives in Itteri and knows many influential people; Raffaella can stay with her, and Orlando can collect her when he returns to Sos Lampidos from Sassari.'

Salvatore said nothing, but took a long draught from his glass. Clearly, Gestinu had other plans for his daughter. A small landowner like Antonio, with little land, for some of his land had been Victoria's dowry, was not among his friend's plans. Poor Antonio would have to look elsewhere.

Salvatore sighed as he walked back to join the rest of the family. He would try to make the best of the rest of the evening.

The celebration passed with the usual feasting and drinking, and later in the evening, Salvatore took down his *Launaddas* and with others playing their guitars, he played the haunting melody of *Ave Maria Sarda* while everyone joined in with the familiar, plaintive tune. When the last note had died away, Ignazio joined Salvatore as he played his accordion, quickening their pace and nodding at Vitoria and Orlando to take to the floor. Soon, everyone joined in as they danced the *Ballu Sardu*. The long, deep, sustained notes droned on, with the quick, successive notes on the higher range of the ancient reed pipe. It was to these notes that the dancers' feet moved in perfect time, their bodies moving to the minute steps, making dresses swing in a rhythmic swaying of heavily pleated skirts as they stepped out the ancient stories that lie concealed in the age-old dances.

The only light came from the dying embers of the fire, and an oil lamp hanging from the ceiling at a crazy angle, its light catching the happy faces and reflecting the gold and silver heirlooms that rested on the lace-fronted shirts of both men and women, giving them the appearance of a Renaissance painting, while all else merged into the darkness beyond that of the light of the lamp.

In this half-light, it proved impossible for the adults to see if the youngsters' fingers were entwined in an intimate fashion, or if their palms rested against their partners'. It was, however, possible in the midst of all this merrymaking to forget that someone had spilt olive oil on the table of the engaged couple, sending Sergio into a fit over such an ill omen. Although everyone tried to play it down, and Sergio had said at least three Hail Marys and fingered his *Mal Occhio* several times to ward off any evil, it had visibly shaken Vitoria and the company.

CHAPTER FIVE

All the ill omens were forgotten the next day as the sun rose in a clear blue sky. Both of the households were busy with the arrangements for the wedding. It had been decided to have the wedding feast at Sos Lampidos as the house was bigger and nearer the church.

Zio Franco Canu was the priest at the small church at Bantadda, his living paid for by his elder brothers, Gestinu and Marco. Father Franco was the one who christened all the new arrivals, and who married or buried the dead of the families in the neighbouring area.

Every one helped with gifts of bread or wine and the occasional lamb when they received the services of Father Franco. He knew their secrets from the confessional and helped them all in every way possible.

At Punta Néula, Vitoria was dressed in the wedding dress she had made over the years. Gabriella had braided her hair and looped it up over her head. Marina entered the bedroom and admired her sister.

'You look wonderful, Vitoria. Are you nervous about the wedding and tonight?'

'No. Oh, Marina, I am so happy. After Mamma has had the baby, Orlando is taking me to Sassari to live with his Zio Marco, so we can be together while Orlando studies for the law.'

'Won't you miss being here?'

'Yes, but it will be wonderful in Sassari. I can't wait to see all the great buildings and meet new people. There is talk of a ball when we get there to celebrate our marriage, and you will be able to come with Gavinu and Raffaella will come with Antonio. Oh, it will be so exciting. I can't wait,' she said, kissing her sister on the cheek.

'Will you be able to go out on your own?' asked Marina.

'Oh no. Zio Marco has people called *Majoli*, they are young men who live in the house to help, but go to university in the middle of the day. It is a way for poorer families to help educate their sons. They will take me out, and take me to mass as well,' she replied, again kissing her sister.

Outside, Antonio collected the horse to take Vitoria to the church. He had groomed the animal so that its coat shone in the sunlight. He had decorated the bridle with fresh flowers and coloured ribbons which Zia Paola had bought on her visit to Ozieri.

He thought of Raffaella and sighed. How long would it be before they too could be married?

A whistle sounded across the valley, and Antonio looked up to Sos Lampidos and saw Sergio standing on the cliff and waving. He waved in return, and went into the house to find everyone ready and chatting together in the large room.

Salvatore, in his best attire, looked smart. Gabriella, too, was in full traditional dress, looked happy, her head was covered with an embroidered shawl, a present from Zia Paola years ago, and still a treasured possession. Her apron rode high on her bump, and she smiled at her husband.

Marina, dressed in her costume, stood looking at Gavinu, and Antonio, watching her, realised that his younger sister was in love with their cousin. He smiled, and turned to see Vitoria coming down the stairs. She took his breath away. She looked lovely, but today she had an ethereal look about her. She stood before Gabriella, who took the white *mantilla* she had kept from her marriage, and placed it on her daughter's head, pinning it with a gold brooch. Tears sprang into Salvatore's eyes as he looked at his beautiful daughter and took her hands in his.

'Be happy, my child, and I wish you both a long and fruitful marriage,' he said as he kissed Vitoria and then, standing back, he put his arm around Gabriella and smiled.

'We must go now. You look wonderful, sister,' said Antonio as he went forward to take Vitoria's hand, and she smiled at him as he led her outside and helped her up onto the horse.

Holding the reins, Antonio put his hand in his pocket and drew out a small silver coin. He took off his sister's little shoe and put the coin inside, then carefully replaced the shoe on her small foot.

'*Buona fortuna*, Vitoria.'

'Thank you, darling Antonio. You next,' she said, squeezing his hand.

The rest of the family came out and climbed into the decorated cart, for it had been decided that it would be better for Gabriella to go in the cart rather than on horseback.

At Sos Lampidos, Orlando paced up and down the large room. He was dressed in a midnight blue three-quarter frock coat. His hair was tied back with a black velvet ribbon, and he wore a silk cravat at his neck.

Gestinu entered the room. He too wore a three-quarter morning coat and carried a grey sombrero in his hand. His parents came from Sassari, and he carried the Catalan stance which, at times, gave him rather an arrogant air, but that impression could not be further from the truth, for he was a generous man and a loving father.

'Are you ready, Babbu?' asked Orlando.

'Yes, I am. Zia Paola is just making sure everything is ready for the wedding breakfast. Where is Raffaella?'

'Behind you, Father,' said Raffaella, as she pirouetted in front of them.

Her black hair that escaped from her headdress shone in the morning light. Her figure now filled her new costume, and she wore little slippers on her feet.

'Well, you look very feminine today,' chided her brother.

However, at that moment, Zia Paola appeared in the doorway. She too wore traditional dress, which made her look taller and more upright than ever.

'Sergio has the carriage outside. We should go, or we will be keeping everyone waiting,' she said in her brisk, no-nonsense way.

Gestinu looked at his son and smiled as they walked out into the sunlit morning.

Vitoria and Orlando stood at the altar of the small church at Bantadda. The bright morning sun came in the east window and the beams of light fell across the old stone floor, catching the specks of dust, which had been sent into the air with the quick sweep by Father Franco before the service.

Salvatore stood next Vitoria, and Gestinu near to Orlando.

Father Franco coughed and took Vitoria's hand, and placed it into Orlando's and gave them his blessing. Orlando took the ring from Vitoria's finger and placed it on her left hand. The two young people made their vows to each other and then joined in a small mass together.

At the altar, they stared into each other's eyes and the priest said, 'You may kiss the bride.'

Orlando pulled Vitoria towards him and kissed her, and then, putting his arm around her, he led her down the aisle.

Zia Paola was standing with her brother Gestinu; they made a striking pair. Behind them stood Raffaella with Sergio and his wife, Elena.

On the other side of the aisle were Salvatore, Gabriella, Antonio, Marina and Gavinu. Gestinu shook Salvatore's hand and Zia Paola hugged Gabriella. Once outside the church, Orlando took Vitoria into his arms again and kissed her.

'Well, Signora Canu, how does it feel to be my wife?'

Vitoria looked up at Orlando and smiled.

'I couldn't ask for more, darling Orlando.'

All the company went forward to embrace the newlyweds. Gabriella threw the plates she was holding onto the ground in front of Vitoria and then embraced her.

'Good fortune, my child, and to you both,' she said, reaching up to kiss Orlando.

A small crowd of well-wishers from the village had arrived and they threw rice and rose petals at the couple, while the older women broke plates in front of them, ensuring good fortune in their marriage.

Orlando thanked the villagers, then picking Vitoria up, he carried her to his horse and mounting, he pulled her up behind him.

Gestinu helped Gabriella up into the carriage, and then gave his hand to Zia Paola to help her into the front with Salvatore. Gestinu then settled himself beside Gabriella. Sergio climbed up on the high front seat and drove the carriage home with his wife Elena perched up beside him.

Antonio walked to his horse, which he had hitched to an old tree, and mounted in a fluid movement. He moved toward Raffaella, bent and pulled her up behind him.

She put her arms around him and hugged him.

'Do you think we can marry here?'

'Of course, darling, maybe in a year or two.'

Raffaella leant against his shoulder and felt the movement of Antonio and the horse as they rode together. He felt wonderful in her arms, and her heart beat like a drum in her chest. She was in love and everything seem so right with the world. She would be able to persuade her father that she wanted to marry Antonio, and she knew, after a time, he would give her his blessing.

Back at Sos Lampidos, Orlando and Vitoria were placed at the head of the table and Gabriella, Zia Paola and Elena organised the food. The meal of cured meats, roast suckling pig and roasted lamb was all washed down with copious amounts of red wine, and carried on for the rest of the day. It was enjoyed by all, and when it was time for the cheese to be put on the table, Zia Paola and Gabriella came and sat down to enjoy the company, as the evening light faded fast.

Orlando stood and raised his glass to toast his father, Zia Paola, Gabriella and Salvatore for all their wonderful work, then picking Vitoria up in his arms, he carried her upstairs to their bedroom.

The room had been decked out with flowers and greenery, and it smelt fresh and cool as Orlando and Vitoria consummated their marriage, while downstairs, the families drank their good health.

When the time came to leave, Antonio went with Raffaella to collect the horse from the stable, and when inside, he took her into his arms and held her in a long embrace. When he pulled away and held her at arm's length, she saw a fire in his eyes she had not seen before, and it caused a thrill of excitement to throb through her body, making her ache for him.

Antonio led the horse from the stable and mounted in his usual fluid movement from the mounting block. He leant from the saddle, and touching Raffaella's cheek, bent to kiss her. She watched as he rode up to the house and then, with shouts of 'Goodbye' and waving hands, he led the cart with Salvatore, Gabriella, Marina and Gavinu aboard.

They returned by the road and by the time they reached Punta Néula, Gabriella was already asleep.

They woke her and sent her to bed helped by Marina, while the men looked after the horses and Gavinu poured the wine.

With everything done, Antonio, Salvatore and Gavinu sat around the long wooden table sipping the dark red liquid.

'It will be strange without Vitoria in the house,' said Salvatore. 'We will miss her.'

Antonio rose and laid his hand on his father's shoulder.

'We will all miss her,' he said, and he made his way up to bed.

CHAPTER SIX

April gave way to May. Orlando and Vitoria became aware of the short time they had at Sos Lampidos, before they left for Sassari and were excused the routine duties by Zia Paola. The others found plenty to do and shared the work, glad to be out of the house and part of the open countryside.

Two days earlier, Antonio and Gavinu, together with Raffaella and Marina, went to the pastures on the higher slopes of Sos Lampidos, to help Sergio get rid of a pair of eagles that had decided to nest on one of the high crags. The alarming loss of young lambs prompted drastic action, so they set out for *Su Spegu*. They found a dead lamb and placed it in an open area, thus attracting the eagles to the easy prey. The great birds swooped in, enabling Antonio and Sergio to shoot them both. Antonio cut off one of the eagle's claws and gave it to Gabriella with pride, for he knew it would ensure an easy childbirth.

Today, however, Antonio, having finished his work, went in search of Raffaella and found her alone in the stable watering the horses.

'How about coming with me to look for some honey for Mamma?' he asked as he took the pail of water she was carrying. 'I need some cork as well, and with a bit of luck, I thought we might even be able to catch some *Apiole* for supper.'

She agreed, glad for the excuse to be alone with him, and added that she must first tell Gabriella and Zia Paola where they were going, and collect something to eat.

'Meet me in the lower meadow by the old sheep pen, *sa sposixedda mia*,' he said as he rode off. Then, as an afterthought, he called, 'And make sure you come on your own.'

Raffaella found Zia Paola busy making the pasta for the evening meal, and told her where they could be found if needed. Then she helped herself to bread, cheese and wine, which she packed into her *bertulla*. A quick kiss to her aunt and a promise that they would not be too late, and she left.

She ambled down the long path to the lower meadow, taking in the gold-green of the valley, and the sweet, heady scent of the drying wild flowers, intensified by the sun, and drugging her mind. It all looked beautiful and so very peaceful. She did so love this land, for its wildness seemed akin to her own wild, restless soul.

Rounding the bend that dipped down toward the meadow, she saw, spread before her, the golden carpet of early summer grass; two large olive trees stood twisted and gnarled by time and climate. At their base were a pile of stones that formed part of the old sheep-pens. A huddle of sheep stood with their heads towards the trunk, their undocked tails swishing in a vain attempt to keep off the ever-nagging presence of the flies. She smiled as she remembered how she and Antonio used to leave messages to one another in the crevice of the large stone.

At that moment, she caught sight of Antonio, and was surprised to see him putting a young chestnut mare through its paces doing the *portante*, an easy gate between an amble and a trot adopted by the Sard horses, done by training them to trot with the two legs on the same side in unison the one with the other.

'Antoneddu,' she exclaimed, dropping her *bertulla*, 'where did you find her? She's magnificent. I haven't seen her at Punta Néula before. Where did she come from and why is she here?' Her unending questions fell out in her usual enthusiasm.

Antonio looked at her and laughed. 'Do you like her?'

'Like her? I love her, she's beautiful. But where did you get her from?'

'I bought her from a Pastore, who breeds horses down on the plain.'

'Then why do you keep her here?' she asked, annoyed by his reticence to answer her questions, but at the same time fondling the animal's soft muzzle.

'Because no one at Punta Néula knows I have her.'

'But why?' she persisted.

'Because first, I bought her with some of my share of my sheep money,' he replied, also fondling the animal, 'and second, I have been busy schooling her with help from Sergio. Anyway, she's a present.'

'A present from you to you. Oh, how lovely,' cried Raffaella in her excitement.

There was a pause, and Antonio laughed. 'No, Raffaella, not from me to me, but from me to *you*,' he said, watching her as she tried to take in what he had said.

'From you to me?' she repeated. 'What do you mean?'

'I mean that she is yours. That is, if you would like her?'

She stared at him, her eyes wide with surprise and disbelief, then suddenly springing forward, she threw her arms around his neck and hugged him, nearly sending him off balance.

'Oh Antoneddu, why? She's lovely. Is she really mine?' she enthused as large tears of joy rolled down her face.

He took her in his arms and laughed. 'You are a funny little thing. Does it mean so much to you, and give you pleasure?'

'But Antoneddu, I've never had such a wonderful gift, never. You know Zia Paola and I have to share the same horse.' She paused and then added, 'I wonder what Babbu and Orlando will say?'

'Does it matter?' he asked. 'After all, you are old enough to have your own horse now.'

'But why have you given her to me, Antoneddu?' she asked, looking up at him.

'Because I know you love horses, and that you would love to have one of your own, and because I didn't want to give you the traditional ring or piglet for a betrothal present.'

She looked up at him. Her voice, when she answered him, was drowned in the whirling of her mind. 'What do you mean, betrothal present?' she asked in a whisper.

He took her hand and led her to the shade of a nearby cork

tree. It was cool in the shelter of its grey-green leaves, through which a small breeze rustled above them. He sat on the dry stones that an old tree had grown out of; the roots making the stones split open. Antonio pulled her down to sit next to him.

'Raffaella, my love, I know I can't ask you yet, and that I should ask your father first, but I must know if you feel enough affection for me to hope that one day, you will marry me?'

She looked into his dark, deep, searching eyes. 'Dearest Antoneddu, you know I have always looked up to you as a brother. We have no secrets from each other, in fact, I've told you things I would never dream of telling Orlando, for he would not understand,' she said.

He took her hands in his and held them close to him,

'My darling Antoneddu,' she continued, 'if missing you and thinking about you all the time is being in love, then yes, I'm in love with you, and if wanting you to hold me and kiss me is being in love with you, and feeling that you were holding me when you were away last winter, and wanting to be with you forever, then I know that I am in love with you. If you want me to marry you, I shall be the happiest woman alive, for I believe you love me too.'

He pulled her closer to him and kissed her. She felt him tremble as he touched her, and the feeling sent a thrill of longing through her.

'I love you, Raffaella, of that you can be sure. I have been aware of it for many years now, but have been afraid to say anything lest I should frighten you, but such feelings can't be hidden forever.'

'Dear, dear Antoneddu,' she said, kissing him on his cheek. 'But you know I can't ask Babbu yet; you must know what his answer will be.'

'I know, I know,' he urged, 'but with the knowledge that you love me, I can wait forever if necessary. I feel I've waited a lifetime already, and now I know I have your love, I'll wait for another if I have to, my dearest little one.' Then, as if to change the mood, he jumped up, pulled Raffaella to her feet and led her to the beautiful horse he had just given her. 'She has been well schooled, so you will be able to ride her all the time,' he said as he helped her up into the saddle, then mounted his horse.

Raffaella turned to him, 'I will marry you, Antoneddu; I promise on my sainted mamma's memory, and by my own Saint Raffaella, I am yours.' And she leant across to him and kissed him.

'Race you,' he called as he urged his horse forward.

It didn't take long to reach the slopes of the neighbouring mountains where the cork trees grew in profusion amid the verdant, tangled vegetation, the shade of the trees giving a longer life to the grasses here compared to the open pastures. The heat of the sun made the scent hang in the air like a sweet-smelling mist.

To one side, the mountains towered above them, shrouded in their blue-grey haze, while on the other side, level ground gave way to the shrub-covered slopes through which cattle roamed. The clang of their cowbells competed with the ever-present rasping of cicadas and the constant chatter of the birds, as the cattle grazed in the coolness of leaf-laden shrubs and tall undergrowth. They were free to roam these lands, and the sound of their bells, mingled with the constant tinkling bells of the nearby sheep. They were only rounded up by their owners to be counted, and the new calves either sold or branded.

Raffaella and Antonio neared the cork trees and dismounted, and he busied himself cutting the cork away from the tree with the caution and skill taught to him by his father, so he did not damage the tree and its valuable harvest. When he had gathered enough for all the various plates, dishes, pails and bowls that needed replacing at Punta Néula, Raffaella helped him pack the cork into the two large saddlebags on his horse.

'Come on, let's go and find the bees,' he said, giving her a broad wink and pointing to a small outcrop of granite that rose from the surrounding trees.

'Do you think we shall be lucky?' she asked, scrambling along behind him. She had tucked her skirt up into her waistband to keep it out of the way, showing her legs under the white cotton petticoat which caught and snagged in the tough grasses.

'I don't see why not, they gave a good harvest last year and they have been left undisturbed since then, so there is no reason to doubt it,' he said, pulling a fine net from his pocket. 'But first, I want to catch a few of them.'

Raffaella helped him as he caught a number of bees, and while he held them by the head, she wound the fine silken thread around their bodies, releasing them when finished. They did this so often together that it was almost routine now, each knowing the other's move before they made it. When she released the last one, Antonio collected a large handful of dry grasses, which he wound into a tight bundle, then taking his flint, he struck it until the grass started to smoke. He breathed hard on it, then added some green leaves, making the smoke come thick and fast.

He nodded to Raffaella, who approached the cork hive with care and lifted off the roof to look inside. Antonio put the smoking grass over the hive to quieten the bees. Sure enough, there was honey, and plenty for both, him and the bees. He handed Raffaella the smoking grass and with deft hands and sureness of movement, he removed one of the combs of honey, gently shook off the bees before placing it into the waiting container he brought for the purpose, and then replaced the cork roof. She had stepped back to watch at a safe distance, and found she couldn't help smiling to herself as she watched him work.

'What do you find so amusing, young lady?' he asked as he collected the container and came towards her, trying to avoid the now-aroused bees.

'Nothing,' she replied. 'I was remembering the time when you first showed Orlando how to catch them and they swarmed. I shall never forget him racing towards the river chased by an angry host of bees. Do you remember?' she said, laughing as he stamped out the smoking grass, making sure there could be no chance of it catching the area on fire. Then, opening his canteen, he poured some water on the smouldering grass, extinguishing it.

'I do, and you shouldn't laugh at another's misfortunes,' he replied, trying to keep a serious tone to his voice, but they both laughed as he replaced the top back on the hive. He left the honey near the hive and went to find the birds. 'Come on, *bellaxedda mia*, or we shall lose our bees,' he called as he ran towards the trees and shrubs.

She followed behind, searching the trees as she did so. 'Look, over there,' she called, pointing to a cork tree. 'Can you see the blue flash against the trees?'

'Yes. I can see it,' he replied, running towards the bird, which flapped in a desperate effort to free itself, but the more it struggled the more entangled it became. Having seen the bees, the bird had swooped down to feast, swallowing the bee whole, leaving the silken thread to trail in the trees and branches to ensnare the poor, unsuspecting creature. Unable to disgorge the bee, the bird became easy prey. They found eleven in this way, and Antonio finished their misery with a sharp blow to the head from the handle of his knife, which Raffaella had given him and he always kept in his belt, and used on every occasion, including at the meal table.

'They should be good for supper,' he said, turning to Raffaella, but she stood with her hands over her eyes. 'Haven't you got used to that yet?' he teased.

'I just don't like it when you kill them,' she replied as Antonio took her hands away from her face. He smiled at her and gathered her in his arms. He collected the honey and his prey and carried her back to where the horses were grazing together.

A clearing near a small rivulet served as an eating area. The horses drank from the crystal water and then wandered to the shade of a nearby cork tree. There they stood head to tail and swished the flies from each other. Antonio and Raffaella splashed the cool water on their faces and bathed their feet before sitting in the shade of a tree to eat their meal. They lay in the shade and watched the sun, which all too soon started to sink behind the mountains, telling them the time had come to make their way back to Punta Néula.

They were entering the lower meadow when a shout went up

from the farmstead that echoed throughout the valley, and was immediately followed by two gunshots.

Antonio and Raffaella looked at each other. 'A boy,' they chorused, and raced up the path to Punta Néula.

There was little room to move in the neat little bedroom. Raffaella noticed that Vitoria, Orlando, Marina and Gavinu were all crowded in one corner, and Salvatore stood at the foot of the bed with the fretful baby in his arms. She noticed too the silver and green *Mal Occhio* that hung from a ribbon around the baby's neck.

She watched as Salvatore spat in each eye and then bathed the child in wine and salt, thus ensuring that evil could not enter through the eyes; the salt representing good fortune and the wine his good health. Having performed this ancient ritual, he handed the baby back to Gabriella, who suckled the fretfulness away.

Salvatore now sat next his wife, looking to all the world as if his heart would burst through his best attire, donned for the occasion. They both took sweets from the dish on the bed, as they had done for the first time on their wedding day. The bed had been moved near the fireplace, as tradition decreed, being a symbolic offering to the saints who protected the house and family. Zia Paola, in one of her lessons, had told them about the offering going back in time to Baal and Tanit, when the firstborn was sacrificed to the fire. Religion in Sardinia became the vehicle through which the ancient rites were still practised as either Christian acts or superstition.

Antonio went forward and kissed his mother on her forehead, at the same time taking a fond look at his new baby brother. He noticed too that his mother wore the eagle's claw around her neck, and was happy that it brought such good fortune. He stood up and put his arm around Raffaella and pulled her toward him, and squeezed her. She looked up into his eyes, and a volume was spoken between them in that moment.

'Well, what are you going to call him?' asked Zia Paola,

returning with another pail of hot water and the bandages for swaddling the baby.

Salvatore stood up and with a break in his voice said, 'We shall call him Salvatore, after me, and Antoneddu, after my firstborn son.'

'Salvatore Antoneddu Sanna,' repeated Raffaella, and then added in a quiet voice to Antonio, 'born on a day I shall never forget, for nothing will ever be the same from now on.' She looked at him, and smiled.

Little did she realise at that moment of happiness, how prophetic her words were to prove.

CHAPTER SEVEN

The day of the ball arrived in early June. Zio Marco's grand house in Sassari buzzed with activity as flowers were arranged in large vases and placed in the elegant rooms. A small boy had been employed to add ice to the water to make sure the blooms didn't wilt in the heat. As the sun dipped and the evening arrived the air became cooler, and a small breeze stole through the streets and into the windows, causing the blinds to flap gently against the panes.

Upstairs in the big house the excitement mounted as they put the final touches to their dresses. The sound of carriages could be heard in the courtyard, and the music drifted up the stairs to where Zia Paola and Raffaella were getting ready.

'Do sit still, Raffaella, how am I supposed to put these flowers in your hair if you keep fidgeting?' said her aunt as she set the last of the flowers in place.

'Oh Zia Paola, I am so excited, I can't wait,' cried Raffaella.

Zia Paola took a small hand mirror and showed her niece how she had arranged her hair. Raffaella looked in the mirror, turning her head from side to side to see better, then jumped up and hugged her aunt.

'Oh, thank you, Zia Paola, it looks wonderful and I know Antonio will love it.'

Ready at last, Zia Paola took Raffaella's hand and led her down the broad staircase to the large entrance hall. People were arriving, the men in cloaks and hats which they handed to the waiting servants who had been hired for the night.

In the hall, Zia Paola and Raffaella were greeted by their hosts. Zio Marco was dressed in the same style as Orlando, in a three-quarter coat, and Zia Madeleine looked elegant in the height of

Continental fashion, in oyster grey silk with pale blue trimming.

Raffaella and her aunt entered the ballroom; the smell of the fresh flowers filled the air with their scent, adding to the richness of the occasion. Raffaella knew Zio Marco's house well, as she had stayed here with her Zia Paola when she was younger.

She caught her breath as she gazed around the room. It had been decorated in duck egg blue and the plasterwork had been picked out in gold. Giant gilt mirrors hung on the walls and reflected all the light from the three large chandeliers which sparkled in the candlelight. Raspberry and gold brocade curtains hung at the windows, and the whole room took on a look of grandeur.

Orlando came to stand beside her.

'It's very grand, isn't it?' he said. 'I would love to have something like this when I have finished my law exams.'

'I don't know if Vitoria would settle here well,' replied Raffaella.

At that moment, Vitoria entered the room with Zio Marco and Raffaella noticed that all the men turned to look at her. She looked very sophisticated, in a red silk dress, embellished with black piping, that hugged her dainty figure. Zia Paola had piled her hair on the top of her head, with small ringlets framing either side of her face. Her olive skin and dark eyes were captivating, and Orlando drew in his breath when she came towards him.

'Why, Vitoria, you look stunning, darling.' He took her arm and went off to introduce her to more of his family and his new friends from university.

Raffaella, left alone, looked around her, searching for Antonio. People were filling the room and music played softly from the balcony above the entrance door.

Zia Paola came toward her. She looked elegant in a midnight blue dress, and her hair piled up on her head with decorated combs.

'Are you all right, my dear?' she asked. 'Have you met anyone yet?'

'No,' replied Raffaella. 'Orlando has just taken Vitoria over to meet some of his newfound friends. Where is Antoneddu? He is coming, isn't he?'

'He is, and he looks so handsome. I do believe that you two will be the best-looking couple here. That dress looks wonderful on you, my dear.'

Raffaella did a small twirl, allowing the pale blue silk chiffon dress to swirl around her ankles, and showed off her beautiful figure. She and Zia Paola had battled with Gestinu as he had wanted her to be in traditional dress, but Zia Paola had argued, and won. The fact that it was a ball, and, probably the only one Raffaella would go to, made a dress far more appropriate. Having won the day, Zia Paola had pulled out all the stops to make sure Raffaella's dress looked outstanding.

Raffaella bent forward and gave her aunt a kiss. 'Thank you, Zia Paola.'

At that moment Antonio made his entrance. Raffaella looked at him. He wore a long-cut coat in fine, dark navy. His hair, pulled back and tied with a velvet bow, and his beard had been trimmed professionally. His embroidered white shirt was held at the throat with two gold buttons, and he wore the bright red silk waistcoat she had embroidered with flowers, under the watchful eye of her aunt. His long, white trousers were pushed into soft black leather boots. She felt her heart skip a beat as she watched him as he walked towards them; she became aware of the women and young girls murmuring, and an excited flutter of fans as Antonio walked toward her. He bowed and asked if they were well.

Zia Paola nodded and smiled at her young protégés.

'Excuse me, you two, I need to see Marco. Make sure you mingle.'

'You look wonderful, Raffaella,' said Antonio, pulling her toward him.

'And you look so very handsome,' she replied, staring up at him.

Orlando came across to see them with Vitoria and another

young man who came from the Continent. He was thin and pale, with watery grey eyes.

'Raffaella, I want you to meet my new friend, Luigi Atzeni. He is studying medicine here in Sassari and I would like you to get to know him.'

Vitoria stood back. She knew a lot about the young man as he and Orlando were always in each other's company, and she felt her husband spent far too much time with the young Piedmontese student. She resented that Orlando always included him in everything they did together, and she had taken an instant dislike to the young man. She pulled away and made a comic face of disapproval to Raffaella from behind Orlando's back. At this, Raffaella found it difficult not to laugh out aloud.

Antonio, seeing her dilemma, stepped in front of her and, excusing himself, asked her for a dance.

He pulled her towards the dance floor and took her in his arms. They did indeed make a striking pair as they laughed together, and Antonio felt very grateful to Zia Paola for her insistence that they all learn to dance and acquire some of the social graces.

Gestinu came across the floor toward them and bowed. 'Forgive me, Antonio, but would you allow me this dance with my beautiful daughter?'

Antonio bowed and released Raffaella into her father's arms.

'You look wonderful, my dear,' he said, looking at his young daughter. 'You look so much like your darling mother.'

Raffaella smiled at her father as they glided around the floor.

The dinner gong sounded and people left the room to find friends and family to sit at the tables.

Orlando approached Raffaella and whispered in her ear.

'I would like you to escort Luigi this evening at the table. He doesn't know anyone and he needs company.'

'Ah, he's your friend, Orlando, you keep him company,' said Raffaella, and took Antonio's arm as he led her into the dining room to sit next to her, quickly changing his name card with Luigi's.

Father Franco said grace and everyone sat down at the great tables, which were covered with fine white linen, cut crystal glasses and silver cutlery.

Raffaella smiled to herself as she noticed that Luigi now sat next to some old spinster who was only too willing to tell the student doctor all her ailments. She also noticed the glowering look Orlando gave her. He showed his obvious displeasure that she and Antonio were seated together. Raffaella shrugged and turned to smile at Antonio.

The meal started with assorted fish in lemon and olive oil, followed by pasta generously flavoured with *bortaga*, a fish roe called Sardinian caviar. The fish course came, fresh and delicious, followed by delicate lamb seasoned with herbs. The whole meal rounded off with an exotic meringue pudding with fresh wild strawberries and raspberries. When the coffee came, the conversation had become a low hum of contentment.

Zio Marco rose and tapped his glass with his spoon.

'Friends and family, this ball is a celebration of my nephew's marriage to his long-term love, Vitoria. We welcome you, young lady, and look forward to getting to know you well.'

A gentle applause rippled round the room, and then Zio Marco continued.

'As you know, their marriage had been arranged at birth, but I am happy to say that it has become a love match. So I ask you, please to raise your glasses to the health and happiness of Orlando and Vitoria. May God bless and watch over you both.'

Chairs scraped across the marble floor as the guests rose and toasted the young couple.

The music started, and Orlando, taking Vitoria by the hand, he turned and bowed to his uncle and aunt, and led Vitoria to the dance floor.

Raffaella leant across to Antonio.

'Will you dance with me? I have marked my card for you, with all the dances,' she said with a captivating smile.

Antonio looked at her. She looked so beautiful in the

candlelight; her black hair and eyes shone with intensity and she had an air of excitement about her.

He rose and held his hand out to her, guided her to the floor and took her in his arms.

Zia Paola watched them, happy in the knowledge that they had learnt everything so well.

'They are a credit to you, Paola,' said her brother Marco as he watched the four of them dancing.

'They are all such lovely children,' sighed his sister.

'Not children anymore,' laughed her brother.

Marco took Zia Paola's hand and led her to the floor, while Gestinu took Madeleine and followed them. Soon they were joined by many of the other couples to the strains of a waltz.

With the first dance over, people returned to their seats to have a drink, or the men to retire to smoke. Orlando came over with Luigi and caught Raffaella's arm, holding it tightly.

'Luigi would like to dance with you. When do you have a spare dance?' he said, trying to take hold of her card.

'If he wants one I'm sure he doesn't need you to ask me. I'm sure he can ask for himself.'

The young man blushed, stammered and cleared his throat.

'Please, Signorina; I would very much like to dance with you.'

Raffaella looked at her card.

'Well, I'm afraid it's rather full,' she replied politely.

Orlando snatched the card away from her and saw Antonio's name written by every dance.

He turned to Luigi.

'It appears she has the next one free, so she is yours, Luigi.'

And with that, he pushed his sister forward into Luigi's arms.

Raffaella threw her brother a murderous look and let Luigi take her to the floor. Antonio stood to rebuke his friend, but then smiled, for Orlando looked like thunder as he watched his sister with mounting anger, as she stumbled and trod on Luigi's foot, making them both look clumsy and awkward.

Luigi couldn't keep his eyes off Raffaella, unaware of her

deliberate mistakes, and looked like a child who had been given a much-longed-for new toy, as he apologised for his mistakes.

Orlando watched his sister as she tried to make a fool of his friend, and it wasn't until Vitoria came and put her arm through his, and asked him for a dance, that he turned and smiled at her, making him forget Raffaella and leaving Antonio with a contented smile on his lips.

Orlando made no further attempt to make Raffaella dance with Luigi, but spent his time with Vitoria, while Luigi sat and watched Raffaella and Antonio with mounting jealousy for the rest of the night.

The evening had been deemed to be a great success, and when all the guests had gone, the family and close friends went to sit in the drawing room for a brandy.

Zia Paola rose first to leave, and Raffaella followed her as they shared a room. Antonio stood to say goodnight to Raffaella, but Luigi pushed him aside, took her hand and kissed it, while he stared up at her.

'I hope to see you tomorrow, Signorina,' he said, unable to take his eyes off her.

Raffaella withdrew her hand, nodded and then turned to Antonio. Wishing him goodnight, she excused herself and went with Zia Paola.

Once upstairs in the privacy of their room, Raffaella turned to Zia Paola. 'If Orlando thinks I am interested in that milksop of a friend, he is mistaken.'

'But did you enjoy yourself, Raffaella?' asked her aunt.

'Oh, Zia Paola, it was wonderful dancing with Antoneddu. Thank you for teaching us all to dance. We owe you so much.'

'It has been a pleasure, my dear. You both made me feel very proud tonight.'

The two of them dropped into bed and talked about the evening, and how handsome Antonio had looked. At last, sleep overtook them both.

The following morning the house buzzed with excitement

as everyone sat in the long room to have breakfast, while the servants packed the bags and men loaded the luggage on the waiting carriages. Final goodbyes were said as Gestinu, Zia Paola and Raffaella rode in the carriage, while Antonio drove it with his horse following.

Once back at Sos Lampidos, Raffaella went with Antonio to Punta Néula to see Gabriella and Marina, who had not been allowed to go as Salvatore had thought Marina too young and, there were concerns about Gavinu being seen by the Carabineri.

After all the excitement of the past week's things settled down into the usual routine in the little mountain community.

Three weeks after the ball, Antonio and Raffaella were down in the lower pasture helping Ignazio and Sergio with the sheep, when a number of shots rang out across the valley.

'Something is wrong,' said Antonio, looking anxious.

Collecting their things, they mounted their horses and raced back to Punta Néula. Salvatore stood in the doorway, his face ashen and tears running down his weathered face.

'Babbu, what is it?' asked Antonio as he dismounted, shocked at his father's appearance, and went forward to put a hand on his shoulder.

'It's Vitoria. We have just heard she has died from the cholera,' he said with a break in his voice

'Where is she now?' demanded Antonio.

'She is at the church at Bantadda. They have put her in her wedding dress and wrapped her in linen with quicklime and closed the coffin.'

'Why is she here?' asked Antonio, stunned.

'The reports from Sassari are bad, so many people have died. There is no one able to bury the dead – the hospitals are full, but there is no one to administer help; no priests for the last rites. There is no meat, no food and no water. The horrors of death are everywhere. Dogs roam the streets, devouring the carcasses. It has all been so quick, and has spread like wildfire. The townspeople are knocking down the city walls to allow the air in,' said Salvatore, trying to talk through his sobs. 'The messenger said Orlando and Zio Marco are coming to Bantadda so they can see her buried, but we will not be able to go near them. Zio Marco is moving his family into the country for safety as Zio Gianni has said they can live at Pinta Longa.'

Raffaella went into the house to find Gabriella. She found her sitting in her chair with young Salvatore in her arms, rocking him as tears ran down her cheeks and dropped onto the youngster. Raffaella went to her and put her arms around her to comfort her as the tears rolled down her own cheeks.

'What happened to her?' she asked.

'She went out with one of the young *Majoli* to mass, as the servant girl in the house had been taken ill. They went out to buy some things for the girl, and had bought some fruit and eaten it. They thought it was just an upset stomach before realising what was wrong with her. Vitoria went to nurse her. The next day she died and Vitoria followed the following day. My poor child. It all happened so quickly.'

Outside, Antonio went to find the horse and hitched it to the carriage. He needed to be alone with his feelings. He loved his sister, and the thought of her not returning to them was more than he could bear. He fought back his tears, but when Raffaella came out to find him, he fell into her arms and wept unashamedly. She tried to comfort him, but the pain of their loss ran deep and was devastating.

They all set out to the little church in Bantadda. Antonio, red-eyed, collected his distraught father Salvatore, and his mother, who held onto her youngest, asleep in her arms. Marina and Gavinu climbed aboard the carriage. She looked stunned as the reality of the death had not hit her yet, and Gavinu put his arm round her to comfort her.

All the families that had stood in the little church two months earlier in their bright costumes now gathered around the grave in black outfits. Zio Marco, Zia Madeleine and Orlando stood away from the others, fearing they may be contagious. Orlando looked drawn; he had large dark circles under his eyes, and he looked pale.

Raffaella watched it all. She wanted to go to her brother and tell him she loved him, but she knew she couldn't. She stood next to her father and took his hand; he looked forlorn, and she squeezed his hand to reassure him. He turned and looked at his daughter and smiled at her with tenderness.

Antonio stood on her other side, and she put her other hand in his and looked up at him. Life was so short, so unpredictable. Vitoria and Orlando should have had all their life together, but she had been cut down so cruelly. What would Raffaella do if something like that happened to her father or to Antoneddu? Her tears welled up, and she fought hard to keep them back, but they rolled down her cheeks, so she had to free herself from the two men to find her hankie and wipe her face.

Father Franco led the service, and with a break in his voice, he gave his blessing for the soul of Vitoria, who had been so full of life when she and Orlando had married. They buried her in the little churchyard with a small wooden cross to mark her passing.

Papa Giovanni, Gestinu's father-in-law, had offered Zio Marco and Zia Madeleine the farmstead at Pinta Longa, and they would remain there until they were sure that they were not infected, and could return to Sassari when the disease had run its course. Zia Paola laid out strict rules that all water had to be boiled. All fresh vegetables should be eaten, and she arranged for Sergio to take the new produce up to them every day, where he left it by the barn away from anyone. Gestinu stopped going to Ozieri as they had cases of cholera reported there, and life as they knew it took on a different aspect.

It was a sombre party that went back to Sos Lampidos after the funeral for the meal for the departed soul, and Raffaella never left Antonio's side, fearful she might lose him.

Death struck on a grand scale in Sassari that year. Many paid vast fortunes to have their families taken to the outer islands. A young man named Giuseppe Garibaldi organised the operation to escape the horrors of the fearful disease; at the same time earning money to fight to unify the Italian states.

Within months, the city of Sassari had changed beyond recognition. Shops and factories closed. The town filled with the sound of tolling bells and the smell of acrid smoke from disinfectant hung in the air. Business and trade came to a standstill; hospitals filled with the dead and the dying, as did the prisons, with nobody to care for the sick and the dead. Medicines were impossible to find and ships could not dock at the ports without a certificate of a clean bill of health for the crew.

The whole community closed down, fearful of strangers and outsiders. Many of the townspeople tried to flee to the countryside, but were met by the peasants with long rifles and sent back to their homes.

At Sos Lampidos and Punta Néula the neighbours exchanged meat for milk, oil for wool, and shared all other produce, and so the small community had been saved from the devastating effects of cholera that spread not just through Sardinia, but the whole of Europe.

PART TWO

PART TWO

CHAPTER EIGHT

Late winter, 1858

A chill in the evening breeze blew in from the mountains. The weather was mild for the time of year, as the little rain that had fallen gave the valley a freshness more common to spring than winter, but the air had a decided snap to it.

Raffaella climbed down from her horse and patted the animal as she tied it to a nearby tree. She stood for a moment and rubbed its muzzle. Her mind went back to the day when Antoneddu had given the horse to her. She smiled as she remembered how cross Orlando and her father had been with her for accepting such a gift from him.

Only after Salvatore and Gabriella had interceded for her had Babbu relented. How long ago all that seemed now. She'd known then that things would be different, but not as much as they had proved to be. Now, whenever she returned from Itteri, she either came here or went to see the Sannas at Punta Néula. She sighed and pulled her cloak around her against the cool breeze, and walked to the side of the small church.

In one hand, she carried a large bunch of wild flowers and grasses which she had stopped and picked on her way to the church. She knelt at a nearby graveside and pulled the wilted flowers from their container, replacing them with her fresh posy. She read the wording on the hand-carved cross as she did every time she came to the graveside, as if to convince herself of its reality.

Vitoria Sanna
Born 1838
Died of Cholera 1855
Age 17 years
Beloved Wife and Daughter

Three years had passed since Vitoria's death; a lifetime gone in a flash, with this small reminder of the life so cruelly cut down. Vitoria had gone to Sassari to live with Orlando and contracted the cholera, and within two days she had died.

Orlando had been wracked with grief, for he believed himself responsible for her death by insisting she came to Sassari. Salvatore remembered his feelings when Orlando promised to look after her, and how he said Heaven would rain wrath down on him if any harm came to her. He told Gabriella of his fears, and she did her best to comfort him.

After Vitoria's death, and when the disease had run its course, Gestinu put his foot down and sent Raffaella to the school in Itteri to stay with his cousin Maria, returning to Sos Lampidos when Orlando came home from Sassari for his vacation. Now, at last, her schooling was finished. Sergio had collected her for the last time so she could be home for Christmas, to help Zia Paola with the extra work. Orlando would be home too in a few days, and at Easter he would be taking up his law practice in Sassari, now free from all the horrors of the cholera epidemic.

A sudden gust of cold wind made her shudder, bringing her back from her thoughts. She pulled her cloak around her for extra warmth as the sun started to dip behind the high mountains, setting the area aflame with its radiant glow. Unaware that she was being watched, she made her way into the small church.

Inside, the air hung cold and dank. Raffaella bowed her head and knelt to the large crucifix suspended above the altar. She crossed herself and moved to the small chapel at the side of the main area, and dropped a coin into the offertory box, taking a candle which she lit from one of the many others that glowed and flickered in the dim, draughty building.

She knelt in silent prayer before the candles; their golden incandescence highlighted her young, fine features and the contrast of her black cloak gave her a nun-like appearance. She did not hear or see the dark figure that came from the shadows. Her whispered *Babbu Nostru* and *Ave Marie* drowned all sound to her ears. He, on the other hand, watched her every move, his heart beating so loudly he was sure she must hear it.

The figure came out of the shadows and walked towards the praying girl. He could see her pearl rosary catching the light as she pulled it through her delicate fingers, and could hear her low incantations. He knelt beside her and she, thinking he was another pilgrim, never took her eyes from her rosary.

'Raffaella,' said an all-too-familiar voice.

She turned toward the figure next to her. For a moment, she said nothing, searching his face to make sure she wasn't dreaming, or that he wasn't some vision sent to her by the blessed Holy Mother.

'Antoneddu,' she cried at last, 'what are you doing here? Sergio never said you were at home. I thought you were on the plains with the herds.'

Tears of joy sprang to her eyes. It had been months since they had seen each other. He had been asked not to visit her at Itteri, as her father hoped the childish infatuation she had for Antonio would disappear with the meeting of eligible gentlemen.

She flung her arms around his neck and wept tears of utter happiness.

'Come, come now, it can't be that bad,' he said, trying to console her and fight back his own emotions.

'How did you know I was back?' she asked between sobs.

'Sergio rode over to see us, and told us that you would be back today. You didn't come to Punta Néula, so I knew you would be here. All I had to do was wait.'

'But Sergio never said anything to me when he collected me,' she said.

'I asked him not to, that's why,' he said, a broad grin spreading across his face.

'But why aren't you away with the sheep?'

'Silly – for the same reason Sergio is at home. The winter has been so mild in the mountains, it hasn't been necessary to go to the plains, and Ignazio is with them. The food here is plentiful, there are heavy crops of sweet chestnuts and grasses, for the snows haven't come yet this year.'

'Oh, my darling Antoneddu,' she sighed, holding him tighter. 'I've missed you so much. Tell me, have you missed me too?' she asked.

'There is no need for me to answer that – you know I've missed you,' he replied, looking lovingly at her. 'But tell me, when does Orlando return from Sassari?'

'He'll be home in a few days, and he's supposed to be bringing that loathsome Piedmontese friend with him for Christmas.'

Antonio pulled her towards him and kissed her, tenderly at first, then with repeated small kisses, which became a mounting passion. Then, as if to check himself, he drew away and held her at arm's length. He released her and fumbled in the pocket of his waistcoat and brought out a small, carved coral hand on a gold chain.

'Raffaella, this is for you. Will you wear it for me, my dearest? I love you, Raffaella, and there are no words to tell you what I want to say to you. I want to cherish you forever. The love I have for you can't be measured. It fills my very being. You are the breath of my life, the beat of my heart, the love of my soul. All the poets in the world can't express the way I feel about you, dearest Raffaella.'

He placed the charm around her neck and kissed her again. 'It's a *bona Fortuna*.'

She made no answer, but turned and looked into his searching eyes. In the glowing light of the candles, the two of them exchanged their vows again to love and cherish each other. They looked into each other's eyes; they had long been able to read their deepest thoughts.

He kissed her hand and then her lips, adding, 'darling, Raffaella.'

'I love you too, dearest Antoneddu,' she whispered.

They each lit a candle and placed them beside each other.

Antonio took her into his arms and kissed her. 'I'll ride with you as far as the river. It will be dark soon, and Zia Paola will be worried about you.'

Antonio led her horse as she rode behind him on his, her arms around his waist. She thrilled to the feel of him as they moved in rhythm with his horse. When they reached the river, Antonio dismounted and helped Raffaella down.

'Now that you are home for good, I want to be able to see more of you. Will you come and see me whenever you can?' he asked, half-entreating, half-doubting her.

'I'll light the lantern in the attic, like we used to, then I'll come and see you the following day at Punta Néula.' she smiled.

He kissed her and set her on her horse.

'Raffaella, *deu volu bene,*' he said, looking up at her.

But before she could tell him she wanted him too, he slapped her horse on the rump, making it leap forward. By the time she gathered her horse and reined in the animal, Antonio had mounted his horse and disappeared into the gathering gloom.

CHAPTER NINE

Christmas came and went with the hateful friend, Luigi, whom Orlando had brought home with him. Raffaella watched the outside world from her bedroom window. Three weeks had passed and she wondered if Antonio had had a good Christmas. She missed him so much. It had been impossible to get away to see him. Snow had fallen over Christmas, making it dangerous for anyone to leave the house, but with the quick thaw the land had, once more, returned to a rich green. Her thoughts were interrupted by a repeated knocking at her bedroom door.

'Come in,' she called, with a vague distance in her voice.

Zia Paola entered the room. 'There you are, my dear child, are you all right?' she asked, looking concerned.

Raffaella sighed. 'Oh, Zia Paola, I hate being cooped up in this house,' she cried. 'All I want is to be able to go out and see Antoneddu, and perhaps help him with the sheep.'

Her aunt laughed. 'I thought that might be the trouble,' she said, her eyes alight with pleasure. 'Then the news I bring you will be good. Gestinu is taking Luigi and Orlando over to Osidda tomorrow, as Luigi has a friend there, a Piedmontese, and they have been invited to go hunting, so they will be away for at least a day. The messenger has just left. So you can go over to Punta Néula tomorrow as I have something I want you to take to Gabriella.'

The smile that beamed on Raffaella's face lifted the whole of her countenance. She hugged her aunt and thanked her with a quick kiss.

That evening, she slipped unobserved into the attic and placed the lighted lantern in the window. She spent a restless night tossing in her bed and thinking of her reunion with Antonio.

She awoke the following morning to the sound of her father

and the men leaving for Osidda. As soon as they left Raffaella made her toilet; she perfumed her hair and rubbed a sweet-smelling oil into her skin. She collected the things from Zia Paola and made her way to Punta Néula. The ride over to the farmstead proved thrilling, and for the first time in ages she felt free; free to be herself.

Salvatore's dogs welcomed her at the farmhouse as they barked about her horse's hooves. Gabriella came to the door to order silence from them, in Heaven's name. Then, holding the horse, she helped Raffaella to dismount. Gabriella embraced the young girl with all the tenderness of her own daughter, which indeed, she hoped one day would be the case.

'My dear young lady, how wonderful to see you after such a long time! It must be six or seven months since you were last here. How you have grown, and what a fine lady you have become. Antonio said that you were no longer a child, and he is right. Come inside,' she said, beckoning to the young girl to follow her.

Raffaella fetched her saddlebag, pleased to be able to hide the flush of joy she knew to be on her cheek at the mention of Antonio's name, and the knowledge that he had noticed the change in her.

Young Salvatore came to the doorway. At nearly three, he was the split image of his father and brother with his dark, curly hair and wide, deep-set eyes.

'Hello, little one,' Raffaella said, picking him up and kissing him. 'Here, I have something for you. Now close your eyes, and hold out your hands,' she added as she put him down.

The child did as she asked, screwing his eyes up tightly, fearful lest the treat be denied him. Raffaella opened her saddlebag and pulled out a carved horse, complete with leather saddle and tack, which she bought for him in Itteri. She placed it in the waiting, outstretched hands.

'You can open them now,' she said, laughing.

An expression of joy and disbelief registered on the little face, and with a hasty kiss and a 'thank you' he raced to the fireside to show Marina.

The two young women embraced each other, and then Raffaella stood back to see her friend.

'My, Marina, you have grown into a woman too. I'm sure you look more grown-up than I did at your age,' said Raffaella, taking in the young girl's fine, mature features.

Marina looked pleased, and swirled in her dress. 'There, Mamma, you see I am a woman now,' she cried.

Gabriella tossed her head and turned to Raffaella. 'I keep telling her there is plenty of time to grow up, but she won't listen to me.'

'At sixteen, I thought I knew everything as well, Gabriella, but since I've been away to school, I realise how much more there is to learn,' said Raffaella. Then, turning to Marina, she added, 'Tell me, Marina, how is Gavinu?'

Marina blushed and shuffled her feet at the mention of her cousin's name.

'Haven't you heard?' cut in Gabriella. 'He is still on the run. After Don diVenti died, the Carabineri have been looking everywhere for him. So far, thank God, he has managed to evade them. They say he's been seen in the area, but his family are the only ones who know where he is hiding. Some say he's gone to the Limbara Mountains with the other *banditti*. Poor lad, I feel sorry for him, for it was his fate to avenge his brother's murder.'

Raffaella watched Marina's face as Gabriella spoke, and could see she knew more about Gavinu than she had told her mother. Marina, recognising what Raffaella was thinking, gave her a pleading look as if to say, not now, I'll tell you later.

'Where is Antoneddu?' asked Raffaella, changing the subject.

'He is at the *pinneta*,' replied Marina. 'He left very early this morning and we don't expect him back until tomorrow.'

'Is Salvatore with him?' Raffaella asked, searching the room for the shepherd.

'No. He has gone to Mores with the idea of buying himself a

new horse, and we don't expect him back for a few days,' replied Gabriella.

Raffaella smiled to herself. 'I'll go to the *pinneta* and find him,' she said, 'but before I do, I have something for you both. This is for you, Marina. I hope you like it,' she said, looking in her saddlebag once more. She took out a small package and handed it to Marina, who took it and examined it.

'Well, aren't you going to open it?' laughed Raffaella.

Marina undid the paper and held out the hand-embroidered silk scarf. 'Oh, Raffaella, it's lovely. Look, Mamma!' she cried, pulling the shawl around her shoulders, and dancing around the room in her excitement.

'Now, Gabriella, we have this for you from Zia Paola,' said Raffaella as she pulled out the handwoven cloth that her aunt had given her that morning. 'Zia Paola has been working on it all winter. There should be enough there for you to make something for yourself and little Salvatore.'

'Such fine work. Zia Paola is so good to us. She is always sending us something over, and is ready to help me. I feel greatly in her debt,' said Gabriella, holding the soft cloth to her cheek.

'Nonsense, Gabriella, she is very fond of you all, and has never forgotten the way you helped her when she first came to the mountains to live, and how you nursed her when she was ill from the fever.'

'She owes us nothing, Raffaella. She has done so much for all my children, what with lessons; it is thanks to her all my children read and write. She is a good, understanding woman. I believe, too, she knows how you and Antonio feel about each other, and is in favour of it. Although she is unwilling to admit as much to Gestinu just yet,' replied Gabriella.

'I know she understands. That is why I'm here today. Babbu has gone to Osidda with Orlando and Luigi to join the hunting party, so I'm alone.'

Gabriella looked at Raffaella with one of her long, searching looks. 'Tell me, Raffaella, how you feel towards Luigi?' she asked, looking at the young girl.

'I don't like him and all that he stands for; he is Piedmontese, a Continental, but he is a guest in our house and therefore commands hospitality. As the saying goes, where there is a stranger, even if he is bad, there, is God. But why do you ask such a question?'

'No reason, my dear, no reason,' replied Gabriella.

She took a large basket from the table. 'If you are going to see Antonio, perhaps you would take this for me? It will save Marina riding down to give it to him. It's just some provisions. He left so early this morning, I didn't have time to do it.'

Raffaella embraced Marina and little Salvatore once more, then they came with her to the mounting block and Gabriella handed up the basket, and with a wave, Raffaella headed off down the narrow path to the ravine.

The *pinneta*, a neat, round stone building topped with reed thatch, sat half-hidden in a clump of grey-green olive trees. The macchia grew thick on three sides of the little hut, while on the fourth side, which faced the river, lay a pale green, sheep-cropped pasture. Sheep grazed everywhere, and their bleating and clanging bells filled the air: together with the birds' song; the gurgling stream and the undying rasp of the cicadas.

Raffaella reined in her horse and stood, taking in the whole peaceful scene that lay before her. A thin wisp of smoke curled from the chimney, and the smell of burning aromatic wood and roasting meat came to her on the intermittent breath of wind that stirred in the scrubland. She sighed, and urged her horse forward down the slope to the small building.

Antoneddu appeared in the doorway. If he was surprised to see her, he didn't show it. He came towards her without saying a word and helped her from the horse. He took the basket and gathered her in his strong arms, as he carried her into the *pinneta*. He pulled the door shut behind him. It was dark and warm inside the hut, with a chink of light coming from the shuttered window. The main light came from the flickering fire. The aromatic wood smoke hung in the warm air, giving it a hypnotic effect.

He put her down in front of the fire and gently kissed her on her forehead. As he did so, he placed the basket on his small, rough table. Antoneddu took Raffaella in his arms and kissed her closed eyes. He rained little kisses on her cheek until he reached her mouth, which he kissed with long, lingering delight, savouring the innocence of her kiss, like that of sweet wine. She ran her hand up to the laces on her cloak, and undoing them, let the garment fall to the ground where she stood.

'Hmm, you smell wonderful.' He sighed.

She became accustomed to the dim light. She could see Antoneddu's eyes clearly, for they were alight with a fire that burnt from deep within his soul. She ached with the longing for his caress, so when he kissed her, she could feel herself melt under his touch. She smiled at him as he carried her to his bed. The smell of the newly gathered grasses and lady's bedstraw, together with the warmth of soft fleeces, filled her senses with a feeling of wellbeing.

Antonio had waited for this moment all his life. Often in his dreams he had held her, wanted her, needed her, even cried out for her, but his need had never been as great as now. Never had he wanted her as he did now. Words being useless in expressing his feelings for her, he could show her how much he loved her. She, too, shared that love, bringing tenderness to his passion.

'You are my first and only love, Antoneddu. There will never be anyone else for me. I have often wondered how it would be with you.' She sighed. 'I love you, Antoneddu,' she whispered as they lay together. 'Tell me, do you remember the first time we pledged our love?'

'I do,' he said, nibbling her neck, 'and young Salvatore is a constant reminder of that day.'

'Oh, Antoneddu, if Vitoria had lived, perhaps everything would have been different. Orlando would have been happy to live here among us all, but he has changed. He still blames himself for her death. He says if he hadn't insisted on her going to Sassari to be with him, she would never have caught the cholera. He has changed, he has become a hard man, eaten inside with a terrible bitterness and dominated by his hateful friend.'

'Father, too, has difficulty coming to terms with her death,' said Antonio. 'I think he blames himself for letting her go to Sassari.'

'Sergio says it was because the people in Sassari were forbidden by the Jesuits to have their Festa, and the religious processions were stopped a few years earlier. He says it was a judgement from God and the saints. That's why they have the festa again. Sergio knew that Orlando and Vitoria's relationship was doomed when someone spilt the olive oil on their table at the *Cujugnu* – don't you remember, he went mad with his outcries of foreboding, and Hail Marys to try to reverse such evil fortune,' said Raffaella, thinking back to that day.

'Come here,' he said, drawing her closer to him. 'I don't want to know about Festa's and Sergio's ravings about ill omens. All I want is you.' He kissed her again. 'Are you afraid, Raffaella?'

She smiled. 'Not of you.'

He took her in his arms and felt her trembling. 'Don't be frightened, *sa sposixedda mia*. I won't hurt you.'

'No, Antoneddu, I'm not afraid. Not when I'm with you.'

He pulled her closer and felt her melt against him. He kissed her on each eye and then ran small kisses down her cheeks until he found her soft mouth. He sensed her relaxing as he again caressed her with profound tenderness. Antonio knew he would have to be gentle with her, and was desperate not to hurt her.

He undressed her, repeatedly kissing her. He lay with her and murmured words of love to her. He caressed her, and she became aware of his heavy breathing as he held her close to him. He lay back, gasping, and then raising himself on his elbow, started to kiss her breasts and ran his fingers over her golden skin. He nibbled her and sent shivers of delight through her. She gasped and rose on the bed as his kisses devoured her. He stood and took off his clothes and then lay next to her again. He kissed her and ran his tongue over her glistening skin, bringing her to a state of ecstasy. Still, he held back as he once again began to cover her in small caresses.

Finally, when she could bear it no longer, she felt the weight of him on her and cried out as he made love to her. The wonderful sensation of lovemaking outweighed any pain she felt, and she put her hands in his hair and pulled his face down to hers. Antonio kissed her with a deep passion and brought Raffaella to a shared joy. They lay in each other's arms, and the tears fell on Raffaella's cheeks as she turned to her lover.

'I never knew it could be so wonderful.' And she buried her face into his chest and wept.

'Darling Raffaella. Are you all right?' he whispered. All his dreams, desires fulfilled as he held her in his arms.

'I love you, Antoneddu,' she said, turning to him to hold him, feeling the warmth of their bodies as she lay in his arms.

'My darling Raffaella. I love you too, and will cherish you forever,' he said as he again pulled her into his arms.

Twilight had fallen when they left the *pinneta*. The day had been spent lost in their love for each other. They shared the day; their love, their feelings and warmth glowed from within both of them. A new kind of love that filled Raffaella with deep contentment. It was wonderful to her, that a man of such strength and inflamed passion could be so gentle and loving.

He had cooked for her and they had eaten together, savouring every moment in each other's company. He now rode with her as far as the small, winding path that climbed up to Sos Lampidos, and leaning out of his saddle, kissed her one last time.

'Until the next time, my love. *Deu cherreru bene.*'

That night Raffaella lay in her bed, still glowing from their lovemaking and longing for times to come. Surely now everything would be all right. Fate would be kind to them and shine on their love, and Babbu would understand and give them his blessing. They would be able to marry soon.

A wave of peace washed over her as she dropped into a dreamless sleep.

CHAPTER TEN

Mid-June, 1859

'They're here, Raffaella. I can see the gig coming up the track. Do come quickly,' called Zia Paola, beckoning her niece to join her at the window, while she lifted young Salvatore up to see his brother driving the gig.

The Sannas had ridden over early that morning as Antonio had collected the gig from Sos Lampidos late yesterday afternoon and left for Sassari, leaving Salvatore and Gabriella to help Zia Paola with the preparations.

Raffaella joined them all at the window to see the oncoming gig. She watched the coloured dust, golden in the afternoon sun, rise from the dry track as it curled up behind the hard-pushed horses, now visible, now disappearing behind the bushes at the roadside. Sergio and Ignazio were busy with the sheep-shearing, so Antonio had volunteered to go and collect his friend.

'Antonio is bound to have pushed those horses hard,' said Zia Paola to Raffaella. 'Be a good girl and tell Gestinu they are home.'

Raffaella left the room and crossed the hall to the small study where her father always retired for a smoke and a brief siesta. She paused at the door, listening for his tell-tale snore. She knocked, and there was a small delay before a muffled voice bid her, 'Come in.'

'Babbu,' she said, opening the door, 'Orlando is here. Zia Paola sent me to fetch you.'

Raffaella smiled as she viewed the fine figure of her father slumped in his overstuffed chair, as he struggled to arouse himself from his brief nap. The air in the small room was still heavy from the smell of tobacco smoke. Her father, a gentle man with a big heart; always ready to help people with their legal problems, whether they could afford it or not. There were many nights when he would be in here with some local shepherd who had fallen foul of the new Piedmontese law, to be rewarded with some wine, meat, oil or whatever could be spared by his client. Gestinu treated everyone the same and was much loved and respected by all, his philosophy being, if you can't help your fellow man, do him no harm.

Raffaella smiled again as she looked around her. She loved this room. There were shelves lined with books, mostly on the law and poetry, and a large encyclopaedia which contained everything any child would want to know and more. She remembered how, when she was young, she would come in here and climb up on her father's lap to recite a poem, or tell him about the lessons they had had with Zia Paola, or present him with one of her drawings of the flowers they had picked that day.

'I'm coming,' he said, raising himself from the chair. He coughed, clearing his throat. 'You know, young lady, those years at Signora Sella's have turned you into a graceful young creature, and one of which your mother would have been proud, God bless her. I think your brother will be well pleased with the result, and his young friend too, of that I am sure.'

'Which young friend?' asked Raffaella, already fearing his answer.

'Why, young Luigi Atzeni, of course; when he sees you again today I have no doubt that he will voice the same opinion.'

Raffaella stiffened. 'How long is he to stay with us, Babbu? Do you know?' she asked, a cold tone in her voice.

'For as long as he wants. You know better than to ask a question like that, my child. He is Orlando's friend, and it's good for you to meet new company at your age, and after his stay at Christmas I thought he seemed taken with you. I know you won't forget the rules of hospitality, will you, Raffaella?'

She bit her lip and leant forward to take her father's arm, allowing him to escort her to the door. His forty-five years were beginning to show a sprinkling of white through his hair, and his trimmed beard and moustache were also smudged grey, giving him a strong, distinguished air.

'It is good of Orlando to come home for the Festa of San Giovanni. I know it means a lot to Gabriella Sanna, for it will be a special day for her. It will be good to go out hunting and fishing together. He has a good month before he goes to Sassari to start with Zio Marco. Luigi is starting with Dr Paddu at Sassari at the same time, so even when they are working they should be able to find time to come back to Sos Lampidos.'

Outside, the gig came to a dusty halt. The immediate family went out to welcome them home. Words were lost in the hubbub of greeting as Orlando embraced them all in turn, and then kissing his aunt, he turned to Raffaella.

'My word, sister, I would not have recognised you. How well you look. I do believe that in these past months you have gained a little weight at last, and it suits you well. How say you, Luigi?' he said, putting an arm round his friend. 'You, my dear little sister, have become a woman in a very short time. It must be your good influence, Zia Paola.'

Luigi took Raffaella's hand and kissed it, while she bobbed a small curtsy. When she looked up at him she became aware that he was still staring at her, and held on to her hand. His clean-shaven, pale olive skin looked like Orlando's, but was in sharp contrast to the other men present, who were dark and bearded. She felt herself blush under his ardent gaze, as his pale grey eyes searched her soul. She tried again to withdraw her hand from his damp grasp.

'It's good to see you again, Orlando,' she said, addressing her brother, at last managing to free her herself.

Orlando came forward and put his free arm around his sister. 'Antonio,' he called over his shoulder, 'you didn't tell me that my sister had matured to womanhood. You've been keeping things from me.' He turned to Raffaella without waiting for a reply. 'It seems that school in Itteri did wonders for you, my dear, and these past months at home with Zia Paola have added an extra polish. You are no longer that awkward, skinny tomboy.'

Raffaella threw her brother a stony look, but before she could say anything Zia Paola came forward, took Orlando by the hand and hugged him. 'Come indoors,' she said, 'you must be tired after your journey. Salvatore and Gabriella are inside. They came over to help me today, and to welcome you home.'

Antonio, glad of the excuse to break away from the group, mumbled that he would look after the horses, and led them to the stables.

Inside, Salvatore and Gabriella greeted Orlando. Marina came forward to kiss him while young Salvatore clung to her long skirt.

'Well, well, and how is my young godson? You have grown up,' said Orlando, sounding a little awkward.

'Yes,' replied Marina, 'he had his third birthday at the beginning of this month.'

'Three,' echoed Orlando. 'Is it three years? It seems like a lifetime.'

Raffaella moved forward and offered her brother a drink, which he took and swallowed in one gulp, and she refilled his glass.

Gestinu went to greet his son, embracing him and kissing him on each cheek; then turning to Luigi, he shook the young doctor's hand.

'Good to see you both again. We will be able to spend time together now.'

Gabriella came forward to say the meal was ready.

Orlando turned to her and said, 'Congratulations, Gabriella, on being elected to be *Comare* to San Giovanni. You must be proud, and the festival is just four days away. Tell me, are you excited?'

Gabriella laughed and tapped him on his arm. 'You're teasing me,' she said, 'but yes, I'm very proud.'

They all found their places at the large table. Raffaella had been placed between her brother and Luigi, while Antonio had to be content to sit opposite her. The meal passed in genial chatter, but Raffaella noticed that Antonio said nothing.

He spent most of the time drinking. He didn't look at her throughout the meal, and was reluctant to be drawn into the conversation, although she made several attempts to include him in their discussions.

'Tell me,' said Luigi, 'what is the election of *Comare* to San Giovanni?'

'It is the honour of being godfather or godmother to the saint for a year. But when you have lived here, you will learn our ways,' said Salvatore.

Luigi, thanked him for his help.

When the time came for the Sannas to leave, Raffaella pulled her lover by the arm into her father's study.

'Whatever is the matter with you, Antoneddu? You haven't said a word since you came back from Sassari. What in Heaven's name is it that is needling you?'

He stared at her.

'Antoneddu, please, I beg you. Tell me what is wrong! What happened on the way home?' she pleaded. 'Since your return you have been like a man eaten by something inside you. Have I done something to upset you?'

'*Boh*. It's not you, Raffaella,' he blurted out, 'and there is nothing wrong with me. I'm not the one who has changed. But by all the saints, those three years have done nothing for Orlando, other than put him under the bad influence of that Piedmontese. He has always been easily led; pliable and willing to bend, but that Continental has him by the nose, by Heaven.'

'For goodness' sake, Antoneddu, what are you talking about?' she asked.

'Raffaella, answer me one thing,' he said, spreading his hands across his chest. 'Do you love me, and still feel the same way you did all that time ago when little Salvatore was born? I know things have changed. You have been away and met other people, broadened your outlook. Do you still love me as you loved me that day in the *pinneta*? Tell me, do you feel trapped by my love and your vows? Would you like to be free to make another choice?

I must know, Raffaella, and I must know the truth, however hurtful.'

She looked into his eyes and saw a pain and anguish reflected there that she had not seen before, and which came from within his soul.

'Dearest Antoneddu, what has brought this about? Do you doubt my love for you? Do I not show you that I love you? My feelings haven't changed, and in your heart of hearts, you must know that to be so. The time I was away proved to me, beyond all doubt, that you are the only man in this world I could ever love. Do you believe that all that has passed between us since Christmas has been anything but sincere?'

'No... No, of course not, Raffaella, I believe your love to be true, but I'm no fool. I may be a shepherd and a rough farmer, but certainly no fool. You must know that I can't give you a home like this, or all the finery you are used to and have come to expect. I know, too, that I am not what your father wishes to have as a son-in-law. I know our children won't be able to go to school in Itteri, nor will they have everything that you had—'

'Hush,' she said, putting her fingers to his lips to stop the flow of words. 'The children will have you to teach them the ways of the land, and I can teach them the ways of the house. They will have our love to watch over them and to guide them, and they will need little more.'

'You say that now...' he cut in.

'Antoneddu, listen to me. When in Itteri I used to wake each morning, look at the mountains and think of you wandering in the flower-filled pastures, our pastures. When the wind blew through the town from those mountains, I could smell the same flowers, our flowers. How it made me yearn for our mountains and our love. At night before I closed the shutters, I used to see the sun throw her crimson fire on the mountains and they seemed to be reflecting my love and desire. Please, Antoneddu, don't doubt my love for you, or the tenderness we have shared.' She paused. 'But why? Why now do you doubt my feelings for you?'

'It's not your love I doubt. But you have loyalties to your father and Orlando. Your brother has plans for you to marry Luigi, and I thought that perhaps you had agreed – not agreed, but, well, felt honour or duty-bound. Oh dear, Raffaella, I don't know what I thought.'

He took her in his arms and buried his face in her dark, sweet-scented hair. He did not see the colour drain from her face, taking the usual bloom with it.

'Don't be silly, Antoneddu, you can't be serious,' she said, trying to laugh it off as a joke. 'Whatever gave you such ideas?'

'They were talking about it on the way home today. How Luigi will ask your father for your hand and the marriage could be arranged to take place in a couple of months. Luigi has already told his parents of his intentions and they will be coming from Milano to meet your father just as soon as everything is arranged.'

She pulled away. She looked pale, and felt thunderstruck. His words felt like a hammer blow, and she found it difficult to recover her composure.

'You're mistaken, Antoneddu, they must have been teasing. Orlando wouldn't do that to me. He knows how I feel about you. They wouldn't talk about that in front of you unless they were joking. I'll speak to Orlando. I'm sure you are mistaken.' But her voice didn't conceal her fear and carried no conviction, for it trembled as she spoke.

'Best speak to the Devil himself for what good it will do you,' he said. Then taking her in his arms again, he said with passion, 'I love you, Raffaella, and I have since childhood. I would rather die than see you married to another, and I would rather see you dead at my feet, killed by my own hand, than see you married to that Continental milksop.' His eyes flashed with anger and jealousy.

'Dearest, dearest Antoneddu, you go home and I will talk to Orlando. Take care and don't worry, for if I can't get anywhere with him, then Zia Paola and Babbu will help me, of that I'm sure. We are already married in the eyes of God, so if all else fails I shall tell Babbu of our promise.'

He bent and kissed her forehead. 'I want to be with you when you tell your father.'

'No, Antoneddu, you must leave it to me. I know how to handle Babbu, even if I can't handle Orlando; at least Babbu is always ready to listen.'

'*Deu volu bene*, dearest love,' he said in desperation as he pulled her close to him and crushed her against him.

'I know, I know, and I want you too,' she whispered, returning his kiss.

Orlando's voice penetrated the room. He was calling Antonio as he burst into the study. He stood for a moment, unsure of himself, and stared at the two still entwined in each other's arms.

'Ah, there you are,' he said, looking awkward. 'Your parents are ready to leave, Antonio, and are waiting for you.'

Antonio gathered Raffaella in his arms once more and kissed her, then let her go. With all the goodbyes said, she went up to the peace and solitude of her room.

Orlando pulled up his chair to be near the fire and his father, at the same time nodding to Luigi to do the same.

'Where is Raffaella?' asked Luigi, looking around him.

'She has gone to her room. I believe she has a headache,' replied Zia Paola, as she put the final touches to cleaning the room after all the guests had gone. 'And if you'll excuse me, I shall follow her. It has been quite a day, one way and another.'

Orlando and Luigi both stood to wish her a good night. When she had gone Orlando helped himself to some more wine and sat himself back in his chair.

An awkward silence fell in the room as Luigi, still standing, drained his glass, cleared his throat and addressed himself to Gestinu.

'Sir, I know I am not yet a fully qualified doctor. Neither am I a Sard, nor a Sardinian landowner, although I inherit land and estates on my father's death. I am, though, a man of independent means, and on my coming of age this year will receive a portion of my estate as an income, which increases on marriage. In time, I am hoping to be able to earn a partnership in the practice in Sassari with Dr Paddu. I could, I believe, offer your daughter a good life as well as the social position of a doctor's wife. I can assure you she would want for nothing, be it money or affection. I would, therefore, be most grateful if you would consider giving me your daughter's hand in marriage, for I understand from Orlando she is not yet spoken for.'

Gestinu eyed the young man, taking in his dark hair which contrasted with his pale skin. He was dressed in the style of the Continentals, and presumably, in the height of fashion. He drew on his cigar and thought for a moment.

'Have you given this matter serious consideration?' he asked.

'Oh yes, sir, I have. Since I returned to university after Christmas, and all I wish for is your blessing, for I know I have that of Orlando.'

'Have you discussed this matter with Raffaella at all?'

'No, sir, I thought – that is we, Orlando and I, thought – it would be more prudent to ask you first.'

Gestinu drew on his cigar again and flicked the long ash into the fireplace. 'You will have to give me a few days to think about it. There is no hurry, as you are, no doubt, to be with us for some time.'

Luigi looked at Orlando, who gave his friend a broad smile.

'Have a drink, brother-in-law,' he said as he stood up and slapped his friend on the back. 'She is yours.'

Upstairs, Zia Paola knocked on Raffaella's door.

'Who is it?'

'Zia Paola. Please, Raffaella, let me in.'

Raffaella drew back the lock and opened the door. She beckoned her aunt to come in and secured the door behind her.

'I had to come, my child,' said her aunt. 'What is wrong? something is troubling you. Have you and Antonio had a row? You both seem so unhappy.'

'Oh, Zia Paola,' cried her niece, throwing her arms round her aunt's neck, 'it's worse than that.' And she burst into tears.

'My dear child, whatever is the matter?'

Raffaella told her aunt all that Antonio had told her earlier. 'And now they are downstairs discussing my future. I can't marry Luigi, Zia Paola, I can't. I belong to Antoneddu, more than Vitoria ever belonged to Orlando. They were promised at birth, but in return for Salvatore having saved Babbu's life, and Mamma wanted it too, otherwise Babbu would never have allowed Orlando to be involved with the Pastore. Vitoria and Orlando were always considered as one, but no one ever gave Antoneddu and me a thought. We were always together too, and our love grew on its own from our childhood dependence on each other, to what has become our adult love and respect. It has grown from the early sweetness to a love neither of us can nor want to control. Grown like the small seeds in the pastures that grow into the big trees with the warmth and affection of the wind, sun and the rains. So our love has grown, and we will not have it cut down and thrown apart to please Orlando.'

Raffaella paused and hunted for a handkerchief to wipe her eyes. 'I know,' she continued, sobbing, 'that when Vitoria died Orlando never forgave himself. He still believes that, if he had not insisted on her going to Sassari, she would never have caught the fever and died, so instead of coming home to emptiness, he would have the warmth and tenderness of her love. He would have let Antoneddu and me marry to bind the families even closer. But now he wants to break away from his past, from the farm, from the country life and drag me with him to his detestable city life. Well, Zia Paola, I won't go. I had enough of that life while at school, and what's more I won't be tied to convention and a dead memory to please my brother,' she cried, her voice rising in despair.

'Hush, Raffaella,' said her aunt, 'we don't want them up here.' She paused for a moment and tried to comfort her niece.

'How do you feel about it?' Raffaella pleaded.

'I, my dear, am with you. I am very fond of Antonio. I have

known him a long-time. He is a kind, compassionate and caring man. A little rough at the edges, but he is intelligent and you and he are kindred spirits, and I know he loves you.

'I, too, thought perhaps the time in Itteri might change you and you might meet another young man. But you haven't changed at all. You are still the same wild young creature you were when you were a child; not the sort to be caged by society and convention. You are going to have a fight on your hands, Raffaella, be sure of that – perhaps not so much from your father, but with Orlando.'

'But I must win,' replied Raffaella, with a defiant air. 'I must – you see, Zia Paola, I have already pledged my love to Antoneddu, and we made our promises to each other and we can't break them.'

'And how long have you been promised to each other?' asked her aunt.

'We made our *Cujugnu* the day he gave me my horse. It was his betrothal present to me. The day young Salvatore was born.'

'But Raffaella, that was three years ago,' exclaimed her aunt in disbelief. 'You were only fifteen then.'

'Nearly sixteen, and age doesn't make any difference,' corrected Raffaella. 'I haven't changed my mind. I still love him, but more now than I did then. Last Christmas, we renewed our promises at the small church.' She paused, to think back to that moment in the cold church when they made their vows and lit candles together. 'Zia Paola, you must help me, please, I beg of you. In the eyes of God, we are already married.' A mixture of desperate pleading and defiance sounded in her voice, tinged with sadness that came from her soul and reflected in her dark, limpid eyes.

Zia Paola sighed and led her to the bed where she tucked her niece into the linen sheets. Such a promise, and before God, she knew to be binding.

'Tell me, Raffaella, have you shared your love for each other?'

Raffaella looked up at her aunt, and tears welled up to sting her eyes. 'Don't ask me that, please, Zia Paola.'

Her aunt bent forward and kissed her niece on her forehead.

'You know the rules, my child. If you love each other, and share the love you have, then you should be married and I for one shall give you every bit of help I can. I give you my word,' she said, squeezing Raffaella's hand. She leant and blew out the candle on the bedside table, and before Raffaella could say any more, her aunt had gone, leaving her to fly to Antoneddu in her dreams.

CHAPTER ELEVEN

The morning of the Festival of San Giovanni broke with usual splendour over the peaceful mountain community. The sun spilled across the still-verdant macchia and caught the last crystal specks of dew on the eastern side of the ravines and valleys.

In the stables at Punta Néula Antonio was already busy rubbing and grooming the horses with an oiled rag. Long fingers of light poured into the narrow gaps of closed shutters and fell in dusty rays through holes in the rough tiled buildings. The slanting beam of light streaming through the uneven tiled roof caught the oiled coat of Salvatore's horse, adding to its luxuriant brilliance.

Antonio had risen in the dark, some hours before sun-up. The now-flickering and smoking lamp hanging on the beam above him had lost its strength with the increased morning light. He took a step back, and wiping the sweat from his forehead, admired his handiwork. He sighed, and content with his work, reached up to the lamp, blew out the weak flame and returned it to the hook on the beam. He collected Salvatore's saddlecloth from the rack and placed it on his father's horse. It looked resplendent with its decoration of paper flowers and silken ribbons. The bridle, too, had multi-coloured ribbons intricately woven through it, with magnificent, elaborate designs. For the past weeks, Marina and Raffaella had worked hard making the delicate ornaments for all the horses' trappings so that everything would be perfect on this special day.

Inside the small farmhouse at Punta Néula everyone helped with the last-minute arrangements. Salvatore had also risen earlier than usual to enable him to help Sergio and Ignazio inspect the flock, and make sure everything was in order, so they could leave for Bantadda in good time.

Marina sat next to her young brother, Salvatore, watching him as he ate his meal, aware of the mounting excitement around them both. She wore her best dress, the one she had worked on under the watchful eye of Gabriella and admiration of Gavinu all those years ago. She toyed with one of the decorated pots standing on the table; her mind miles away.

She knew Gavinu would be at Bantadda today, and she couldn't wait to see him again. For the past year he had come to her in secret. At first he hung an oak branch under her window to show his affection for her, and then he had become bolder, spending more time talking to her from her window; all the time watching the area, lest he should be seen by some passing Carabineri. There would be long periods of time when he never came to see her, which sent Marina into moods of deep depression.

Gavinu had been keen not to involve the Sannas, not now he had been outlawed. Since that fated night when he arrived at Punta Néula three years ago, he lived in fear of capture. Three weeks after he shot Don diVenti in revenge for his brother's death, the Don had died of the gunshot wound. It had been a long and painful death, for which Gavinu, in all honesty, could show no regret; but as a result found himself outlawed and hunted. Doomed to roam the mountains, begging for his food and seeking shelter wherever possible, with either friends or relatives who were willing to help him. True, he managed to spend some of the time at Pinta Niedda, moving on when the Carabineri came searching.

He fell in with another band of outlaws, but when they moved to Gallora he decided to remain near home, preferring the land he knew well to the mountains of the Limbara. Condemned to this existence until he could prove his innocence of the murder charge, and enter a plea of justification for self-defence. Marina knew that against the Piedmontese it would be difficult to gain such a plea, and from the Carabineri a miracle, but she prayed each night to her saint and to the Holy Mother for help, so her lover could achieve his freedom, and enable them to live together as husband and wife.

At the Festa they knew they would be safe to meet, for there was a general amnesty for the *banditti*; a gathering of all the local people, and the Carabineri found themselves shunned on these occasions, and kept away from the festivities. The families were reunited with their outlawed husbands and lovers, and the increased number of babies nine months later bore witness to such meetings. Although they were safe during the festivals, great care had to be taken by the outlaws on returning to their mountain hideouts, lest they should be followed by the Carabineri or someone seeking their vendetta.

Marina was bought back from her thoughts by her mother chiding her for letting Salvatore spill his milk. Gabriella was in a fever of nervous excitement and had been since she had been chosen, at the beginning of April, to be one of the *Comare* or godmothers to San Giovanni for the coming year.

This year Francesco Piddis had been made *Uvriere*, the man who organised the whole Festa by giving the food and wine to all the attending company of the local area. He had asked for the privilege from the village elders, the *Cussorgia*, for thanks in the safe delivery of his wife from the dreaded *impeiere* fever. He felt, too, that he owed his wife's life to Gabriella. He had to beg her to come to the Festa, for Gabriella had been frightened that if praised, she may lose her powers of healing. But now Efisia was strong again, and as thanks for such a blessing Francesco, or Zizzu, as he was known in the community, asked Gabriella to be godmother as a small sign of his gratitude. She, in turn, had accepted with grateful thanks to the saints for her powers.

'Such an honour for all the family,' Gabriella had repeated, trying hard to disguise her obvious delight and pride.

At the end of April, she planted the grains of corn and flax in small pots, made from the cork bark by Antonio and Marina. Gabriella showered tender care on the seedlings as they grew into the strong shoots. Then, when Antonio had gone to Sassari to collect Orlando, he had first stopped to buy his mother metres of multi-coloured ribbon to decorate the plants and pots in the ancient tradition, and her delicate work now took pride of place on the table and the balcony outside, waiting to be taken to Bantadda for the Festa.

The Festival of San Giovanni is like so many in Christian lands where the old heathen rites are cloaked in the respectability of the saint's days. Zia Paola had told them the growing of seeds in pots and throwing them against the temple walls went back to Phoenician times and the midsummer rites of Astarte. Such deep-rooted traditions were nurtured with as much tenderness as the plants themselves.

At last they were ready to leave. Salvatore had left Ignazio in charge of the sheep, as he did not like festivals, but favoured his own company. So with his work finished for the day, Salvatore collected his horse and took it to the mounting block where he helped Gabriella onto the back of the decorated animal. She looked very young, sitting sideways on the horse, her long dress falling over the animal's haunches. She clutched the decorated pots that Antonio handed her.

'You look wonderful, Mamma, so happy,' he said, taking her hand and squeezing it. 'Like an angel, Mamma.'

Salvatore echoed his son's sentiments, his pride and delight welling up inside him at the sight of his beloved Gabriella looking so contented and serene. He climbed up in front of her, and swung his leg over the animal's neck. He sat astride the great horse so his wife could hold on to him as they rode together.

Young Salvatore was dressed in his best attire, mirroring in miniature the clothes worn by his father and elder brother. The embroidered white shirt, caught at the neck and cuffs with gold filigree buttons, which were a present from Orlando, his godfather, at his baptism. The shirt stood out crisp and clean against his black waistcoat. His white trousers contrasted with the short black kilt and his dark leather boots. The only difference in the three being the red waistcoat worn by Antonio, which Raffaella had made and embroidered with wild flowers, and given it to him for a present.

Antonio, too, mounted his horse from the granite block and

pulled young Salvatore up to sit in front of him. He turned to look for Marina. She stood staring down the ravine, her hands shading her eyes against the brightness of the morning sun. She seemed to be searching the narrow path that climbed from the ravine below. Antonio followed her gaze and caught a glimpse of someone approaching on horseback. It was difficult to make out the face as the overhanging trees shielded the on comer from prying eyes. Antonio noticed the flash of happiness dart across his sister's face, and smiled.

'It's Gavinu,' she cried. 'He said he would come, for it will be safe for him at the Festa.'

Everyone welcomed their cousin, and after a brief exchange of greetings, Marina climbed up to sit behind Gavinu on his horse. At last they made their way to the bridge, where the road divides to wind its way up to Sos Lampidos. At the bridge all those from the house were waiting.

Gestinu, in his festive clothes, was mounted on his great white mare. Zia Paola, in her finery, sat on her docile bay and Orlando on his grey, while Raffaella sat sideways behind Luigi on her chestnut mare. They were all dressed in festive attire except Luigi. He wore a long leather coat and breeches with the Catalan-type fedora, making him stand out from the other men, who sported the long stocking *berrita*.

Antonio felt a sharp stab of jealousy at seeing Raffaella seated behind the Piedmontese, on the horse he had given her on their secret betrothal. But as she explained later, she had no choice. Babbu and Orlando insisted on it as a mark of hospitality. But the barb of jealousy soon passed to Luigi, for in the confusion of the meeting and greetings of the old friends, and the pleasure of seeing Gavinu again, no one noticed Raffaella drop from her horse and clamber up behind her lover and his young brother.

Though annoyed at Raffaella's open defiance of their wishes, neither Gestinu nor Orlando wished to upset the happy mood on such a special day and let the matter lie; just as Raffaella had banked on, and she smiled to herself. With pleasure, she watched her brother lean over to put a restraining hand on Luigi's arm, fearing he might make a scene out of the incident.

The party moved off, eager to hear what Gavinu had been up to during his exile. Marina laid her head on Gavinu's back and listened to him chatter on, content just to hold him in her arms again.

The road to Bantadda lay ahead, and she could feel the sun warm on her back and a gentle breeze cool on her cheek. She, at least, was at peace, and in love.

They found the village alive with people. Awake from the early hours, they had dragged long tables from their houses, with numerous chairs and benches, setting them in rows for the feasting that would follow later in the day. In the centre of the piazza stood a huge bonfire waiting to be lit for the night's revelry.

The group made their way to the familiar house of Zizzu and Efisia Piddis where they were welcomed with warm open affection, with the usual hugs and kisses at the meeting of old and dear friends. Orlando introduced Luigi to Zizzu and Efisia; then to their four daughters, Francesca, Giovanna, Istervan and Caterina, and last of all to their son, Zizzeddu. Luigi smiled at each of them in turn.

As a mark of respect for Gestinu's guest, Zizzu had asked a visiting Jesuit to his house. The priest was a small, thin-faced man with parchment-coloured skin and thin grey hair. He came from the mainland, and happened to be passing through the village, inspecting the various churches in the area to make his report for the Vatican.

'I thought you might feel at home with a kinsman from Savoy,' said Zizzu to Luigi. 'It will be a comfort for the priest to have someone who speaks his native tongue, for I fear he has difficulty in understanding our language.'

The priest seized Luigi with a pale, long, bony hand and drew him into the corner where they could talk undisturbed. Raffaella watched Luigi's face drop at the prospect of such company. She turned to Antonio and smiled in response to his broad, knowing wink.

The music being played outside invaded the room where they were all gathered. The youngsters were eager to see what was happening, and to join in the festivities. Giovanna, the second and most striking of the Piddis daughters, gave her father a pleading look, and he laughing, waved his hands to shoo them off.

'Not too long, mind. We want to go to mass before the meal, understand?'

They all nodded and chorused their affirmation.

Raffaella and Marina seized the opportunity to make good their escape with Antonio and Gavinu. But Raffaella couldn't resist a backward glance to see the annoyed expression on her brother's face, and the look of jealous contempt on that of Luigi as the old Jesuit tried again to engage him in polite conversation.

The youngsters hurried out into the cool, shaded courtyard of the impressive grey stone house, with its small garden of pots and climbers, which ramped and fell in colourful profusion all over the granite walls. They hurried out of the large gates and into the piazza. The bright sunlight on the vibrant colours of the milliard of costumes were breath-taking. Young women in their delicate dresses of reds and violets contrasted with the fine whiteness of their shirts. Filigree-worked gold or silver buttons and jewellery flashed in the brilliant sun as precious heirlooms glinted in the clear, warm light, worn against smooth olive skins or black velvet bodices.

The men, too, looked handsome with their air of rugged, wild independence. Some wore red waistcoats over white shirts, others the black, woolly *Mastrucca*. But all wore the *berrita*; each man wearing it in his own characteristic manner. The bachelor at a cheeky, jaunty angle, with all the confidence of youth. The engaged man in a proud, haughty way; and it thrilled Raffaella to see that Antonio wore his *berrita* in this way, as did Gavinu. The married men wore them rolled up in a dignified mode, while the widowers let them hang over an ear or down the nape of their necks in a hangdog fashion, giving them the appearance of not caring. Some of them carried their tobacco hidden in the depths of the long stocking so it could be retrieved when needed. All the men wore beards which, whether long or short, were groomed and trimmed for the great occasion.

Widows, clad from head to toe in black, looked like ravens as they walked or hobbled among the youngsters, and were in stark contrast with the vibrant colours worn by the youths. The widows made their way towards the church, and as they neared the building, they drew their shawls around them and clutched their rosary beads in the same tenacious way they clung to the traditions. Once inside the church they would make their confessions or give thanks for favours asked, and pray for their departed loved ones. Some formed small groups and moved together in a large, black sea of mourning. Others, widowed early, had young children hanging on their black skirts or enfolded in black arms.

Raffaella took Antonio's arm and squeezed it hard. Half out of fear for the unknown which the widows represented, and half out of the joy radiated by the young people with their passionate love of life.

'Isn't it exciting, Antoneddu?' she said, still squeezing his arm. 'I know it's the same every year, but I never tire of seeing it.'

Antonio gave her a loving smile, and wound his fingers through hers and hugged her arm to his side. He didn't have to say anything to her. He could read her every thought, and the familiar thrill of such intimacy shot through Raffaella.

Marina and Gavinu called to them. A group had started to dance the *Ballu Sardu,* and as they snaked their way round the piazza they added to their numbers as more and more joined in. Raffaella and Antonio joined Marina and Gavinu with the Piddis girls; their tiny steps in perfect time to the wailing notes of the *Launaddas.* Again, Raffaella felt that wonderful warmth flow through her, as Antonio once more entwined his fingers with hers, this time in full view of everyone. Such an open demonstration of affection was thrilling, as she knew that, if Babbu or Orlando saw it, they would be furious at such a blatant exhibition of intimacy.

But to the world they were already promised to each other; only the family could not, or would not, accept this fact.

Suddenly the piazza was full of young men on horseback. The clattering hooves on the dry ground drowned all sound of the music, and the dancing stopped. Youths from all the surrounding areas, eager to prove their courage on such an occasion, had arrived dressed in their finery. After the procession they would race three times round the church, the winner having the honour of becoming another of the saint's *Compare*.

The families heard the noise in the piazza, and with Luigi and the old priest, joined the youngsters to attend the mass. Inside, the small church was packed to bursting, but the Canus and the Sannas all had seats, being the honoured guests of Zizzu Piddis. Those who couldn't cram into the church gathered on the outside. The great doors of the building were opened wide, so all could join in the mass. Neighbouring priests, including Father Canu, helped administer the communion, so that everyone who wanted to, could partake of the sacrament.

At the end of the service, the priests followed the great silver cross down the crowded aisle. The smell of incense that had filled the church now hung in the warm midday air. Everyone followed the cross as the priests made their way round the church. The *Comare* and *Compare* carried their treasured pots of flowers with them. On the third time round they stepped forward, and smashed their offerings against the old walls of the building. A great cheer went up from the entire crowd as the cork pots fell into fragments, and Gabriella looked excited as she threw her pot with the others.

Then the young men leapt to their horses and demanded a gangway. Antonio was among the men who went to find their horse, and on his return to the piazza, Raffaella gave him her amulet, which she had blessed with holy water in the church.

'*Buona Fortuna*,' she whispered, as he leant from his saddle to kiss her.

The crowd fell back, frightened of being crushed under the pounding hooves. Zizzu stood alongside the wide line of horsemen, a banner in one hand and a rifle in the other. A loud shot rang out, and the great, teeming mass of men and horses surged forward amid the fevered cries of encouragement from the crowd. A huge column of dust rose from the horses' hooves, making it impossible to see who was where. The route to be raced was longer than the one the procession had taken, but in no time at all, the men were thundering past the crowded piazza. Before the dust had time to settle the pounding hooves again whipped it up into another choking cloud. The riders were still bunched. But Raffaella knew that the third and last time round sorted the men from the boys. They flashed past for a second time, again throwing the dust heavenward into the still-choking air like some sacrificial smoke. She saw Gavinu flash past as she searched for Antonio.

Zizzu raced across the course after the last horse. Behind him, he trailed the ribbon which would be snatched by the winner. It fluttered in the warm breeze and then, with the deafening return of the riders and a roar from the crowd, it was snatched by the winner. Seconds later Antonio reined his horse before Raffaella, the ribbon in his hand. Raffaella jumped up and down in her excitement, and Marina hugged her as they danced together, sharing the moment of joy. Antonio dropped from his horse, and watched by the entire crowd, he placed the ribbon round Raffaella's hair and tied it in a great bow. The crowd showed their delight with a roar of approval and a round of gun fire for such a popular winner and gallant gesture.

That evening, after all the main festivities had taken place and the eating and drinking were being enjoyed, they lit the great fire in the piazza. The godfathers and godmothers lined up on either side of the fire. The men held long sticks, which they handed to their partners. Thus united, they passed the sticks over the fire three times, binding them in their responsibilities to the saint. Antonio chose his sister for his partner, much to the surprise of Orlando. But Antonio knew that if Raffaella became his *Comare*, he would not be able to marry her during the following year. For such is the responsibility of godparents; it was not allowed to be shared by the young close to marriage.

Later, everyone sat and watched the flames die while small children ran and jumped over the fire, their little faces catching the remaining light from the embers, highlighting the joy on their innocent features. In this half-light, warmed by the thrill of the day, and weary from the excitement of all the happenings, they were lulled by men singing the songs that were as old as the mountains and steeped in tradition.

In this serenity, Raffaella let the scene pass before her as if she were in a dream. Antonio pulled her to him and kissed her on her lips; unobserved by her father or Orlando. But the kiss did not go unnoticed. Luigi, who had been in the constant company of the priest, watched Raffaella's every move. Their open display of affection angered him, as he felt the bitter gall of jealousy tinged with revenge sweep through him.

CHAPTER TWELVE

The morning started before sun-up on the day of the hunt. While there had been great activity at Punta Néula for the Festival of San Giovanni, the Canus had been working on the final arrangements for this social day. The beaters were out the previous night, stopping the runs in the nearby valleys and on the mountain slopes.

Before dawn Raffaella woke to the sound of people collecting in the yard of Sos Lampidos. *Agricoli*, *pastore* and friends from all the neighbouring hamlets joined Gestinu at his invitation.

Everyone brought his own hunting dog, and the strange assortment of *Cari Pertialzus*, large, short-muzzled dogs known as *Dogo Sardo*. The ears were cropped and the tails docked. The strange animals were topped only by the variety of stories claimed by each proud owner about the capability of their dog in the chase.

The men bred the dogs for hunting, and their excited chattering, with the dogs' constant yelping, made it necessary for everyone to shout to be heard above the ever-increasing racket.

The serious talk among the men was of the news from Solferino. The Sardinian Brigades had distinguished themselves with their fighting. Their victory under Victor Emmanuel II, with the French Army under Napoleon III against the Austrian Emperor Franz Joseph I, had been long and bloody. Horrific stories were told of the deaths of the soldiers, not just in battle, but on the battlefield after the conflict was over. The men crossed themselves, while others fingered their amulets, grateful not to have been involved.

Raffaella dressed in the half-light and went downstairs to help Zia Paola with any last-minute preparations. By six o'clock, all the men were present and ready to leave. Again, their colourful outfits of red waistcoats and white cotton shirts were in stark contrast to the pale morning light. The men carried guns slung across their backs and cross-bands of ammunition. The brass ends of the cartridges glinted and flashed in the morning light as the sun started to rise along the mountain ridge.

They all carried *Sa Leppa*, the dual-purpose knife which the Sards find so indispensable. The knives were made by one of the men present, who came from Pattada. He and his family were known throughout the island for their skill and handiwork, and it had been to him that Raffaella and Zia Paola had gone to make Antonio's knife for his birthday. Men also carried a pair of cross-pistols in their belts to give them added protection.

Luigi spotted Raffaella as soon as she made her appearance. He had not left her alone since the festival, and this morning proved to be no exception. He followed her everywhere as she wandered among the many visitors, talking and chatting in her usual friendly manner. She managed to give him the slip when her father took Luigi and introduced him to one of the neighbouring farmers, who had many friends in Piedmont.

She lost no time in finding Antonio, and gave him her eagle's foot tied up in her handkerchief as a token of good fortune. He leant from his horse and kissed her on the mouth. The fullness of his beard sent a renewed thrill through her. He looked so handsome with his *berrita* tipped over one side, and his black woolly *Mastrucca* over the clean cotton shirt Gabriella had made for him. He, too, carried his gun on his back with his ammunition. For one split-second Raffaella saw him not as her lover, but as a romantic bandit, a role she found exhilarating.

She knew Luigi was watching her, and again she smiled up at her lover. She was pleased when she saw the jealous venom sweep through Luigi as he stood clenching and releasing his knuckles as he tried to control his emotions. She watched him as he swung on his heels to go in search of her brother.

He found Orlando in conversation with Gestinu and Salvatore as they tried to decide which way the party should approach the selected hunting areas.

'Alvos is the best pass,' said Gestinu, 'then on to Cazza Noa where we can stop for a meal by the stream. Agreed?'

The others nodded.

Luigi drew Orlando to one side, and Raffaella overheard his whining words to her brother. 'Your sister shows far too much interest in that peasant Pastore,' he said, nodding his head toward Antonio.

'She always has, my friend. We have all known each other since childhood. Don't worry; it's nothing serious,' replied Orlando, trying to reassure him. 'She will grow out of it. He is like a brother to her, that is all.'

Gestinu mounted his horse and called to Orlando and Luigi to follow. Raffaella looked up at her father. He looked so smart in his hunting outfit; his *berrita* pulled down onto his forehead with the long stocking falling down his back. His vivid red waistcoat stood out under his Mastrucca. She ran forward and jumped up to kiss him goodbye, then stood with Zia Paola to wish them good hunting as they set off.

The mountains in late June had lost much of their lush greenness. The early morning coolness soon gave way to the heat, which intensified the sweet smell of the grasses that nodded in profusion in the gentle morning breeze. The route had been arranged so that they could go on the sunny side of the valley to catch the warmth of the sun.

Once up in the macchia-covered mountains the chase was soon in full cry. It wasn't long before they were on the heels of the deer and moufflon, and soon bagged many rabbits and a couple of small boars. By lunchtime the catch had been considerable, with enough game to share among the many men present.

The party gathered in small groups at the preselected eating spot. Antonio dismounted and let his horse loose to wander near the stream with the other animals. He took his saddle and dumped it in the shade of some trees near his friends.

Sergio had collected a small boar from the first kill, and had stripped branches off some myrtle bushes, which he had laid in the bottom of a pit that he had dug. He had placed the gutted boar on the prepared branches and then covered it in the same way, adding wild thyme and parsley for extra flavour. This, in turn, he covered with earth and then lit a huge fire over the top. Around this, Sergio placed pheasants and rabbits on long spikes to cook in the glowing heat. The fire was burning well, and many sat around watching the embers glow.

'Why do you bury it in the earth?' Luigi asked Orlando as they sat drinking the cooled wine which Sergio had placed in the stream.

'It cooks quicker and is much tastier. All the *banditti* and poachers do it this way, so nobody knows. I dare say there is many a shepherd who has warmed his hands over the fire that cooked his own sheep,' said Orlando, laughing.

One of the shepherds came forward to the fire with a long stick, on which he had placed the heart, liver and kidneys of the wild boar. He had tied them to the stick with the washed intestines, which he had wound round the animal fat and the meats, and placed in the embers to cook. The smell of the roasting meat hung in the air and whetted the men's appetites.

When at last they decided the boar was ready, they dug into the fire and the animal was lifted onto the wooden dishes. Sergio took his knife and pushed it into the cooked flesh and then placed the blade on the back of his hand. It was hot, and therefore, the meat would be cooked.

The men came forward and helped themselves to pieces of the herb-flavoured meat with their knives. Luigi watched as all the company put the meat into their mouths and, instead of biting it, would cut the piece away with the long knives, a habit he found distasteful to say the least. The bones were thrown to the waiting dogs who rushed on their prize, dragging it to the cool of the shade to lick and savour their treat.

Antonio sat under a myrtle bush with his dog and watched the present company. He fondled his faithful companion, *Bandidu*, as he licked the bone he had given him. He also watched the familiar faces locked in conversation and gossip. He couldn't help comparing Luigi, who looked pale, with the dark skins of his father and friends. Even Orlando's skin was a little darker – not a lot; it was true. The time in Sassari, always indoors with his studies, had made his friend's skin more pallid than usual. He watched as Gestinu talked to Orlando and Luigi, while Salvatore lay sprawled in the sun-baked clearing.

After a restful two hours the beaters started to collect their belongings together and the silent dozing became a burble of activity. They decided they should cut across the river and return via Punta lillischeddos and sweep down the long valley to Sos Lampidos where they had started from that morning. They also agreed that Antonio and Orlando should head the right-hand sweep, while Gestinu and Salvatore headed the left drive; the beaters dividing according to their friends and various farmsteads.

'You come with us, Luigi,' called Gestinu, signalling to the young man.

Luigi urged his horse forward grateful to be included somewhere.

'If you ride behind us, you can help us if we miss anything,' said Salvatore, laughing. 'We will see you back at Sos Lampidos, Sergio.'

Sergio waved and set about clearing everything away.

So the parties set out hunting once more. The breeze freshened a little, adding a cool relief to the heat of the afternoon, and the promise of a glorious evening.

It wasn't long before the dogs were in full cry again, and the men followed behind. The yelping from the other side of the valley gave a clear indication that the dogs had wind of something.

Gestinu and Salvatore reined their horses near a ridge to watch the chase in full cry below. They could follow the boar's movement as it weaved and crashed its way through the undergrowth and up the steep escarpment, heading straight towards their side of the valley.

'We can head her off down there, Salvatore,' cried Gestinu in a fever of excitement as he spurred his horse down the narrow goat path to meet the oncoming sow.

Salvatore followed his old friend, throwing all caution to the wind in the thrill of the chase.

The heat of the moment made both men blind to the dangers; after all, they had hunted together for many years, and only received minor injuries in falls, or cuts as branches whipped back in their faces.

In a clearing, below the ridge where they had watched the sow, they dismounted and waited for the beast to break cover. She hadn't looked too big, a medium-sized sow, but for all that she would make good eating for the house.

Luigi came into the clearing and was about to dismount when a huge boar broke cover, crashing through the bushes. Clearly not the one they had seen from above. This one was a male. A great brute of an animal, with two sets of massive tusks rising on either side of his gross snout. Gestinu's dogs rushed at the beast, but with a roaring snort and a swift turn of the animal's mighty head, one fell to the ground, blood spurting from the severed artery in its neck. The other lay yelping, its leg gored.

Gestinu ran forward and aimed his gun, but the boar proved too quick for him. The animal, now wild with pain from the large, tearing wound one dog had managed to inflict, charged at Gestinu, throwing him off balance. The retort from his gun echoed round the clearing, with an anguished yell of pain from him as he fell to the ground. The boar became more frantic with the constant yelping and the retort from the gun, and tore savagely into Gestinu's leg.

Salvatore took careful aim. He didn't want to hurt his friend, and knew the shot had to be good. Luigi, on the other hand, seeing his host fall, aimed wildly and fired, wounding the animal. The boar, by now incensed with terror and pain, swung round and drove its tusks into Gestinu's side. A split-second later, another shot rang out and the boar fell dead on the spot. This shot came from Salvatore, who had been shaken by the wild shot from Luigi.

Luigi dismounted and ran forward, his gun at the ready.

Salvatore hurried to Gestinu's side and yelled at the young doctor. 'Shoot the dog, for pity's sake.'

Luigi did as he was ordered and the yelping stopped, leaving a morbid silence over the horrific scene.

'There was nothing I could do,' whined Luigi. 'Why didn't you fire earlier?'

'I didn't want to injure the boar. I wanted to kill it. Don't just stand there, for Heaven's sake. You're the doctor, help Gestinu!' cried Salvatore.

Luigi, now recovered from the initial shock, took off his shirt and tore it into strips, calling on Salvatore to do the same. He folded Salvatore's shirt into a large pad and bound it round Gestinu's waist to try to stem the bleeding. Luigi now bound the leg as tight as he dared, and then tied the two legs together to act as a splint.

At that moment Orlando and Antonio came into the clearing. Having heard the shots and the yelping, they had come to see what had happened. The carnage that met them made Orlando sick to his stomach, and he retched violently.

'Holy Mary, preserve us,' cried Antonio as he crossed himself and jumped from his horse. 'What on earth happened, Babbu?'

Salvatore just looked up into his son's eyes. His face registered all the pain and anguish he felt for his injured friend. Antonio put his hand on his father's shoulder to comfort him.

Orlando pulled himself together and went to kneel beside his father. He looked from his father to Luigi with a pleading expression. Salvatore broke the silence by explaining, as best he could, what had happened. But he had become confused by the shock of seeing his old friend felled in front of him. It had been terrible to see Gestinu brought down like that, and Antonio tried to comfort his father as best he could.

'Luigi, how bad is he?' asked Orlando.

'Bad,' replied Luigi. 'You will have to get some of the men to ride to Sos Lampidos to get water and linen ready, and the kitchen table scrubbed. Tell Zia Paola to fetch my bag of instruments from my room. They must be boiled and left in the water until I need them. Do you understand?'

Orlando nodded and turned to the men, who had followed him to the clearing. There was no shortage of volunteers, and minutes later they were riding hard, on their way back to Sos Lampidos with their instructions.

Those that remained helped Antonio and Orlando lift the now semi-conscious Gestinu up onto the horse, into the arms of Luigi, so he could support him on the ride home. He could also reach the rough tourniquet to be able to release it when necessary. Orlando rode beside Luigi in numbed silence, while Antonio walked with his father as they led the horses back to Sos Lampidos.

At the house, Zia Paola opened the door in answer to the repeated banging and the men told her what had happened to Gestinu, at once offering her their help. Together they busied themselves building up the fire and collecting more wood.

Raffaella, fighting back her tears, scrubbed the table and then tore the linen into long strips for bandages. She then collected her best healing herbs and laid them out on the chest near the fire. Zia Paola, meanwhile, collected the bag from Luigi's room and boiled the instruments as directed. One of the men rode to Punta Néula to collect Gabriella, for her help would be needed. She had come with many of her special herbs and an amulet for Gestinu's sure recovery.

CHAPTER THIRTEEN

Darkness began to fall and Raffaella became more and more worried. She kept going to the door, to see if she could hear or see anything. Her mind went back to her youth when her uncle had been killed in a hunting accident. The memory frightened her, and she went to the door again and peered into the darkness. Then, out of the gloom, she saw them coming up the bottom meadow in a long procession. She ran down the rough track towards them, and saw at once that Antonio was leading her father's horse. Oblivious to everyone, she ran sobbing into her lover's arms.

'Come now, Raffaella,' he whispered, putting his arm round her and leading her with the horse, 'pull yourself together. You don't want your father to see you like that.'

She looked up at her father. His gaze was that of a man half in this world. From him she stared at Luigi, who cradled Gestinu in his arms. Her father's head rested against Luigi's white, naked, hairless chest, which was smeared with his blood. The mare had streaks of blood over her matted coat where Gestinu's wound had opened, and the blood seeped through the rough bandages on his leg and side.

Raffaella bit her lip hard and stood back as strong hands came forward, reached up, and lifted her father down. She watched helplessly as they carried him across the threshold and placed him on the clean table.

Inside the house Zia Paola had already poured boiling water and vinegar into bowls and was organising more fresh water. Gabriella, too, busied herself as she prepared her different herbs.

Luigi washed his hands, then turning to the men, said sharply, 'He has been unconscious most of the time, which is in our favour.

What I have to do will be painful, and you will have to hold him down.'

Orlando stepped forward to help, but Luigi shook his head. 'Not you, nor your aunt, or you, Raffaella. You are all too close to him. I want someone I can shout at if needs be.'

Two volunteers stepped forward.

Luigi took a small phial from his case and administered a measured amount of the opiate to Gestinu. 'Hold him,' said the young doctor, and without much ceremony took a sharp knife and cut off the Gestinu's leather boots and cotton gaiters. He cut up the already torn trousers, revealing all of the damaged leg and the blood-soaked bandages. As he unwound the cotton from the wounds they gaped wide, causing them to bleed afresh.

Gestinu moaned. Luigi looked at one of the men and nodded. The man took a bottle of *fil 'e ferru* from Gabriella and put it to Gestinu's lips. The wounded man gulped feebly at the strong drink and fell back in a semi-conscious stupor.

Luigi worked as quickly as possible to clean the wound as best he could. 'Needle and gut, Zia Paola,' he ordered.

Zia Paola watched as Luigi passed the needle through the flame of a nearby candle and started to sew up the hideous wound. Gabriella, too, watched the young doctor at his work. She was not impressed by what she saw. She did not like doctors and their new-fangled ideas. They always charged exorbitant prices with little or no result. That wound in the leg was far too bad to leave just stitched, and she knew trouble would come from such treatment.

'You will never save his life that way,' she said at last.

'What would you suggest then?' asked Luigi, in a sneering, superior manner.

'Cut off his leg now, before the damage spreads. Wash it in spirit and put maggots on the wound to clean it. If you take it off just above the knee you will save his life,' she replied with an edge to her voice. There came a murmur of approval from the men.

Luigi laughed. 'That's silly. There should be no need to take off the leg. It will be all right and then you will have taken off a good leg for nothing.'

'Better to do it now while there is time, rather than wait until it is too late; for if the poison spreads up the leg, you will never be able to take it off at the hip and his life will be lost,' retorted Gabriella.

'With my modern medicine and balms it will be no problem. All he needs is rest and good nursing. Now if you will excuse me, I will attend to the other wound.'

Luigi undressed Gestinu, cutting away the rest of his clothing. The tear in his side yawned open as the young doctor pulled away the clothing. Gestinu again moaned, and the man with the spirit administered another heavy dose until he fell back unconscious again.

'And I suppose you suggest we should cut this out as well?' sneered Luigi.

'No,' replied Gabriella indignantly, 'but it would be better to wash it in spirit and again put maggots in it, then cauterise it rather than stitch it. Then bind it in lemon and honey.'

The other men nodded agreement with her. She had saved many of them from death with her skill in herbal medicine.

'Look, Gabriella,' cut in Orlando, 'I know you are good, but Luigi has all the modern techniques. They are better than the old practices. You will see, everything will be all right,' he said with impatience.

Luigi took some balm from his case, and spread it on the wound. He then set about stitching up the great, gaping hole, while all present watched him in intense silence.

'I need more light here,' he called.

Zia Paola came forward with a large lantern which she held up over Gestinu. When Luigi had finished, he ordered the men to carry Gestinu to his bed to rest. Zia Paola had already remade the bed with fresh linen and draw-sheets underneath, so they could change them without disturbing him too much. Once the patient was in bed, Luigi ordered extra bedding to be placed round him to stop Gestinu turning over and reopening the wounds.

Raffaella followed them upstairs, where she stood at the foot of the bed and stared at her beloved father. He looked so pale, so frail under the tallow candlelight. He looked nothing like the brave, strong man, that waved goodbye to her earlier that day. Tears welled up in her eyes and ran down her face. She felt lost and helpless. Antonio, sensing her feelings, came toward her, and put his arm round her in an attempt to comfort her.

At this, Luigi stepped forward and pulled Antonio's arm away from Raffaella. 'Leave her,' he said with an icy tone. 'There is nothing you can do now. I will comfort her and her family. She does not need you.'

Antonio's eyes flashed with anger.

Salvatore, who had helped carry Gestinu to his bed, watched everything from a distance, moved forward and put his hand on his son's shoulder to restrain him. 'Come, Antonio, we must go downstairs. There is nothing we can do at the moment. Gestinu is in the Heavenly Father's hands now, and with the good work of Luigi–'

'Good work? Good work, you call it, Father?' snarled Antonio. 'If he had been quicker on the draw, perhaps none of this would have happened; him and his fancy ways.' He took a step towards Luigi. 'Where were you when it all happened? Cowering in the shade of the trees, no doubt?' He paused, his anger mounting. 'If you are going to practise medicine in the country among the mountain people, you will have to get used to mangled bodies. It's not like the city, where all you have to deal with are cut fingers and fits of the vapours from bored women, and treat the pox for randy old men. And you would be well advised to listen to the old women of the villages, who have to live without doctors and their fancy prices. To you their methods may seem crude, but they have saved many a life with their knowledge, handed down from mother to daughter. Never be too proud to ask anyone'

'Antonio, please. You are forgetting that I was there too,' cut in his father. 'I couldn't shoot the animal either. If I had been just that bit quicker… It all happened so fast. We weren't expecting a boar. We thought it was the sow you were chasing up the hillside. In our excitement, we forgot the rules of safety.'

'You are old, Babbu; allowances have to be made for the old.'

'Antonio,' roared his father, 'first I would remind you that Luigi is a guest, like you, in this house, and second, that without his help Gestinu would have bled to death by now. For none of us could have helped him.' Salvatore turned to Luigi and added, 'For my son's lapse of hospitality, I apologise. We have all been under a great deal of strain and the shock has made us forget our manners.'

'Don't you dare apologise for me!' cried Antonio. 'Don't ever apologise to him or his kind. He is a Continental. He's a rat, vermin. Have you forgotten what his kind did to Gavinu's brother Ugo? They killed our cousin and that makes us bitter enemies, and you apologise for me? I spit on his kind, and on him. He is a coward.' At this Antonio spat on the floor at Luigi's feet and swung out of the door and clattered downstairs.

Salvatore rested his hand on Luigi's arm. 'It is true, I owe no friendship to the Piedmontese, for as Antonio said, one killed my cousin. Also, the Carabineri gunned down my own brother. But you have helped save a good and dear friend of mine, and for this I thank you from the bottom of my heart. If your medicine proves good and he lives I shall have much to be grateful for, but if your medicine fails, and he dies, I shall carry it on my conscience forever that I wasn't quick enough to help him, and that I didn't insist on Gabriella looking after him.'

'There was nothing else anyone could do, old man,' replied Luigi, still shaken by Antonio's outburst. 'I have done more than your wife could do for him. If you want to do something I suggest you try some patience and pray.'

Orlando, who had stood back during the whole outburst, came forward and took Salvatore to the door of the bedroom. The old shepherd looked up at Orlando, and took his hand squeezed it hard.

'You know, Orlando, if your father dies I shall have his death on my hands, as much as if I had pulled the knife on him myself. All it can do is split our families, for you are bound to hold it against me.'

'Dear Salvatore, my father already owes his life to you for the time when you saved him all those years ago. I believe Luigi; have no fear on that score. You are blameless, I know that. If anyone is to blame, perhaps I am for letting you two go off together. It could have been you lying there. Go down and see Gabriella and try to calm Antonio. I beg you.'

'If it had been me, Gabriella would have done what should be done. I hope your faith in that young man proves to be well-founded,' mumbled Salvatore as he took Raffaella's hand and led her downstairs.

CHAPTER FOURTEEN

That night, the men who decided to stay at Sos Lampidos sat round the fire in the large downstairs room and kept a constant vigil. Some who had stock to feed returned to their homesteads, promising to come back in the morning.

Elena supplied endless cups of coffee and wine for the men while Zia Paola, Raffaella and Gabriella took it in turns to sit with Gestinu as he lay motionless on his bed, his breathing so shallow they had to listen for signs of life. Luigi visited his patient every half hour, noting any change and taking his pulse.

It was Raffaella's turn to be with her father when Luigi and Orlando came up for the evening visit, and to inspect the bandages. Luigi pulled back the linen sheet and looked at his handiwork.

'Tell me, Luigi,' whispered Orlando, 'how bad is he?'

'Well, there is no fresh bleeding. The bandages look clean so there is little oozing. His head is hot and feverish, but his skin is cold and clammy. I fear the fever will have to run its course; when it breaks we will know if he is out of danger. As long as we can keep him still we have a good chance.'

Luigi covered the semi-conscious patient and turned to Raffaella. 'Would you go to your aunt and ask her to bring cold water? Then will you both bathe his head and arms to try to keep the fever down as much as possible?'

Luigi drew Orlando to one side and said in a low voice, 'I know it's late, but I want you to send someone to the doctor at Mores. Ask him for this,' he said, scribbling a note on a small piece of paper. 'Make sure you give it to the doctor himself and tell him it's urgent. Ask him, too, if he could come himself; I would be grateful. Tell me, how long will it take someone to ride there, do you know?' added Luigi.

'I'll go. I know the way and it will take me a couple of hours, even in the dark. I'll be back as soon as I can,' replied Orlando, and he prepared to leave.

Luigi grabbed him by the arm and added, 'Find the priest and bring him too. We will need him if this fever doesn't break.'

Orlando looked shaken by his friend's request. 'But you said he would be all right. That it would just be a matter of stitching. You said you could look after him.'

'He will be all right. It's just a precaution, that's all. I need that medicine, though, if I am going to help him with the fever. Hurry now, for pity's sake,' hissed Luigi.

Orlando stared at his friend in disbelief.

'Well, don't just stand there. Go and get the medicine. Hurry!' cried Luigi.

Orlando pulled himself together and disappeared down the stairs.

Raffaella heard her brother call to Sergio to collect their horses. She heard, too, Sergio's garbled protest about the dangers of riding at night, and how he had heard the small owl hooting outside, and that nothing would induce him to go out with such an ill omen. Someone else volunteered to go with Orlando. She heard the door slam and the sound of horses retreating into the black night.

Luigi, unsure of himself, paced the room.

'We will call you if we need you,' Raffaella said to Luigi, dismissing him, and he went downstairs to join the other men.

Raffaella sat by the bed and watched her aunt as she bathed Gestinu's head. Zia Paola looked calm enough. Her lifestyle would change very little if Gestinu died, for she would still have to look after her and Orlando.

She looked at her father lying in the big carved-oak bed. It had been a gift from his father as part of his wedding present. Gestinu had made love to his wife on it. Orlando had been born in it; Raffaella had been born here too, but her mother had also died here. She crossed herself as she thought of her.

It worried Raffaella; she knew if her father died, she would not be able to get round Orlando in the same easy way she could her father. Babbu had always spoilt her and she managed to get what she wanted, even if she did have to bide her time. After all, when Antonio gave her the beautiful horse Orlando had not minded at the time, but now he showed his disapproval, saying it should be returned. Gestinu, on the other hand, wasn't too happy about it at the time, but when he saw how much pleasure it gave her, he let the matter drop. He would not hear of her having to give the animal back now. Orlando would still make her give up her most precious gift, of that she was sure.

She knew, deep down, that in time Babbu would come round to her way of thinking and let her marry Antonio. It would be just a matter of time. The one thing it seemed she had lost at the moment. When Orlando became head of the family it would be very different. He would insist on her marrying Luigi. A chill ran through her, and she shivered. She couldn't marry him. She and Antonio were bound together, both morally and physically. It would be impossible. The thought of Luigi touching her filled her with cold horror. Babbu would understand. After all, he had given up the city life to marry Maria and they had been happy together.

Raffaella was aroused from her thoughts by her father as he stirred. She took his hand and felt the sting of tears as she kissed his pale skin. His face was no longer relaxed in the numbness of oblivion, but contorted with the pain that now wracked his whole body and mind.

Zia Paola tiptoed across the room and went to the top of the stairs, where she called to Gabriella, who came to her side in moments. As they entered the room Gabriella's face dropped. She looked frightened.

'What is it?' asked Zia Paola, concerned.

'The smell, can't you smell it?'

'No. What is it?'

'It's slight, but it's there: the distinctive, sweet odour of moist gangrene,' replied Gabriella.

'Oh no. God, no, not that,' cried Zia Paola, crossing herself.

Gabriella went to Gestinu. He had become restless, and she felt his pulse, which was rapid. She opened his mouth, but his tongue was clean.

'It can't be,' snapped Luigi, who had followed them into the room. 'The bandages are all clean. There is no sign of any oozing.'

Gabriella sighed. 'I told you the leg should have come off,' she replied in her usual soft way. 'You have wasted valuable time.'

'I have sent Orlando for some medicine. He will be here soon,' said Luigi, trying to keep ahead of the situation.

Gabriella leant over Gestinu and removed her charms and sacred amulet from around his neck. Then, taking a small phial from her apron, she put it to Gestinu's lips.

'Thank you, Gabriella. I know why you have come,' wheezed Gestinu.

'What are you giving him?' snarled Luigi.

Gabriella smiled sardonically as she looked at the young man. 'We have a saying here: *bivi de miegu e mori miserable*, meaning, who lives by the doctor dies miserably. I have given him laudanum to help his pain and removed the charms, for it is better he goes quickly.'

Gestinu put his hand up to her. 'Gabriella, before you do what you must do, I must have paper and pencil,' he gasped.

Zia Paola went at once to fetch what he requested.

Luigi came forward and bent over his patient. 'You mustn't exert yourself, Signore Gestinu. I beg of you to lie still. I have sent for the doctor at Mores. Please wait until he comes,' he urged.

But Gestinu waved his hand to dismiss the order and turned to Gabriella. 'Dear Gabriella. I know you would have taken off the leg. It is too late, dear friend, for that. My leg feels heavy and there is a stinging pain shooting through it. You have come to give me the sweet death, but go and fetch Antonio. I must see him.' Gestinu fell back on his pillows. His eyes were sunk into the back of his head, and there were large, dark circles under them.

Gabriella left the room and returned with her son to sit by the bedside.

'Raffaella, are you there?' croaked her father.

'Yes, Babbu. I'm here. What is it you want?' she asked as silent tears rolled down her face.

'Antonio. Is he here too?'

'Yes, Gestinu. I'm here,' replied Antonio.

Raffaella looked to Antonio, but he nodded and smiled.

'And Orlando?'

'No, Babbu, he has gone to get some medicine from Mores.'

'Give me your hands, children,' said Gestinu, reaching towards them.

The young couple did as they were bid.

'I know,' croaked Gestinu, 'I know, Raffaella, that you love Antonio, and I know too how he feels about you, and for how long he has held that need for you.' Gestinu started to cough, his breathing shallow, and he found it difficult to catch his breath as it came in short bursts. He wheezed and fell back on his pillow, exhausted.

Luigi stepped forward, his concern for his patient overshadowed by his jealousy of Antonio. 'Look, Signore Gestinu. You must lie still. I can't be responsible for what happens if you keep moving. Please, you must listen to me,' said Luigi with a sharp edge to his voice.

'You are already responsible for what happens to me,' replied Gestinu, as he struggled for breath.

Luigi turned to Raffaella. 'If you have any thought for your father, I beg you to leave him to rest.'

But Gestinu held her hand, even tighter. His eyes were deep and compelling. 'There is nothing you can do for me now. I am a dead man. But for pity's sake, at least let me speak to my daughter in peace,' he said, drawing Raffaella closer to his ashen face. 'I know, my dear, what binds you two together, so no one can drive you apart and I give you my blessing. I must sign the paper, for you will need my consent to marry Antonio.'

She bent forward and kissed her father. 'Oh Babbu, my dearest Babbu, I'm sorry if I have hurt you. I love you so much. Thank you.'

Gestinu held on to his daughter and she became aware of his rasping rattles as he struggled for breath.

At that moment Zia Paola entered the room carrying the paper and pencil, but she was not alone. The Pastore had returned before Orlando, with Gestinu's brother the priest.

Gestinu raised himself up and made an effort to reach the paper Zia Paola had in her hand. But in that moment all the strength left him. It all proved too much as he cried out in pain and fell back. His face distorted in agony, then relaxed as he slumped back, dead, on the pile of pillows.

Luigi felt for a pulse but found nothing.

Gabriella pulled back the bedclothes to enable her to examine the wounds. The shock of the sweet smell and the sight of the blood and liquid pus-soaked bandages made them all gasp in horror. Large black pustules stood up on Gestinu's upper leg, which had turned a livid red. In his effort to sit up, he had reopened his stitches on the infected wounds and the pain had been more that his heart could cope with, as the toxins spread throughout his body.

'Moist gangrene,' said Gabriella.

The women stood, crossing themselves, and mumbled prayers under their breath.

Raffaella clung to Antonio as the priest, her uncle, chanted the last rites over her father as his remaining life's brown blood drained onto the bed. She felt powerless as the candle of his life was snuffed out so untimely. He was dead. Gone from her forever, gone to join her mother and the other spirits in the peaceful meadows of Asphodel.

When Orlando and the doctor returned, Gabriella, Zia Paola and Raffaella had washed and dressed Gestinu in his finest suit and then wrapped him in a linen winding cloth, and laid out his disfigured body on his bed. They placed him on his *tapis*, a special rug for the dead, and covered him with more clean, fresh linen. They moved the bed so as to point the dead man's feet towards the door, as custom dictated, allowing the departing soul to pass, unheeded from the soles of the feet. All the soiled sheeting was then burnt and the fires extinguished.

The doctor demanded everyone leave the room, except for Luigi, and examined Gestinu. When he had finished, he turned to Luigi and said quietly, 'Next time listen to the women, then whatever happens you can't be blamed.'

With that he took his leave of the family, eager to return home.

The loud incantations from the priest echoed throughout the house as the family and friends thronged into the room, now heavy with incense and herbs. The news would travel fast and everyone would be here to pay their respects to their dear friend.

Antonio came forward and took Raffaella's hand, and she fell into his arms as silent tears fell down her cheeks.

'I can't believe he is dead. Yesterday he left for his hunting trip so full of life. Now he has gone, everything has finished for him. His comforting words, advice, help, and most of all his special love have all gone, denied to me forever by a single act of fate,' she cried, holding on to Antonio.

Salvatore shuffled forward to kiss his old friend. Raffaella noticed, with shock, how much he had aged over the past day. His bearded face looked pale and his eyes were sunk deep into his head.

The priest finished his incantations and people left the room one by one, each shaking hands with Orlando as they did so. The mourners staying, to carry on their wailing that would continue throughout the night and the following day.

Raffaella had been unable to say anything to Orlando on his return. The shock of finding his father dead closed in on him, and her bitterness at him and Luigi melted at seeing the pain on her brother's face.

'Might I be allowed to be alone with Gestinu for a moment, Orlando?' asked Salvatore in a low voice. Orlando looked at the drawn figure and nodded. He ushered out the mourners and closed the door behind them all.

Outside Raffaella could hear Salvatore's heartfelt sobs as he begged his old friend to give him mercy. His sobs grew louder.

'In God's good grace, have pity on my soul and grant me peace of mind so nothing will ever happen to divide our families.'

She moved away from the door, and noticed when Salvatore came out that he looked as if his spirit had been broken. Without a word he went downstairs to find Gabriella.

Raffaella went to follow him, but Antonio caught her arm.

'Leave him be, my love. He needs to be on his own,' he said as he drew her toward him.

CHAPTER FIFTEEN

People came from all through the valley. They came in a long procession, chanting their laments, which droned up the valley and echoed in the mountains. Even the birds gave up their frenzied singing to the wailing of the mourners. On entering the house, the women, who were dressed in black from head to toe, continued up the stairs to the bedroom. On seeing their dead friend, they started their wailing and lamenting with renewed vigour. The men followed, chanting in deep voices, told of the virtues of their dead friend and called on the Holy Mother to care for his soul.

Raffaella knew the lamenting and chanting would continue now throughout the day, and she felt as though she would go mad with the constant droning in her ears. She fled from the house to the edge of the cliff-like drop which fell away to the river below. The first blush of day tinted the trees and grasses with an eerie glow. In the half-light, she could just make out the river's winding course by the thick reeds and flowering oleander bushes that grew in profusion at its brink. She leant against the gnarled old olive tree to steady herself, feeling faint. A sweet-scented breeze tossed the silver-grey leaves above her and blew through her hair. It felt so pure, so fresh after the stifling, stench-ridden atmosphere of her dead father's room. She sighed.

'Mind you don't fall,' said a gentle voice from behind her, and a pair of arms enfolded her.

'Oh, Antoneddu,' she sobbed, seeking the comfort of his arms, 'why did it have to happen? I shall miss him so. He did understand, you know. He understood all about us.'

'Hush, my love. Don't cry, my darling,' he said as he rocked her in his arms.

Her hair glinted in the dappled light as he stroked it. She

sobbed as if her heart would break, and he tried to comfort her as best he could. The words were hard to find, and she noticed a break in his voice when he spoke.

'Oh Antoneddu, he knew all about us and gave us his blessing. Gabriella is witness to that, so Orlando can't make me marry Luigi now.' The thought frightened her, and she cried anew. Antonio held her close to him, and kissed her forehead.

'Darling, darling Raffaella, no one will ever take you away from me. I promise.' He kissed her again on her mouth, and she responded, safe in the comfort of his love and strength that filled her entire senses.

They became aware of someone calling their names. Zia Paola came hurrying toward them, beckoning them to come to her.

'Orlando is looking for you both. Quick, now, come inside with me.'

Again the wailing of mourners filled and numbed Raffaella's senses, drowning all thought of everything except the death of her father. Her brother came towards them. Did he look even more arrogant now? Raffaella could not be sure, but of one thing she was positive: nothing would ever be the same now her father had gone.

'I have arranged for Father Franco to bury Babbu at Bantadda tomorrow morning. Zio Marco will be coming from Sassari today, and we expect him this evening. We will take Father to the church tonight for the vigil and the reception.

Zio Marco will also be able to settle Father's estate. Sergio has ridden there with the news. I shall be returning to Sassari with them after the funeral. You will stay here with Zia Paola and look after Luigi. Is that clear, Raffaella?'

She nodded in acquiescence.

Later, Raffaella stole away to the stables; she needed to be on her own. She wanted to make a straw dolly for her father. Men were traditionally buried with straw dollies placed in their pockets to represent their grandchildren. She fashioned the straw into her doll, taking time to make it perfect, and when she was happy with her work she slipped, unseen, into her father's room and placed it in his waistcoat pocket for her unborn child.

Sergio returned in the late afternoon with Zio Marco and his wife Zia Madeleine. He had ridden hard, staying in Sassari for the night. They had left in the morning, as the shepherd needed to be back at Sos Lampidos by nightfall. Sergio feared the dark, when the spirits walked, and, he knew they lingered behind trees, waiting to chase him.

At Sos Lampidos the men loaded the coffin onto the cart. Antonio offered to drive all of them to the small church, where they were met by Father Franco. The soft light of the candles in the church caught the stonework and illuminated the saints. They set the coffin on two trestles, said their private prayers, and left Gestinu in the hands of his God.

At Sos Lampidos the table was crowded for the evening meal. Zia Paola had asked the Sannas to stay, as Marina and Salvatore had come over after Gabriella. The women worked all day helping with the preparations for the enormous meal, prepared and eaten in the company of the dead spirit, to fortify him on his journey to the other side.

They all sat at the table, with Gestinu's place laid at the head of the table. A solitary candle flickered by his place, with food and wine, in case the departing spirit should need refreshment to aid him on his long journey. For should he come to the table and find no victuals that would indeed be a blight on the family's hospitality.

Luigi remarked on the quaint custom as a heathen act of barbarism, but found himself being stared at with stony silence, making him feel isolated. There wasn't even the usual rush of defence from Orlando, which made Luigi withdraw further from the unforgiving stares.

Raffaella, unable to stomach food or the constant wailing from the mourners, excused herself from the table. Antonio watched her every move, but, it was Luigi who rose and arrested her path up the stairs. She turned and looked at him in complete contempt. His grip grew stronger on her arm.

'You are hurting me, Luigi. Let me go,' she hissed.

'You will come with me to the funeral tomorrow. I want to take you. Orlando, I'm sure, will give me his permission,' he said in his oily manner which made her flesh creep.

'I shall go with my family, and you are not family,' she retorted, and she tossed her hair away from her face. 'In Sardinia, it is the women who go to the burials; the men stay at home to hide their grief, but if you wish to join the women that is your choice.'

Someone laughed at the table, and Luigi swung round, unsure of himself.

'It would be good for you to have an escort, sister. Luigi comes from a country where it is normal for the men to attend funerals. I give him my permission to take you,' replied Orlando in a triumphant manner, for he saw that it had been Antonio who laughed at the idea of Luigi joining the women.

Antonio stood to defend Raffaella, but Luigi, bowing to the better part of valour, let her go with a sickly smile. Raffaella noticed that Zio Marco placed a restraining hand on Antonio's arm. She threw him an acknowledging smile and fled up the stairs to her room.

Once inside she bolted the door, threw herself on her bed and wept until sleep hushed her cries and drove the fear of events to come from her tormented mind, aware now, of the life of Antoneddu's child that moved inside her.

The funeral was brief. Father Franco gave a short sermon praising the virtues of his brother to the gathering, followed by a blessing. Sergio came to help with the burial, and stepped forward to fill in the open grave.

The coffin, made by one of the shepherds, had been roughly hewn, and merged with the baked earth, as it lay in the yawning hole. Father Franco stepped forward and sprinkled the coffin with holy water, and again gave his blessing to his brother. Zia Paola came forward and bent to pick a handful of soil, which she threw onto the coffin. The deep, hollow thud of earth falling onto the wooden box sounded like a moan from the depths of the earth itself.

Raffaella watched the whole scene dry-eyed as if she were merely an observer, and not connected with the play that unfolded before her. Elena handed Sergio a wooden cross. It had been given to her by some of the hunters, who had carved Gestinu's name on it, along with his birthdate and the day he died. Sergio took the cross and knocked it into place with the back of his shovel. The women then surged forward to place their flowers around the terracotta-coloured grave, then melted out of sight as they began to make their way back to Sos Lampidos to join their menfolk.

Raffaella approached the grave. She dropped down on one knee and placed her small bunch of wild orchids, picked that morning, next to the wooden cross. She stared at the grave. Now here in this small churchyard lay her father, mother and dearest friend Vitoria. At that moment, she felt cold, and a terrifying feeling that they were beckoning her to join them. She shuddered. The peace that descended on the place was eerie, but at last she could hear the birds singing again, which had for so long been drowned out by the constant wailing of the mourners.

She rose and sighed, then turned to the gig. She had managed to come with Zia Paola and Zia Madeleine, but they had gone. She searched for Antonio and Sergio, but they, too had left to find the men to help them fill in the grave. She suddenly became seized by panic. Her worst fears were realised as Luigi walked round from the far side of the gig and came toward her. With unusual resignation and without any argument she allowed herself to be escorted to the carriage, and climbed up while Luigi arranged her skirt around her feet. He then walked round the gig and climbed up beside her, and urged the horse forward.

It was a little while before he broke the silence. He took her acquiescence, to be a sign that she might be in a friendlier frame of mind, which for him proved a grave error of judgement.

'I'm sorry about your father, Raffaella, really I am. I did everything in my power for him. You must believe that. I know he meant a lot to you. I know, too, that you people in these mountains have little faith in doctors. Sergio has made that very plain. But I can assure you no one could have done more.'

She sat without saying a word, but smiled to herself, as she could just imagine what Sergio had said to Luigi. He would not have minced his words. Served him right.

'You should have taken his leg off.'

'It would have made no difference. He bled internally, and there was infection in his side as well as his leg. I could have taken the leg off, but he still would have died.'

'Where are Zia Paola and Zia Madeleine?' she asked, with a flatness to her voice.

'Orlando told Sergio to send them straight back to Sos Lampidos after the funeral.'

They drove on in silence, Luigi encouraged by the fact that she made no serious objection to his presence. Orlando had been right. Now that her father had gone, she would realise that she would be better off with a good marriage. He decided to press his case. They reached a clump of cork trees and Luigi reined in the horse under the shade, glad of some relief from the now oppressive heat. He turned to Raffaella and cleared his throat in his usual irritating way.

'I know I haven't been able to capture your love, and perhaps this is not the time to talk to you, but I have a great affection for you, Raffaella. I can take you away from all this and make you happy. We could even go to Piedmont to live. I have lands there, and you can ride the finest horses and have everything you want. My father and mother would, I know, welcome you into the family. You would make me very happy.'

She sat listening to him without saying a word, but inside, her anger was rising. She turned to look at him, and almost spat her words at him. 'You, Luigi, are Orlando's friend and a guest in our house, and this forbids me from telling you what I think of you. But I will say this. You don't know me and I know nothing about you, and have no wish to know you better. So how can you expect me to have feelings for you?'

But Luigi would not be put off, and continued. 'Feelings come later. They are not necessary for a good marriage. Your schooling in Itteri has given you all the charm and poise needed for a doctor's wife, and you are indeed very beautiful. Any man would be proud to have such an asset. I am a man of the world. I know that these schools teach you young women to be coy and play at coquetry with your suitors.'

He leant forward and tried to kiss her with a fumbling lust, which made her sick with fright and anger. Freeing herself from his clammy grasp, she wiped her hand across her mouth. Her eyes flashed with vengeance.

'How dare you take advantage of me?' she cried. 'You may know women who trifle with men's affections, but up here in the mountains we say what we mean.' She raged, her whole body trembling with anger. She had a wild passion about her now, which made Luigi lust for her, making him more determined to have his way.

'I have more to offer you than that peasant shepherd Antonio. I can assure you that any thoughts of him that you call love will soon vanish when you have the graces of fine linen and silk clothes. He can't offer you that; even your father never gave you that. You can't fool me, Raffaella, you are not the innocent young woman you make out to be.'

'Don't you dare speak to me like that, you pig, you're not worthy of mentioning my father's and Antonio's names in the same breath. You have poisoned my brother's mind with your fancy ways. You call yourself a man? Sergio was right. You should have left Father to the women, they would have saved him. They knew what should be done. They would not have shrunk from cutting off his leg, or cutting out the flesh. You are to blame for his death as much as if you had knifed him.'

Luigi watched her in her fervent anger. His lust for her made him bolder, and he again leant forward to grab her, but this time Raffaella was too quick for him. Seeing her chance, she grabbed the whip and hit out at him, causing him to reel back from the pain of the lash mark she laid across his face. Then, grabbing the reins, she urged the horse forward into a feverish gallop.

The gig swayed from side to side as it bumped and lurched on every rut and stone on the arid road. The wind took her headdress and freed her hair, which streamed out behind her in waves of black light.

Luigi clung to the side of the gig, begging her to slow down as they would both be killed. With a sudden sharp turn Sos Lampidos jumped into view, perched high on its steep escarpment and overlooking the valley below. Again she urged the horse on, but the steady upward climb slowed his pace. Outside the house she reined the horse in amid a cloud of dust. She jumped from the gig, leaving Luigi to collect his senses.

He called after her in desperation, 'Raffaella, your brother has promised you to me, and I am prepared to wait.'

She turned to look at him. The whiplash stood red and angry on his face, with a small trickle of blood where the leather had snapped at the delicate skin.

'I'll see you in Hell first,' she replied as she swung on her heels and went indoors.

Friends, from the neighbouring farmsteads now joined the men. The mourners, too, mingled with everyone, mercifully quiet at last as the garbled chatter filled the room. Raffaella couldn't help noticing how drab they all looked in their black clothes. Like carrion crows, she thought; such a change from their bright daily costumes.

She glanced around the room, thankful that Zia Paola had enough help, so hoping not to be noticed, she went upstairs.

The sudden knock on her door, therefore, made her start.

'Who is it?' she asked.

'Orlando. Let me in, Raffaella.'

She unlocked the door and let him in.

'I've just seen Luigi. Have you seen what you have done to his face? You little vixen, how could you whip someone like that? You're a vicious little cat. I understand from Luigi that you are being most uncooperative, and I warn you now, you are trying my patience, Raffaella.' His eyes were narrow and mean-looking.

'Why did you make me come home with Luigi? Why couldn't I have come home with Zia Paola and Zia Madeleine? Where is Antoneddu? I want to talk to him.'

'Antonio is downstairs, and I do wish you would call him by his proper name, and not that stupid pet name that you insist on calling him.' Orlando leant towards her and wagged his finger at her menacingly. 'Now you listen to me, young lady. I have had a serious talk with Salvatore and told him that I have plans for you, and they do not include his son, is that clear, Raffaella?'

She sank onto her bed. Her legs felt weak and his words came like rifle fire on her mind.

'As for Zia Paola and Zia Madeleine,' he continued, 'I needed them here. Now make sure you listen to me, Raffaella. Zio Marco and I are leaving tomorrow for Sassari. Luigi has asked if he can come as far as Mores with us. It seems he has some work there, but he will be back here within the week and you, Raffaella, will do your best to make him feel at home. Do you understand?'

She stared at her brother, unable to believe that he was the same person who had enjoyed all the fun the four of them had shared all those summers ago.

'You've already been through this, Orlando,' she said, sighing.

'Raffaella, if you give Luigi half a chance,' he droned on, 'you will find out how kind and gentle he is. What is more, he is in love with you and will make you an excellent husband.'

'Who are you to tell me who I should like or love?' snapped Raffaella, finding her courage. 'Babbu gave me and Antoneddu his blessing on his deathbed. You weren't there. You were too busy racing round the countryside finding another doctor to patch up the mess this one had made, instead of asking Gabriella to help. But I tell you, Orlando, Zia Paola and Gabriella will vouch for it, and with that blessing I shall marry Antoneddu.'

'They would say anything in your favour,' he replied. 'I have asked Luigi and he denies any knowledge of Babbu giving you his blessing, and he was with you all the time.'

'He's lying,' she retorted. 'He went out of the room for most of the time; he was downstairs by the fire. You ask the others. Gabriella, Zia Paola and I were the ones who bathed Father'. We were the ones who sat with him until he came round. It was then that Babbu called for Antoneddu and we were given his blessing. Luigi came back when we called for Gabriella, and he heard Babbu when he gave his consent because he tried to intervene.'

'There is little doubt, my dear sister, that Babbu wasted his money sending you to Itteri. I thought that perhaps schooling in the academy would have made some sort of a lady out of you. In fact, when I returned this time I thought you had at last grown into womanhood. It seems I was mistaken. What in Heaven's name do you see in Antonio that isn't in Luigi? Antonio is a brotherly love. It's not healthy, and he can't offer you anything in the way Luigi can. His family is much respected in Piedmont, and with the estates and titles and money, what more could you want?'

Raffaella stood and faced her brother with all the defiance she could muster.

'Since you went to Sassari, Orlando, all you can think about is wealth and position. Since I went to school, I have learned that we Sards have been dominated by the barons of Piedmont for too long. They have drained our people dry and crushed their spirits. Feudalism is supposed to be abolished, but still we are bent under their domination. A few years ago, the people, our village included, took up the cry for liberty against Carlo Alberto by uprooting vines and burning olive trees. In the words of Francesco Mannu:

Ipsos inoghe incotrana	*The Piedmontese have here contracted*
Vantagiosos imeneos;	*advantageous marriages;*
Pro ipsos fin sos impleos,	*for them were all employments,*

Pro ipsos fin sos honores	*for them were all distinctions*
Sas dignidades magiores	*the greatest dignities*
De Cheja, Tòga, e Ispada:	*of the church, the robe and sword:*
Ea su Sardu restada	*To the Sard was left*
Una fune a s'impaccare	*a rope to hang himself.*

'For Heaven's sake Raffaella, that was twenty years ago,' cut in her brother.

'But it is the same today. No Sard can hold any office of importance. We have always been pawns in other people's wars. We have not been able to rule our land since the Phoenicians came. We have always been under someone's heel; someone else's laws. Even the *Carta di Logu* has gone. The Continental Carlo Felice has replaced the laws that were given to us by Eleanora d'Aborea, and which we have lived by for centuries and were for the Sard people, with laws which favour the Piedmontese. Our lands are stripped. We have been forced to speak their language, although we struggle to keep our own. Our taxes go to the Continent and still we have nothing, only the rope.' She paused, trying to hold back her tears of anger. 'Even our flag looks to the left, and is blindfolded so as not to see what the intruders do to our land. All I can say is, it's a good thing Vitoria died, because she would never have followed you into the Sassarese society. When you were together you were happy to savour her kisses and caresses and share her love; the open love of a poor shepherd girl.'

Orlando looked taken aback by his sister's outburst. 'What do you mean?' he stammered.

'Don't be an idiot, Orlando. I know you and Vitoria were lovers before you were married; we knew you couldn't resist her wild eyes and her beauty.'

Orlando felt his hand twitch in anger, but couldn't bring himself to strike his sister. 'But Raffaella, what is the matter with Luigi? Tell me, for pity's sake,' he roared, uncertain of his ground.

'Apart from the fact that he is a Piedmontese, you wouldn't understand. You couldn't, not in a thousand years.'

'Try me,' he replied, the venom melting in his veins. 'I want what I think is the best for you, and I want to see you happy with lovely things around you, Raffaella. I want to see my dear friend happy too, and I know he will care for you.'

'What about your friend Antoneddu, don't you want to see him happy, too? Orlando, I don't even like Luigi, but I love Antoneddu, and what's more, he loves me too.'

'But so does Luigi, and with so much more to offer you,' cut in her brother.

'See? I told you wouldn't understand. You're not even prepared to hear me out.'

'I'm sorry. Carry on.'

'When I went away to Itteri I tried hard, really hard, to be the daughter that Babbu wanted, and to do the things he expected of me. I wanted to be an elegant young lady to please him. As a result, I can dance, play the piano and embroider with the best of them. But my heart wasn't in it. All the time I kept thinking about the mountains that overlook our home. I remembered the wonderful times we all used to have, playing in the streams or rounding up the sheep and goats. Dancing reminded me of the times when we came together to dance the *Ballu Sardu*. Orlando, my heart belongs to this place, among my mountains, and Antoneddu is part of that belonging. I couldn't live in Itteri or Mores, let alone Sassari or the Continent; away from all the people I know and love. I am a Sard and proud of my heritage. For pity's sake, Orlando, don't uproot me from my homeland and make me marry Luigi.'

'All very fine sentiments, Raffaella, but still no real reason why I should go back on my promise to Luigi. We all have to grow up at some time, and now is your time.'

'Orlando, please, I beg you,' she pleaded. 'You and I are different. You are like Babbu, you have Sassarese blood in your veins, but I favour Mamma; I am a pure mountain Sard. Babbu gave up his lifestyle to marry Mamma and I know he never regretted it.'

'You forget, Raffaella, that this farm came as her dowry and Babbu was obliged to come here as much for the money as for his love for Mamma. Just as I would have done for Vitoria. When you marry there will be no dowry, there is no money for that.'

'I don't care if there isn't a bean, and it will make not a jot of difference to Antoneddu. You know that as well as I do.'

Orlando turned to go; he was not going to get any further with his sister. Raffaella pushed in front of him and barred his way.

'Please, Orlando, you must understand this: when we were children Antoneddu and I shared our secrets, our treasures, our hopes and even our kisses. Nothing has changed for us, our feelings have grown deeper. You and Vitoria had everything arranged for you. You were to marry from the outset. No one ever gave Antoneddu and me a thought. We used to go everywhere with you and Vitoria, always in each other's company. Is it any wonder that our feelings for each other grew? Now we share a wild love. Don't think that we didn't know that you and Vitoria knew the same feeling of love. That love she had for you is doubled, no, trebled a thousand times in the love that Antoneddu and I share. Orlando, whatever you try to do, you will never stop that. Perhaps if Vitoria had lived you wouldn't be so against me marrying Antoneddu now. It's your bitterness, that I have the warmth of her brother's love, while all you have are her memories for cold comfort. I pity any woman you marry, for you will only want her money or position. Luigi has changed all that. He has made you want things that are above you. Remember, the Piedmontese are courteous, but false. He wants something, and it's not just me.'

Orlando stood before his sister, shaking with rage. 'You little fool. I am head of the family now and you will do as I say, and I say that you will marry Luigi and the sooner we can arrange it the better it will be for everyone. Babbu has left very little estate and you must be provided for, and this is the best way I know.'

Raffaella looked up into her brother's eyes. They were hard and unmoving. All the sparkle and depth had gone from them since Vitoria's death, as if he were possessed by a jealousy that ate into his very being. Money and position seemed to be the only way to placate his craving soul.

'Orlando, I ask you again. I beg you. Please don't make me do this, or I shall be forced to go against your will and that would be hurtful to me.'

'You will marry Luigi, Raffaella, and you will go with him wherever he wants you to go. There is no good in pleading with me, I have made up my mind. One day you will thank me for this, I promise,' he replied, now deaf to all her pleas.

'Get out!' she shouted, seeing the fruitlessness of her entreating, and aware of her frightful situation. 'Get out, GET OUT, and I tell you, if that man so much as lays a finger on me again, his face will be unrecognisable,' she shrieked, and picked up her hairbrush and hurled it at her brother, who managed to dodge the object and make good his exit.

She sank onto her bed, buried her face in her hands and wept bitterly. The desperation of her plight frightened her. She knew now that she would have to tell Zia Paola and Antoneddu about the baby.

That evening Zio Marco and Orlando sat together in Gestinu's study. A portfolio of deeds and papers lay on the desk together with Gestinu's handwritten will, a bottle of wine and two glasses. The two men sat opposite each other across the large mahogany desk.

Zio Marco poured the wine into the two glasses and handed one to Orlando. Taking a long draught of his wine, he turned to his nephew.

'You know, my father, Zio Carlo always remembered the day Papa Giovanni came to his office in Sassari with young Maria, your mother. He always went to our father as he didn't want anyone from Ozieri to know his business. As you are aware, he owned an extraordinary large portfolio of property. As people left the land, so he bought their farms, adding to his vast estate. Papa Giovanni adored his daughter, and when she met Gestinu that day, he knew he had lost her to him.

'He had bought Sos Lampidos and gave it to her for her wedding gift, as he wanted her to be near him and the family. When Raffaella was born, he gave her the lower valleys in trust so she would have some income, but it has always been run with the farm and paid for her schooling. All that opportunity, and my brother never took advantage of it. All he ever wanted was a small practice and his family; such a wicked waste of opportunity.

'When your mother died, Papa Giovanni was beside himself with grief. So he and Gestinu went to your grandfather, Papa Carlo, to ask for Paola's release from the convent. The sisters released her, after a large donation to the convent, and she looked after you and Raffaella. And, I might add, my sister has done a wonderful job of it.'

Orlando rose and paced the room.

'You know the family has always been close,' continued his uncle. 'His son Gianni has always been fond of Paola and that is why he made her godmother to his daughter. He is also a trustee for Raffaella and Paola's land. Papa Giovanni arranged for Gestinu to work at the lawyers in Ozieri, where he dealt with small clients for him but gathered a large clientele for Gestinu. He also managed Zia Paola's and Raffaella's property.'

'Yes, I know, I wanted to ask you about that. Do you think I will be able to take over that work?' asked Orlando.

'Nothing has been said. I don't know, but you can always ask Gianni as he runs all his father's estates.'

'So everything else comes to me,' said Orlando, a note of triumph in his voice.

'Well, Orlando,' said his uncle, settling himself back in the large leather chair, bringing the tips of his fingers together as if in prayer, 'you know that you inherit Sos Lampidos. It has many hectares and should be enough for your needs with your salary as a junior lawyer.'

'But I have part of Punta Néula, the Sannas' land, too. That came as Vitoria's dowry, didn't it?'

'No, that has reverted to the Sannas as your father never

signed the documents; he always said he couldn't take another man's living, but we might be able to sort something out.'

'Well, there is the land in the lower valley and Pinta Longa that comes in under Sos Lampidos, doesn't it?'

'No, Orlando, when Papa Giovanni gave Maria and Gestinu Sos Lampidos, he gave them the farmstead and the surrounding hectares.'

'And the land at Pinta Longa?' asked Orlando, concerned.

'Papa Giovanni gave it to Paola in trust for her life, or to become hers on marriage. As I said, it was in thanks for looking after you children, and he felt she should be independent of the family. Why, do you have something in mind for the lands?'

'I understand there is good money in the sale of timber, and I thought I could sell the trees on Pinta Longa and Raffaella's land.'

'How would you organise it?'

'Luigi's father is an estate manager, and has all the contacts for the felling and the sale of timber.'

'Does he now? That is interesting. Perhaps we could come to some arrangement on the deal. I could see to the release of the land and you organise the sale. It would buy your partnership in my law firm. Think it over, we could make ourselves a handsome profit. I can see we have a bright future together,' said Marco with a broad smile on his face.

Zio Marco drained his glass and stood up. 'Now if you will excuse me, Orlando, we have a long journey tomorrow back to Sassari and I would like an early night.'

Uncle and nephew shook hands and wished each other goodnight.

When Zio Marco had left, Orlando dropped into the leather chair vacated by his uncle and poured himself another glass of wine. He would have to see Gianni and organise the timber, he thought, sighing hard.

The knock on the study door made him look up.

'Who is it?'

'Luigi. Can I come in?' he said as he entered, holding a glass of wine in his hand. 'Dear fellow, have you inherited all that you wanted? Now we will be able to do everything we planned.'

'Not quite,' replied Orlando.

'What is the problem?'

Orlando told him everything Zio Marco had said.

Upstairs, Raffaella couldn't sleep. The air was humid, and her head ached. She climbed out of bed and pulled on her nightgown. She needed to see Zia Paola; she would have some potion to take away the thumping in her head. She tiptoed along the landing, not wanting to wake anyone. She noticed the door to her father's study was open, and paused to hear if Zio Marco and Orlando were still talking. But it was Luigi's voice that carried up the stairs.

'What does it matter if you can't have their land? Fell the trees anyway. I can organise the removal and shipment before anyone has time to realise what has happened. The money will be in your bank and no one will be able to do anything.'

'What will happen then?' asked Orlando.

'You're the lawyer; possession is ninetenths of the law. They can't touch you. Don't worry, we will sort it out. It will be no problem,' said Luigi, leaving the study. 'See you in the morning.'

Raffaella stood rooted to the spot. Her brother and the hateful Luigi were going to fell the timber on the land so they could make a fortune from them, and then leave the land to become barren.

She darted back along the corridor to her room, her headache forgotten. She would have to see Antoneddu in the morning.

CHAPTER SIXTEEN

Orlando and Luigi left for Sassari with Zio Marco and Zia Madeleine in the early hours of the following morning, without bothering to see Raffaella. They had said their goodbyes to Zia Paola the night before, and Orlando had given her strict instructions to keep Antonio away from the house, and that the relationship between him and his sister should be discouraged as much as possible.

Raffaella woke from a fitful sleep to the sun streaming in through the holes in the shutters. She was soon out of bed to look at God's glorious morning. She glanced at herself in the mirror as she passed. Her face was still flushed and swollen from the tears shed the previous night.

Throwing open the shutters, she looked across the valley. The once-green vegetation had a golden aura about it where the relentless sun dried the numerous grasses, which were flecked with the evergreen olive and cork trees. The breeze that brushed her face was sweet and scented, like new-mown hay. Reminiscent of the fresh grasses in Antoneddu's *pinneta*, when he first made love to her earlier that year. She sighed with contentment, as she watched a hawk wheel and circle in the morning light, and felt a momentary pang of envy for the bird's winged freedom.

On the far side of the valley rested Punta Néula, bathed in the bright sunlight: it stood proud above the half-covered slopes robed in olive groves which encircled the small farmstead. The vines she had helped Antoneddu to plant all those years ago ramped their way across the roofs of the nearby stables, over the trellis and onto the house itself.

How many times had she stood here as a child and looked across the valley, and wondered if Antoneddu was looking at Sos

Lampidos? She wanted to see him now; to tell him all she had heard last night. Now that Orlando and Luigi were gone, they would be free to spend time together, like the time before Orlando came back from Sassari. Antoneddu had returned to Punta Néula last night with his family, before she had time to say goodbye.

Zia Paola entered her room, making Raffaella jump at her sudden appearance. 'Hurry and get yourself dressed,' she said to her niece.

'Oh, Zia Paola, you startled me!' cried Raffaella, laughing.

'Antonio is downstairs and he wants to see you,' said her aunt with a smile.

Raffaella's heart leapt. 'I won't be long, give him some wine. I'll be down in a moment,' she cried, delighted by the news.

She bundled her aunt out of the door and dressed herself in her long black dress as custom demanded after a death in the family. She pouted at herself in the mirror and pinched her cheeks to make them rosy, and bit her lips to bring some colour to them. She hated herself in black. It reminded her of crows, ravens and widows.

Downstairs, Antonio stood in front of the window, and looked out at the same view that she had been admiring moments earlier upstairs. Raffaella walked towards him, her eyes fixed on his broad back. He swung round, and collecting her up in his arms, showered her with quick, successive kisses until he found her mouth, kissing her with passion.

'I've missed you,' she said when he released her.

'I've missed you too. I'm sorry I couldn't see you after the funeral, but they would not leave me alone. I couldn't get away,' he said.

'I know, they watch me here like a hawk, but he has gone for a while. Oh Antoneddu,' she murmured as she put her arms round him, 'Orlando has changed so much since he first went away to Sassari. It's not like it used to be when we were all so happy together. He has said that I have to marry Luigi. They are going to fell the trees in the valley and Pinta Longa for the timber. What am I going to do?'

She felt his hold on her tighten, and he kissed her on her forehead.

'Hush now, you won't have to marry him, not while I'm with you. I will see to that, and you must tell Zia Paola, she will know what to do. What is this about felling trees?'

She pulled away and looked up into his face, and told him all she had heard Orlando and Luigi discussing last night.

He held her close to him and said, 'Don't worry, *sa sposixedda mia*, we won't let it happen, I promise you. But you haven't even asked why I'm here.'

She looked up at him and smiled. 'Well, why are you here?'

'Because I've finished my work on the farm and Babbu doesn't need me at the moment, so I am having a day in the mountains with my sweetheart.'

Raffaella's eyes became alive with expectation, as she turned to her aunt for her approval.

'As far as I'm concerned, I think it's a great idea,' she replied, 'so it's up to you, young lady.'

'I have the picnic basket outside,' said Antonio, grabbing her hand, eager to be gone.

'One thing before you go, Raffaella,' called her aunt, 'you can't go out riding in that black dress. You will ruin it.' Then, smiling, she added, 'Run upstairs and put on your woven skirt and your cotton blouse, they will be more comfortable. But please, Raffaella, wear your headscarf.'

'Oh, Zia Paola, thank you! Don't you think it will matter if I'm not in black?'

'Who is to see you?' replied her aunt, as Raffaella gave her a big kiss and hurried from the room to change.

The young lovers were on their own mounts, and they had raced each other along the narrow tracks and across the open meadows; through the cork trees and over the ridge to the valley beyond. Raffaella had pushed her horse to the utmost and succeeded in winning. A feat to be well proud of, for Antonio was an excellent horseman, as he proved at the Festival of San Giovanni.

Now at a leisurely pace, the horses ambled along side by side as they settled down to enjoy the countryside and all its glory. Antonio pulled her horse's reins toward him and leaned over, putting his arm around Raffaella, and drew her to him, kissing her with passion. She leaned in to him and returned his kiss.

They headed for the small stream tributary which wound down to the river that ran through their valley. Here they dismounted and set the horses free to roam the lushness of the meadow near the stream. They walked hand in hand without saying a word, happy to be alone with each other again. Their horses followed behind; stopping to bite some lush grasses or drink at the stream.

The luxuriant growth of the meadow soon gave way to the coarse, harsh grass, parched under the sun's intense heat, the stalks standing up like brittle clumps of straw. Wild flowers grew everywhere at the water's edge in a nodding profusion, among the short shrub land, and the air smelt dry and sweet under the golden heat.

Raffaella walked through the grass trying to catch a large butterfly, and sent clouds of small insects and butterflies into the air around her. Antonio stood and watched her; she had a halo of light around her, with a mass of buzzing insects that gave her a hazy appearance. She had removed her headscarf and he noticed too how her long black hair shone in the sunlight, and that her olive skin had turned a rich, deep brown over the past weeks. She looked well, more rounded; she had filled out into a woman, and it suited her. She had grown up in the past months. As he watched her, he became aware of his desire for her, and Raffaella, looking up at him, recognised the fire in his dark eyes.

'No, Antoneddu,' she scolded, and ran towards the small ruin that lay half-hidden among the rock outcrops and entangled vegetation. They often came here to be away from the world, in this small, disused *pinneta*, once the home to some unknown shepherd, and a sanctuary to the young couple.

Raffaella ran towards the low doorway and threw herself on the soft, moss-like grass. The roof had long since gone, and it was cool in the shade of the walls and the overhanging olive tree. Antonio fell beside her and pulled her towards him.

'God, I love you,' he whispered in her ear as he nibbled it gently.

'Do you, Antoneddu? Really love me, enough to stand by me through everything?'

He sat up on one elbow and looked at her. His voice was solemn, with a touch of sadness. 'Do you doubt me, *sa sposixedda mia*? I've loved you all my life. I've never thought of anyone else other than you. I have never loved any other woman other than you. All my love and tears and joy, they are all yours and bind us closer. I want you, and shall fight Orlando and Luigi for you if I have to." He paused, and looked at her. 'Do you doubt me?'

She looked up to him, searching his deep dark eyes, and shook her head.

'Then what have you to be afraid of, my darling?' he asked, as he bent to kiss her again. 'We pledged our love that day when young Salvatore was born, and he's a living reminder of that vow every time I look at him.'

She sighed and took his hand. 'Tell me something, Antoneddu. Did you know that when Babbu arranged with Salvatore for Vitoria to wed Orlando, he would take part of your land?'

'Yes, I did. Babbu told me after Vitoria died.'

'Why didn't you tell me?'

'Would it have made any difference to us if they have taken part of the farm as a dowry? I still have the flock.'

'But doesn't it worry you that my father tried to take your inheritance away from you? It was my father who owed his life to Salvatore, not the other way round.'

'Raffaella, it wasn't like that, and we still have three quarters of the farm. When Babbu and Mamma can no longer manage it, it will be shared with young Salvatore and our sons.'

'You know when I marry you I shall have no such dowry, don't you? Orlando would never agree to lose his lands to you now.'

He bent over and kissed her with tenderness. 'I don't want anything else. I have all I want right here in my arms.'

She returned his kisses. She had missed his caresses and passionate lovemaking during the weeks Orlando had been at home. Luigi had kept a constant watch over her and followed her everywhere like a trained lapdog, making her more and more sullen and unresponsive to him. She despised the puppet of a man and all he stood for. Her love for Antonio, on the other hand, burst into flower from the moment he had taken possession of her in his *pinneta*. The now-familiarity of his touch still thrilled her and filled her with a wonderful feeling of completeness in their union. She felt again the mounting desire of their love and their joy in the moment of fulfilment.

Snuggled in his arms, she watched the branches of the olive tree through the open roof as it dipped and danced in the small breeze. Everything seemed so perfect, and she felt secure as she lay in her lover's arms.

'Antoneddu, I have something to tell you. I wanted to tell you before, but I wasn't sure,' she said.

'Tell me then, darling,' he said, pulling her even closer to him with his powerful arms.

'I was almost sure before Orlando came home, but now I know for certain I'm going to have a baby.'

He turned and faced her, his eyes alive with the fire of his overpowering love for her. 'Are you sure? Oh Raffaella, dearest love, don't you see? Now they will have to let us marry. Orlando can't stop us now, and Luigi will never marry you knowing you carry my child. Tell me, does anyone else know? Have you told Zia Paola?'

'She may well know. I haven't told her. I'm sure, though, that Babbu knew, and that is why he gave us his blessing. If you remember, Zia Paola knew that Gabriella was pregnant with young Salvatore, and no one would believe her. So I think she knows, and that she may have told Babbu. She knows that we have been promised for three years, because I told her and she promised to help us.'

'My little love, you have made me so happy. I'm so proud of you and I love you, dearest Raffaella.'

He held her close to him, and she sensed the great joy he felt in the knowledge they could now be married.

'When is the baby due?' he whispered.

'About January, I think.'

The hot, languid days of July slipped by. Antonio never left Raffaella's side. He wasn't needed with the sheep as Sergio and Ignazio spent their days with the flock. Antonio and Raffaella did everything together. Young Salvatore went with them too, and when she could be persuaded Marina would go and help round up the sheep. Antonio and young Salvatore collected the milk and made cheese, and ricotta, refusing to let Raffaella do any of the hard work.

'Are you coming fishing with us this afternoon, Marina?' asked Raffaella as Antonio finished preparing the ricotta he was making.

'No, not today. I'm riding up to the *pinneta* at Mataldara to see Babbu and take him some food,' she replied with a slight blush on her cheek.

When she had gone into the house, Raffaella turned to Antonio.

'Marina spends a lot of time riding to Mataldara or up into the forests of Sa Mela. Is there someone special over there? Does she go to see Gavinu?'

'I doubt it. She always has been one to favour her own company.'

'Can I come fishing with you?' asked young Salvatore, pulling on his brother's trousers.

'You most certainly can, tiddler.'

The three of them collected bunches of wild euphorbia that afternoon. The bright yellow-green splashes of colour made it stand out in the drying vegetation, and when they had enough, they made their way to one of the small pools in the river Enas. Antonio took the herb and crushed it with a stone, letting the white juice run into the swirling water, turning it a milky colour.

Within minutes the trout came to the top, stunned by the poison. Salvatore ran and splashed in the water as he collected some of the fish, while Raffaella caught them up in the crude net Antonio made to make it easier for her. She stood thigh-deep in the water, her skirt tucked up into her waistband, and felt with delight the coolness of the stream as it passed by.

In the evening, they returned to Sos Lampidos, weighed down with the bountiful catch of fresh fish. Zia Paola was delighted with their harvest, for some she would salt down, but first she took four of the fish and cooked them all supper over the open fire. Later that night Antonio returned to Punta Néula with the rest of the catch for Gabriella, and a sleeping brother in his arms.

Long days were spent away from Sos Lampidos, either at Punta Néula or in the mountains among the sheep and goats, and upon returning from one such excursion they were met by Zia Paola, looking worried.

'What's the matter?' they asked as they approached her.

'A messenger came from Zio Marco this afternoon. It seems that Orlando has been taken ill in Sassari and won't be back for some time. Marco has called in the very best doctor and it seems he might have *Impeiere* as there is an outbreak in the town, but they confirm that it's not cholera.'

Antonio put his arms around both the women and led them into the house. 'Don't worry. He'll be all right. He's strong and in the best of hands, and Luigi isn't there to nurse him!' He laughed. 'Is the messenger still here?'

'No.' said Zia Paola, 'he left after a meal. It seems that he wanted to be back before nightfall. The Carabineri is out in force; they are searching for a band of *fiorri leggi* in the area and he wanted to be back on the road before any trouble. I believe the entire Sassarese think that we are a wild band of pagan brigands in the mountains. But about Luigi you are wrong: he is supposed to be in Sassari with Orlando.'

'Better send the Devil,' said Antonio, and they laughed.

Antonio rode over to Punta Néula to return his young

brother to Gabriella, and told her not to expect him until late. That evening Zia Paola cooked special pasta followed by fresh fruit. After the meal they sat round the fire, and in the light of the flickering tallow Antonio worked on the wooden platter he was carving, while Raffaella sat at her loom. Zia Paola made herself busy by spinning on her distaff from the pile of freshly sheared wool Salvatore had sent her.

'Did the messenger say who the Carabineri were looking for?' asked Antonio.

'No,' replied Zia Paola, shaking her head, 'and I tried to find out from the village when Sergio went to take some wool to his mother. Tell me, has there been any word from Gavinu since he took to the mountains after the Festival of San Giovanni?'

'None,' he replied. 'All I know is that he is with a bandit gang from Gallura and living either in the Limbara or near Ollolai. So they won't be looking for him, pray God. They must be after someone else. But why do you ask?'

'No reason, other than Sergio is under the impression that someone had seen Gavinu back at his farm at Pinta Niedda.'

'Surely he wouldn't go there. That would be the first place they'd search,' said Raffaella.' Are you sure he isn't at Punta Néula, Antoneddu? After all, they hid him there before when the Carabineri were after him. You have not been there recently, you wouldn't know if he was there or not.'

'True. But Babbu would have said something to me if they had hidden him. But I think you are right about Marina, and that is where she goes when she goes riding. The other morning, I noticed that someone had pinned an oak branch under her window.'

'You never told me!' enthused Raffaella. 'Do you remember when you used to pin such love tokens under my window?' She laughed.

The warm, idle chatter and speculation continued into the night, interspersed with singing and laughter. Zia Paola watched the young lovers with a contented heart and peace of mind, sure in her heart of hearts that on Orlando's return, she could tell him the news and he would relent in his obsession for Raffaella to marry Luigi. Also, if she told Orlando what she knew to be true about Raffaella, she knew Luigi would never consent to marry her. But that was to be her trump card.

Outside in the darkness, hidden from view in the heavy shadows, stood alone, dark figure near the window of the big room, who watched their every movement. Rumours from the village people at nearby Bantadda and Mores, and overheard gossip, told Luigi about the love Raffaella and Antonio had for each other, and how they were always together. Some even said they had married in secret. Luigi's need for Raffaella now drove him to desperate lengths to find out whether these stories were true or not; so he had returned to Sos Lampidos to see for himself.

When it came time for Antonio to leave, the dark figure, still under the cover of the shadows, watched with mounting jealousy and hate as the lovers bid each other a tender goodnight. In that moment Luigi vowed he would follow them and report all he saw to his friend Orlando. He would know how to deal with both his aunt and his sister for disobeying his wishes.

July passed into August, with glorious days spent in each other's company. Raffaella and Antonio took young Salvatore with them on picnics and visits to the hidden pool to teach him to swim in its cool, refreshing water. Every morning Antonio arrived on horseback with his young brother sitting astride behind him. But on this particular morning Raffaella was surprised to learn from Zia Paola that they had not yet arrived from Punta Néula.

She went to her window and peered across the ravine to the farmstead, shielding her eyes against the onslaught of the bright light. Sure enough, above the brilliant sunlight, she could see the red light shining from the attic window.

Raffaella hastily dressed, and kissing her aunt, she hurried to the stable to collect her horse. Anxious to know what had happened, she urged the animal down the narrow pathway of the ravine, on across the river and up the steep track to the farmstead she knew and loved so well.

Once there, she found the Sannas in a terrible state. Gabriella had been crying for some time, judging by the heavy red colour of her eyes. Raffaella went in search of Antonio and found him in the stable saddling his horse.

'Hello, darling,' he said, as he came around the animal and kissed her on her cheek. 'Gavinu came here last night,' he continued, without stopping his work. 'He has taken Marina with him. It seems they have a perfect hideout in the mountains and she wanted to be with him. He has been seeing her on and off for months now, but she never said anything. No wonder she always wanted to go to see Babbu with the provisions, and to be on her own. The Carabineri is closing in and he must return to his hideout, and she has decided to go with him. As you can imagine Mamma is upset, and is sure harm will come to them both.'

'What about Salvatore?' she asked.

'I rode down to collect him this morning when we found her gone. He would rather Marina had stayed at home, but knows the Carabineri are searching the whole place. He gave them his blessing years ago, so he can't go back on it. Marina is in love with Gavinu, it would be cruel to keep them apart.'

'So the Carabineri the messenger from Sassari saw, are looking for your cousin after all,' she said, sighing. Then added, as an afterthought, 'If your father promised Marina to Gavinu, that was before he turned outlaw. Doesn't that cancel everything?' But she knew the answer before he replied.

'Wouldn't you marry me, my love, if I were outlawed for fulfilling a vendetta in vengeance of a relation's death? Gavinu killed Don diVenti in revenge for killing his brother. Remember, the law would do nothing to help him.'

'I think I would marry you whatever you did,' she replied, and reached up to kiss him. 'And where are you going now?' she added.

'Up to the pool to take food there, so Gavinu and Marina can rest there for a while before setting off to the mountains. With good luck the Carabineri will be gone in a few days, and then they will be free to travel back to the Limbara.'

'Antoneddu, I beg of you. Take care of yourself,' she implored, frightened by what had happened. 'You know if they find you helping them the Carabineri will shoot you. Remember, I need you too now, darling.'

'I shall be back this evening, so when you go to bed don't close your shutters and I will come to you, and we can spend a night together.' He drew her close to him so she could feel his breath warm against her neck. 'You arouse a passion in me, *sa sposixedda mia*, like a fire. Every smile, every touch, you consume me in your pure joy and love.'

'My darling Antoneddu,' she cried, throwing her arms around his neck, 'I can't wait for tonight.'

He cradled her in his arms and kissed her. They were so engrossed with each other that neither of them noticed the dark figure who had followed them throughout the past weeks. They were lost in their own world. Such total absorption made things easy for the dark figure. Now this same figure stole from the shadows of the stables to his waiting horse in the ravine below. Only Salvatore's dogs gave any indication of an intruder, for they barked from their kennel.

'You will come tonight, won't you?' she whispered, her dark eyes pleading from the depths of her soul. 'We have shared our love in open fields, under the light of the open sky, but I want to lie with you in the darkness of night and share the coolness of the mountain breezes and the soft moonlight in my bed.'

He kissed her half-closed eyes, and then, reaching for his horse's reins, he walked her out into the brilliant daylight. He swung into his saddle. She noticed that his saddlebags were full of food, and his rifle butt stuck out from one. He blew her a kiss and with a wave of his hand, headed down the path to the ravine below.

Raffaella went to bed early that night, feigning a headache.

She had returned from Punta Néula late in the afternoon after helping Gabriella and comforting her as best she could. She also found time to play with young Salvatore, who seemed at a loss to know what was going on. On her return to Sos Lampidos Zia Paola listened to the story, and told Raffaella she would ride over to Punta Néula in the morning to see Gabriella.

In her bed, Raffaella tossed and turned, waiting for the sound of horse's hooves on the dry ground. She couldn't help thinking about the news Sergio gave her on her return when she went to see him about some milk.

'Dottore Luigi is back, then?' he had said in an offhand manner.

'No,' she replied, 'not yet.'

'But I saw him last night, waiting by the stables. I went to ask him if I could help him, but when I crossed the yard, he had gone.'

'You must be mistaken, Sergio. He is in Sassari with Orlando.'

'It was him, as sure as I stand here now. I thought he went into the house, but there was no sign of him or his horse anywhere. Then I saw him ride down the road and thought he was going over to Punta Néula, and thought you must have told him to follow you.'

Raffaella tossed in her bed again. Why would Luigi come back and not come to the house? Zia Paola hadn't said anything. She would have mentioned it if she had seen him. Sergio must have been mistaken; he always saw shadows and weird creatures which more often than not came from his fertile mind, or too much of his own wine.

She rose from her bed, went to the open window, and looked out over the valley in the vain hope she would see Antonio. The bright moonlight spilled over the nearby barns, and down the rough pathway to the narrow track below. On the far side of the buildings the silver-washed meadows gave way to the blackness of the void that fell away to the river below. The big olive tree stood like a large ghost, with the already silver leaves double-dyed to give it an ethereal appearance as it shook and shimmered in the night's breath; its branches appeared like long arms that beckoned her to it. She shivered. On the other side of the valley she could see the pale outlines of the olive grove at Punta Néula, and the trees stood like ghostly sentinels in their neat rows. Everything seemed to be bathed in the silvered wash of moonlight, and the curling mists from the valley added to the mystical quality.

Her horse snorted in the stable, attracting Raffaella's attention. She became aware of someone walking towards the house. She drew back against the bedroom wall and peered out to see who it could be, cautious lest it should prove to be one of Sergio's strange creatures, or perhaps Sergio himself on his way home from seeing the sheep.

Her heart leapt in delight at seeing Antonio. She watched as he scaled the vine-clad wall with thrilling agility, and she welcomed him into her waiting arms.

'Oh, darling, I've been so worried, so frightened. You've been ages.'

'I know, my dearest, but the Carabineri are everywhere, so I doubled back round the mountains to the back of Sos Lampidos. If you look over there, below Punta Néula, through the valley, you can just see their fires. They have a camp on the far side of the ridge too, so they are watching both homesteads.'

Raffaella followed the direction of his pointing finger. She could see the golden light of the flickering flames and the ashen, curling smoke which hung in the almost breathless night that she had earlier mistaken for the mist.

She shivered, and Antonio, gathering her in his arms, carried her to the great carved bed and laid her down. He kissed her with tenderness, and then with a mounting desire, he untied the ribbons of her white cotton gown, revealing her naked beauty.

'My beautiful, beautiful love,' he whispered as he fell into her warm embrace.

Lost in their overwhelming passion and love, the day's troubles slipped from their minds. They spent the night awake in fervent lovemaking, or sleeping in the sheer joy and contentment of their love for one another. Even the baying of Gestinu's dogs and the hooting of the *barbagiannu* owl, both regarded by all mountain people as the worst of ill omens, couldn't touch them in their total union.

But Sergio and Ignazio heard the omens, and spent the night chanting their Hail Marys and interceding to the saints, to ward off the evil they knew hung in the air.

CHAPTER SEVENTEEN

It was late afternoon when Luigi neared Sassari. He had pressed his horse and his journey had proved unbearably hot, long and dusty, but the coolness of the olive and orange groves around the city, were in sharp contrast to the gaunt prickly pears, fig trees and the heavy-scented thyme, rosemary and tamarisks, making the last dreary miles more tolerable.

He urged his horse on towards the great city. The large walls, that once surrounded it, had been knocked down when the plague took hold to allow fresh air into the narrow streets. Men returning from their work in the outlying fields and groves now filled the road, and their laden horses and bullock carts teemed in all directions. The men looked gnarled, and stooped from the affliction of malaria, so rife every year in this area.

He soon came to the large city entrance and went up the narrow streets of outer houses, trying to avoid the lines of washing that dripped or flapped in the rare gust of wind that passed through the ravine-like buildings. The cobbled stones underfoot made his horse stumble as ragged, barefoot young children ran beside him with outstretched hands, begging for money. Luigi threw down a handful of small change and the children fell to the ground to retrieve the offering.

Women, heavily veiled, sat in dark doorways sifting flour from one large basket to another, while the vegetable sellers called their wares. Young, half-naked boys with donkeys laden with water barrels sold their prized commodity by the litre or by the ladle, and were always in demand. Braziers burnt, sending up showers of sparks as the men prodded the ashes to keep the heat up for the meats they roasted.

The narrow streets gave way to the wider, more fashionable

area, and the buildings began to take on an air of prosperity. Although most of the houses remained unpretentious, some sported handsome facades with carving on the doors and over the windows. It was at such a house that Luigi reined in his horse and turned into the spacious courtyard. He dropped from his saddle and handed the reins to the young stable boy who jumped to his feet at the sight of a visitor.

Luigi beat the dust from his trousers with his crop, and hastened to the large pair of doors that crowned the short flight of marble stairs. His mind went back to the first time he had come here, when Zio Marco had had a ball and he met Raffaella. He sighed. This was the living he was used to, with fine houses and refined customs. The roughness and lack of fashion in the mountains depressed him, but here everything was different. Raffaella had sampled the fashionable life, but it could not compare with what he could offer her. Orlando liked the good life too. It would only be time before Raffaella came round to his way of thinking, and those dark, smouldering eyes and luscious lips would be his forever; together with her land which was worth a small fortune. He smiled to himself.

His knock at the door was answered by an elderly servant woman who admitted him to a large white marble hall.

'Dottore Atzeni. How good to see you. Have you come to see Signore Orlando?' she asked as she signalled him to enter.

Luigi nodded.

'You will be pleased to know that he is much better, and should be able to return to normal work in a few days,' she added, closing the big doors behind him.

'Thank you,' replied Luigi. 'Can I see him now?'

'No doubt he will be glad of the company. But would you like to freshen up first?'

'Later,' replied Luigi with a sharp edge to his voice.

At that moment, a large door opened across the hall and an elegant woman stepped forward. Orlando's Aunt Madeleine was dressed in the height of fashion, in grey silk embellished with black silk cord. Her hair was pulled back into a bun and the severity of the style gave her an immediate air of authority.

'Dottore Luigi, how good to see you again. Orlando has been asking for you for the past week. He has missed you being here.'

'Signora Canu, I am sorry I have had to be away on some private business. I must apologise for the state of my dress at this hour of the day, but I have ridden hard from Bantadda and it is important I see Orlando at once,' he said, taking the Signora's hand and kissing it. The perfume of her toilet and the rustle of her silken dress put him in mind of his own mother back in Torino.

'Orlando is in the study. You will find him much improved and almost ready to go back to university. Although I hope you will be able to stay and sample the delights of Sassari society for a while.'

Luigi bowed and took his leave of Orlando's aunt, and went into the study where he found his friend sitting in a large chair in front of a small table, on which he was playing patience. He still looked a little pale, but there was little sign of any fever.

'Luigi, my dear friend, how wonderful to see you. What have you been doing? I've missed your company just when I needed it most of all. It's been dreadfully dull playing patience on my own,' he said, rising from his chair. 'Come and join me in a glass of this excellent wine. There is no doubt Zio Marco keeps a good cellar in the house. I shall have to get his advice when I start mine.'

Luigi accepted the invitation, took the wine and sat beside his friend.

'Now tell me what you've been doing,' continued Orlando. 'Not that I need to ask. Have you made all the wedding arrangements? Is everything all right and ready to go for our return? No doubt that sister of mine will be ready to see sense by now. The time it has taken you to make arrangements, you must be going to have the most celebrated wedding Mores has ever seen.'

'Orlando, listen to me,' cut in Luigi. 'I went to Mores for a couple of days to organise everything, as you know. While I was there I heard rumours about your sister and her relationship with that shepherd.'

'What rumours?' demanded Orlando.

'The villagers say that they are in love, and that they are already promised to each other. There is even a story that they were married secretly in the small church at Bantadda. Everyone took it for granted the wedding arrangements were for Raffaella and Antonio, and were deaf to the fact that she and I were the ones to be married.'

'Oh that, is that all? You needn't worry about that, it's peasants' talk. You know what those people are like. You must know it isn't true, Zia Paola would never let that happen. She would not go against my wishes,' replied Orlando.

'But it's all I've heard since I went back to Mores. So I decided to go to Sos Lampidos to see for myself. When I arrived late in the evening Antonio's horse was in the stable. I looked through the window. Zia Paola is not with you, Orlando, for when that peasant embraced your sister, she just watched it all go on. He was allowed to be alone with her so he could embrace her goodnight. The following morning they were together again.'

'What in Heaven's name do you mean, together?' roared Orlando.

'He rode over from Punta Néula to see her. They have spent hours together out in the pastures with the sheep. They are always together, unchaperoned,' whined Luigi. 'They go fishing and spend long hours in each other's company with the boy.'

'By all the saints, Luigi, I thought you meant they had spent the night together under my roof. They have always spent the days together, they have done since they were children. They are like brother and sister. Although I told Zia Paola not to let them go together, they have young Salvatore with them. They wouldn't do anything wrong with him around. They are both too fond of him for that.'

'Orlando, they do not act like brother and sister when they are alone. I know, I have followed them. Brothers and sisters do not spend time lying in each other's arms and kissing and caressing each other. They may not have slept together under your roof yet, but they intend to. Antonio has gone to help a cousin or somebody who is in need, and when he returns, he is going to Sos Lampidos. Raffaella is in agreement with this, but it appears that Zia Paola knows nothing of the arrangement. Orlando, if we return now, ride through the night, we will be there in time to put a stop to it. You will be able to see for yourself, for it is sure they won't expect your return yet. I beg you to please help me. I want her, and I hate that peasant shepherd she is with, for I swear, if he has touched her I shall seek my revenge.'

'Antonio is a good man and Raffaella is headstrong, just like her mother. Go and ask Zia Madeleine if we can organise the stable lad to saddle my horse. We'll leave as soon as we can.'

Luigi left the room and Orlando poured himself another drink, taking it down in a single draught. He felt the tension in his muscles ease. He thought of his mother; she had died giving birth to Raffaella, and although in his darkest moments he blamed his sister for his mother's death, they had a happy childhood, thanks to Zia Paola.

He poured himself another drink and wondered if Antonio did, in fact, have tender feelings for Raffaella, or if it was just an animal lust. The gall of bitterness and jealousy swept through him, leaving its sour taste, and he shuddered. Why should Raffaella have what she wanted, while he had nothing?

He tried to console himself about the state of the farm and the estate left by his father, for the funds had dwindled. It had been a shock to find that he didn't have Vitoria's land, Raffaella's or the land at Pinta Longa. The promised marriage of Raffaella to Luigi would answer all his prayers. It would not be necessary for him to provide his sister with a dowry, for that had been agreed with Luigi. Better still, he would not have to give her an income from the farm, as she would be well provided for with the wealth in Luigi's family. The money from the estate could be reinvested in the farm and bring it up to a better standard. If he could sell the timber in the valley and the land at Pinta Longa, which had always been considered the poorest living, but by a turn of fate had now turned to gold, he would be wealthy beyond his dreams.

Orlando sighed. With the money and the law practice, he would be able to gather more lands and even raise his position so he could live in Sassari all the time. He knew Luigi had been thinking the same, since he had been looking for a permanent position with Zio Marco's friend, Dottore Paddu. There was always Zio Marco's law practice in Sassari, which was growing and would soon need a younger partner, and he would be able to pay for that partnership. Also, there was Gestinu's firm at Ozieri.

Orlando knew that neither Zia Paola nor Raffaella knew of their inheritance. Luigi would not say anything and Zia Paola was not likely to marry. He would see that they never found out – after all, what would they do with such wealth? Yes, Raffaella would have to toe the line. But in all honesty, he couldn't see what Luigi wanted with his sister. He had little success with the women of fashion, yet he was determined in wanting Raffaella.

He was brought back from his thoughts by Zia Madeleine's scolding him as she entered the room, with Luigi, following close behind her.

'Orlando. You can't be serious in your intention to return to Sos Lampidos tonight. You are not well enough to ride all that way, especially at night.'

'Zia Madeleine, I shall be all right, I promise. After all, I have Luigi to look after me. I couldn't be in better hands. How many men travel with their own doctor? It seems I am needed at home as Raffaella is proving insufferable.'

'That doesn't sound like her, she is always such a willing young woman. Can't it be dealt with by Zia Paola?'

'I'm afraid not, Zia Madeleine, but we shall all be back soon, for I hope to be able to announce the good news of Raffaella's engagement and we shall all be together at Mores for the ceremony.'

'Oh, have Antonio and she decided to name the day? That will be news indeed.'

'No, Zia Madeleine,' replied Orlando, now a little unsure of himself, 'Luigi has asked for her hand and I have granted his wish.'

'Why, that is wonderful,' cried his aunt. 'You mean you have managed to win her affection, Luigi?' she said to him. 'I'm pleased for you, and for Raffaella. You must be a proud man to have snatched her from Antonio's grasp. Perhaps we shall see more of you in the future, for I'm sure you will not stay forever in Mores.' She turned to Orlando. 'You must be pleased that Gestinu sent your sister to that school in Itteri. It must have changed her outlook.'

Orlando looked at his aunt and nodded.

So, after a huge discourse, Orlando finally persuaded his aunt of the prudence of his journey, with an agreement to eat before they set out on the return.

Orlando and Luigi left later that evening on the long trek to Sos Lampidos. The night air proved cool, and the track difficult, even though the full moon sailed in the clear black sky. Orlando, feeling weaker than he had realised, forced the pace to be slower than his friend hoped, making Luigi worried and irritable.

CHAPTER EIGHTEEN

Dawn broke in the mountains, filling the bedroom at Sos Lampidos with its warm golden light. Antonio stirred, and Raffaella, who lay awake, watched him as he slept beside her. His dark hair lay like a halo on the pillow and his long lashes made his eyes look heavy in repose, and she smiled at the thought of their lovemaking.

He opened his eyes and for a split second, she saw a worried look on his face as he tried to recollect his surroundings. Then, seeing Raffaella he smiled and sighed with pleasure, and drew her close to him. She felt again the strength and warmth of her young, virile lover.

'You feel so warm, so soft,' he murmured as he lovingly kissed her neck.

'And you feel so warm and strong,' she replied as she snuggled closer to him.

Antonio propped himself up on one arm, as he always did when they lay together, and ran his fingers across her cheek to her mouth, where she kissed them. He held her close to him, almost crushing her in his desire to possess her.

'I must go, before Zia Paola finds me here. I don't want her to be involved in any way.' He sighed a deep sigh.

'I don't want you to go. Oh, darling Antoneddu, hold me just a little longer, please,' she pleaded.

He held her close again and kissed her forehead. 'When Orlando returns, I will tell him we are avowed to each other and that you are with my child. We can then have the formal side of the contract drawn up and we can be together as husband and wife. We can pay the fine for living together and then we can go to Father Franco and be married at Bantadda. You will be free to come to me. We can build our own home at Punta Néula, down in the bottom meadow near the stream.'

'I'm frightened, Antoneddu,' she cried, clinging to him. There was so much she wanted to tell him, so much she wanted to say.

'No harm will come to you. Not while you have me, never forget that, *sa sposixedda mia*. We are already married in God's eyes and that is good enough for me.'

'Where are you going now?' she asked, trying to fight back her tears.

'I'm going to see Sergio and Ignazio and I shall be back later, so make sure you are up and ready. We can go down to the river fishing if you like, and I promised young Salvatore I'd show him how to shoot.'

With a quick kiss, he slipped from her grasp and she watched him as he dressed. His slender and lithe body, and the looseness of his movements pleased her. She pulled on her cotton nightgown and flung her arms around his neck.

'I love you, dearest Antoneddu, but we are going to have a terrible battle with Orlando.'

'Don't cry, my love. I don't like to see the mother of my son unhappy.'

He lingered to kiss her lips again, then grabbing his pistol, he put it into his belt. He swung a leg over the windowsill, and catching the entangled vine, he dropped to the ground.

She watched as he hurried toward the small clump of trees. She felt warm and secure from his lovemaking. She was about to wave to him when two men stepped out from behind the barn. Her heart missed a beat and her blood froze in her veins as the sickness of realisation swept through her. It was Luigi and her brother. Sergio's warning, that one means trouble, rang in her ears with a vibrant clarity. She had meant to tell Antoneddu last night about Luigi being at Sos Lampidos, but in their unbridled love she had forgotten all about it. Now there would be trouble and she was to blame.

Raffaella noticed, with horror, that both Orlando and Luigi

were armed. She cried out to warn her lover, but it was too late; with a yell Orlando stepped out and seized Antonio. Terrified, she fled from her room and down the stairs, all the time begging her brother to let Antoneddu go and calling to her aunt to help. She turned the corner of the barn and saw Orlando drag Antonio, struggling, to the edge of the ravine.

As she watched Antonio she realised by his expression that he believed her brother meant him no harm, and put up little resistance. Orlando threw Antonio to the ground at the edge of the ravine. Luigi, still mounted, watched Antonio, his pistol aimed at the ready. Antonio stood up slowly to face Orlando, and was clearly not prepared for the blow he received from his old friend, which sent him reeling dangerously near the ravine. In that split second Antonio realised his position, and drew his pistol and fired it into the air in the hope of bringing his assailants to reason.

Raffaella stood rooted to the spot. Sheer terror gripped her as she watched the dreadful scene unfold before her. She became helpless as her feet turned to clay, and her mouth went dry, so beseeching moans were all that issued forth. She noticed Luigi, who looked like a hawk; he didn't miss anything and eyed his victim like a hungry bird.

In a second he took in the horror registered on Raffaella's face, and noted her inability to do anything about it. Hatred for Antonio welled up in him like bitter gall, and he became seized by the jealousy that his peasant rival was still warm from the bed of his promised bride. He also saw, in a flash, a chance to rid himself of that rival and have Orlando forever in his debt for the loss of his sister's chastity. He aimed, but his horse, unnerved, jigged just as Luigi fired. The shot rang out over the whole valley. Orlando watched in horrified silence as Antonio fell to the ground.

'My God, Luigi, I meant to frighten him, not kill him. For pity's sake, do something to help him!' yelled Orlando, unable to believe what he saw.

Raffaella ran forward, half-mad with hysteria, and threw herself on Antonio, desperate in her effort to stem the flow of blood from her lover. Frantically, she dabbed the wound with her nightgown. Her hands, face and hair soon became covered with his blood as she kissed him again and again. Her sobbing turned to wailing as she tried to get some response from him.

'Oh no, Antoneddu, no, please God, no, not Antoneddu, please, Holy Mother, I beg you to hear me, not now when I need him so.'

The sound of her wailing drowned the heavy plod of approaching horses, and a shot rang out with a command to stand with arms raised. Orlando and Luigi did as they were bid, and the two Carabineri, who had arrived on the scene, covered them with their rifles.

'In the name of the King of Sardinia I command you to give an explanation,' cried the older of the two men. 'Who is the dead man?'

Raffaella, covered in her lover's blood, stood up and walked towards the two mounted Carabineri. She looked as if she had committed the bloody deed herself. Then she cried hysterically. 'It was him,' she screamed, pointing to Luigi. 'He has killed my lover out of jealousy. For God's sake, avenge my dead lover's life, I beg you.'

Without questioning, the younger of the two Carabineri aimed his rifle at Luigi, but the older man checked him.

'Is this right?'

But before he could reply, Luigi, seeing his plight, lowered his arms and took a shot at the officer, hitting him in the thigh and frightening the horse. Another shot followed and Luigi too fell to the ground, felled by the young Carabineri's gun. A volley of shots followed. Orlando, seeing his friend gunned down, fired twice. The first barrel, loaded with a single shot, missed. The second blast struck the young Carabineri in the heart and he fell back, lifeless. The sudden rush of warm blood over its coat made the horse rear up, and seized with terror, threw the young man from his saddle, but his foot remained caught in the stirrup. The horse, maddened by fright, bolted, dragging the man across the meadow.

The injured officer collected his horse and followed his young recruit, his oaths of vengeance ringing through the valley. Orlando stared in horror at the ground, now red from the blood of his two friends, and was physically sick.

Zia Paola, who had heard the shouts from Raffaella and the volley of shots, came running from the kitchen, still covered in flour, and went forward to help. Everything had happened so quickly she didn't have time to realise what had caused all the commotion. At the bloody scene she crossed herself and muttered her Hail Marys. Her first concern was for Raffaella as she lay beside Antonio. She shouted at Orlando to pull himself together and ordered him to carry his sister indoors.

'What in God's name happened? What are you doing here?' she demanded once inside.

Orlando, still weak from shock, tried to explain to his aunt how Luigi had come to collect him from Sassari. He told her in short bursts as she collected the smelling salts and clean water to try to wash the blood from her niece.

'Antonio fired at Luigi; he wanted to kill him. Raffaella and Antonio were lovers, Zia Paola,' Orlando said at last.

'I know. They have been since last Christmas.'

'And you allowed it to go on? Did Babbu know?' he replied.

'I think perhaps he did. They were close, you know. I don't think she told him; she didn't tell me. I just knew, and I think Gestinu knew too, and that is why he gave them his blessing on his deathbed.'

'It's disgusting,' retorted Orlando.

'Why? She is a woman. It's no more disgusting than your relationship with Vitoria before you married her, and she was a lot younger,' she replied, a cut in her voice.

Orlando looked taken aback.

'My dear Orlando, don't think we didn't know that you two were lovers. We did, but we turned a blind eye. You were to marry Vitoria, so what could be more natural? But look what your pride and greed have done. If you had left these two alone, they would have been happy together. Raffaella is right. She said that Sassari has changed you, and that Luigi was a bad influence on you, making you want things that were above you. Thank Heaven that school in Itteri didn't change her. Why were you so determined for her to marry Luigi? What difference could it have made to you if she married Antonio? She needed nothing else. Now look what you have done.'

'I didn't mean him any harm. I wanted to frighten him so he would leave Raffaella alone. I took him to the ravine. I wasn't going to throw him over. I just wanted to make him realise that she wasn't his by right. But he drew a pistol on me and fired at Luigi. The next thing I knew, Luigi had shot him and he lay bleeding at my feet. Everything was so confused from then on. The Carabineri arrived out of nowhere and threatened us.' He paused for a moment and then added, 'Zia Paola, please take care of Raffaella. I must take Antonio's body to his father, it's the least I can do. If the Carabineri come back, hang a white light in the attic when it is safe for me to return.'

'Orlando, pull yourself together. You can't go to Punta Néula; the Carabineri will be here any moment. It won't take them long to find out what happened when the two injured men turn up at their camp.'

Orlando felt sick and weak; his illness and the sudden shock catching up with him. 'Antonio fired the first shot at Luigi; he wanted to kill him. There was nothing I could do. It was all Antonio's fault, you know how hot-headed, he is,' he repeated.

'You must ride to Pattada and find Luigi's friends; they will need to collect his body for the burial. Take food and blankets and go to Zio Franco at Bantadda, I beg you, just until it is safe,' urged his aunt. 'For if they come here now they will find no mercy for you, that is sure.'

Orlando looked at his aunt and then went downstairs. She heard him raid the larder. She watched him as he lurched his way to the stables, where he mounted his horse and headed round the back of Sos Lampidos toward Bantadda.

No one saw Ignazio leave the kitchen, or heard him as he ran to find his father.

Sergio left Ignazio with the sheep; he was in no state to do anything. His father had sworn him to secrecy and left to collect the donkey that they used for grinding the corn, and approached Antonio. Sergio rolled him over to try to haul him up onto the small animal. He leant down and put his hands under Antonio's arms, and tried to haul him into an upright position. As he did so Antonio let out a low moan. Sergio, thinking the spirits had come to get him, leapt away and immediately let him drop back onto the ground as he started on his Hail Marys.

'Help me,' came the weak voice, and Sergio, realising that Antonio was still alive, dragged, pushed and heaved him onto the donkey and started down the ravine, leading the animal behind him, convinced the Devil himself was in pursuit.

When Sergio reached the farmhouse at Punta Néula he started calling and wailing in such a mad way that Salvatore and Gabriella came rushing to see what had happened. They both crossed themselves when they saw the limp body of their son across the donkey, and Salvatore went to help Sergio as he pulled Antonio to the ground. They carried him inside and laid him on the table.

'He was alive when I left Sos Lampidos,' wailed Sergio. 'Orlando swears it was Antonio who shot at Luigi, but Ignazio says he is lying, it was the young recruit. He is in a terrible state. I must get back to him; he is with the sheep.'

Salvatore thanked Sergio and made him swear on the Holy Bible that he would tell no one of Antonio's survival. They needed to know what had happened first. If Orlando was believed, then Antonio would be accused of murder.

Gabriella felt for a pulse. It was there – very faint, but it was there. She examined Antonio, and found a large wound on the back of his head where he had hit it on something sharp. It was still bleeding. She asked Salvatore to fetch her salves, bandages and splints; all kept ready for such accidents. She cleaned the head wound with care and then bound it with linen bandaging. She knew that it was not serious, but head wounds always bleed profusely. He would have a thumping headache when he came round.

Gabriella removed Antonio's shirt and saw the bullet had nicked the skin near his left upper arm and passed out the other side, thank the Lord. She asked Salvatore to make a splint, and strap the arm to his side so it would not move and open the wound. He had lost a lot of blood, but thanks to all the saints, he was a strong and fit young man, so he should survive.

They worked quickly, and then put Antonio in the hiding place in the cask. Gabriella took all the bandages and Antonio's shirt and burnt them in the fire.

After Sergio had left, Salvatore made a rough coffin, filled it with stones and covered them with linen. He then dug a grave near the large olive tree by the stables and buried it, so everyone would think his son was dead. Returning to the house, he put his arms around his wife and consoled his young son.

'There is a red lamp in the attic room, they need help up at Sos Lampidos,' said Gabriella.

They agreed that she would go to Sos Lampidos. So, taking the donkey, Gabriella retraced Sergio's steps back to the house, where she found Zia Paola in a terrible state. She had put Raffaella to bed with a fever, and Zia Paola was at her wits' end as she had no idea what was wrong with her. Gabriella went to see Raffaella at once and examined the young girl. It took her no time at all to realise that she was pregnant, and that she was carrying a dead child which was poisoning her.

The air at Sos Lampidos became full of the sound of hooves with the arrival of the Carabineri. The tall Captain dismounted and strode towards the house. He knocked on the door. He had been here a few years before, he remembered the house now, and they had come here looking for a young Sard who shot some landowner nearby. He wracked his brain: Don diVenti, that had been the landowner's name.

Zia Paola opened the door.

'Where is the man who shot my men?' he commanded.

Zia Paola pulled herself up to her full height and addressed the Continental. 'First, I would remind you that I am a Sard, and not one of your countrymen or a member of your troop, and second, I would be obliged if you removed your hat when you address me.'

The Captain, used to dealing with the pastore and men of the area, was somewhat taken aback by the dignified Signorina who stood before him. He removed his hat and apologised, at the same time bowing and clicking his heels. He felt awkward; he remembered how he had treated these people before. He had been rude and arrogant and the thought made him feel ashamed.

'There is no one here, only my niece, and she is in bed having seen her fiancé gunned down by the Piedmontese, who is also lying out there with Antonio. I have no one to help me. I would be grateful if your men could bring them into the house so I can lay them out.'

The Captain went to the door and snapped orders for his men to collect the two bodies. Zia Paola found a winding sheet and laid Luigi's corpse out. The Captain then ordered his men to bring in the other body, and then find timber from the outhouse to make two rough coffins.

Zia Paola gave the Captain some coffee and bade him to sit at the dining room table while his men carried out the work. She sat watching him. He was tall, like most of the northern Continentals. He sported a fine, full beard, neatly trimmed to the sides of his face. Gone was the thin, waxed moustache of three years ago. It made him look more like a Sard than a Continental. His eyes were heavily lashed and his brows strong. She found him interesting, and stared at him.

She roused herself, and making an excuse, went upstairs to see Raffaella.

'Could you please tell me what happened?' asked the Captain, rising from his chair when Zia Paola returned and joined him at the table, his manner much subdued by this striking woman.

'I was called from the kitchen by my niece's screaming to see Antonio lying dead on the ground, together with Luigi, and the two Carabineri were charging off. I didn't see what happened,' said Zia Paola with a break in her voice. The Captain rose and poured her a cup of coffee, which she took thankfully.

At that moment one of the young Carabineri came to the door and asked to see the Captain. After a brief few words, he again disappeared.

The Captain returned to the table and addressed Zia Paola. 'Don't distress yourself, please, Signorina,' he said, looking concerned. 'Where did the other man go? The fiancé – Antonio, you said his name was – where is he?'

Zia Paola looked at him with genuine surprise. 'Is he not there? My shepherd must have taken him.'

The Captain sighed and thanked Zia Paola for her help and hospitality, and replacing his hat, he bowed. 'Thank you again, Signorina, we will be back to speak with your niece when she is better.'

With all the work completed, they laid the young doctor in the new coffin and nailed it down. Zia Paola thanked them all and bid good day to the Captain.

She hurried upstairs to help Gabriella, who had mixed some herbs which had brought on labour. Raffaella and Antonio's stillborn son was delivered late that night, the cord wound around his neck, and Raffaella now lay sweating and breathing heavily, having lost a lot of blood. Gabriella gave her feverfew and waited for the fever to subside. She was frightened that she would haemorrhage like her mother had done. They put draw-sheets under her so they could change them without disturbing her too much.

In Raffaella's fevered mind, she called upon the saints to help her, and upon all the spirits to curse her brother for his hand in the deaths of her child and her lover. In the early hours of the morning, the fever broke and Raffaella now lay exhausted on her bed.

Zia Paola collected the soiled sheets and wrapped the dead child in them, first making the sign of the cross and adding a benediction for the lost soul. She went into the garden and lit a huge fire and burnt everything.

Upstairs, Gabriella smoothed Raffaella's forehead and cooed to her. 'He is alive, Raffaella, do you hear me? He is alive.'

But there was no response from the young girl.

Raffaella regained consciousness in the early hours of the morning. She became aware of the flickering candle on her bedside table, and struggled to collect her thoughts. Then the sickening reality entered her numbed mind. She rose from her bed and made her way downstairs, drawn by a compulsion of which she was not sure. Noiselessly she opened the door to the large room. The dawn light fell in at the open casement, and on the long table in the hall, on which lay a rough-hewn coffin.

Zia Paola slept in a chair near the coffin. She was still dressed, and had fallen asleep during her long vigil. Raffaella walked towards the table. She was shaking and felt a cold shiver run down her back.

The coffin lid was nailed down, and fresh wild flowers were placed on top. She bent and kissed the coffin, the tears coming hot on her cheeks. The tears turned to sobs as she took in the finality of death.

Zia Paola, hearing her sobs, roused herself. 'For pity's sake, child, what are you doing here?' she asked, and taking Raffaella by the hand, she led her away.

'Oh, Zia Paola, he always said everything would be all right while we had each other; he would look after me. Now he is gone, what am I going to do? I curse Orlando for what he has done. Curse him by all the saints. I don't want to see him, promise me, Zia Paola,' she wailed.

'Hush now,' said Zia Paola as she gathered the young girl in her arms and led her to her bed. 'That is not Antonio, that is Luigi's coffin.'

Raffaella looked at her aunt, unable to comprehend what she was saying. The room became dark and she fainted into her aunt's arms.

The Captain arrived at Sos Lampidos the next morning and knocked on the heavy oak door.

Zia Paola came to see him, and he could see from her face that she was distraught. He immediately removed his hat and bowed.

'I'll not trouble you now, but is there anything I can do for you or your niece?' he asked with obvious concern. 'Can I get our medic to look at her?'

Zia Paola smiled at the Captain. 'Thank you, but Signora Gabriella Sanna is with her, she rode over this morning and is our healer. Would you like a coffee? I was about to make one.'

'Thank you, if it is no trouble.'

She opened the door wide to let the Captain in and led him to the table. He was about to sit down when Gabriella came into the room, having come down from upstairs.

The Captain went forward to meet her. 'Signora, I believe I owe you an apology,' he said, bowing.

'Whatever for, Captain?' replied Gabriella, looking taken aback.

'Three years ago I came to your house looking for Gavinu Piddu and I was rude and condescending to you and your family. I was a raw recruit and still not familiar with the ways of the Sard people. I hope I have learnt a lot since then, and that you will find it in your heart to forgive me.'

Gabriella came forward and shook the Captain's outstretched hand. 'We all have things to learn, but thank you, Captain,' she said with a warm smile. 'You have an excellent memory.'

'You don't forget bad manners, and I have often thought of that day,' he replied, looking uncomfortable.

'All forgotten now,' replied Gabriella, and touched the Captain on his arm.

'Sit down,' said Zia Paola, smiling at the Captain as she poured the coffee for the three of them and bid him sit at the table next to Gabriella.

Gabriella turned to Zia Paola. 'Raffaella will be all right, and

I will come and see her in the morning. If you need me, put the lamp in the window.'

The Captain sipped his coffee and watched the two women, so typical of the mountain people, self-sufficient and independent. He finished his coffee, and not wanting to outstay his welcome, he wished them a good day and replacing his hat, bowed again.

'I will come back tomorrow to see if there is anything I can do, if that is all right with you. Are you sure you don't want me to bring our doctor with me?' asked the Captain.

'Thank you, Captain, that is very kind, but we can manage,' said Zia Paola, again struck by his kindness and the difference in his manner now from the first time he called.

She saw him to the door and watched him as he walked outside and took his horse from the waiting soldier. He mounted, and giving her a small salute, they left.

When Zia Paola returned to the table Gabriella smiled at her.

'I think our Captain has taken a shine to you, Paola,' said Gabriella with a wicked twinkle in her eye.

'*Boh*, don't be silly, Gabriella,' she retorted, but was surprised that she felt her heart skip a beat.

CHAPTER NINETEEN

For two nights Orlando rode to the spur of the mountain to see whether the lamp in the attic had been lit by his aunt, but every night was the same. A dark, uninviting void was all that awaited him. Then, on the third night there it was, shining dimly in the attic window. Orlando's spirits rose as he urged his horse down the mountain and up the familiar narrow path to Sos Lampidos. He had been to Pattada to find Luigi's friends who had collected his body for burial, and had stood with them and wept for his friend at the graveside.

Orlando dismounted at the stable and walked across the courtyard, searching for signs of life. His father's dog came forward to greet him and Orlando bent to fuss the animal. There were no other visible lights in the house, so he let himself into the kitchen. He found a lamp and lit it. The light flickered across the room, and he went upstairs to his sister's room. He opened the door without making a sound, and entered the room, which smelt of thyme and lemon. It was lit by a small, flickering candle that stood on her bedside table.

Orlando walked towards the bed, his gaze fixed on the motionless form of his sister. Her eyes were shut as if in deep sleep. He put down his lamp, and searched the bed for some movement, breathing or life, and then in a panic, he took hold of her hand. To his horror, the skin was cool to his touch. A shudder ran down his back and he felt the hair move on his scalp. He stared at her in growing disbelief. Was she dead? But she couldn't be. Why? She hadn't been hit. Why had she died? A thousand questions fell on his now-befuddled brain. Horror filled his panic-stricken mind. He fell to his knees, making the sign of the cross, and called to her.

'Take pity on me, Raffaella, and forgive me,' he cried, taking her almost lifeless hand in his. 'I beg you in your kindness to forgive me. By all the saints and their mercy, I beseech you to forgive me.'

His sobs and pleading deafened him to the sound of Zia Paola as she rose from the chair near the bed, so her gentle touch on her nephew's shoulder made him cry out in his terror.

'Hush, Orlando, it's me, Zia Paola,' she whispered. 'There is nothing more we can do for her at the moment.'

'What happened?' he asked, his voice flat and dry; the words sticking in his throat.

'The shock of seeing Antonio gunned down was too much for her. She went into labour and lost the child she was carrying. Unfortunately, the child, a boy, was born dead with the cord wound round his neck; there was nothing we could do for him. She haemorrhaged, just as your mother did all those years ago. Gabriella and I did everything we could for her. She had a terrible fever for a while, but at last the fever has left her, though she is very weak.'

'Did she suffer?' he asked, his voice trembling.

'It wasn't easy for her. Gabriella gave her laudanum to try to kill the pain, but she didn't put up a great fight. She has lost the will to live and she hasn't tried to pull herself through, but now the fever has broken, she has at last managed to get some rest.'

'Did she, by any chance, ask for me?'

He looked his aunt in the eye. She turned away; she was drawn, and looked pale, in the light of the flickering candle. She made no answer to his question.

'Zia Paola, I beg you, please tell me,' he pleaded, rising from his knees and standing before her. 'Please tell me that she forgave me.'

He searched her face for some clue to her reply, but all he could see was pity.

'Why didn't you hang the light in the attic earlier? I would have come, regardless of the Carabineri,' he demanded. 'I could have spoken to her, made her understand how I felt and that I meant Antonio no harm.'

'The Carabineri left two days ago,' said his aunt coldly. 'She didn't want you to return and she made me promise not to light the lamp.'

Orlando looked at his aunt, and then at his young sister in her coma, and then back to his aunt. 'Did you know she was carrying his child?' he asked.

'I had a good idea. You can't keep something like that hidden forever. She and Antonio have been promised to each other for a long time, in fact, since the day that young Salvatore was born. That is why he gave her the horse. It was her betrothal present.'

Orlando looked at his aunt with disbelief. 'But that was over three years ago. Do you mean to say that you have known about this all that time and you never said anything to anyone? Did Babbu know about the child?'

'I believe he did, and that is why he wanted to sign the papers so she could marry the man she loved and not the one you insisted on tying her to. He knew the state of his affairs and there wasn't any money for a dowry. But to Antonio and Raffaella it wouldn't matter.'

Questions and answers whirled in Orlando's mind, and a look of comprehension spread across his face. 'So that is why Raffaella was so adamant about not becoming young Salvatore's godmother,' he said slowly. 'Because the Sannas wanted Antonio as godfather she knew she could never marry him. How stupid of me not to realise. It was the same at the Festival of San Giovanni this year, when Antonio chose Marina to be his *Comare*.'

'Orlando, you must realise that they have been in love all their lives and you couldn't, or wouldn't, see it. You were too busy in your selfish obsession with Vitoria. When she died and Gestinu went too, you could see a way to build an empire at Raffaella's expense. Then you became jealous of her happiness and became obsessed with the idea that she must marry Luigi, to open so-called doors in society for you. I tell you, Orlando, you have a lot to answer for.'

'You should have known better than to encourage them, Zia

Paola,' he said, trying to keep any authority he might have had. He tried to take in all his aunt was saying, but his mind seemed unable to absorb the words. 'I didn't want Raffaella to have to work hard for the rest of her life. If she married Luigi she could have a good life without worries and hardships. She could have lived like a true *Bourgaise*, dressed in silks and respected by other people of the same standing. She could have lived in Sassari or Piedmont and mixed with people of similar education; married to Antonio she would have nothing other than poverty and misery, and would waste all the time and money Babbu lavished on her with her schooling.'

'And you would not have had to pay for her. But she has nothing now. She loved Antonio in a way that you couldn't even begin to understand,' replied his aunt.

'She told me that before, and I heard the points she put forward and they made no difference. She would have grown to despise Antonio in his old age, with his poverty.'

'And who are you to say that she would have been any happier with Luigi?' demanded his aunt.

'At least she would have been unhappy in comfort. Which is more than can be said with Antonio,' he snapped.

'Raffaella only needed Antonio,' she replied.

'Oh for pity's sake, Zia Paola, what would you know about it?' he replied, feeling trapped. 'Tell me how long were they lovers. Do you know?'

'It is my belief that he never touched her until she came back from Itteri. It was while they were away from each other that they realised how much they loved each other. If only you hadn't tried to make her marry Luigi.'

'Why didn't she tell me she was having Antonio's child? I would have seen everything in a different light, and Luigi wouldn't have wanted to marry her then.'

His aunt laughed. 'You say that now, but you would never have understood before. Why should she have to tell you that? She felt you should respect her wishes as her brother. You should have been aware that she wanted a life of her own. Listen, Orlando, you can't stay here. Go to Zio Marco, he will know what to do. He will protect you.'

Footsteps on the stairs made Orlando look up to see Sergio standing in the doorway.

'Are you all right, Signorina Paola? I saw a horse and wondered if you needed any help.'

'It's all right, Sergio, it's me,' replied Orlando.

The shepherd turned toward the familiar voice. Orlando watched as the colour drained from Sergio's face and he stood there wide-eyed and open-mouthed.

'Whatever is the matter with you, Sergio? You look as if you have seen the Devil himself.'

Sergio stepped back and glanced at the doorway, eager to make his retreat. Orlando, annoyed by such open hostility, stepped forward and tried to catch his arm, but he cowered away, a look of fear stamped on his face.

'For Heaven's sake, man, what is the matter?' demanded Orlando.

'Don't come near me, stay away,' wailed Sergio as he crossed himself in rapid succession and frantically fingered his *Mal Occhio*.

Zia Paola stepped between them. 'That will do, Sergio. You can go now,' she said in a quiet but firm tone.

Orlando made a grab for him again, and this time managed to hold on to him.

'Please,' cried Sergio, 'please let me go. Signorina, please don't let him touch me.' Terror seized him, and he looked like a hunted animal awaiting the final death blow from its captor.

'Tell me!' yelled Orlando, shaking Sergio so hard that his teeth rattled.

'You're cursed, you're cursed,' repeated the shepherd, whimpering. 'Cursed, I say. Your sister, God bless her, condemned your soul to the Devil and to everlasting damnation on the death of her son. Cursed, cursed.' The words hissed on his lips.

Orlando let him go. The impact of Sergio's words crashed in on him. He looked at Zia Paola; there was no need to ask her for confirmation of the shepherd's words. He could see their truth written on her face.

He felt faint and wretched, and the oppressiveness of the room closed in on him. He pushed past both of them and clattered downstairs and out into the cool night, where he paused to draw in the sweet, fresh air. He found his horse and mounted it, yelling at it as he rode like a man possessed; indeed, as if the Devil himself were on his tail. Oblivious to anything around him, he urged his horse on, up into the mountains once more, deaf to the entreating calls of his aunt, but with Sergio's words still hissing in his ears and searing his brain. He needed help, and there was only one person he could trust: his Zio Marco.

The narrow path to Sassari from Sos Lampidos was difficult enough to negotiate in daylight, but the pale light of a half-moon was bound to spell disaster. Orlando spurred on his horse, even though he couldn't see the pathway clearly, while his horse was reluctant to be driven on at his master's pace, tried to slacken the speed.

In the flash of a moment, a white form darted out from the shadows, causing the already nervous horse to whinny and shy. It reared up, and losing its balance on some loose stones, tried to regain its footing. Orlando, seeing the white object was no more than a mountain goat, tried to calm his horse; he reassured it again and again. Realising his plight, he held on to the creature's neck and mane, giving words of encouragement all the time to quieten the animal.

Slowly, like an extended nightmare, the horse lost its battle against the crumbling ground as shale, rocks and boulders showered into the ravine. With a last desperate effort, the frightened animal lunged forward, but the ground gave way under its weight and exhausted, it fell with a heart-rending whinny as it crashed through the shrubs and undergrowth into the gorge below.

CHAPTER TWENTY

When Orlando regained consciousness, he became aware of a flickering light that came through his still-fogged mind, and out of the indistinct, grey darkness came the outline of a heavily bearded face. His eyes tried to adjust to the smoky light as he made out the swarthy features of a man in his early forties. The face was half-illuminated by the flickering light of a candle which the stranger held close to Orlando's face.

'I'm Gian Porqueddu,' said the stranger in a deep but kindly voice. 'I was the one who saw you fall and rescued you.'

Orlando tried to sit up, but was arrested by a severe pain in his head.

'You will have to rest many more days yet. You have broken your leg and you received a heavy blow to your head, but you are safe with us and lucky to be alive.'

'Who are you? And who else is with you?' asked Orlando, aware of another shadowy shape moving in the semi-darkness. 'How long have I been here?'

'So many questions,' laughed the stranger. 'You have been with us for a week. We are all like you, fugitives from the law. We are all your friends here, and some of us you know well.'

As he said this, Gian turned from Orlando and beckoned to a young girl who had been waiting in the shadows. Orlando strained his eyes to see who it was who came forward.

'Hello, Orlando. You remember me, don't you?'

'Vitoria, is that you?' asked Orlando in a desperate manner.

The young girl turned to Gian. 'He thinks that I am my sister, his wife, but she is dead. He is still sick and delirious.' She turned to Orlando and smoothed his head. 'It's me, Marina. You are all right now, Orlando,' she whispered. 'Gavinu is here with me. I joined him two weeks ago. He has been here for months, but we eloped from Punta Néula and were married by an old priest in a small chapel in the mountains.'

Orlando tried hard to recall all she was saying, but his mind seemed caught in a whirl, and none of her words made any sense to him. 'Dear Vitoria, stay with me please, please don't leave me,' he said, grabbing Marina's arm.

'You must rest now,' cut in Gian, 'or you will never regain your strength.'

Orlando slept for the main part of the following day, woken only by Marina to be fed and cared for. Gradually, the sleeping hours grew shorter, and the longer waking hours became more bearable, the pain in his head at last easing. The herbal tea that Marina prepared and gave him, helped to ease the dull, aching thud that was his constant, nagging companion. The pain, when it came, filled his body and mind and drove out all the past events. But in sleep, he found no such peace. The torture of horrific events overwhelmed him, rising from his subconscious, and became a nightmare that he fought to forget.

One night, after his first conscious recollections, when he had mistaken Marina for Vitoria, he lay tossing on his straw mattress. His restlessness worried Marina, and she sat beside him to try to comfort her old friend. She fetched water from the container in the cave and cooled his feverish head. Orlando stirred and opened his eyes. He looked wild, and not of this world.

'Raffaella, is that you?' he asked, searching the young girl's face. 'Do you remember nursing Babbu like this? You were the one that cared for him, with Zia Paola and dear Gabriella. You were so good to him, and he loved you. You were always his favourite. Dear Raffaella, I have such terrible dreams. Haunting nightmares, when I see you go away from me. When you hate and despise me. Tell me you don't hate me.' He grabbed Marina and pleaded with her in his despair. 'Sergio says you have cursed me, but you wouldn't do that to me, would you, dear Raffaella?'

He fell back, exhausted, and Marina continued to bathe his fevered head.

'There, there, Orlando, you are safe here now,' she whispered, fearing he would wake all the others in the cave.

'Vitoria, is that you?' asked Orlando, his voice rising to a fearful crescendo.

'Hush, hush, Orlando, or you will wake everyone.'

His mind wandered in its fevered ramblings, and Marina found it difficult to understand everything he said to her. He was tormented by the idea that she was Vitoria or Raffaella, and as if he was afraid of something terrible happening to her.

The ravings that were commonplace at last gave way to more wakeful nights, and then sleep came from sheer exhaustion. As days and long, weary nights passed, he became well enough to sit up during the day. Finally, he could leave the confines of his bed. He hobbled around in the dim light of the cave with the help of a crutch made for him by Gian.

Marina was grateful to see him on the mend, and confided with Gavinu about some of Orlando's strange ravings.

'The mind does funny things when upset with a heavy knock,' he comforted her. 'Don't worry, he will tell you soon enough if there is anything wrong. Just give him time. He's not used to living in such rough conditions as this, and it's all very strange to him.'

So came the day, late in September, that Orlando, finding the cave empty and with the aid of his crutch, ventured to see the outside world and free himself of the cave that had been his prison for the past weeks.

The entrance to the cave was narrow and covered by a thick myrtle bush and a tangle of smaller shrubs, obscuring any view from outside. He hobbled out of the cave. He was not prepared for the light that flooded into his eyes, making him shade them against the torrid rush of searing brightness. He allowed himself to become accustomed to the vivid glare until he absorbed all the intense colours that had been denied him for so long in the dark cavern. He looked around and found himself in a narrow ravine intersected by a small brook on which the light sparkled and glinted as it murmured its way through the confined area. Orlando was so occupied by the colourful spectacle that he didn't hear Marina come out of the cave.

'How do you feel now that you are outside again?' she asked, putting her hand on his arm.

Orlando jumped and swung towards her. 'Sorry, what did you say? I didn't hear you; I was miles away and taking in all this light and scenery.'

She repeated her question, adding, 'Funny, I didn't think you ever liked the wild outdoors.'

He ignored the remark and replied, 'I feel much better now, thanks to your constant nursing and help.'

Marina led him to a rock and signalled to him to sit beside her, which he did, eager to rest his arm from the crutch which he let it fall to the ground at his feet, and an awkward silence fell over them both. He stared at the plaster still on his leg. It was made of a mixture of chopped straw, horsehair and mud.

'Did you plaster my leg like this too?' he asked.

'No, Gian did it. His mother was the local bone-setter and she taught him how to do it from childhood. It is useful up here to have someone to do work like that. I have Mamma's salves and herbal remedies, for they are easy to make up here as everything grows in the area.'

'Where are all the others?' he asked.

'Some are deep inside the cave, sleeping. The others are out hunting with Gian and Gavinu. They should be back soon,' she replied, then added, 'Tell me, Orlando, what news is there from home? How are my parents? Are they well?'

It was the first time she had been on her own with him since he had become himself again, and she now longed to know the answers to all the questions that she knew Gian was anxious, for some reason or other, for her not to ask.

Orlando nodded. 'Do they know you are here with Gavinu?' he asked, trying to evade her question.

'They know we are together and safe, but they don't know where we are. It would be wrong for them to know that, for what they don't know they can't tell.'

'Whoever told you that?' he asked, surprised.

'Gian – he has been a bandit for many years, and this is his home. We live here in safety because no one outside the band knows where we are. True, he goes home to visit his wife and children and comes back with food, oil and wine and many other good treats, but even his family doesn't know where he lives.'

'How long has he been a bandit?'

'For many years now, but he has a good life and sees his wife regularly. She gave him a new baby last year, which made him very proud, and the Carabineri furious, because they know he visits her but haven't been able to catch him.'

'Tell me, Marina, are you happy here?' he asked.

'I have Gavinu and he is safe, so for that I am happy. We can't see any way of him receiving his pardon for killing Don diVenti, so we are doomed to stay in the mountains for our lifetime. I can assure you, Orlando, if there was any way I could regain Gavinu's freedom, believe me, I would.' She sighed. 'But tell me, how are Babbu and Mamma, and my brothers Antonio and little Salvatore – how are they? Are they all well?'

Orlando hesitated. 'Yes, they are well. At least your parents are.'

'And Antonio, how is he? Are he and Raffaella to marry? They must be so happy…'

Her words trailed off as Orlando buried his head into his hands.

'Stop it, for Heaven's sake, stop it!' he shouted.

The pounding in his head was returning, and the nightmare of the past weeks came back with a vivid reality. Antonio's death; Raffaella lying on her bed, pale, looking at death's door; the terrifying ride from the house as if the Devil was with him in the saddle, and Sergio's words still hissing in his brain. No longer were they figures of his dark, troubled dreams, but he knew them now for what they were: pictures of the truth. He felt a dull sickness in his stomach, and beads of sweat stood out on his face while the water trickled down his back.

'For pity's sake, Orlando, whatever is the matter?' pleaded Marina. 'Tell me what is wrong.'

Orlando struggled with the words in his brain, but his mouth stayed mute. The full horror of the scene came back in his mind's eye. He could see Antonio lying in a pool of blood, and Raffaella, weeping and bloodstained. For weeks he had fought the nightmare, clinging to the hope that it was nothing more than a terrible dream. But the reality of his surroundings and the company of *fiorri leggi* confirmed his innermost dread. Luigi and Antonio were dead, together with the Carabineri, and the full horror of all its consequences came in on him with a frightening clarity. He heard a ringing in his head as the world darkened around him.

Marina put his head between his legs when she saw the colour drain from his face, frightened that he was going to faint.

'Something terrible has happened at home. You must tell me,' she cried, shaking him with violence and bringing him to his senses.

'Marina. Antonio is dead.' His mouth was dry with fear and the words clung to the back of his throat. 'Raffaella is alive, but she has been very ill – she haemorrhaged giving birth to his stillborn child.'

Marina was stunned, her mind in turmoil. Everything was disjointed, but at the same time formed a pattern from the pieces she had gleaned when Orlando had raved in his fever. She seemed resigned to the news.

'Why... How did he die? He was alive when I left Punta Néula. Who killed him? When did it happen?' she asked, her voice flat and unemotional.

Orlando braced himself and told her what happened. 'Luigi shot him. He was in love with Raffaella,' he said. 'I... I didn't realise he was so jealous of Antonio. He wanted to marry Raffaella, but I told him he couldn't; that she and Antonio were promised to each other,' he lied. 'True, at first I thought Luigi would be a good match for Raffaella. But on this last visit home, I gave my consent for her to marry Antonio, for I could see they were more suited. I had returned from Sassari with Luigi to tell Raffaella she could marry Antonio. But Luigi was jealous and shot him. There was nothing I could do.'

Marina looked her old friend in the eye. The colour once more left his face, to return again with a burning fury at the lie he told, and at the thought that Marina may not believe him.

'And Raffaella?'

'She saw it all happen. I would have done anything to stop her from seeing such a terrible sight. The shock sent her into premature labour. I didn't even know she was pregnant. She didn't talk to me like she used to in past years.'

Marina rose to her feet. 'And Luigi, what happened to him?'

Orlando thought for a moment, frantically searching for the right words, but it was Marina who answered her own question.

'Of course,' she cried, 'you must have avenged Antonio's death by shooting Luigi, and that's why you are outlawed.'

Orlando made no reply.

'Thank you, Orlando. It must have been difficult for you to shoot a friend like that. At least I know that my brother's death was avenged. Babbu would find it difficult to avenge anyone, he is so gentle, and I would have to teach vengeance to young Salvatore, which is something I would not want to do. Antonio will at least lie in peace now. The thought of him restlessly searching for vengeance as a lost soul is more than I could bear. I'm glad you have told me, Orlando. We have known for some time that something was wrong because you used to cry out in your fever for Raffaella, and you thought I was Vitoria.'

Orlando felt a cold shiver run through him. He was about to ask what else he had said, when they were interrupted by the sound of hooves on the dry ground. In seconds, the quiet ravine became a hubbub of activity, with horses panting and men dismounting and chattering amongst themselves. They stood around in various form of dress: *mastrucca, berritas* sported at rakish angles, and various colours for waistcoats. Their guns were slung across their shoulders, with belts of ammunition. They were all bearded and long-haired. Some had game slung across their horses' withers, while others had their catch hanging from drab, homespun saddlebags.

Gavinu came forward and picked Marina up in his arms and gave her a large hug. 'We've brought back a large wild boar, so tonight we can celebrate the renewed health of our friend,' he said, swinging her round in his joy. He put her down and looked at her. He was not prepared for her reaction, for she leant forward, flinging her arms round his neck, and burst into tears. Her sobs came in uncontrollable waves, and Gavinu threw a questioning glance at Orlando, who with the aid of his crutch, hobbled over to join them.

'I'm afraid I had some bad news for her. I hadn't told her before because I wasn't sure until now whether the dream that haunted me day and night was just a nightmare or reality. You see, Antonio is dead. I have been wretched, and prayed it wasn't true,' said Orlando, panic rising in his voice.

'We knew there was something wrong, for you told Marina in your fevered raving. We have been waiting to see what you had to say. The realisation of the truth has just hit her.'

Gavinu took Marina in his arms and comforted her by bestowing small kisses on her tearful face.

That night Orlando found no solace in sleep, but lay tossing on his straw bed. His leg ached, and the pounding in his head was not eased by the racing in his mind. No one had witnessed the fight at Sos Lampidos other than Zia Paola, and she wouldn't give him away. Certainly not to the Sannas, of that he was sure. Zia Paola would need their help while he was away, for Sergio would be worse than useless. The Carabineri that came on the scene that morning hadn't come back while he was there, so they must both be dead and dead men can't talk. So it was his word that mattered now.

If he could get Gavinu and Marina to believe that it was he who had avenged Antonio's death, then everything would be all right. They, in turn, would then convince Gian of his innocence, and more important still, Gabriella and Salvatore. After all, he had only meant to frighten Antonio and bring him to his senses over Raffaella. Why had Luigi been so stupid and hot-headed? Orlando sighed.

Now that his health was on the mend, he would go back to Sos Lampidos and see if Zia Paola could do something about securing his pardon with the help of his Zio Marco in Sassari. He was bound to be able to help; he had a good standing in Sassari and many of his friends had high-ranking jobs in the city. Orlando had been introduced to some of them during his stay with Zio Marco while at university. They all knew him to be an outstanding student of the law and would never believe that he was an outlaw, a murderer. Living with this band of *fiorri leggi* would go against him, for an innocent man didn't need the help of bandits. In that moment, he made up his mind to go back to Sos Lampidos as soon as he could.

CHAPTER TWENTY-ONE

At Sos Lampidos the velvet night fell with a star-filled sky. Raffaella lay in her bed in that half-sleep when the mind plays tricks on the soul. She heard her bedroom door open, and turned to see who it was who entered, but she could see nothing. The moon had hidden behind the scurrying clouds, leaving the room in darkness. She felt someone near her and became paralysed with fear as her heart beat in her chest. Not just from fear, but a feeling of nearness she knew so well.

'Raffaella, my darling, it is me, Antoneddu,' he whispered.

She stiffened and was about to call out when he put his arm around her and smothered her mouth with kisses.

'You're dead,' she whimpered as she pulled away. 'What have I done to make you come back to me?'

'Darling Raffaella, I am alive. Don't be frightened, my love. Luigi shot me and when I went down, I struck my head on a rock and passed out. The wound in my arm was not deep. Sergio took me to Punta Néula and Mamma and Babbu nursed me. Orlando has told everyone that I fired the first shot to kill Luigi, and that I was shot in self-defence.'

'But that's not true, I saw what happened. Orlando was going to throw you over the ravine and Luigi shot at you – if you had aimed to kill Luigi he would have been dead. You are too good a shot to miss.'

'Yes, but you have not been well enough to testify, and anyway, with you being so close to me they won't listen to you.'

The sudden realisation that Antonio was alive and that he was with her came to her, and she fell into his arms and sobbed.

'Every prayer I could pray has been answered. Oh my darling, Antoneddu, I love you so much.'

She sat up and lit her candle and held it to his face in wonder. She touched his cheek, his eyes and his mouth, as if to convince herself that he was alive and with her, and not as a spirit. Putting the candle back down, she fell back into his arms and wept tears of utter joy.

He held Raffaella and lay on the bed next to her. 'I am going to Pinta Niedda to stay with Gavinu's family. With Gavinu away and two of the boys dead in the war, they need help.'

'No, please don't go away, I need you here. You know I lost our son. I can't lose you, not now. Please hold me, darling.'

'I know,' he murmured as he held her closer to him. 'Mamma told me all about it, darling. We will have all the time in the world to have more, my sweet. But if they believe Orlando – and why shouldn't they; he has many good connections in Sassari, and with your uncle a lawyer, they will pay good money to secure his papers – you know the saying: *Chie hat dinari cumparit innocente.* I have no such friends or money, so how will I prove my innocence if they believe it was self-defence?'

'Gabriella was here. She said, "He is alive," but I didn't realise it was you she was talking about. Oh Antoneddu, my love,' she said, the tears flowing again in her joy.

He put his uninjured arm around her and drew her to him again. She lay there, happy and contented to know he was alive.

'Hold me, Antoneddu, please hold me.'

He pulled her even closer to him and whispered to her. 'I will leave you a message in the top *pinneta* and we can meet at the pool. If I am looking after the sheep, it will be easy to come down to the lower meadows. But remember, Raffaella, only my family know I am alive. You will take care, won't you, darling?'

'I won't say anything, I promise, and I will leave you messages too in the old olive tree, like we used to when we were younger. Oh Antoneddu, I can't believe you're alive.' She sighed, and smiled through her tears.

They spent the night together, each one absorbed in the other. 'I will spend my life thanking my beloved Saint Raffaella and the Blessed Virgin Mary, for they must have interceded for you, Antoneddu.'

In the morning, when Raffaella awoke, she had the wonderful feeling that she had slept in her lover's arms, so when she turned to find he was not there she was frightened it had all been a dream. It was then that she noticed a small bunch of flowers on the bedside table. Her heart leapt with joy – Antoneddu was alive. She remembered he had said he was going to Pinta Niedda to help Cousin Gavinu's family. She fell back on her bed as hot tears rolled down her cheeks. He was alive; Luigi had not killed him. She would go to the little church at Bantadda and light a candle in thanks to her beloved saints and the Holy Mother.

It was a warm autumn morning, about a week after Orlando had left for Sassari, that a messenger arrived on horseback at Sos Lampidos with a letter from Zio Marco, saying he was worried that he had not heard from Orlando, and that he was expected in Sassari four days ago, as he was supposed to be in court to represent a client.

Zia Paola sent the young man to see Elena for something to eat and drink, while Ignazio looked after his horse. She went into the study to write a letter in reply.

> *Dear Marco,*
> *I am alarmed to learn that Orlando has not returned to Sassari, as he left on horseback last week and I had assumed that he was back with you.*
> *Please let me know if you have any further news.*
> *Your sister,*
> *Paola.*

When the messenger had eaten and the horse had been watered, the young man once more set off for Sassari.

Later, Zia Paola was in her vegetable garden tending the

vegetables and herbs. Her mind was far away, and she was concerned about Orlando.

She did not hear the Captain arrive, nor see him dismount.

As he walked toward her, Zia Paola became aware of him watching her as she bent to water the plants. She stood to see him. He went to her, and without a word, took the pail from her, and went to refill it from the large tank that collected all the water from the roof of the house and stables.

He returned the brimming pail to her and asked, 'What else needs watering?'

They stood and looked at each other, and then, blushing under his stare, she gave him a warm smile.

'Thank you, Captain,' she said, her smile broadening. 'Just this row of carrots, and I have finished for the day.'

He went forward and emptied the pail along the row where Zia Paola showed him. She watched him with pleasure as he set about his task.

When he had finished, she took the pail from him. 'Thank you, Captain. That is kind of you. Please come inside and we can have some refreshment. Wine, lemonade or coffee. Which would you prefer?'

He followed her into the house, where she showed him the sink and they washed their hands.

'Are you alone here? Do you have anyone to help you?' asked the Captain.

'I have Sergio, when he is not with the sheep and his wife Elena, who helps me in the house, and their son Ignazio. Now he is sixteen, he helps Sergio all the time. He is always around somewhere, coming from the most unexpected places. One minute he is here and then he has gone.'

The Captain smiled at Zia Paola.

'Please, Captain, sit down. Now, what would you prefer to drink?'

'Coffee, if it's not too much trouble,' he replied, looking at her.

She went through to the kitchen to find Elena to ask her for coffee and *amaretti* and then returned to sit with the Captain. Elena returned with the coffee and biscuits, and left Zia Paola to do the honours for the Captain.

'Tell me, what news do you bring us? How are the Carabineri who came here?' she asked as she poured the coffee and passed it to the Captain, at the same time pushing the plate of *amaretti* toward him. 'Help yourself.'

The Captain sipped his coffee and bit into one of the biscuits. 'Mmm… these are wonderful, did you make them?'

'Yes, I did,' she replied, a blush rising on her cheeks at the praise. 'You were going to tell me your news?'

The Captain sipped his coffee again, and replacing the cup on the saucer, turned to Zia Paola. 'One, the young Sard recruit, I'm afraid, is dead. When he was shot, his horse bolted and he fell, but his foot was caught in his stirrup. It seems he was dead before he fell, thank heavens.'

Zia Paola crossed herself and fingered her rosary which hung from her waistband. 'I am sorry to hear that. And the other man?'

'He was shot in the thigh. He has given a statement to my superior, but I haven't been able to see it yet. Unfortunately, an infection set in and he has also died. So it looks as if young Antonio is wanted for two counts of murder.'

'But that can't be right,' said Zia Paola with alarm. 'Antonio was already down on the ground before they even arrived.'

'Did you see that?' asked the Captain.

'He was lying there when I went to see Raffaella.'

'But did you see the shooting?'

'No, but Orlando told me,' she replied.

'Where is Orlando now?'

'He was supposed to go Sassari to see my brother, Marco, who is a lawyer there. But a messenger came here this morning from my brother; Orlando was supposed to return to him over a week ago, but he hasn't and I can't imagine what has happened to him. I am worried lest he has come to some harm.'

'We have not had news of any trouble in this area. Perhaps he stopped off to see friends.'

'I don't know, but it is unlike him to go missing. He was supposed to be in court with Marco.'

The Captain sighed, and toyed with his coffee cup. 'I would like to talk to him when he returns. Can you arrange that for me, please? In the meantime, I will listen out for any news about him.'

'Yes, of course, and thank you.'

'Is there any chance anyone else could have seen anything? What about Sergio or his wife, or maybe Ignazio?'

'I don't know, they haven't said anything.'

'Is Raffaella with you?'

'No, she went riding today; she said she wanted to be alone for a while. She will probably go and see Ignazio as she loves to be out with the sheep.'

'How is she?' asked the Captain.

'She is much better. She has taken on a new lease of life. She is putting on a brave face; I was so worried that Antonio's death would affect her. But she is much better. She seems to have rallied.'

Raffaella reined in her horse at the *pinneta* and dismounted. Antonio's horse was already grazing in the lush grass near the river.

He appeared from the ruin and went toward her, and enfolded her in his strong arms.

'You found the note, then.'

'Yes, in the crevice under the old olive tree, where we always used to leave them. Darling Antoneddu, it is wonderful to see you. Hold me tight.'

He held her closer, and she felt safe in his strong embrace. He pulled away and looked at her.

'I love you, Raffaella.'

She leant into him and sighed.

'It is so good to be in your arms again, to feel you close to me. Your arm is obviously better, and I have missed you so much, darling.'

He took her hand and led her to the river. 'Yes, it is completely healed, thanks to mamma. Come on now, let's go for a swim. It is so hot, and it will be refreshing,' he said, taking off his shirt.

Raffaella dropped her skirt and blouse, and catching her hair up in her combs, she headed for the river in her petticoat and camisole.

'You don't need those on. There is no one around, we can swim naked,' he said as he dropped his cotton trousers, and ran bare into the water. Raffaella stripped off her clothes and the two of them splashed and played in the river.

Raffaella watched as he swam, and saw his love turn to desire. She splashed out of the water, and up to the *pinneta*, where she flung herself on the ground. Antonio, concerned about her health, gently made love to her, and she loved the touch of his nakedness close to her after such a long time.

'I have missed you, missed making love to you, my darling. I want you so much, darling love of my life.' she whispered.

Antonio kissed her, and again his need for her welled up and he made love to Raffaella again.

Afterwards, as they were lying in each other's arms, he asked, 'How are Mamma and Babbu?'

'They are well. Little Salvatore is at a loss to know what has happened, with Marina gone and now you. Are you all right at Pinta Niedda? Are they looking after you?'

'Yes, of course.' He pulled her closer to him and kissed her with profound tenderness. 'I will be back down here in seven days. Will you come and find me so we can be together again? Dearest, love. I need to know I can see you and I can come down here from Pinta Niedda.'

'Of course. I will count the days, dearest one,' she said, smiling, and kissed him.

The night was closing in when Antonio rode with Raffaella to the bottom meadow, and kissing her again said, 'In seven days, my love.'

And with that, he disappeared into the gathering mists.

CHAPTER TWENTY-TWO

Back at the cave, it was a warm, languid day in late autumn when Orlando, armed with a gun, set off from the hideout in search of food. He was now well enough to help with the everyday routine. His plaster had been removed and now exercise was considered good for the weakened muscles.

A mist hung in the valleys, while on the mountains the sun shone, giving warmth to the morning. Orlando found it an eerie experience coming out of the mist into the bright sunshine. The delicate vapours hung in the valley, so it was possible to see the peaks of the neighbouring mountains rising above the wispy whiteness, into the welcome sunlight. It reminded him of Sos Lampidos, when the mists hung in the valley and the houses sat in the sunshine.

He spurred his horse on, eager to check all the traps he had set the previous day with Gavinu. Who with Gian, had tried to show him their various methods of trapping and hunting. Gavinu snared rabbits with horsehair snares and Gian showed Orlando the way to find the runs of the wild boar, but Orlando found the work demeaning.

He hated this crude outdoor living, and longed for the comfort of Sassari. He came to the first of his traps and found it empty. The second was the same. He felt despondent. But the third one proved to be more successful. The dead rabbit lay with a silken sheen of dew on its grey coat. He loosened the horsehair snare and reset it, then placed the stiffened animal in his saddlebag.

He was about to remount his horse when the tinkling of sheep bells distracted him. Through the mist came the grey, woolly creatures, bleating and calling to one another. Orlando eyed them as possible meat and felt in his saddlebag for his knife. When he turned round, he found himself looking down the wrong end of a shotgun, held by a young lad. The sun was shining straight into Orlando's eyes, making it difficult for him to make out the features of his captor, for most of his face was covered by a homespun scarf around his neck, and a *berrita* pulled down over the forehead, but Orlando couldn't help noticing the profound, dark eyes that had him fixed in their gaze.

A twig snapped and the gun was momentarily lowered as his captor turned in the direction of the sound. In that split second, Orlando seized the gun and grabbed his captor, with the blade of his knife against his throat. A terrified squeal came from the youngster, and Orlando reached up to pull off the *berrita* to inspect his catch more closely. A flood of raven black hair fell over the youth's shoulders and down to the waist. The dark eyes now looked frightened and at the same time appealing.

'But,' laughed Orlando, 'you're a girl! What on earth are you doing here?'

The young woman gave him no answer, for terror flowed from her eyes.

'Don't be frightened of me,' he said, realising he must look a fearsome sight with his long beard, unkempt hair and barbaric dress. He put his knife away and placed her gun on some nearby rocks. 'Please don't be afraid,' he repeated, 'I won't hurt you, I promise. Tell me what your name is?' he asked as he sat on a large rock and signalled to her to join him.

'Rosanna,' came her reply in a half-whisper, and she went to sit near him.

'Well, Rosanna, tell me why are you out here. Have you no brothers to help with the sheep?'

'My brothers are away fighting with the rebel Garibaldi and there is no one else to do the work.'

'What of your father, can he not help?'

'My father is dead. He died of the fever many years ago.'

'I'm sorry,' he replied. 'So you stay with your mother and do the work?'

'She is dead too.'

'I'm sorry for that too,' he said, feeling the inadequacy of his words.

'Please don't be. I have two aunts who look after me and my brothers, when they are home. We are luckier than most,' she replied. 'And what is your name?'

'Canu, Orlando Canu.'

'You are a stranger in this part of the world, as I have not seen or heard of you before.'

'Yes, I am.'

She drew back from him, the look of fear returning to her face.

'I won't hurt you. You have my word on that,' he said, still trying to reassure her.

'Where do you come from? Where do you live? Are you alone?' asked the young woman, looking around her.

'I come from Sos Lampidos near Bantadda, and I live up here in the mountains at the moment,' he said.

'In the mountains?' she repeated. Her eyes round with surprise. 'You must be one of the *banditti* that are said to be dangerous!' she exclaimed.

'None of us are dangerous, of that I can assure you. We are all victims of our own circumstances. People crossed by fate.'

'But you don't deny that you are one of the *banditti*.'

'No, I don't deny that,' he replied, with complete honesty.

'What do you mean, victims of your own circumstances?' she asked, again looking around as if she expected to see the whole bandit gang.

'I am alone, I promise you. That snap of the stick was one of the sheep as it walked away.'

Orlando shifted on the rock and turned to Rosanna. He told her his story. How he had been to university to study law. How he hoped his sister would marry a fellow student, who was rich, and in a position to look after her. How she wanted to marry the shepherd whom she had known all her life and, she said, loved since childhood. He told her of the terrible row, and how jealous his friend, Luigi was, and how Luigi had killed the shepherd, and that he himself, had killed the Carabineri who had killed his friend to avenge his death.

The young woman listened to Orlando as he poured out the whole story. He told her of Raffaella's illness. It was like confessing to an unknown priest, and he felt cleansed. When he finished the young woman turned to him and smiled.

'Surely your sister realised that you were trying to do what you thought to be best for her. Are you so sure she would have been happy with her shepherd lover?' It must be terrible living up there in the mountains like a hunted animal,' she said.

'It has taught me that I was right about Raffaella: she would never have been happy with Antonio,' replied Orlando.

He fell silent. He had told her the truth about the shooting. He hadn't needed to lie, as he had to Marina, and he wondered, why he found it so easy to talk to, this young girl. He looked at her long and hard. She had the same simple, gentle look as Vitoria. He was surprised by the peace of mind he found by simply looking at her, and into her deep eyes with their trusting appeal.

'If you come here every day,' she said, taking his hand, 'I'll bring you food and we can talk. Since my brothers went away, I have no one of my own age to talk to and I get lonely out here with only the sheep as company. When I return home, my aunts are no better, as all they talk about is the bread they have baked or the local scandals they have heard while washing in the river.'

He smiled at her. She rose from the rock where they sat, and went to a nearby bush, where she had dropped her *bertulla* to enable her to take a better aim at her captive. She collected the small, embroidered bag. Inside were her daily food ration and her ammunition. She opened the food package and they shared its meagre contents.

'My eldest brother, Umberto, is in Alessandria with the King's troop. He has always been interested in the army and left home at an early age to join. He used to come home with such tales of the life and what went on that he fired the imagination of my younger brother Sebastiano. He heard about a man called Garibaldi, who lives at Caperna in the north of the island, and went to join him. He has joined Garibaldi's red shirt brigade, and is fighting in Sicily for what they call the unification of the Italian states. It seems that Garibaldi wants to make the King of Sardinia the King of all Italy so we can prosper as one country rather than divided states as we are now. I don't understand it, but they say it will happen soon.'

Orlando laughed. 'How do you know so much about all this, Rosanna?'

'Oh, I listen to all that my brother tells me. Sebastiano is very special to me and we have always got on well together, so it is right that I know all he's doing. Occasionally I get a letter from him and he tells me what is happening and how they fare. It seems that some of the fighting has been hard, but he says they are sure of victory with Garibaldi leading them.'

'And Umberto, do you hear from him too?'

'Very seldom, he is a loner. He has a friend and they went to war together. Since my father died, Umberto has taken on the role of the head of the family, and Mamma used to lean on him for all the decisions.' She paused and smiled at Orlando. 'So you can see, life can be very lonely here too without friends and family.'

They passed the day with stories of their families, and laughed at the similarity of their aunts who now looked after them. They talked, little heeding the sun's warning of the closing day, as it started to dip behind the distant range of mountains. The sudden cold breeze of the fast-approaching night made them aware of the lateness of the hour.

It was Orlando who rose. 'I must go and check the rest of the snares while there is still enough light, otherwise there will be nothing for us to eat at the camp tonight. It will be dark before I return to the hideout and I'm not too sure of the way yet. I can't begin to tell you how wonderful it is to speak with you. I have not had any good company for ages. Thank you.'

They stood and faced each other, neither wanting to be the first to break the spell between them.

'Will you come tomorrow?' she asked.

'I will. God willing,' he replied, and with a quick stride, he caught his horse's bridle and mounted, then swinging the animal round to face Rosanna, taking in her striking beauty as best he could. Then, with a quick jibe into the animal's side, he disappeared into the thick macchia.

CHAPTER TWENTY-THREE

At Sos Lampidos, the sound of hoof beats broke into Raffaella's awareness, and she rose to look out of her bedroom window to see who had arrived at this early hour. She smiled to herself as she recognised the tall Captain as he dismounted and walked towards the house. He was carrying a posy of flowers and a small package for Zia Paola. He had been a regular visitor since the shooting, and Raffaella was sure the Captain was fond of her aunt. She smiled again – the thought pleased her; it would be wonderful for Zia Paola to have someone to care for her and fight her corner against Orlando.

True, Raffaella had difficulty in accepting the Captain to begin with, as he represented everything she hated about the Piedmontese and the Carabineri. But Zia Paola had seen something different in him, and she had decided to make an effort for her aunt.

She washed and dressed, and entered the large day room, the Captain and Zia Paola were sitting drinking coffee, and the aroma filled the room. The Captain rose as Raffaella came towards the table.

'You look so much better, Raffaella,' said her aunt. 'You have some colour in your cheeks at last. Look, the Captain has brought us some new coffee beans.'

Raffaella sighed and smiled at her aunt, and accepted the cup of coffee the Captain held out to her. She sat down and looked from her aunt to the Captain.

'How wonderful, thank you and good morning, Captain. It is good to see you here.'

'Good morning, Raffaella, and thank you for that. I must say I have been a bit concerned, as being Piedmontese, I thought you might hold it against me.'

Raffaella blushed, feeling that he must have understood what she had been thinking.

'You are different from all the others I have met. You are more like us, and you even speak our language,' she stammered.

'You are different now from when you first came to the island; when you came here looking for the Sannas' cousin Gavinu,' said Zia Paola, a tender smile on her face.

The Captain shifted in his chair.

'So tell us why you came to Sardinia?' asked Raffaella, as she helped herself to a small bread roll and honey.

'I was sent to Sardinia from my regiment in Piedmont. I stood up for a young recruit who missed roll call; I knew he had lost both his father and his brother in a campaign, and was planning to go to see his mother. My father is well known in military circles, and rather than cause a scandal, they sent me here, out of the way. At first I resented the move, but later I came to love the Sards and their land.'

'What changed your idea of us?

'I fought with them in Tchernaya.'

'Ah… I understand it was terrible,' said Zia Paola, lowering her eyes. 'Will you tell us about it?'

The Captain sighed, as he thought back to those days.

'The sickness outweighed the casualties; men died like flies from cholera, and others were just lost in the mud, it was heart-rending. I was billeted with a Sardinian regiment and one of them, Giuseppe Pisceddu, took me under his wing. His mother was the village herbalist and she sent him all sorts of herbal teas and tisanes, and insisted on him boiling all the water that he drank. She had noted that they always boiled the water at the local convent and they were never ill.'

'We always boiled all our water at the convent,' said Zia Paola with a smile.

'Were you there at the school?'

'Yes, my father put me there at the age of seven, after my mother died, as he couldn't look after me. Franco was already at the seminary taking his orders, and I was supposed to remain there, but when Raffaella's mother died, her father and my brother went to the mother superior and asked her to release me. I had not taken my vows, so they let me go, and I have looked after the family ever since. But sorry, please go on with your story.'

'Where was I?' he asked as he stared at Zia Paola.

'You were boiling water,' said Raffaella with a broad smile.

'Yes, Giuseppe's mother insisted that he took a kettle with him and promised to boil all his water. I believe it saved many of us from cholera and fever. I was lucky to have him. He taught me his language, as he came from near here, in the Logodoro. I used to argue with him that we were making great improvements for the island, but he soon showed me the error of my ideas. It was he who explained what the Piedmontese were doing to Sardinia and her lands. He opened my eyes to the rape of the countryside, and I became ashamed of my countrymen, who only seemed interested in the big profits that were to be made from stripping the land of all its wealth.'

Raffaella looked at the Captain. 'You do understand.'

'There is still a lot to learn. As you know, we are still on the lookout for outlaws. There are many more these days. The laws of Carlo Felice go against the laws of the Sardinian people, which they have held for centuries. The *Carta di Logu* had everything in it the Sards needed, but since the new laws more and more people fall foul of the law for no good reason.'

Zia Paola rose and went to see Elena to ask for some fresh coffee and some pastries.

'Please,' said the Captain when she returned, 'I should not keep you.'

'Nonsense, Captain, we don't often get company here, so you are always welcome. Please continue.'

The Captain sighed. 'The taxes from Piedmont are high; the landowners can't pay them and the government takes over their estates, leaving the land to return to nature or become barren once more, or absent Piedmontese landlords move in and strip the lands.

Since 1760, you have had to speak our language. One advantage is that islanders can now understand one another, but my fear is that you will lose your languages altogether, and as someone once said, whoever loses his language loses his soul. But the Sardinians are unique in the way they hold on to their traditions and culture, as they are held in the hearts and souls of all the people.'

A silence fell around the table, and Elena returned with a new pot of coffee and some *amaretti*.

'Now,' continued the Captain, 'I came to cheer you up, not to be thoughtful.'

They drank the coffee, and then the Captain rose. 'I thank you both for your hospitality, but I must get back to the camp or they will send out a search party for me.' And popped the last *amaretti* in his mouth.

'Thank you, Captain, for the flowers and the coffee, it was very generous of you,' Zia Paola said with a smile.

Raffaella remained seated, allowing Zia Paola to escort the Captain to the door.

'Thank you again, Signorina, for your company. I hope I will be able to return the compliment. Perhaps you could join me for a ride one day when you are not too busy, and if Raffaella would like to come too?'

'That would be lovely, thank you very much.'

He paused, searching her face, and then replacing his hat, he bid her good day.

'I think he likes you, Zia Paola,' said Raffaella when her aunt returned to the table.

'Nonsense, child,' she retorted, but she felt the blush rise on her cheek and Raffaella smiled to herself.

CHAPTER TWENTY-FOUR

At the cave, Orlando now volunteered every day to do the rounds of the snares, and as the weeks passed, he met Rosanna every day. On this particular morning, he woke with a new sense of urgency and a feeling of wellbeing.

'I'll do the snares, Gian,' he called in his usual bright manner as he collected his horse. 'It's good to be away from the camp for a while.'

Gian nodded as he lit his pipe and sat back by the fire. 'Be careful, that's all I ask.' He said smiling, and engulfed in a cloud of white tobacco smoke.

Orlando laughed and mounted his horse.

Outside the ravine, the world seemed bright and colourful. The autumn air was still warm, and the sound of bees as they buzzed in the trees and herbs collecting the late crop of nectar was a familiar one. For this was the season of the bitter honey, from the Corbezzo tree, and the thought pleased Orlando, for he preferred it to the sweeter variety made in the springtime. He picked his way through the now-familiar route of thick *macchia*, following the narrow goat and sheep tracks and listening for the sound of tinkling bells of the grazing sheep. He reined in his horse, dismounted, and walked to the small sheep-cropped meadow where he knew Rosanna would be waiting for him. The sight that met him took his breath away. There she was, seated on the outcrop of rock where she always waited, but instead of her usual breeches and jacket she wore her festive costume. The gold thread of the fine embroidery caught the sunlight, making it glint in its reflected brilliance against the dark background of the fine cloth. Her hair was covered by the formal headdress which was caught up with a silver clip at the side, thus covering her mouth as protection from the dreaded fever.

Orlando stood and drank in the scene. The effect made his legs weak and his head spin at the same time, stirring his blood from deep within him. Rosanna turned and looked up to where he was standing.

'Oh, Orlando, you have come. You are late and I thought perhaps you couldn't come today,' she cried, standing and holding her hands out in welcome. 'I have brought food for both of us so we can spend the whole time together, and I want to take you somewhere.'

He walked towards her, captivated by her spell. He unclipped her headdress, letting her long tresses of hair fall over her shoulders in a black cascade. Then gathering her in his arms, he held her as he searched the depths of her limpid eyes and tenderly kissed her. He felt her struggle for a moment under his searching kiss, and then relax. In that moment he knew she was his for the taking. But something held him back. He pulled away, and looked into the young, trusting face. Her eyes, wide with innocent expectation.

'What is the matter?' she asked. 'Do I not please you?'

'You please me very much, dear Rosanna, but...' He paused; his mind had become a jumbled array of flashes. He saw Vitoria come back to him, sweet and soft in the grass, just as she had been when he first made love to her. He saw her cold and emaciated, dressed in her wedding dress, lying in the bare coffin. He saw, in stilted visions, pictures of Antonio lying dead, Luigi beside him and Raffaella ghoul-like, with blood over her hands and face. Her happy laughter when with Antonio, contrasted with the stillness, and the deafening silence of her lying on her bed, ill from the delivery of her son. So much havoc wrought by one man. Here he was about to start all over again with Rosanna. He stared at the young woman in front of him with a blank expression as the colour drained from his sweating skin, while beads of sweat stood out on his forehead.

'Orlando, are you all right?' she asked, looking concerned. She put her hand in his and held it tight. 'Tell me, am I the first woman you have had any affection for since Vitoria?'

He was taken aback by the forthrightness of the question.

'I understand, dearest one, really I do. I will help you to live with her memory and find a new meaning of life with me. There will be no need for you to fight the fear, we can face that together.'

He smiled at her and put his arm round her tiny waist. 'I haven't eaten since last night. What do you have with you today, young lady?' he asked, happy to change the subject.

'You will have to come with me. I've got everything in a small clearing further up the mountain.'

Orlando mounted his horse and pulled Rosanna up in front of him so that he could put his arms round her slender waist. She took the reins and guided the horse where she wanted it to go. Orlando took in the landscape with its autumn shades. The seared brown grasses with the dark-green contrast of the myrtle bushes. The brittle sound of the snapping grasses as the horse picked its way through the hay-like stalks of vegetation. Clumps of trees gave shady relief for the short, stubby bushes that were trimmed by the wild animals and the grazing herds that frequented these remote areas.

At last, they came to a place where the grass was uncropped, and its stalky appearance looked out of place as it fuzzed the edges of the distant bushes. It was almost surrounded by an outcrop of rocks, and a large, twisted olive tree overhung part of the area, giving shade from a still-strong sun. His mind was in a whirl. He had loved Vitoria when she was young, and everything about her was familiar as they had grown up together, but Rosanna was a new experience. She was an independent girl, impetuous and in love with him. He found her irresistible, and knew he wanted her above all.

'Are you all right behind me?' asked Rosanna, aware of his silence. 'I found this place when I was young and whenever I want to be alone, I come here,' she said with pride. 'It is the home of some ancient Sardinian family from the mists of time, and I love it,' she said as she dismounted.

'Did you and your brothers used to play here?' asked Orlando as he too dropped down from the horse.

'No, never. They don't know of this place. I came here when

Babbu died, and then when Mamma died, and when my brothers went away. I always come here to read and when I want to be alone. That's why I want to share it with you.'

He pulled away, and again looked into the young, trusting face. Orlando took her in his arms and kissed her, gently at first and then with a passion. The two lay on the ground and Orlando slowly undressed her. The whiteness of her skin filled him with a mounting desire as she pulled his shirt from him. It was impossible to check their need for each other. Rosanna begged him to make love to her and he, only too willing to answer her call, took her in a long, sweet embrace.

They lay in each other's arms, all love spent, while tears ran down the young woman's cheeks.

'Answer me, Rosanna. Are you not happy?'

'You have opened my eyes to a new world, a world of loving and being loved; of wanting someone and being wanted by them.'

'But that is what love is, Rosanna. You have taught me that too. You have shown me the same feelings and that is something no one can take away. When I secure my freedom papers, we can be married, and we shall have the whole of our lives together in the knowledge of that love.'

'If only it was as simple as that.' she sighed.

'But we can. It may take a little time, Rosanna. My Zio Marco will get my papers through. Then we can be married and go to live at Sos Lampidos.'

'No, Orlando. I can't. I can't,' she cried in desperation. She looked up at him, held him and added, 'You see, Orlando, I'm already spoken for; therefore, I can't and never will be able to marry you.'

Her words fell like hammer blows on Orlando's ears and drove into his brain. He pulled himself free of her embrace, and sitting up, he looked at her in stunned disbelief, anger welling up inside him.

'Why didn't you tell me all this before you let me make love to you? Why are you here with me when you belong to another man?'

'Please, Orlando, please don't be cross with me. Hear me out at least,' she pleaded.

'I don't understand, Rosanna. Why do this to me? I have done you no harm.'

'Orlando, you must listen to me, I beg of you,' she said, sitting up and taking his hand. There was a pleading look on her face, the like of which he had seen once before, when Raffaella had pleaded with him to try to understand the love she had for Antonio.

'I'm listening,' he replied.

'Dominicu is a friend of my brother, Umberto, and the one that has gone to fight with him at Alessandria. They have been friends all their life and Umberto has promised me to his friend. Just as you did with Raffaella – now perhaps you can understand why I understood how you felt about your sister. But that was before I fell in love with you and knew the other side of the story. Now I know how Raffaella must have felt about being made to marry Luigi. I was quite prepared to marry Dominicu until I met and fell in love with you. You have changed all that. But I know where my duty lies, and I must marry Dominicu. I don't have the strength of character that Raffaella has. The one thing I wanted to know was what it was like to be held in the arms of a man I love and who loves me. I wanted to be made love to by someone I wanted to make love to me, rather than just a man chosen for me by my brother. If I did wrong, I am truly sorry. But I knew if I told you about Dominicu you would never have made love to me.'

Orlando looked at her through haze-filled eyes. He felt as if someone had taken his world and tipped it upside-down. He sat in stunned silence.

'Orlando, please don't be too hard on me. I love you with all my heart, but my brother will insist on me marrying Dominicu, and if he thought I had been with another man he would demand revenge.'

'Tell me, Rosanna. If I gain my freedom, would you come to Sos Lampidos with me. I would go back to law I could support you.'

'Our word has been given, and you know what that means, Orlando.'

He kissed her. 'I love you, Rosanna.' He held her close to him. Fate couldn't be so cruel as to bar him from the little happiness he had found. 'I'll travel to Sos Lampidos and see Zia Paola, for she will know what has happened by now. Tell me, when are you expected to marry Dominicu?'

'The wedding is set for the spring. By then my brothers hope to be home for a short time.'

'That gives me about five months, plenty of time for me to get my papers and have everything arranged at Sos Lampidos. If your brothers won't give us their blessing, we can elope together to the Continent. We can be married in Savoy, for they don't need written papers for people under twenty-five there.'

'I'm frightened, Orlando.'

'Don't be, my love. You must be strong, for I shall be away at Sos Lampidos for some time. Be patient and I promise I will come back for you.'

She clung to him, and under the darkening sky they made love to each other again, each experiencing the depth of the other's feelings.

CHAPTER TWENTY-FIVE

The autumn mists lingered in the valley below, while the sun shone above the vaporous clouds and lit up both Sos Lampidos and Punta Néula. Zia Paola was up as usual, and having done all her daily chores, she collected her basket to go and look for fungi. She loved this season of bounty, and there was so much to do to get ready for the winter. She looked up at the two houses, which stood proud in the sunlight.

She found her shawl and set off to the meadows to look for her favourite mushrooms, and wandered through the lower meadows which were still shrouded in a mist.

After several hours, and with a basket full of mushrooms, Zia Paola was about to turn toward home when the sound of hoof beats made her stop. The sun had now broken through the mist, and she caught sight of the rider.

The Captain, seeing Paola coming toward him, reined in his horse and dismounted. 'Good morning, Signorina.'

'Good day, Captain, and what brings you here today? Do you have any news for us?'

'Not at the moment, but I have received a parcel from my parents with many of my books, and I thought you might like to borrow one.'

'Why, that is thoughtful, thank you.'

The Captain put his hand into his inside coat pocket and pulled out a small book and handed it to her.

'Oh,' she cried, 'Italian poetry, what a treat, thank you.' A slight blush rose on her cheeks.

They walked together side by side. He took the basket from her and she carried the book he had given her; his horse following behind them as they discussed the poems. The path started to rise to Sos Lampidos and Zia Paola, looking up at the house, saw Raffaella waving, and she tripped. The Captain caught her with his free arm and held on to her.

'Are you all right?' he asked, still holding her and looking concerned.

'Yes, thank you, Captain,' she replied, but made no move away from him, and felt the flush on her cheeks spread across her face.

'Would you like to ride?' he asked, catching his horse and swinging it round so he could help her up into the saddle.

At Sos Lampidos Raffaella watched the scene below as the Captain led her aunt up the pathway to the farmstead. When they arrived in the yard the Captain reached up and helped Zia Paola down, and gave her the basket of fungi he had been carrying.

'Please come in, perhaps you would join us for some lunch.'

Zia Paola entered the house and took the mushrooms into the cold room where she would dry them later, then called to Elena and asked for lunch for an extra guest.

The Captain took his horse to the stable and Ignazio came forward to take the animal. The Captain studied the young lad, then searching in his saddlebag, he withdrew a knife and held it out to Ignazio.

'Tell me, do you like my new knife? I bought it the other day and would like your opinion on it.'

Ignazio, wide-eyed, came forward, his eyes fixed on the exquisite object. 'It is one of the finest I have seen. I am saving for one, but I will not be able to afford one so fine, Captain. Did you buy it in Pattada?'

The Captain nodded and handed him the knife. 'I would be happy to give someone such a knife if he had some information.'

'What sort of information?' asked the young lad, looking from side to side.

'Information that only that man could give me,' replied the Captain.

'I don't know anyone, nor do I have such information,' he replied, looking to see if anyone else was around.

'Oh, but I think you do,' said the Captain, watching Ignazio intently.

'I am sorry, Captain, but I know of no one who can help you; and there is always the fear of reprisal.'

'If someone has that information, there is no possibility that anyone would know where it came from, I can give you my word on that.'

'What makes you think I have such information?'

'How did Sergio know to go and get the donkey if you didn't tell him?'

The young lad hesitated for a moment, and then turning away, said, 'I am sorry, but I can't help you.'

The Captain took the knife back from Ignazio and returned it to his saddlebag. 'If you should change your mind, let me know,' he said as he turned to go out of the stable.

Ignazio watched the Captain go into the house, and touched his *Mal Occhio* several times before returning to his work.

Lunch proved genial, and there was much talk about Sardinia and her future, of poetry, and about Orlando.

Later that evening, after a relaxing time in good company, the Captain collected his horse and said goodbye to Raffaella and Zia Paola. He turned down the road to the lower meadow. The light was beginning to fade. He was deep in thought. His feelings for Zia Paola were growing; he found her captivating, and he wondered if there was any chance she had any feelings for him.

At that moment he became aware of someone calling him. He looked round and saw Ignazio under a clump of cork trees. He was signalling to him. The Captain reined in his horse and turned to the young lad, who went deeper into the grove.

'Captain, good evening.'

'Good evening Ignazio. What can I do for you?' he said, dismounting and walking toward the young man.

Ignazio stared at the Captain for a moment, and then, looking around him, beckoned him to follow.

The Captain, leading his horse, followed as he was bid and

came to rest under the shade of a huge oak tree. 'Can I help you?' he asked.

'May I see the knife again? Do you still have it?' asked Ignazio, his eyes large and round.

'I do,' replied the Captain as he put his hand inside his saddlebag and drew out the beautiful object. The Captain opened his hand and showed it to Ignazio again, who eyed it with love. It was carved horn with a decorated blade. He would be the envy of everyone with such a knife.

'What was it you wanted to know of someone?' he asked, not taking his eyes off the object of his desire.

'Come now, Ignazio, I believe you saw what happened that morning, and for whatever reason, someone has sworn you to secrecy.'

The boy looked frightened, but the sight of the knife was such a temptation. 'I was there. Father had forgotten his knife and I went back to find it. I saw Signore Orlando and the Dottore Luigi at Sos Lampidos.'

He broke off, turning around again to see if anyone was listening.

'Go on,' said the Captain, putting the knife back in his bag again.

'I saw Signore Antonio climb down from Signorina Raffaella's bedroom. I saw Orlando go forward and he knocked him to the ground. I saw Antonio's look of surprise; he was not expecting anything from his friend. But when Antonio stood up, Orlando pushed him toward the ravine, and until that moment, I swear Antonio thought his friend was joking.'

Ignazio paused and looked around him again, and then continued. 'When he realised that Orlando was serious, he took out his pistol and fired it into the air. It was obvious it was a warning shot.' Ignazio drew in his breath and continued. 'But the Dottore Luigi, he was intent in what he did and shot at Antonio. Thank the Lord, he was not a good shot, but Antonio went down. Raffaella was with him, she was covered in his blood. Then the Carabineri arrived; after a short discussion the older one aimed at the dottore but Luigi shot at him, wounding him in his thigh. The young recruit then fired at Luigi and he fell to the ground.

Orlando shot the young recruit in the chest. His horse reared up and dragged him, with the other officer following him. He was swearing oaths of vengeance on Orlando.'

'Whatever happened then?' asked the Captain.

'After they had gone, Signorina Paola took Raffaella and Orlando into the house. I heard Orlando say it was all Antonio's fault, that he, Orlando, was innocent; but I knew better, and I raced down to see my father and he returned with the donkey. I was too frightened to do anything, and Father swore me to keep it a secret.'

'So you were the only one to witness the whole thing?' said the Captain.

'Yes, sir, but if Signore Orlando finds out he will dismiss my family, or worse. If you say it was me, I will deny everything. I am afraid, Captain.'

'I understand. You have earned the knife, but if you can wait a while, it would be better, for if anyone finds you with it, they will want to know how you earned it. Meanwhile, I have this for you.'

He searched in his pocket and brought out a small working knife used by the shepherds every day. 'I give you my word, Ignazio, as an officer: I will give you the other knife when I have cleared Antonio's name, and Orlando is brought to justice.'

Ignazio took the small knife. 'I believe you, Captain, and thank you.'

The two men shook hands, and the young lad went into the wooded area. The Captain remounted his horse and turned to look for Ignazio, but he had disappeared into the gloom.

The Captain turned his horse and made his way back to the camp. He went over what young Ignazio had said. There must be some record at the camp. When the older Officer man came back there must be some report, and his account of what happened. He decided he would look at the notes.

With that, he spurred his horse on to the camp.

CHAPTER TWENTY-SIX

It was well after dark when Orlando returned to the ravine hideout. Across his saddle was slung a sheep given to him by Rosanna for all his friends whom she had not yet met. Some of the band gathered round him, eager to see what was new, while others, engrossed in the ancient game of *Morra*, were unaware of his return. Shouts of delight went up as one of the men beat his opponents, in the intriguing game where they have to guess the total number of fingers each man has shown.

Orlando dismounted and pulled the carcass to the ground. Strong hands came forward to take the magnificent beast.

'You have done well, Orlando; that will make good eating to be sure,' said one.

A voice boomed across the ravine, stopping Orlando in his tracks.

'Where in creation's name have you been?' demanded Gian. 'Were you followed here? Have you seen anyone on the mountainside? Any Carabineri?'

Orlando was surprised by the barrage of questions. 'No, I've not seen the Carabineri and I wasn't followed. Why do you ask?' he replied, a little nettled by the interrogation.

'The Carabineri have been sweeping across this area and we can't afford to have them find us.'

Orlando bent down to pick up the sheep to carry it inside the cave.

'Where the hell did you steal that from? Not from near here, I hope?' demanded Gian.

'No, it came from the other valley. I did not steal it either. Where is Marina?'

'She and Gavinu have left. They have gone back to Punta

Néula. They left this morning. It seems that Marina is pregnant and doesn't want her child born in the mountains. The winter up here is no place for a woman at the best of times, and certainly not a pregnant one. We have been lucky with the weather so far; it has been warm, but the snow will come. It always does. Gavinu has gone with her and hopes to work with Salvatore for his keep. But tell me, if you didn't steal that sheep, where did you get it from? I don't want some irate shepherd calling out the local *vendetta* on sheep-rustling.'

'Suffice to say that it was given to me,' snapped Orlando. He was taken aback by the news of Gavinu and Marina's departure to Punta Néula. He had no idea that Marina was expecting a child, but then, he couldn't even see that in his own sister. They hadn't said anything about returning home either. It was imperative that he returned to Sos Lampidos to see Zia Paola at once.

'Gian, I have to talk to you,' he said, grabbing the man's arm. 'I want to leave as well. I want to return to Sos Lampidos to see if Zio Marco has managed to secure my freedom papers. Over the past weeks I have been meeting a young girl from the other valley and now I want to marry her. But I can't until I'm a free man and have title to my lands again.'

Gian looked at him for a moment and said nothing, eyeing the young man up and down. Then he replied, in his usual direct way, 'I can understand you wanting her. She is indeed beautiful.'

Orlando's jaw fell open. 'How do you know?' he asked, dumbfounded.

'My dear Orlando, you have been out regularly for weeks. Always eager to do the round of traps, never letting anyone else go. I wanted to know what else was keeping you. When I discovered it was a young girl, I left you alone,' he said with a large smile.

'Who on earth did you think I was seeing?'

'Come now,' replied Gian, putting an arresting hand on Orlando's shoulder, 'I knew nothing about you when I found you. I brought you here to my hideout without knowing who you were. True, Marina and Gavinu vouched for your character. But in your fevered ravings, you called out about death and shootings. I needed to be sure you were not off, perhaps, to avenge some killing, or inform the Carabineri of our whereabouts.' He put up his hand to stop any abuse from Orlando. 'Let me finish. I have not just myself to protect here, but many others; those here now and, those that will come in years to come, as more of our people fall foul of the new laws that will be imposed when all the Italian states are united. For all I know you might have come from Salvatore and Gabriella to try to send their daughter home.' Then, placing his hand on Orlando's shoulder again, he added, 'My friend, when do you want to leave?'

Orlando smiled at Gian. 'You're right, and I'm sorry. I would like to go tomorrow at first light, if that's possible. I should be back in Bantadda by late afternoon. As to the horse, I will send it back with Gavinu when he returns.'

'If I don't see you in the morning, Orlando, *bae in bon ora*, may God go with you,' he said, shaking Orlando's hand.

'Thank you, Gian, for everything. I shan't forget you, and remember, if you are ever in the Bantadda area, you will always be welcome at Sos Lampidos. There is one last thing I would ask of you. If you followed me, you know where I go, so will you go to the meeting place and tell Rosanna that I have gone to Sos Lampidos and will be back as soon as I'm free? Gian, if ever she needs help and comes to you, will you send word to me so I can come at once? Will you promise me that?'

'You have my word on it, I promise, my friend. I shall give her instructions on how to contact us.'

That night, the men sat around the fire. The smell of roasting lamb on the spit whetted their appetites and it wasn't long before they were sitting in the cave, eating the prize and drinking large amounts of wine. Soon bellies were full and the noisy chatter turned into a steady murmur, till it died to a contented deep breathing interspersed by the occasional loud snore. Good food and the warm fire had worked their usual magic.

The following day, Orlando reined in his horse and looked

across the spur of the hill to the farmland below. It was almost dark, and he would soon be able to cross the river and climb the path to Sos Lampidos under the cloak of night. He had rested at the secret pool since mid-afternoon, where he bathed and washed his clothes, leaving them to dry in fading autumn sun, wrapping himself in his horse blanket until he was ready to move on.

He made his way up the long pathway. Once at the top, he led his horse to the stable where he found food and water for the animal. Raffaella's horse stood there with Zia Paola's, and he could hear their contented ruminating, and smell the warmth of their bodies, which somehow comforted him. He took the saddle and hung it on the rack and then made his way towards the house. His father's old dog growled and barked at the intruder, and then recognising him, came whimpering toward him in greeting.

'Down, boy,' he whispered, holding the dog back and fondling him roughly. He patted his hand against his thigh to call the dog with him as he went toward the house.

He crossed the yard and let himself in via the kitchen door. He searched for a candle, which he lit. Familiar objects came into view as he swept the room with the flickering light. Home comforts, so often taken for granted, now seemed all-comforting, all-important in their neat places. He walked through the house, savouring the familiarity of the rooms and enjoying the smell of homemade beeswax polish. The feeling of childhood security swept over him, and he felt at peace.

He made his way to the stairs and climbed them as quietly as possible. On reaching his aunt's room, he paused and listened at the door to hear her regular breathing. He tapped on the door and there was a low moan and a rustle of cotton bedding.

'Who is it? Is that you, Sergio?' came the voice of his aunt.

'Zia Paola, it's me, Orlando. Can I come in?'

There was a gasp of astonishment and a cry of surprise. 'Come in, come in,' she called, the sound of relief in her voice.

He opened the door and went in to greet his aunt. She beckoned to him to come and sit by her bed and patted a place for him next to her. Putting his candle on the bedside table, he sat where he was bid, first bending to kiss her on the cheek.

She looked well. Her hair was long and in two thick plaits, giving her an angelic look in the candlelight. Orlando took his aunt's hand in his; it felt warm to his touch.

' But where on earth have you been? I sent Sergio out to look for you, but with no luck. Zio Marco came here about two weeks ago. He has your freedom papers. His testimony, together with the good words from your professor at the university and a large payment, has freed you of murder and upheld the plea of self-defence. You have been bound over and must keep the peace for a year, so you can stay here at Sos Lampidos or go to Sassari with Zio Marco has been worried, and has sent people out looking for you. You were supposed to be at court with him for an important case.'

'I know,' said Orlando, and began to tell his aunt all that had happened over the past weeks.

'Zia Paola, I have met such a wonderful girl.' He told her about Rosanna, their meeting, and the way in which she cared for him. How they had fallen in love. 'We want to marry and come here to Sos Lampidos to live. Now that I'm a free man, I can ask her brother for her hand. She is from a farming family and we can work together to build this place back up, as Mamma once helped Babbu. You will be looked after too, and not have any of the hard work anymore.'

'That's wonderful news, Orlando. I'm so pleased for you. She has changed you. You are more the Orlando of your childhood. I'm afraid Sassari did you no good, not with the company you kept. Luigi was a bad influence on you. No doubt the time living in the mountains has taught you many things, and how to fend for yourself. What about your law practice?'

'When Rosanna comes here, we will fill our time with looking after the farm and all the new stock I intend to buy. I intend to go to Sassari to practice law. Rosanna is more than capable of running the farm with Sergio.'

'Oh, still selfish, I see, Orlando. People here know you are a free man as it has already been read in all the surrounding churches. You have a chance now to make amends by coming back.'

He ignored his aunt's remark and squeezed her hand.

'You must make peace with Raffaella,' she whispered.

'How is she? Is she all right now?'

'She is still grieving for Antonio. I think you will have to give her time, Orlando.'

'I will, I'll give her all the time she needs and I will help her. I hope to go back after Christmas. I can go back over the mountains and collect Rosanna, and she will be company for Raffaella.'

His aunt smiled at him. 'Did you know Marina and Gavinu are home too? Did you travel with them?'

'No, they left earlier. Marina is expecting a child and she wanted to be with Gabriella when it's born.'

'It will be like old times,' mumbled his aunt as she sank back on her pillows. 'Gabriella and Salvatore will come here again now you are back, for they know you are innocent of the reported crime.'

In his room, Orlando opened the shutters and looked out across the wide expanse of darkness. The stars hung in the black sky and the air was full of the night time sounds of nature. He looked across to Punta Néula. Sure enough, the lights were shining from the small farmhouse, perched as it was on the other side of the ravine. It was difficult to make out which were its lights, and which were the low stars on that clear night. He thought about Marina and Gavinu, and if he could go and see them now that he was home. Would they believe his story, or had Gabriella and Salvatore come to the right conclusion? Was that the reason they had not been over to see Zia Paola? He would ride to Sassari tomorrow to see his Zio Marco for help and his protection.

That night, in the comfort of his bed, Orlando found peace for the first time in months. The knowledge that he was now a free man again, and the oppressive burden of being hunted like an animal being lifted from his mind, allowed him to relax. Now he could ask Rosanna to come to be his bride. He had lands to offer her, and could free her from her arranged marriage. Now he could find some of the happiness that he craved so much, and that up to now had been denied him. Surely the gods would, at last, smile on him and his new venture.

In her room, Raffaella lay awake. She had heard her father's dog bark, and had looked out of the window to see Orlando cross the yard. With Orlando back, it was going to be difficult to get away. She was worried, too, that she had not heard from Antoneddu for weeks now. She had ridden up to the pool, as they had planned, but he wasn't there. She had searched the places where they left notes to each other, but she had not found anything.

She had been to Punta Néula to see Gabriella, but she hadn't heard anything either, and they were at their wits' end. It was not like Antoneddu not to contact them. She had toyed with the idea of riding over to Pinta Niedda, but knew the place was being watched as the Carabineri searched for Gavinu.

She would have to confide in someone and ask for help. She decided she would ask the Captain. Perhaps he could help.

Orlando left for Sassari the following morning to see his Zio Marco, much to the relief of the household.

Raffaella went to find Zia Paola, who was busy in the garden.

'Did Orlando tell you where he has been?'

'Yes.' And her aunt told Raffaella what Orlando had told her. 'But he has gone to Sassari, which is good. Tell me, Raffaella, you saw Gabriella yesterday – how is she? I haven't seen her in ages and I want to know if she is all right. How is she coping?'

Raffaella took her aunt's hand, her tears welled up and ran down her cheeks.

'Raffaella, whatever is the matter?' said her aunt, putting her arm round the young girl.

'Zia Paola, I am sorry I haven't told you before, but Gabriella and Antoneddu made me promise not to say anything as they are afraid.'

'Antonio? What do you mean, child?'

'Luigi did not kill Antoneddu, he is alive and I have seen him. He came to my room not long after the accident when I was in bed, and we met up at the pool over two weeks ago. He told me to see him in seven days, but he hasn't been back. Oh, Zia Paola, I am so worried, and so is Gabriella.'

'But why couldn't you tell me he was alive?'

'Orlando has sworn it was Antoneddu who fired the first shot, and they are all afraid that if Orland knew Antoneddu was still alive he would be in danger.'

'But you don't think that Orlando would harm Antonio! No, Raffaella, that is not possible.'

'He tried to push him over the ravine, and they are frightened, Zia Paola, really frightened.'

Her aunt sighed, 'I will go and see Gabriella today and reassure her, and I promise to keep your secret, but my dear, I am so happy for you.'

Raffaella kissed her aunt and wiped her tears. 'Thank you, please don't be cross about them not telling you, but they thought it would be easier than you having to lie to Orlando.'

Her aunt laughed. 'They are probably right.'

The Captain arrived, and was unaware of Orlando's return and subsequent departure to Sassari, but Zia Paola had gone over to Punta Néula to see Gabriella, and to take her some produce. He found Raffaella in the house where she was writing another letter to Antoneddu.

'Good day, Raffaella. I hope I find you well. Is your aunt here?

'I'm afraid you have missed her, she has ridden over to Punta Néula to see the Sannas.'

'Ah… then would you do me the honour of walking with me?' asked the Captain.

'Thank you,' said Raffaella. 'That would be wonderful.'

They walked down the long track towards the river. The air was fresh and a gentle breeze blew from the mountains. The sheep bells sounded across the valley, and Raffaella sighed.

'My, that was heartfelt,' said the Captain, looking at her.

'Raffaella, you said that I was different from the other Piedmontese. I want you to know I am very fond of your Zia Paola, and I would like to share my life with her, but I would not like to do anything that could bring about a rift between the two of you.'

'Have you told her how you feel?'

'No, I needed to know your reaction first.'

'Captain, for my part, I wish you the best in the world. I can think of nothing better. She is such a wonderful person. You might have a fight with Orlando – he has returned, but gone to Sassari to see Zio Marco – but as far as I am concerned I am very happy. You will have to go carefully with her; remember she is still a nun in her mind. She will find the fact that you care for her difficult, but I will help, I promise. You should know that people here believe that with a kiss, the soul passes from one to another in the breath. So if she is a bit reticent, you will know why.'

The Captain turned to Raffaella and smiled. 'Thank you. I appreciate that, and if there is anything I can do for you, you only have to name it.'

'No one can help me. Orlando has laid the blame of the shooting at Antoneddu's feet. I know it was Luigi who shot at Antoneddu; if it had been the other way round Luigi would have been dead, as Antoneddu is such a good shot.'

The Captain looked at the young girl. 'You said *is* a good shot,' he said, slowing watching her every move.

Raffaella blushed at his gaze, and drew in her breath.

'Don't worry, your secret is safe with me. I promise. I am so pleased for you, Raffaella. Know you can always confide in me. Does your aunt know?'

Raffaella looked at him, and burst into tears.

'My dear girl, whatever is the matter?' said the Captain, concerned.

'The Sannas were afraid Zia Paola would find it difficult to lie to Orlando that Antoneddu didn't die in the accident. I told her today as I was sworn to secrecy, as they are all afraid that Orlando will find out and there will be trouble. Antoneddu was knocked unconscious and received a small shoulder wound. Gabriella nursed him after Sergio took him back and they swore him to secrecy. Ignazio had seen it all and heard Orlando blame Antoneddu. I saw him once after he had left; he came to see me at Sos Lampidos. He went to Pinta Niedda to help the family as Gavinu was away in the mountains, and then we met up at the *pinneta* and said he would see me at the pool in seven days. I went there, but he wasn't there and I haven't heard from him since. I have been everywhere looking for him and Gabriella hasn't heard anything either. He hasn't left me any notes in our secret places, and he hasn't been to the pool. I'm desperate to know where he is.'

'Has no one seen him?'

'No, and I am so worried. I'm at my wits' end.' She sobbed.

The Captain put his arm around Raffaella. 'I will put out a word for you.'

Raffaella turned to him and said, 'Thank you. I feel we are so lucky to have someone like you.'

That night the weather broke and winds came in from the north. Snow would cover the mountains and the land would be impassable. Raffaella wept bitterly, for she knew, that it would be impossible for anyone to survive out in the mountains for any length of time in this weather, and her fear for Antoneddu's safety clasped her heart.

CHAPTER TWENTY-SEVEN

At Punta Néula, preparations for Christmas were well underway. The weeks since Marina and Gavinu's return had slipped by, lulling them into a sense of security so all the family went about its daily business with little thought of the Carabineri.

Gabriella and Salvatore were delighted to see their daughter and new son-in-law, and thrilled at the prospect of becoming grandparents in the New Year.

Gavinu, who had been back to Pinta Niedda, gave the Sannas news of Antonio when no one was around. He had gone to see to the sheep on the higher slopes, but had not returned. They had all searched for him, but there was no trace of him. Gabriella begged them all not to say anything to Raffaella as she was frightened it would make her ill again, but she found time to ride over to see Zia Paola and tell her the news.

Marina found plenty to occupy her, what with making clothes for the new arrival and helping Gabriella with the everyday chores. She also undertook the job of teaching her young brother to read and write as best she could.

Gavinu and Salvatore spent most of the days away from the farmstead, working with the sheep in the lower meadows. They had been moved to the further valley, for the exceptionally dry autumn and winter had resulted in flash fires near the homestead. The great, black scars stood out against the distant green vegetation, so far untouched by the fires. The olive trees, some brown and burnt, stood like gallows between the ones that had been fortunate enough to only be singed, depending on the direction of the wind that fanned the flames at the time. It had all happened so quickly, there had been nothing they could do to rescue some of the livestock or avert the fire. Salvatore and Gabriella had watched helplessly as it roared and crackled its way through the valley, jumping walls and fields and licking at the highest trees, leaving the black, arid waste land with the occasional green patch in the middle where, for some reason, it hadn't burnt. But they all knew from previous fires that come the spring, there would be a newness of growth and a lushness that would be rewarding in its beauty, and the bonus of an increase in the milk yield of the herd.

One evening, about ten days before Christmas, Marina crossed the yard to the storeroom to collect one of the cheeses she had made on her return from the mountains. A light fall of snow covered the ground, and the strong moonlight caught the continuously falling flakes, making them glisten in its silver luminescence. She pushed opened the storeroom door and held up her lantern to put it on a hook. Marina reached up to take the cheese from its usual place, when she became aware of someone behind her. Before she could cry out a strong hand fell across her mouth, stopping any sound she might try to make. Terror seized her, and she felt her heart racing as the fear coursed through her veins.

'Don't cry out,' said a deep voice behind her. 'If you do, I shall have to hurt you and I don't want to do that. Now listen to me carefully. I have been watching your husband for the past weeks, and seeing you together, I'm sure you want him at home with you for Christmas and when your baby is born, don't you?'

He paused, and Marina nodded.

'Now, before you cry out, give me a chance to speak. If not, I will turn your husband over to the Carabineri. Do you understand?'

She nodded again, but her heart sank. She felt the man behind release his hand from her mouth, at the same time lessening the grip he had on her arm. She swung around, turning on her captor.

'Who the hell are you? And what do you want?' she snarled, looking at the intruder, whose features were caught by the lamplight. Her face registered surprise at seeing a young man in his early twenties. She had expected him to be older, judging by his voice and strength.

'My name is Franco Melli, brother of Giovanni Melli.' He paused. 'Doesn't that name mean anything to you?' he asked.

'No,' she replied, wracking her brain for the connection. 'No, should it?'

'You have been in the company of Orlando Canu for some time now. Did he never mention that name?'

Marina shook her head.

'Giovanni Melli was the man Orlando Canu gunned down in August,' he said.

Marina gasped. 'But what do you want of me, then? I had nothing to do with that affair, and neither did Gavinu. We were miles away from here at the time. I understood your brother killed Luigi Atzeni; if that is so, he has paid for it with his own life. Why should I offer help to the Carabineri? It was they who ambushed my husband's family at Don diVenti's and shot his brother Ugo. We owe you nothing,' she snapped.

'I'm not from the Carabineri, and yes, it was my brother who killed Luigi.

There were two Carabineri there that morning: one a Piedmontese officer and the other a young Sard recruit, my brother Giovanni. They found Antonio dead on the ground and told Luigi and Orlando to surrender their arms, but it seems Luigi was frightened and shot and wounded the officer badly, so badly that he died of his injuries. That is why it took them so long to find out where it happened, for they had to wait until the men at the camp reported their crew missing. My brother killed Luigi in revenge for his officer, and in self-defence. It was Orlando who killed my brother, and his horse dragged his body to Bantadda. Even my mother wouldn't have recognised him when they found him.'

'Oh please, don't go on,' begged Marina, 'just tell me what all this has to do with Gavinu and me.'

'It's simple. Antonio's death was not avenged by Orlando as he claims, but by a raw Sard recruit, who paid for it with his own life at Orlando's hand. All I want is Orlando's whereabouts so I can avenge my brother's death.'

'You can find that out without me. He has received his freedom papers from the courts in Sassari, so he will be home before too long. Have you been to Sos Lampidos?'

'I don't want to gun him down on his own ground, not if he has papers.' He paused and looked at her. 'Tell me, Marina, do you think it is fair that a man like Orlando should go free, just because he has friends in the right places who have paid out large bribes for his freedom, when your husband has to watch over his shoulder night and day, living like a hunted animal? Do you want your son forever watching over his shoulder in case the baby son of a Sard recruit takes it in his head to avenge his father's death? Is that what you want?'

'But Gavinu had nothing to do with all this. You said it was Orlando who killed your brother. Why do you want to drag us into it?'

'I know there is a gang of bandits living in the mountains, and that you lived with them for a while. If you don't give me Orlando's whereabouts I shall swear it was Gavinu who was involved, and with his record with Don diVenti he will be shot on sight. Now, are you going to help me?'

'And what is in it for us?' she snapped.

'I have papers which I found among my brother's things that state that it was an ambush that killed your husband's brother. That Don diVenti paid good money to the Carabineri for their help. With these papers I can set your husband free to live here without any trouble. All you have to do is tell me where Orlando is, and if you tell me where the hideout is in the mountains I promise you I will leave all the others untouched. I will also see about freedom papers for them as well. As a fellow Sard, you must know the importance of revenge.'

At that moment the two of them were interrupted by Salvatore calling from the house. 'Marina, are you all right? Do you need any help?'

'No, Babbu, I'm fine. I'm just trying to find a good cheese,' she called, her heart again leaping with fear.

247

The young man grabbed her arm. 'I also know there are rumours that your brother is still alive. What do you know about that?'

'That's not possible. I would know if Antonio was alive.'

'And Raffaella, have you seen her?'

'No, she is not well and Zia Paola won't let us see her. But how can you do all this?'

'I have a job in the court office, that's all you need to know, and I am a patriotic Sard. Tell no one I've been here, and think about what I've said. I'll give you a couple of days to think about it, but think hard before you answer. Remember, your whole future and that of your husband and child lie in your answer.'

'Where shall I contact you?' she asked.

'I'll contact you. One more promise. No one will ever know it was you that gave me the information. Do you understand?'

She nodded.

He reached up, and took the lantern from the hook and gave it to Marina. 'Now tell me which one of these cheeses you want. A girl in your condition shouldn't be reaching up and carrying things like that.'

She stared at the young man, and then held up the lamp he had given her. 'That one,' she said, pointing to a large, ripe one in the far corner.

He took it down. 'I loved my brother, just as you loved Antonio. But my brother was married with a baby son, and all they have is a small piece of land to live off with a small pension, and the soul-destroying knowledge that his killer is still alive. All I ask is for the sweetness of revenge. I also love my country, and I will do anything to help my fellow men who become more and more oppressed by the new laws from Piedmont.'

Marina said nothing, but took the cheese from the young man and made her way back across the snow-covered yard to the house.

That evening the young man's words kept going round and

round in her head, fogging her mind. So feigning a headache, she left the table and went to bed early.

She lay thinking about those far-off days when she and Antoneddu had played together, shared everything, and they had all been so happy. When Vitoria was alive, and Orlando and Raffaella were always at Punta Néula, or they were at Sos Lampidos. Everything had changed so much after her sister's death, and when Orlando had gone to Sassari.

Gavinu came to bed at last, worried about Marina's health. He placed his lamp on the bedside table.

'What is the matter, my love? You have been miles away all evening. You look so pale. Do you feel all right?'

She forced a smile to try to reassure him that all was well. 'I'm a little tired. The baby is weighing heavily on me at the moment. I shall be all right after a good night's sleep.'

Gavinu blew out the lamp, climbed into bed next to her, and drew her close to him.

'Are you happy, dearest Gavinu?' she asked in a low whisper.

'Of course I am. Why shouldn't I be?' he said, drawing her even closer.

He was soon asleep, oblivious to the racing in her mind. The peaceful rhythm of his breathing comforted Marina as she lay in his arms.

Orlando had lied about his involvement when he told her what had happened. But Orlando was a lifelong friend. He hadn't shot Luigi as he said, but a young Sardinian recruit whose brother was now bent on revenge. The law of the mountain people was a savage, wild justice, and Gavinu would be a free man. But if she told of the hideout she would be breaking the silent code of *Omerta*. She would be no better than Orlando. Her baby stirred in her, and she turned over to find the solace of sleep.

CHAPTER TWENTY-EIGHT

With a brief break in the weather the Captain arrived at Sos Lampidos in the late morning, and left his horse with Ignazio and assured him everything was going well.

He entered the house, and found Zia Paola balancing on a stepladder as Sergio and Elena passed her the various ornaments she was placing on the festive tree.

'Can I do that for you?' he asked, going forward to help.

'Oh Captain, how kind; no, I have finished. Would you like something to drink? I am in need of a coffee.'

She climbed down the steps and Sergio, mumbling a greeting to the Captain, took them away, while Elena collected the boxes that had contained all the decorations, and left the room.

'You are not in uniform, does that mean you are free?' said Zia Paola.

'I have a few days off and I thought I would come and see you.'

'Can you stay for lunch?'

'That would be lovely. Thank you.'

Zia Paola went to make the coffee and told Elena the Captain would be staying for lunch, and that they would be eating in the dining room.

When she returned, the Captain came forward and took the tray from Zia Paola and she went to sit next to him at the table.

'Is everything all right here at Sos Lampidos? Is Raffaella all right? And you? How are you coping?

'Yes, I am fine, but I am worried about Antonio. Raffaella said that you knew he was alive.'

'Yes, the poor girl let it slip. Have you still not had any news?'

'No, they met at the *pinneta*, but she has heard nothing for the past three weeks. Gabriella came over yesterday to say that Gavinu had been back to Pinta Niedda to ask about Antonio, but they haven't seen him for three weeks. When he first went missing, they sent out a search party for him, but they have found nothing. Captain, I am worried, and I haven't said anything to Raffaella about Gabriella coming here because she will insist on going to look for him.'

'Leave it with me, I will go to the camp and see if anyone has heard anything. We always have a list of people who are missing or have been abducted.'

'That would be wonderful, thank you.'

'Where is Raffaella now? Is she here?'

'No, she has gone out riding again to see if she can find him and leave him a note, or if he has left her anything in their hiding places. I begged her not to go out in this weather, but she is headstrong and determined to try to find him.'

When Raffaella returned at dusk she found Zia Paola and the Captain reading poetry and chatting together and she was happy for them, but her search had not brought her any nearer to finding Antonio, and wanting to be alone, she retired to her bed.

She looked out into the darkness and listened to the wind that whined in the trees and echoed in the large caves, giving it an eerie moan as it passed by. It would become still, and silence would once more descend in the valley, only to be woken again by the next howling gust of wind.

Raffaella was reminded of the time when she was about twelve, when she had climbed the olive tree so she could see Antoneddu coming up the meadow. The wind had come up the valley and taken her headdress, and while trying to rescue it, she had stepped on a branch that had cracked under her weight. Antoneddu had caught her and said he would always be there for her. A lump came to her throat and she sobbed uncontrollably. He was gone, and was no longer there for her. How would she ever cope without him and his love?

Downstairs, Zia Paola sat in her chair near the hearth, while the Captain stood in front of the roaring fire. The evening had a decided chill as the wind picked up and roared around the house as it screamed up the valley and rattled the shutters. Sergio had made up the fire in the sitting room, which was now warm and inviting.

'I have something for you,' the Captain said, pulling a small book from his pocket and going toward her.

Zia Paola took it and opened it the first page. The poem was handwritten in his neat writing. 'Captain, this is wonderful, thank you, and they are *Sardi poesi*, which I love.'

'I hoped you would.' He hesitated. 'Do you think you could call me Luca?' he said, looking at her intently.

She looked at him.

'Thank you, Luca, and will you please call me Paola?' she replied, blushing.

'You know, Paola, I look forward to our times together, and find myself wanting to come and see you more and more.'

'And I look forward to seeing you too,' she said, looking into his eyes.

'Would you let me read a poem to you? It is a special one. I'm sure you know it, but it says all I want to say to you.'

Paola handed him the book and he came and sat in the chair next to her. He opened it at his chosen page and began to recite the poem he had copied out.

Pro te so, bella mia,	*For you, my love,*
Bortende su cherveddu	*I'm impatient for every hour.*
Dogn'hora e dogn'istante;	*Every moment;*
Intender ti cheria	*I want to hear*
Unu bellu faeddu,	*Your beautiful words,*
Chi pro me ses constante	*That you love me.*
Cando alzat s'istella	*When the star rises*
A su bonu manzanu	*in the morning*
dat grande rislendore;	*spreading a serene splendour;*
dimando a tie, bella,	*I hope, beautiful one,*
chi mi tocches sa manu	*to take your hand*
in signale de amore	*as a sign of love.*

When he came to the second verse, she quoted it with him, and they laughed.

'Giommaria Piu from Padria,' she said, looking at him.

'I knew you would know these poems well.'

Luca stood up and pulled Paola up to stand in front of him. 'You are the most amazing woman I have ever known, and you have captured my heart, dearest Paola.'

'Luca,' she replied, a little breathless.

He pulled her toward him, and cupping her face in his hands, he stroked her cheeks with his thumbs and stared into her eyes. She did not pull away, so he bent and kissed her cheek, and then tenderly on her mouth.

'Raffaella told me that you believe that our souls unite when we kiss. I hope you believe that, dearest Paola.'

Then releasing her, he took her hand and went down on one knee. 'Paola, I am in love with you, and want to look after you. Do I have any chance of winning your affection? Would you consent to be my wife?'

Paola drew away and looked at him; she could feel the blush spread across her face. 'My dear Luca, I can't believe that someone as wonderful as you could want me. You are so special, and yes, I do believe that souls unite in a kiss.'

'I love you, Paola.'

'Oh Luca, I believe I love you too, and yes, I will marry you, but…'

'But what, my dearest?'

'I can't do anything until Antonio is found. Please understand.'

'Of course I understand, but is there anyone I should ask for your hand?'

'Yes, my guardian Giovanni Piras. He lives in Ozieri.'

Luca pulled her into his arms and kissed her again. Then, looking into her eyes, he added, 'Are you happy, darling?'

'Beyond my wildest dreams, dearest Luca.'

The sun shone the following day, and all traces of the night's storm had died down. Luca, who had been persuaded to stay the night, slept in Gestinu's room, after some mutterings from Elena, who had made up the bed and a warmed it with the stone hot water bottle. She also placed a *braccere* at the end of his bed, filled with the ash from the fire to make sure he was warm enough.

After breakfast, Luca and Paola took the gig and drove to Ozieri to see Giovanni, Raffaella and Paola's guardian. Raffaella had been adamant that she wanted to see Gabriella, and set off after kissing her aunt and asking her to give Cousin Gianni her love.

Ozieri sits on a steep hillside, like an amphitheatre in dense woodland with its wide, tiered streets, wonderful paving and small terraces and squares. This morning it looked magical with its dusting of snow. The streets kept clean as the water from the fountain at the top of the hill flows into the first set of troughs, which are for human drinking, then on into a lower one, used for the horses and animals, and the final one used for washing by the women of the town, and down through the centre of the street.

Luca stopped the gig outside the convent, and helped Paola down with all the various parcels and packages, which she had collected for the sisters over the months. He carried them to the door and waited until someone answered Paola's ring on the great bell.

Having seen her inside, he mounted the gig, and went in search of the address Paola had given him.

The large archway to the building was open, and as he climbed down from the gig, a young lad came forward to take the horse and carriage through the archway, where he unhitched the horse and placed it in a nearby stable. A manservant came forward to escort Luca into the house.

The marble hall was large and impressive, and Luca, looking around him, removed his hat and gloves and handed them to the waiting servant with his calling card, and a sealed letter from Paola. The servant bid him wait and went into one of the rooms. Luca stood in front of a roaring fire in the hall and warmed his hands. The manservant left the room and returned to informed Luca that his master would not be long. He didn't have long to wait, as the door to the room opened into the hall and a tall, swarthy man came forward with his hand outstretched in greeting.

'Captain Ferrero, how good to meet you. I am Giovanni Piras, but everyone calls me Gianni. Please, do come in,' said the man, showing Luca into the room and closing the door behind them.

'The pleasure is mine, Signore,' replied Luca.

The two men shook hands and Luca was shown to a large leather chair opposite a mahogany desk, where he sat down.

'Vernaccia?' asked Gianni.

'Thank you.'

The room was warm and welcoming, with a roaring fire and book-covered walls, and Luca watched as his host collected a decanter from the sideboard and poured golden liquid into two glasses.

'Your health, Captain, but I think you should call me Gianni and I will call you Luca.'

Both men toasted each other and downed their drinks, and Gianni refilled their glasses.

'Is Paola not with you?'

'Yes, she is, but she wanted to leave some produce and linen at the convent. She will be along later.'

'She is always doing something for the sisters, I hope they appreciate what she does. Well, that is good as I have told my manservant to ask my wife to arrange for us to have lunch together, so it will be good to talk to you both. Now, what can I do for you?'

'I am sure you know what I have come for. Over the time I have known Paola I have come to love her and I wish to marry her. I love her very much and she is precious to me. So I have come to ask you for her hand.'

Gianni rose and paced the room.

'Yes, she did mention it in her note,' he said with a broad smile. 'You know about her? She was supposed to enter the convent for life, but when my sister, Maria, died, my father was beside himself with grief at the loss of his beloved daughter. He went to Carlo, Marco and Gestinu's father, to beg him to allow their sister Paola to look after the children. It was all arranged after a good payment to the convent, and I think she has been happy at Sos Lampidos.'

Luca sipped his drink and listened to Paola's guardian.

'When Maria and Gestinu married, my father, Papa Giovanni, gave them Sos Lampidos as he wanted to keep his daughter nearby. Orlando was the firstborn, and would inherit the farmstead. When Raffaella was born, Papa Giovanni saw his daughter in her all over again, and made over the valleys adjoining Sos Lampidos. She has had the income from it; it paid for her schooling and clothing and it has been run together with Sos Lampidos. He also bought the neighbouring farmstead, Pinta Longa, and gave it to Paola in trust until she marries, when it will be hers outright. Now Orlando is asking Marco about the lands. He has some idea that he could sell the timber and raise a lot of money. I have to ask you to make sure that neither you, Raffaella nor Paola sign a paper or document or anything that might look legal in any way. My father never trusted Marco or Orlando, and I am afraid I am of the same opinion. If he can get his hands on the lands and timber, he will fell every tree on the estate and leave it to become a barren wasteland.'

'I understand. Don't worry, I will see that no one signs anything,' said Luca.

'Now tell me, how is Raffaella?'

'She is well, but Antonio is missing and she is desperately worried about him.'

'But I thought he was dead?'

'He survived the shot from Luigi and went into hiding, as Orlando has sworn he was to blame for the shooting and they are all worried about his safety. Antonio went to Pinta Niedda to help their cousins as they were short-handed, what with the war and Gavinu on the run. Raffaella is worried as she has not heard from him in weeks. They met once after he went away and they planned to meet in seven days, but he hasn't contacted her or been seen since then. I am worried, and I am looking into the matter.'

Gianni put his hand on Luca's arm.

'Take care, if Orlando and Marco are together, make sure that Marco is not behind it somewhere.'

Before Luca could answer there was a tap at the door and Paola entered. Luca rose and she went to Gianni to give him an affectionate kiss. Giovanni took her into his arms and kissed her.

'Congratulations, my dear Paola, I am so happy for you both and I give you my blessing.'

With smiles all round, Paola went to Luca, who kissed her on her cheek, making her blush once more.

Lunch was a family affair, with Gianni's wife Caterina and his two sons, Gianni and Giuseppe. All the family ate together, as they did at Sos Lampidos, which was still considered unusual in the country, as women usually ate away from the men.

Gianni turned to Luca. 'The boys help run the estate, and if ever you need any help or any advice, just ask them. If you need any help for anything, contact me at once.'

Later that afternoon, they all said farewells, and Luca drove Paola home to Sos Lampidos as she snuggled up beside him.

The following day, Luca opened the door to his commanding officer's room. It was big and airy, dominated by two huge bookshelves on either side of two large windows that overlooked the camp. His commanding officer had been taken sick a few days earlier, and it had fallen to Luca to look after running the day-to-day affairs.

He had sorted out all the various orders expected of him, and in the evenings, he had gone through the papers to see if there was any reference to the shooting. He had been through all the files in his Colonel's room. He had even searched through his desk, but had found nothing. He had spoken to the surgeon who had been on duty that day, and he confirmed there had been a report, as he had signed it, and had personally given it to the Colonel.

Luca went through the drawers in the large cupboard in the Colonel's room, and having found nothing, sat down in the Colonel's chair and put his feet up on the desk. He stared round the room, and let his eyes wander over the shelves of books and ornaments. Looking along the rows, he noticed a mahogany box sitting amongst the books. Luca rose and went over to the box on the bookshelf, took it down and tried to open it.

He searched the drawers of the desk to see if there was any sign of a key. A large walnut ink-stand stood on the desk, with two cut-glass ink-wells. Luca noticed a small draw under the place where the pens were laid. He opened it, and found a small key inside. Luca pulled it out and tried it in the box. It turned, and opening it, he pulled it toward him as he sat to look at its contents.

Personal letters lay with assorted documents. He lifted them up carefully, so as not to disturb them. Underneath was an envelope marked *report*, and he opened it to find the detailed statement from the surgeon about the slain Carabinier; it was almost word for word the same as Ignazio's story. He pulled all the letters out, and at the bottom of the box was a velvet bag, which Luca took out and laid on the desk to the sound of coins clinking. He opened the drawstring and tipped the contents onto the desk. Five gold 100 lire coins lay there, with a note in bold handwriting.

With sincere thanks, dear friend, in return for services. Marco Canu.

Luca sat back, allowing his mind to go over the evidence before him. So Marco Canu had visited the Colonel and paid him a handsome amount to lose the report, so Orlando would be free and Antonio deemed guilty.

Luca put everything back into the box except for the report and the note, which he put in his breast pocket.

He replaced the box, and the key in their rightful places, and left the office to go and find one of the young recruits who knew everything that was going on, and always gave information for payment.

Luca found him lounging in a chair, reading the local paper.

The young man sprang to his feet and saluted his Captain.

The Captain waved away the salute. 'At ease, please. Tell me, Guido, have you had any report of a young man being kidnapped or held for ransom?'

'There are two over near Nuoro, a shepherd and a young teacher. Negotiations are going on at the moment and they will be freed in a couple of days, once the monies have been paid.'

'Nothing over Pattada way, or at Pinta Niedda? If you hear anything about a Signore Sanna, Antonio Sanna, I would be grateful if you could let me know at once.'

'No, Captain, not so far, but I will make enquiries for you.'

'Thank you, there will be a good drink in it for you,' replied the Captain as he walked out of the room.

CHAPTER TWENTY-NINE

At Sos Lampidos, Orlando was roused from his sleep by a commotion in the yard below his room, and rising from his bed, he hastened to the window. He flung open the wooden shutters to let in the morning light. He had returned to the farmhouse to tie up a few loose ends before going to see Rosanna. With Christmas past, the promise of spring was everywhere. He saw Sergio rounding up the dogs and trying to make himself understood to the long-suffering Zia Paola.

'What in Heaven's name is the matter with you, Sergio?' roared Orlando.

The old shepherd stopped his stream of babble and searched for the familiar voice.

'I'm here, Sergio,' called Orlando, banging on the shutters to attract the shepherd's attention. 'For pity's sake, whatever is the matter?'

Sergio caught his master's eye and started his babble again. The confused words fell in a torrent of unholy abuse. Orlando caught the odd one as Sergio became more and more hysterical.

'Revenge... Abandoned and wandering souls...'

The stupid fool was off on his superstitious ramblings again, thought Orlando, and he watched as Sergio scattered corn round the door of the house and by the windows.

He had seen it all before as a child. It had been amusing then, hearing the stories the shepherd told, with such utter conviction, about the evil spirits coming to the house, and how upon finding the grain, they would stop to count it. Then dawn would come and the light would frighten them all away. It was the same with a broom, for they would stop to count the bristles. Orlando couldn't remember a time when a broom hadn't stood outside the farmhouse door.

He pulled on his trousers, grabbed a shirt and fled downstairs. He pushed past Zia Paola and grabbed Sergio by his *mastrucca* and shook him like a woolly rug. The old man's eyes widened to such an extent that Orlando was sure that they would fall from their sockets.

'Now, Sergio, calm yourself and tell me what it is this time that is troubling you. What's all this nonsense about *vendetta* and being cursed?'

The poor man stood there, opening and closing his mouth as if to speak, but nothing came out. All he could do was point to his horse standing near the stables.

Orlando stared at the animal with growing horror, and let Sergio go with a push. Over the tree of the saddle was slung a dead lamb, its neck slit almost in half.

'How many?' he demanded.

'Six of the new born lambs,' snivelled Sergio.

'When was it done?' shouted Orlando, feeling trapped and uncertain of himself.

'Late last night or early this morning, I'm not sure. I checked them before turning in last night, and that was late because I had a ewe in difficulty, and was up most of the night with her. It is a warning, Orlando, someone knows you're back. I knew no good would come of it. I told your aunt so,' wailed the shepherd.

'*Boh*,' retorted Orlando, turning on his heels and walking towards the house. 'People have known I've been back for weeks now. You'd better go back and bury the lambs and bring the herd closer to the farm,' he called over his shoulder, and slammed the door behind him.

Once inside, he poured himself a long draught of wine from the cask in the kitchen.

'Do you think it's a coincidence, Zia Paola, or do you think it was planned for some reason?'

'I don't know, Orlando. There have been some strange happenings over the past week or so, but I dismissed them as nothing.'

'What sort of things?' cut in Orlando.

'Stones thrown at the windows, and a stranger who rides a black horse has been seen in the area a lot. Then last week I found a pile of asphodel leaves at the kitchen door.'

'Why on earth didn't you tell me all this before?' he demanded, taking another draught from the cask.

'I didn't like to worry you. You are a free man now. Someone has made a mistake. It's nothing.'

Orlando tried to put it all out of his mind, and busied himself with the many preparations he still wanted to do before returning to Rosanna. *Vendetta* warnings were hard to ignore, and he found it difficult to go out without looking behind him; often reining in his horse to hear if he was being followed by some other horsemen.

On a trip to Bantadda to see his uncle, the priest, to arrange for the calling of the banns, Orlando stopped on several occasions, convinced that someone was following him. For the return journey, he decided to go down through the valley rather than return through the thick wood in the gathering gloom.

But all this fear was cast to the wind on his return. Waiting for him was his friend Gian Porqueddu, the outlaw. Zia Paola had already made him welcome, and Orlando fell on the neck of his friend, who congratulated him on his freedom.

'They must be getting free with the papers these days,' laughed Gian. 'My family has notice that they are reconsidering my case.'

Orlando shook his friend firmly by the hand. 'That's wonderful news. But tell me, what brings you here, Gian?' he asked as they sat to eat.

'I have come to collect my horse, and to give you this letter from Rosanna. It seems it's important. She gave it to me a little over a week ago now, when she came to see me. I told her I would not be able to see you until now, but she seemed happy with that.'

He handed Orlando the crumpled-looking letter. 'I'm sorry about that, but I slept with it in my jacket and it was with me all the time. I was frightened I might lose it,' he said, looking rather sheepish.

Orlando took the letter, opened the red seal, and sank back in his chair to read her news.

January 1860
    Dearest Orlando,
I am writing this letter first to tell you some sad news. I had a letter from Umberto's commanding officer. It seems that both he and Dominicu were killed in action. They died bravely, and with honour. The loss of my eldest brother has been a severe blow, but the death of Dominicu, though a loss, has released me from my promised marriage.
    If this news is of any joy to you I hope I shall see you soon. Free man or not.
    Your own,
    Rosanna.

Orlando stared at the letter, rereading it to make sure that what he had read was correct.

'Good news?' asked Gian.

'Yes and no, Rosanna's brother has been killed in action with the man she was supposed to marry, thus freeing her from her marriage promise. She's mine, Gian, she's mine! Zia Paola, you will have a wedding in the house as you wished.'

They spent the rest of the evening celebrating, finally calling it a day when Gian fell into a noisy sleep.

But Orlando found sleep an elusive bed partner. Instead, he lay tossing in his bed. The year's events trooped before him. When he did find sleep it was filled with dreams of being hunted like a wild animal. He dreamt he was back in time. He saw Antonio and Raffaella locked in each other's arms, lying in the long, cool grasses by the river. He saw their shared love, and the way in which they looked into one another's souls. He saw the terrible fight all over again, with Raffaella weeping for her lover. He saw their two spirits rise from their bodies, Antonio going towards Punta Néula, while Raffaella remained chained to Sos Lampidos.

He heard them crying for each other, heard their desperate calling and entreating, the one for the other; and through it all he could hear Rosanna lamenting and calling to him.

He woke in terror, and sat up in his bed. He was soaked in sweat, and leaping from his bed, vomited into his wash bowl. His legs gave way under him and he fell back on his bed in a dead faint. The lack of sleep and the fear of the night had taken their toll.

The following morning he rose, and went down to the kitchen, to find Elena to make him coffee, to help clear his head. Gian joined him; his eyes were bloodshot from the night's heavy drinking.

'My God, Orlando, you look worse than I feel. Are you going to ride today?'

'I must go, and the sooner the better,' he replied.

Orlando organised Ignazio to prepare Gian's horse together with his own for the journey. They returned to the mountains in silence, Gian still nursing a bad head and Orlando deep in his private thoughts, and leading the spare horse. He felt that once Rosanna was with him everything would be all right, and the terrible nightmares would be banished forever. She would drive the dreams and the demons from his troubled mind. He knew, too, that she understood his troubles and loved him just as he was, even in the knowledge of all the things he had done, which he regretted. Such was her love for him.

They reached the ravine and Gian bid Orlando goodbye and wished him all the best. Orlando thanked him for his kindness in looking after him and for bringing the letter, and wished him good fortune with his pardon. He also made Gian promise that he would come and see him again when they were settled, and Gian agreed. He took the spare horse from Orlando, and with a hand shake, they parted.

Orlando pressed his horse on, content in the knowledge that he would see Rosanna by nightfall. Inwardly, he defied fate to hurt him anymore, for he had borne all the pain he could stand.

It was evening when he at last reached the farm. There was

a small lamp burning in an upper window. Orlando knocked at the farmhouse door and waited, then seized by his impatience he knocked again, but louder. It was one of Rosanna's aunts that answered the repeated knocking. A small, stooped little woman peered round the door to see who was calling at such an hour. She held a lamp to Orlando's face so she might see the caller better.

'Good evening, Signorina. I am Orlando Canu. I have come to see Rosanna. Can I please see her? I believe she has told you of me,' stammered Orlando.

The woman looked at the stranger with his neat-cut clothes and clipped beard.

'I have ridden far. Please may I come in? I have come to tell her I am a free man now, and in answer to her letter. I am in love with your niece and wish her no harm.'

'Come in, come in,' repeated the old woman.

Orlando entered the house, and as the light fell on the woman's face he noticed how drawn it was. 'Rosanna has told you about me, hasn't she?' he asked again.

'She has. In fact, she has spoken of little else since she met you, but–'

'Please may I see her?' cut in Orlando. 'I have ridden all day and I have so much I want to say to her.'

The old woman took his arm and looked with tenderness into the young man's eyes. 'Orlando…' She paused. 'Rosanna is ill. She has *impeiere*. The herb-healer has been…' She broke off, trying to stifle the tears that came in sobs. 'She says there is nothing more she can do for her. I've sent for the local doctor. He will be here in the morning.'

Orlando's blood turned to ice in his veins as he became aware of the strong smell of thyme and lemon, that had been present in Raffaella's room when she had been so ill after losing her child.

'Where is she? Please, I must see her,' he begged, his panic rising.

'You can't – the healer won't allow anyone with her other than my sister or me. She is afraid of it spreading.'

'I don't care. I've nothing left, only Rosanna. Please, I beg of you.'

The old woman took Orlando's hand and led him up the narrow stairs to a small, ill-lit room, which had the strong smell of the thyme and lemon. Rosanna lay motionless on the bed, her long hair spread over the pillow. Orlando turned to the other aunt who rose from the chair beside the bed.

'How long has she been like this?'

'Three days,' she replied.

'I'll stay with her now,' he said. 'You get some rest. I want to be with her, if you don't mind. I'll call you if there is any change.'

The two aunts left the room, closing the door behind them.

Orlando took Rosanna's hand and kissed it once, and then with repeated little kisses. His tears mingled with the sweat that stood out on her pale skin.

'Oh, Holy Mother and all the saints, by Christ's dear blood, I have already paid dearly for my wrongdoings, my pride and my jealousies. Don't make Rosanna suffer because of me, I pray you. Give her life and strength and I will go away and leave her if that is your wish. Lord, don't take this young life.' He wept bitterly.

He sobbed, unaware that Rosanna could hear his entreaties through her semi-consciousness. Through the night he lay on the bed next her, his arms round his love while she slept. He watched over her, and when she was troubled with the fever he caressed her forehead and bathed her with cool water and a damp cloth.

At about midnight she stirred and came to.

'Orlando, is that you?' she wheezed.

'Yes, dearest Rosanna, I'm here. My dearest, dearest love, I've come back a free man. We can be wed as soon as you are well enough. We can go back to Sos Lampidos and become husband and wife.'

'Dear Orlando, that will be wonderful,' she gasped. 'We can start our life anew. I shall give you sons and you will be so proud of them, I know.' Her breath was short, and rasped as she spoke.

'Don't talk. I've missed you so much these past months. But

I have everything ready for us at Sos Lampidos, and Zia Paola is looking forward to meeting you.'

'Orlando, please hold me in your arms again, my love,' she panted as her breath came in short bursts. He held her and kissed her feverish cheek, which felt as if it had been burnished by the sun.

'Dearest Rosanna. I love you so much. You have changed my life for ever.'

'Dearest Orlando, I love you too. Come, you look tired. Lie here with me, for we have all our life in front of us,' she whispered weakly.

He was tired from his journey, and the shock of seeing Rosanna ill made him accept her offer. He pulled her to him and lay with her in his arms, where he slipped into a brief, dreamless sleep.

He woke with a sudden start, to find Rosanna lifeless in his arms. Stunned panic washed over him. He felt frightened and alone. Then anger welled up inside him. He felt angry that she had to suffer, angry about life and its injustices. Angry that fate had dealt him such a bitter blow. Why him, why Rosanna? He thought of Vitoria, he thought of Raffaella and Antonio, and a wave of sudden remorse swept over him. He was cursed all right, he had even challenged the gods to do their worst, and now they had, by making the one he loved suffer. Sergio was right: he had brought all this on himself. He was doomed to suffer all his life. If he had been more understanding, perhaps life would have looked on him with a kinder grace and not have dealt such a cruel blow.

He looked at his young lover with the life gone from her, and saw again Vitoria as she had lain in death. He took his knife from his belt and cut a large lock of Rosanna's hair. He kissed her on her cool lips, and then fled from the room, not wanting to see anyone.

He ran to the stables in search of his horse, still numbed by Rosanna's death. He hadn't taken it all in, but the brute force of the events suddenly came to him, jolted by the sight now before him. During the night, someone had entered the stables and hamstrung his horse. The poor animal lay bleeding from its hindquarters.

He took his gun from the saddlebag, and gathering his shaking nerves, he shot the wretched animal. He watched, emotionless, as it crumpled to the ground in front of him. Half-mad with fear and shock, he grabbed the nearest horse and rode for all his worth towards the mountains.

His mind was now in a fever, for he shouted obscenities at the passing trees and yelled at bemused sheep. 'God in Heaven, you can't hurt me anymore. Raffaella, do you hear me? You have had your revenge. I am in your hands now,' he yelled at the top of his voice.

It was late in the afternoon when he reached the small graveyard at Bantadda. He slid from his horse, fell to the ground and crawled towards the graves on all fours, at the same time calling to Raffaella and Antonio to forgive him.

The first grave he came to was that of his father and mother, then Vitoria's. Orlando fell weeping on her grave. He stood and cried again and again, and begging his sister.

'Raffaella, take away your bitter curse and leave my soul alone to give it the peace it craves.'

A stick cracked behind him. He swung to see who was coming towards him. The fading light made it difficult to see any features on the faces, but he could make out the outlines of a man and a woman. His half-demented soul and tormented mind saw them as his sister and her lover.

'Raffaella, Antonio, you have heard me. Please, please, in your mercy, hear my plea and free me from this living death.'

The figures came towards him through the evening mist. Orlando walked to meet them. A shot rang out and echoed round the graveyard, silencing the birds and leaving a morbid stillness in its wake. Orlando fell to the ground, clutching his chest. A second shot rang out, and then there was nothing.

A young man came forward and looked at Orlando. He rolled him over on his back and bent down to see what it was Orlando had clenched in his fist. A long lock of black hair had sprung from the now-limp hand. At his throat was a small leather pouch, which the man cut from his neck. Inside were Orlando's freedom papers, secured by Zio Marco. The young man returned to the woman, who was waiting in the shelter of the trees.

'You can rest at ease now. Your husband, my dear brother Giovanni, has been avenged. Your son can now hold his head high. Go home, before anyone comes. I have one other job to perform, then I shall be back. Kiss my nephew goodnight for me.'

Later that night a stranger rode to Punta Néula and asked to see Marina. It was Salvatore who answered the door to the late caller.

'It is impossible for you to see her. She is asleep. She gave birth to her son last night, and is in need of her sleep.'

The stranger smiled at the shepherd. 'When she wakes, give her this package,' he said, handing Salvatore a large cheese and a document sealed with red wax. 'Tell her I hope her son lives long and that I wish you and your wife the best of health and happiness, and her husband, Gavinu, the peace of knowing he is a free man with an honest pardon for Don diVenti's death. You will find it all legal in that document.'

Salvatore tried to take in all the young man was saying. He took the cheese and was about to ask the stranger a question, but the young man had remounted, and bidding Salvatore goodnight, headed for the track where he vanished into the darkness.

Upstairs the young baby cried, and Gavinu gently rocked its fretfulness away. Salvatore went into the room, and putting his arm round Gabriella, he laid the cheese on the bed. There were large tears in the shepherd's eyes as he bent to kiss his daughter.

'Well, Gavinu, it looks like you have a permanent home here now. That document is your pardon. You are a free man.'

The baby cried again, and Gabriella took it and nursed it. Gavinu looked at Marina sleeping peacefully in their bed.

'Thank God,' he said, and wept on Salvatore's shoulder. 'Free at last.'

CHAPTER THIRTY

They buried Orlando in the small churchyard at Bantadda, next to Vitoria and near his father and mother. It was a sombre gathering on that cold day. The sun was reluctant to show itself from behind the mist-laden clouds, and a sharp wind snapped at the air.

Father Franco had found his nephew, cold and lifeless, early on the morning after the shooting. He laid the young man out in a makeshift coffin in the church and had ridden over to Sos Lampidos with the news.

Now all the families were there; Zio Marco looking shaken as he stood with his wife Zia Madeleine, who had come from Sassari. They were joined by the Sannas from Punta Néula. Salvatore and Gabriella stood with young Salvatore, while Gavinu and Marina had stayed at Sos Lampidos as women were not allowed in the church until forty days after a birth, and not before they had been back to the priest to be cleansed. Antonio was still missing, and Luca stood next Paola and Raffaella to give them comfort and support.

Father Franco performed the service, and Raffaella watched it all unfold before her. Life seemed so brief, and in the lap of the gods. Sergio was right: it was all down to fate.

She felt the Captain take her arm as he led her away from the churchyard to the awaiting carriage.

'Are you all right, Raffaella? We are all going back to Sos Lampidos. Paola and Elena have organised a meal for everyone, and I understand Zio Marco and his wife are returning to Sassari later today.'

'Yes, I'm fine,' she replied with a wan smile.

When they all reached Sos Lampidos the women went inside and busied themselves putting the final touches to the meal.

Luca led his horse to the stable, and was surprised to see his young Sergeant waiting for him by the stables talking to Ignazio, and went to join them.

'Captain, I have this letter for you from Guido Maspero. He said it was urgent, and that he thought there was a large drink in it.'

Luca laughed, and took the letter and opened it. He read it, and then told Ignazio to take the Sergeant to the kitchen, and to make sure he had something to eat and drink.

'Before you go, who is the commanding officer at Nuoro?' Luca asked his Sergeant.

'Colonel Don Vincenzo Corte, sir.'

'How long before they are shipped out?'

'I understand it to be imminent, sir.'

So Marco had sent Antonio to the military service to get rid of him and free his nephew. But how did he know Antonio was alive? Luca sighed. Two could play at that game.

He read the contents of the letter again, taking in all the details; then folding it up, he went into the house to find Paola.

She was in the dining room, and noticed at once the strained look on Luca's face.

'What is it?'

'We have to leave, I'm afraid, darling. Something has come up and I am needed at once.'

'Will you be long?' asked Paola, looking up at him.

'I don't know. But I must see Marco before I leave.'

'He is in Gestinu's study.'

'My Sergeant is in the kitchen. I have asked Ignazio to see he has something to eat, and can you pack us some food to take with us, please?'

Marco had just settled himself into a comfortable chair in Gestinu's study to have a quick smoke before lunch, when there came a knock at the door.

'Enter.'

Luca opened the study door and let himself in.

'Good day, Captain. I believe congratulations are in order. I understand Paola has consented to be your wife,' said Marco without rising.

'Yes, sir, it is wonderful news, thank you. But Orlando's death is dreadful, we shall, of course, be looking into it.' Hesitating a moment, he added, 'Sir, I have something I need to ask you.'

'What is it?'

'When Orlando came to see you in Sassari, you knew he was guilty of shooting the Carabineri, didn't you, but you defended him and paid for his freedom. You are a man of the law, why would you do that?'

Marco took a long draw on his cigar and blew out the smoke. 'You don't understand, Captain. Orlando was wasted here. He was a bright young man. I have no children, and I saw myself in him; I wanted him to have all the advantages that I had when I was young. His father, my brother Gestinu, married well, but he did nothing with his life; he was content to be just a county lawyer, with no ambition. But Orlando was different, he was ambitious and liked the finer things in life; so when he came to me and told me what had happened I went to the Colonel, who is a friend, and I paid him a handsome sum to lose the papers. It gave Orlando a new chance in life.'

'Did Orlando know what you had done?'

'No, I didn't think it was necessary to tell him.'

'What about his conscription papers?' asked the Captain, looking Marco straight in the eye. 'You also paid the Colonel to send out Orlando's papers in the name of Antonio Sanna, and then told him where he could be found. When they couldn't find him at Punta Néula, you sent out your henchmen to find him at Pinta Niedda and take him to Nuoro, where he was conscripted to the army waiting to go to the Continent. How did you know Antonio was alive?'

'I have contacts everywhere. Orlando had heard a rumour that Antonio hadn't died in the shooting, so I put out a reward for information.'

'What about Antonio?'

'What about him?'

'We have an innocent man in the army who is still wanted for Luigi's death, and I want Antonio's freedom guaranteed, and him returned here before he is shipped off to the Continent.'

Zio Marco puffed on his cigar again, allowing the white smoke to envelop him. 'You will find that difficult to prove; that I can assure you, Captain. It is of no matter now – with Orlando dead it is all over.'

'But it is not over, not for Antonio.'

'You ask too much, Captain,' said Marco, rising and throwing his cigar stub into the fire. 'As far as I am concerned the matter is closed now Orlando is dead. You are in no position to do anything about it, and as I said, you will find it impossible to prove.'

'I don't think so. First, I have your letter giving all the details of your dealings with the Colonel, and second, I have my father in Piedmont. He, like you, has many contacts, and I know that one of his business associates and friends is one of your largest clients in Sassari. I would not like to see you lose such a client. Now if you will excuse me, I have to see my Sergeant.'

With that the Captain clicked his heals and left the room, leaving Marco to consider his position.

Luca found his Sergeant in the kitchen where Elena was busy packing food for them.

'Thank you, Elena. Look after Paola for me.'

The Sergeant went to the stables where he found his Captain's horse and waited for him, watched by Ignazio.

Luca found Paola. 'I am sorry about this, but it is imperative that I leave at once. Take care of yourself, darling. Look after Raffaella and try to comfort her. I don't know when I will be back, but it could be days. One thing I need to know: does Antonio have any distinguishing marks?'

Paola looked at him and smiled. 'He has a nasty scar on his left arm, he cut it when shearing the sheep.'

He took her in his arms and kissed her, then went in search

of his Sergeant. After mounting his horse, and with a wave of the hand, they were gone.

To the surprise of all the family, Zio Marco and his wife made their excuses to leave before the meal, stating that he was not feeling too well and that he needed to return to Sassari.

Paola, at a loss with all the comings and goings, called everyone to sit at the table to share the meal for Orlando's departed spirit.

Later that night after they had left, she climbed the stairs to bed. The flickering lamp caught the pictures and tapestries on the wall and threw a glow on the rough plasterwork.

As she neared the top she became aware of the sound of weeping, and going to Raffaella's door, listened to the young girl's sobs. She knocked on the door, and entered her niece's room. The lamplight picked out the old carved chest and danced over the handwoven rug which covered a good part of the floor.

Raffaella sat up in her bed. 'Are you all right, Zia Paola?' she asked with a sob.

'I heard you crying, child, is there anything I can do?'

'Oh, Zia Paola, I am so worried about Antoneddu, and now Luca has gone, what are we going to do? It's cold out there, please come into my bed,' said Raffaella as she pulled back the bed linen to allow her aunt to join her in her bed.

Her aunt put her lamp on the chest next to the bed, and climbed in with her niece. Zia Paola plumped up the pillows and pulled Raffaella into her arms.

'I don't know what to say to comfort you, Raffaella. Now Luca has gone too and I don't know when he will be back.'

'He will be back, Zia Paola, there is no doubt about that, for he loves you so much. Has he told you how he feels, and have you told him how you feel about him?'

'Yes and no. Yes, Luca did tell me he loves me, but it is all such a new feeling for me and I'm not sure of myself or my feelings. How do I really know if I am in love with him?'

'Tell me, Zia Paola, is he your waking thought, your sleeping dream? Is he the breath of your life, the beat of your heart and the love of your soul? Because if he is, then you love him.'

Zia Paola sighed. 'I do believe he is.'

'Then if that is so, you can't deny your feelings. If a love like that comes into your life, you are truly blessed. How many people marry the person of their dreams, hopes and desires? And has he asked to marry you?'

'Yes, but how do you know how he feels about me?'

Raffaella laughed. 'I can see it in his eyes when he looks at you. It is the same soul-searching, heart-rending look that Antoneddu gives me.'

'He asked me to be his wife, but I'm not sure I am worthy of him.'

'Of course you are. He wouldn't ask you if he didn't think so. You are so well suited, you both enjoy the same things. What did you say?'

'I told him that I wouldn't do anything until Antonio was found.'

'When he comes back, and when he asks you again, for it is sure he will, you must say yes; please don't let the chance of true happiness pass you by. There is nothing quite like the love of a man you love and adore. I can assure you, when the man you love takes you in his arms and tells you he loves you, all the world goes away. It is just the two of you and there is nothing like that shared love. Promise me, Zia Paola; whatever happens, don't let him go. You are so good for each other.'

'And you, Raffaella, have you heard from Antonio?'

'No. I've been to all the usual places. Gabriella says Gavinu has been to Pinta Niedda, but he hasn't been seen again. I am at my wits' end. I miss him so much, his kisses and his warm embrace. What am I going to do if something has happened to him?' Her sobs caught in her throat, and her aunt pulled her closer toward her.

'He will be all right, I am sure. Meanwhile I will pray for us all.'

Zia Paola lay back on the large pillows and thought about Antonio and Luca, as Raffaella fell into a restless sleep. She had decided not to tell her that Luca had asked her if there were any distinguishing marks by which he could recognise Antonio, in case it sent her into a deeper fit of depression. She pulled her arm out from under Raffaella and slipped out of the bed, and then taking the lamp, tiptoed out of the room, closing the door behind her.

She walked back down the corridor to her room, where she climbed into her own bed, and blowing out the lamp, went to join Luca in her dreams.

CHAPTER THIRTY-ONE

Spring returned to the valley, and the two houses sat perched above the mists, bathed in glorious spring sunshine above the vaporous clouds.

Paola was working outside, where she was trying to plan the new vegetable garden, collect the eggs, and generally potter.

Her mind was not on her work: she had not seen Luca for three weeks, and was concerned as she had heard nothing from him either.

Raffaella came toward her with a box filled with packets of the different seeds they had harvested last year, ready to plant.

Paola watched her niece as she walked toward her. She had lost weight, and looked thin and gaunt. It was obvious she was pining for Antonio. Both of them had heavy hearts, and were short on conversation as they struggled with their private fears about their men.

The sound of approaching horses made them turn to see who was coming. The clouds still hung low in the valley, making it impossible to see the riders. Slowly they appeared out of the swirling mists; two men on horseback. One dressed in full uniform, the other heavily bearded and in a large Greatcoat.

Paola, recognising Luca, stood and watched him as he came nearer. Her heart was pounding and she felt weak, but she had a wide smile on her face.

'Luca,' she breathed with a sigh.

Raffaella watched her aunt and then turned to see the men who came into the yard, and watched as they dismounted. Luca went to Paola and kissed her. Raffaella turned to the other rider. He had dismounted on the far side of his horse and she could not see his face. She turned to speak to Luca, but stopped and turned again to look at the other man. Sudden realisation hit her, and dropping the box, she ran toward him.

He turned, and the next moment she had thrown herself into his arms.

'Antoneddu, oh Antoneddu, my darling, where have you been? I've been looking everywhere for you. I have missed you so much. I thought something terrible had happened to you.'

Antonio folded her into his arms and kissed her with a breathless passion.

'Luca found me,' he said, drawing away and looking at Raffaella.

'How? Where? Oh, my darling Antoneddu. I thought I had lost you forever.'

'It's a long story, and Luca and I are in need of a wash and clean clothes.'

Luca turned to Paola.

'Is Sergio or Ignazio here? Could one of them ride to Punta Néula to get Salvatore, Gabriella, and all the others? I am sure we could all do with something to eat, and we need a bath. I have been on the road for three weeks.'

Paola looked up at him.

'Thank you, dearest Luca.'

Luca dropped her a kiss and handed his horse to Ignazio, who had appeared from the back of the house. Ignazio went forward and took Antonio's horse as well, and led them to the stable.

'Take care of them for me, Ignazio,' said Luca. 'They have been ridden hard these past weeks.'

Ignazio turned to the Captain and nodded.

'Oh, and Ignazio, this is yours,' the Captain said as he put his hand into his uniform pocket and pulled out the knife he had promised the lad.

Ignazio's face lit up with an enormous smile, and he took the knife in a reverential manner.

'Thank you, Captain,' said the young man, overwhelmed.

'You earned it,' said the Captain as he headed toward the

house. 'When you have rubbed the horses down and watered them, would you ride to Punta Néula and collect all the family please?'

Ignazio nodded, and again thanked the Captain.

Indoors, Elena was busy putting kettles on the fire to heat the water.

Upstairs, Zia Paola dragged the tin bath into Orlando's old room. She found fresh linen for the men.

When Antonio and Luca arrived upstairs they were met by a steaming tub of water, with extra kettles on the side. Soap and towels were laid out on the washstand with flannels and scrub brushes.

The two men looked at each other, and closing the door, began to take off their dirty clothes amid calls of approval.

Downstairs Zia Paola was busy organising *pane frattau*[viii], large cuts of cold meats and enormous amounts of vegetables.

Raffaella laid the table and stood back to admire it all. She stood near the crucifix that hung on the wall by her father's desk and gave silent thanks to her saint and the Holy Mother for the safe return of Antoneddu.

Salvatore and Gabriella arrived with Ignazio and young Salvatore, and Marina and Gavinu with the new baby, and greeted Zia Paola and Raffaella with hugs and kisses. Salvatore brought a large cheese and some of his special wine for the meal. Gabriella had a clean set of clothes for Antonio, and went upstairs to lay them outside the bedroom door. Zia Paola had found some trousers from Gestinu's wardrobe with a shirt and waistcoat for Luca.

When Luca and Antonio entered the room, they smelt of fresh soap and water. Gestinu's trousers were a bit short on Luca, and they hung above his ankles, giving him a waif-like appearance. Zia Paola's heart went out to him, and she sighed.

Antonio went to Gabriella and kissed his mother and hugged his father, and then, picking up his little brother, gave him a big kiss.

Marina and Gavinu came forward and showed Antonio his new nephew.

'What have you called him?' asked Antonio, looking the beautiful boy.

'Gavinu Franco Salvatore. He is so special,' replied Marina, holding the young child close to her.

Raffaella went and put her arms around Antonio and turned to Luca.

'Thank you, Luca, for I know you are the one who made all this possible,' she said.

Zia Paola insisted that everyone sit down, as she put the large plates of sliced sausage and cheese with pane carasau on the table, and said grace, thanking God for the men's safe return.

Young Salvatore sat wide-eyed as he watched the Captain and Antonio.

On such a special occasion, Elena and Sergio, joined by Ignazio, sat at the far end of the table so they could help with the serving and clearing of plates.

The men fell on the meal; devouring the *salciaccia* and cheese, followed by the *pane frattau* and then the cold meats and vegetables before rounding the meal off with fruit.

Luca pushed back his chair, blew out his cheeks and looked at Paola.

'Thank you, that was wonderful. Neither of us has eaten properly in days.'

'What happened?' asked Raffaella, eager to know.

Luca filled his glass and sat back in his chair to tell them the story.

He had read the letter that Guido Maspero had sent him. It had stated that he had found the papers in which it was clear that Marco Canu had paid for Orlando's name to be taken off the conscription list, and Antonio's put on instead. It was common practice among the wealthy to pay to have their sons replaced by other young men for payment, and let them join the army and fight on the Continent instead, but it was usually by mutual consent and following a good payment.

After confronting Marco, he and his Sergeant had ridden to Nuoro, to find the troop had already left for Terranoa, and would be embarking for the Continent soon.

Luca had decided to go on his own, but the Sergeant insisted that someone went with him. He found another Sergeant who had to take papers to the port, and so they had left to follow the troop. It had been a hard ride and taken them three days until they arrived at the small port, which was teeming with troops and men, either returning wounded or waiting to leave. From outside the port men were everywhere; their encampments were alive and the smell of battle-weary soldiers and fear from the young recruits filled the air.

Men sat in groups playing cards or *Morra*; others slept on kitbags while sailors milled around, loading supplies and animals onto the ships. The noise was deafening, with men shouting and horses whinnying, and it brought to mind the time when Luca had embarked for the war at Tchernaya. It all came back as a vivid memory, and he had felt the sweat of fear as it trickled down his back.

Luca found the commanding officer and put his case forward, but he had met a brick wall. No one was interested; men were being lost at the front and were needed as things were getting worse, so his words fell on deaf ears.

He took two rooms in the small boarding house and set about trying to find where Antonio might be. The Sergeant went in among the men and returned with the news that an Antonio Sanna was indeed at the port, and expected to embark the following day.

Luca went to the dock to see if he could find the person in charge, but everyone was too occupied in the job of loading the vessel to give him any help.

As he was about to return to the inn someone yelled for him to look out. He turned sharply, just in time to avoid a rolling barrel, and bumped straight into an old soldier, who immediately stood to attention and saluted.

'Captain Ferrero, sir, what are you doing here?' asked the soldier.

Luca turned to see an old Sardinian campaigner he had served with at Tchernaya.

'Predu, what are you doing here?' he asked, amazed at seeing his old friend. 'I thought you had retired, you old dog.'

'I was retired from action due to the wound I received, but I help with the troops here. So many young men away from home for the first time, and not knowing what the hell they are heading for. God help them. And you?'

'I am looking for a young man who has been sold to the army. He was kidnapped and sent to replace someone else.'

'What is his name?'

'Sanna, Antonio Sanna. He comes from Bantadda.'

'Where are you staying?'

'At the inn as you come into town. I will see you right on this, Predu.'

'We'll find him. Good friend, is he?'

'He is my fiancée's niece's betrothed.'

The two men shook hands and parted.

Luca returned to the inn and found the Sergeant in deep conversation with a young woman who was the landlady's daughter, and not wanting to disturb them, he ordered a meal and took it to his room.

He thought about Paola; he had not been able to get word to her, and knew that she and Raffaella would be worried. He toyed with his food and decided to go back down to the quay again to watch the activity there.

The hustle and bustle of the place, the crowds of men in uniform, and young women saying their goodbyes once again put him in mind of his time in the war, and the same feeling of fear crept upon him again and he shuddered.

He saw Predu, who whistled to him and went to see him.

'You'd better come with me,' he said, turning to walk up a narrow alleyway.

Luca followed close behind, frightened he would lose his guide in the crush of people.

They turned into a square, where there were more soldiers huddled together, waiting to embark.

Predu went up to one of the officers and said something to him. The officer nodded and waved him away. Predu went over to a group of men, and bending down over one who was fast asleep, woke him.

'Sanna, Antonio?' demanded Predu.

The young soldier jumped to his feet and saluted.

'Sanna, Antonio from Bantadda?' barked Predu.

'Yes, sir.'

'Come with me. We have papers for you to go with the Captain.'

Predu marched Antonio over to Luca.

'Take him, Captain. I told the officer he was wanted, and that you had papers to escort him to prison. If you leave at once they will never check, not with all this loading to do.'

Antonio watched the two men, weary of their actions.

Luca turned to look at the young man. He looked battle-weary before he had even started. His eyes had lost any lustre they might have had. Luca knew that, although they were brave in battle, many Sards died of homesickness on the Continent.

'Show me your left arm,' said the Captain, turning to Antonio.

Antonio undid his shirt cuff and put his arm out for inspection.

'That scar – how did you get it?' asked the Captain.

'I cut it when shearing sheep, sir.'

'Thank you, Predu,' said Luca, and he put his hand in his pocket and drew out two large gold coins which he gave to the old campaigner, who took them, touched his cap and then put them in his mouth and bit on them.

Luca raised an eyebrow.

'Sorry, Captain, bad habit, but I have learnt to trust no one,' he said with a wide, toothless grin.

'Thank you, my old friend and companion,' said Luca with a laugh.

'Ever the gentleman, Captain Ferrero.'

The two old friends embraced, and Luca escorted Antonio back to the inn.

Once there the Captain called for coffee with *fil'e ferru* and sat down with Antonio.

'Who are you, sir?' asked Antonio.

'My name is Luca Ferrero, and I am a Captain in the Carabineri. A good friend of Paola and that is why I am here.'

Antonia was shocked. 'I can't thank you enough, Captain, but how did you manage to find me?'

'It is a long story, one I can tell you on the way home. Also, as we are going to be related, in a roundabout way, by marriage, I think you should call me Luca. *Salude!*' called Luca as he downed his drink in one.

He collected his things and paid his bill.

'Have you seen my Sergeant?' he asked the landlord.

'He is out in the kitchen with my daughter. I will fetch him for you.'

The Sergeant returned with the landlord and looked sheepishly at his Captain.

'Found your man, Captain?'

'I am returning to Bantadda. You are on leave as of now. Watch out for yourself. But I need your horse; you can always get yourself one from the camp when you need to return to Nuoro.'

The Sergeant saluted.

So Luca and Antonio started on the long journey from Terranoa to Bantadda, a journey of two days, to arrive at Sos Lampidos that morning.

Raffaella rose and went round to Luca.

'Thank you for bringing him home; we shall be forever in your debt.'

Paola took Luca's hand and smiled at him. It was a smile that told him she loved him, and he lifted her hand and kissed it.

Antonio rose and nodded at Luca, who stood up and the two men hugged each other. A bond had been formed between them which would never be broken.

'And you, Antoneddu?' asked Raffaella. 'What happened to you?'

'I was up in the high meadows at Pinta Niedda with the sheep when a man came. He said he had a message from you, Raffaella. I went to see him and take the letter which he was holding. He pushed me to the ground and the next thing I knew, there was another man and they put a sack over my head and bound me. They slung me over a saddle and we started a long journey. I was handed over to another gang of men who fed me on a diet of bread and water. Five or six days later, they handed me on to another set of men who took off my sack and bindings. They were all in uniform, and I was accused of trying to dodge my conscription.'

Antonio looked at Luca.

'I was put with all the new volunteers and conscripts. We went through weeks of strict training, and then we were marched to Terranoa. The one good thing was that I was put in charge of the horses, but it was like all Hell had been let loose. I have never seen so many men, not even at the large festival at Sassari. Wounded men being unloaded from the waiting ships, and soldiers being loaded ready to fight. I have had a glimpse into the nightmare you must have endured in the war, Luca.'

A silence fell over the table, and Zia Paola, took his hand and smiled at him. 'Will you tell them, Luca?'

Luca looked around the table. 'Before I went away, I asked Paola if she would do me the honour of becoming my wife.'

A gasp of joy slipped from Raffaella as she looked at her aunt.

Luca smiled at her and continued. 'I am proud to say that she accepted my offer, but said she wanted to wait until Antonio was home.'

Turning to Paola, he went down on one knee. 'Now that he is home, will you marry me, dearest Paola?'

'Yes, dear Luca, I will,' she said, as the gentle blush on her cheek spread across her face.

A cheer went up from all the company.

'A toast to the happy couple!' said Salvatore.

'A double wedding celebration,' said Antonio, taking Raffaella into his arms.

It was late when they finished celebrating.

'You can't go back to Punta Néula tonight, Gabriella,' said Paola 'We can make up the bed in Gestinu's room; you and Salvatore can sleep there and we can put the old cot in there for young Salvatore.'

She turned to Elena. 'We can put Luca and Antonio in Orlando's room.'

Linen was fetched, beds were made, and after a final nightcap, the house settled down for the night. Antonio lay in his bed, listening to Luca's deep breathing. He found it difficult to adjust to the fact that he was safe and that Luca had, by some miracle, found him before he was due to be shipped to the Continent. His mind turned to Raffaella, and a wave of affection and desire washed over him.

He rose quietly from the bed, so as not to wake Luca, and tiptoed across the large rug that lay on the wooden floor.

Luca stirred, and Antonio froze.

'Be back before dawn. You lucky devil,' said Luca as he turned over and fell back into a deep sleep.

Antonio smiled to himself. Luca had become a good friend, and he knew that he was in love with Zia Paola. It would be good for her to have someone like Luca to care for her, and there was no doubt she would be good for him.

Antonio let himself out of the room and crept down the corridor to Raffaella's room. He opened the door and let himself in. The room was hung in darkness; the stars and moon were hidden by the misty clouds. He crossed the room and felt for Raffaella in her bed.

'My darling,' she said as he fell into her arms. 'I was hoping you would come. My life has been so empty without you.'

'Did you think of me, Raffaella, *sa sposixedda mia*?' he said as he pulled her into his arms.

She sighed. 'Every morning when I woke I thought I could see you lying beside me, your hair tousled on the pillow just as it was that fateful morning at Sos Lampidos. At night I lay with my bedding wrapped around me and made believe it was your arms around me. Oh Antoneddu, love of my life, I have missed you so.'

He held her close to him, feeling the softness of her young body next him. He kissed her gently at first, and then with a fevered passion.

To Raffaella the strength of him; the smell of him, fresh from his bath, filled her senses with longing, and she held him close.

'There were times when I thought I might never see you again,' he said, kissing her and feeling the tears on her cheeks. 'Tears, *sa bellaxedda mia*? I'm home now, and we will never be parted again. I told you long ago I would always be there for you.'

He took her into his arms again, and made love to his beloved Raffaella.

CHAPTER THIRTY-TWO

April light filled the house at Sos Lampidos. The meadows were filled with spring flowers and the sound of the streams could be heard, rushing and gurgling with the added water from the melting snows in the mountains. Raffaella sighed as she looked out of her window. She loved this time of the year.

Everyone had been busy for days, cooking and preparing food for the joint wedding, and it was now laid out in the large dining room covered by huge linen cloths. The meats were roasting out in the yard under Ignazio's watchful eye. The smell of the meat wafted on the flower-laden air and filled Raffaella with a sense of wellbeing.

Marina came into the room which she was sharing with Raffaella. She stood and admired her lifelong friend and soon-to-be sister-in-law.

'You look lovely, Raffaella. Here, these are for you,' she said as she handed Raffaella a bunch of hand-tied wild flowers.

'Oh Marina, they are beautiful, thank you.'

Marina went over to the chest and collected the box she had put there earlier, and opening it, took out the lace mantilla and carefully shook the veil, which had been Raffaella's mother's, placing it on Raffaella's head. She pinned it with a gold brooch, then stood back to admire her handiwork.

At that moment Gabriella came in to see if there was anything she could do, and stood there admiring her soon-to-be daughter-in-law.

Tears welled up in her eyes, and she kissed Raffaella.

They all turned to see Paola come into the room. She was dressed, like Raffaella, in traditional dress, and she wore a beautiful handmade lace mantilla that Luca's mother had sent as a wedding gift. Although in her mid-thirties, she looked like a young girl. She radiated happiness.

Raffaella went forward, and aunt and niece embraced each other.

Gabriella gave each of them a silver coin to place in their shoes for good luck.

'It's time we were on our way,' said Zia Paola.

Outside, Sergio stood by the gig, waiting for the family. He was dressed in his Sunday best and had combed his hair down close to his head before pulling on his berrita.

All the family clambered into the gig to join the Captain and Antonio in the little church at Bantadda.

Gianni and his wife Caterina were already waiting at the church. They had been invited after the two couples had gone to Ozieri with the news and the date of the wedding, and to get their marriage licence. The little church hummed with the chatter of friends and family in the hub of greeting.

Sergio returned to collect the two brides. There was a tear in his eye as he helped Paola into the gig, and then turned to help Raffaella. The two women, who had been lifelong friends, held each other's hands.

'I'm so happy for you, Zia Paola,' said Raffaella. 'I hope Luca knows what a lucky man he is to have such a wonderful wife.'

Zia Paola smiled at her niece and held her hand harder.

'And you have your love at last. Antonio will, I know, make you very happy.'

Father Franco welcomed them at the church, and Salvatore took Raffaella's hand while Gianni took Paola's arm to escort her into the church.

The sun shone into the little church, the beams of light catching the old brickwork, casting a warm and welcoming glow.

The men were all in their finest shirts, cloth kilts and white linen trousers, their waistcoats of black velvet or brocade contrasting with the vibrant colours of the women's costumes of the region.

Paola, on Gianni's arm, now stood with Luca, who looked so handsome in his uniform, and very tall among the present company.

Salvatore took Raffaella as she joined Antonio.

The wedding service in Latin was simple as they exchanged their vows and rings, and had a short mass when they shared their first communion as a married couple.

Father Franco then gave them his blessing.

Luca took Paola into his arms.

'My darling, Signora Ferrero I love you,' he said, kissing her with tenderness.

Antonio pulled Raffaella to him and kissed her with a long, passionate embrace.

Gavinu and Marina then stepped forward for the short christening of their new baby.

'Name this child,' said Father Franco as he took the young baby from Marina.

'Gavinu Franco Salvatore,' said Gavinu, pride welling up in his chest.

After the services all the families walked out into the sunshine once more. Elena and Sergio came forward and smashed plates at their feet to ensure happiness for the newlyweds.

Raffaella placed her bouquet on her parents' grave, and pulling some flowers out, set them on Vitoria's grave. Paola put hers with Raffaella's in memory of her brother Gestinu.

Father Franco joined them in the gig as they made their way back to Sos Lampidos. Raffaella and Antonio rode together on his horse.

At Sos Lampidos, all the doors and windows had been thrown open to allow the breeze to steal through the house.

Gabriella removed the covers from the food and everyone was invited to sit at the large table.

Luca turned to Gianni.

'One thing I have noticed; the Sards do not need much of an excuse to have a wonderful meal and a gathering of friends.'

Gianni laughed.

'I believe we owe you a great debt for getting Antonio back. I told you to be careful with Marco. He was always ambitious, and recognised the same ambition in Orlando.'

'I am happy that everything turned out so well,' replied Luca.

'I have all the papers with me. I shall need Paola to sign the documents as she will take over the ownership of her farmstead and land at Pinta Longa. I am pleased to say that women can still own land in Sardinia under the old *Carta di Logu*. But you know if you ever need any help or advice, I am always at Ozieri. Take care of her, won't you? She is precious to me.'

'You know I will, and thank you, Gianni, your friendship is much appreciated.'

The meal passed in great celebration, with everyone enjoying the assortment of meats and delicacies, washed down by copious amounts of wine that was set before them.

Late in the afternoon, as the fires started to burn down and people became mellow, Gianni asked Paola and Raffaella to join him in Gestinu's study.

The two women sat before him on the other side of the desk. Gianni looked at them and smiled.

'You are both my favourite girls, and what I have to tell you gives me great pleasure. You both remember my father Papa Giovanni, and as you know, he gave Maria Sos Lampidos as her marriage present. He also bought the farmstead nearby which has been in trust for you, Paola, but now becomes yours by right on your marriage. The income you received over the years from Gestinu was from the farm at Pinta Longa, but Gestinu always farmed it. I have spoken to Luca and told him the land is yours, and he is happy with that. I understand he is thinking of leaving the army and wants to settle down at the farm. I have told him I will always be here if he needs any help.

'As for you, Raffaella; Papa Giovanni left you the valleys, so they will now join Sos Lampidos and become yours now you are married. You too had the income from them, as they paid for your schooling as your father ran them together. I know you and

Antonio will run it all well, with the land foremost rather than fat profits.'

Paola looked at Raffaella, and they hugged each other. Sos Lampidos and the valley would be safe.

Back in the dining room, Salvatore had his Launaddas and joined Ignazio, who played the guitar with Sergio. Their music filled the house so people could sing or dance.

Raffaella left the room, and walked across the broad sward to the large olive tree overlooking the ravine. She looked down into the valley where a small mist was curling its way up the lower meadows, as the sun started to ride along the top of the mountains before it would dip behind them.

Antonio came and put his arms around her.

'It's all yours now, Raffaella,' he whispered as he kissed her neck.

'No, it's ours, and Punta Néula goes back to Gabriella and Salvatore, and Zia Paola has her land, which is wonderful. We have Sos Lampidos and it's all I have ever wanted – that and you.'

Antonio took her into his arms.

'I would have had you with nothing, I love you so very much, my darling.'

She leant up and kissed him, and he, picking her up, carried her to the stables where his horse was saddled and waiting. He placed her on its back and mounted from the mounting block in his usual fluid way, and headed the horse down towards the pasture.

'I want to spend our first night of married life in the *pinneta* where I first made love to you, darling Raffaella; just the two of us, away from everyone.'

She leant against him and felt the movement of him as she rode behind him.

Paola and Luca had come out to find Antonio and Raffaella, and watched them as they disappeared into the mists in the lower valley.

'You know, I can see now why, in Ozieri, you up here, are

called the children of the mists, watching them disappear into the valley like that,' said Luca, taking Paola into his arms. 'Happy?'

'My darling Luca, I never realised that I could be so happy. I count my blessings and thank God every day that we have found each other, and that you have helped all the family. Darling Luca, what would we have done without you?'

He pulled her closer to him and kissed her, and saw the awaking of her desire for him. And picking her up in his arms, he carried her indoors.

In the *pinneta*, Antonio pulled Raffaella into his arms, as they lay on the freshly made bed of wool and sweet-smelling lady's bedstraw, and made love to the only woman he had ever loved.

EPILOGUE

After the wedding, Antonio and Raffaella settle in at Sos Lampidos, where Elena and Sergio help them. Over the following years their joy is completed with a family of four boys and two girls, all of whom are the apple of Antonio's eye.

Gavinu and Marina build a house for themselves at Punta Néula, and work helping Salvatore and Gabriella, who slowly hand everything over to the young ones. They now spend time looking after their grandchildren, two boys and two girls.

Paola and Luca have a much-loved son. Paola opens the old schoolroom at Sos Lampidos, and spends her time teaching all the young family. Luca, having retired from the army, has taken to farming with the help of Antonio and Gavinu.

With all the new families in the houses, the valley rings to the sound of young children, who are still known as the children of the mists.

AUTHOR NOTES

i. *Sa sposixedda mia* (sa-sposi chedda mia) a term of endearment

ii. *Sa Bellaxedda mia* (Sa-bella-chedda mia.) Another term of endearment; 'my beautiful little one.'

iii. *Accadadora*; 'She who ends', usually a widow who receives no payment from the family, but alms from the villagers for her services. She removes all sacred images and beloved objects from the room of the dying to help the spirit leave the body, and usually suffocates the patient or hits him/her on the back of the head with a large olive-wood club (on mazzolu), which she carried as a walking stick. She is known as the ultimate mother, as only women can perform this act as they bring life into the world, so only they can take it away. It is a dolce morte; a sweet death.

iv. *Sebadas*. (Seadas) Famous dessert; originally second course. Typical of Sardinian shepherd families. In the past women would dress in their finest dress and serve Sebadas to their husbands on their return from the plains with the sheep. The name comes from the Sard word seu; an animal fat used to make candles, referring to the shimmer of the fritters coming from the honey and the sugar.

v. *Cujugnu* (coo gee noo) Is the betrothal, like an engagement, but is not binding.

vi. *Pane Carasau* Sardinian bread, baked like a crispbread and taken by the shepherds when they go to the plains.

vii. *Malloreddus* Is the national pasta dish of Sardinia. Also known as gnocchetti Sardi, sometimes made with a pinch of saffron. Malloredus alla Campidanese is usually made with added Sardinian sausage. On a personal note, ot is one of my favourite dishes.

viii. Pane Frattau Is a Sardinian dish made from *pane carusau*, together with lamb broth, tomato sauce, grated pecorino cheese, and egg. Although found throughout the island in different versions, it is a typical dish of the Barbargia.

Dear Reader,

Thank you for taking the time to read *Children of the Mists* and I hope you have enjoyed the story of Antonio and Raffaella.

If you have any comments, good or bad, I am very happy to hear from you, as I love to have contact with my readers.

Getting feedback is always rewarding, and a review can sometimes help persuade other readers to choose one of my books for the first time.

For news please go to my website: www.lexadudeywriter.co.uk

If you wish to leave a review please go to:
http://www.troubador.co.uk/shop_booklist.asp?s=lexa%20dudley

Best wishes,
Lexa

BY THE SAME AUTHOR...

The Whispering Wind

Also set in Sardinia, this novel won finalist in the Romance category at the Next Generation Indie Book Awards 2014, and at the National Indie Excellence Awards 2014 for Romance and Literary Fiction.

PROLOGUE FOR *THE WHISPERING WIND*

A gentle breeze fluttered through the peach grove, but gave no respite from the midday sun. The rows of peach and lemon trees offered no shade, and the branches of the tall cypress trees surrounding the orchard seemed to trap and intensify the relentless rays, creating an overwhelming heat that pervaded everything. Only the strident call of the cicadas broke the unnerving quiet that descended over the parched land.

One exception to the dryness was a small area at the end of the garden where an old standpipe dripped, making the ground damp. This area was bordered by giant prickly pears, and growing through their great spines were masses of pink and white wild roses, together with honeysuckle; their strong sweet scents mingling languorously in the oppressive air.

The rows of peach and lemon trees, planted with military precision, gave way to a mantle of green vineyards, which in turn blended into fields of golden barley, before finally fading into the hazy, distant mountains that rose from all sides of the Campidano.

This hard-baked Sardinian soil, that has drained the strength of all who have worked it since pre-Carthaginian times, produces men as tough and durable as the ancient land itself, and the two brothers working in this grove were no exception. The elder of them leaned heavily on his shovel and surveyed the work that the two of them had done. He watched his younger brother as he put the finishing touches to the hoses and turned on the water from the huge standpipe in the centre of the grove, allowing the water to gush into the newly dug trenches before being swallowed up by the thirsty earth.

He had promised to help in the peach grove today, but now he was tired, having lain awake most of the night listening to music, drinking whisky and trying to fight the demon depression that lurked in his mind. He had kept his promise to his brother, but now he needed to sleep.

'Are you alright? You look awful.' asked his younger brother looking concerned.

He didn't reply. He was busy undoing the rough bandaging on his normally well manicured hands. His mind went back to the time when, as a child, he had worked beside his father in this same grove; when he returned home at night his mother had bathed his hands in salt water to harden them and ease the pain. He shoved the bandaging into his pocket and sighed as he put his hands up to his brow to try to stop the relentless pounding in his head.

'I don't know how the hell you stand this heat all the time.'

'Probably because I don't drink like you do and, I am used to it.'

The elder brother shrugged and walked to the bottom of the grove to collect his shirt. Nearing the hedge of prickly pears, he became aware of the suffocating, heavy scent coming from the roses and rampant honeysuckle. The sun dazzled between the leaves of the overhanging lemon trees and the ever-changing light was mesmerising. The summer heat closed in on him and he felt weak. His feet turned to clay as he became rooted to the spot and beads of sweat stood out on his forehead as an icy chill ran down his spine. He felt unable to breathe and a dull, sick feeling welled up in the pit of his stomach.

Coming toward him through the now blurred lines of trees, and moving slowly, as if in a dream, was a young woman, her arms outstretched to greet him. Her long, golden hair flowed over her shoulders, glinting in the sun, and her white cotton dress seemed to intensify the bright light. He put his hands up to shield his eyes from the glare as the girl came nearer. He turned to see if his brother was there, but seeing no one he looked back and was surprised to see that the young girl now appeared to be beside him. He knew her. He knew her so well that all his senses cried out as he stared at her once familiar face.

Stirred memories and lost dreams rushed in on him from days long gone, and a deep yearning filled his soul. He found it difficult to catch his breath with his heart pounding as if it would burst. The world about him began to spin and tears sprang to his eyes.

'I've come back, darling,' she whispered, laying a soft, cooling hand on his fevered skin.

Everything fell out of focus as he reached forward, in desperation, to embrace his long-lost love, crying out as he fell to the ground.

'I always knew you would!'